DEAD SCARED

DEAD SCARED

S. J. BOLTON

WHEELER PUBLISHING
A part of Gale, Cengage Learning

Detroit • New York • San Francisco • New Haven, Conn • Waterville, Maine • London

GALE
CENGAGE Learning®

LIBRARY OF CONGRESS CATALOGING-IN-PUBLICATION DATA

Bolton, S. J.
  Dead scared / by S.J. Bolton. — Large print ed.
    p. cm. — (Wheeler Publishing large print hardcover)
  ISBN 978-1-4104-5107-1 (hardcover) — ISBN 1-4104-5107-0 (hardcover)
  1. Large type books. 2. Women detectives—England—London—Fiction.
  3. Suicide victims—Fiction. 4. Students—Crimes against—Fiction.
  5. University of Cambridge—Fiction. 6. Cambridge (England)—Fiction.
  I. Title.
  PR6102.O49D43 2012
  823'.92—dc23   2012020599

Published in 2012 by arrangement with St. Martin's Press, LLC

Printed in the United States of America
1 2 3 4 5 6 7 16 15 14 13 12

In memory of Peter Inglis Smith:
kind neighbour, great writer,
good friend.

What are fears but voices airy?
Whispering harm where harm is not,
And deluding the unwary
Till the fatal bolt is shot!
                    William Wordsworth

Prologue

Tuesday 22 January (a few minutes before midnight)

When a large object falls from a great height, the speed at which it travels accelerates until the upward force of air resistance becomes equal to the downward propulsion of gravity. At that point, whatever is falling reaches what is known as terminal velocity, a constant speed that will be maintained until it encounters a more powerful force, most commonly the ground.

Terminal velocity of the average human body is thought to be around 120 miles per hour. Typically this speed is reached fifteen or sixteen seconds into the fall, after a distance of between five hundred and six hundred metres.

A commonly held misconception is that people falling from considerable heights die before impact. Only rarely is this true. Whilst the shock of the experience could cause a fatal heart attack, most falls simply don't last long enough for this to happen. Also, in theory, a body could freeze in sub-zero temperatures, or become unconscious due to oxygen deprivation, but both these scenarios rely upon the faller's leaping from a plane at significant altitude and, other than the more intrepid skydivers, people rarely do that.

Most people who fall or jump from great heights die upon impact when their bones shatter and cause extensive damage to the surrounding tissue. Death is instantaneous. Usually.

The woman on the edge of one of the tallest towers in Cambridge probably doesn't have to worry too much about when she might achieve terminal velocity. The tower is not quite two hundred feet tall and her body will continue to accelerate as she falls its full length. She should, on the other hand, be thinking very seriously about impact. Because when that occurs, the flint cobbles around the base of the tower will shatter her young bones like fine crystal. Right now, though, she doesn't seem concerned about anything. She stands like a sightseer, taking in the view.

Cambridge, just before midnight, is a city of black shadows and gold light. The almost-full moon shines down like a spotlight on the wedding-cake elegance of the surrounding buildings, on the pillars pointing like stone fingers to the cloudless sky, and on the few people still out and about, who slip like phantoms in and out of pools of light.

She sways on the spot and, as if something has caught her attention, her head tilts down.

At the base of the tower the air is still. A torn page of yesterday's *Daily Mail* lies undisturbed on the pavement. Up at the top, there is wind. Enough to blow the woman's hair around her head like a flag. The woman is young, maybe a year or two either side of thirty, and would be beautiful if her face weren't empty of all expression. If her eyes had any light behind them. This is the face of someone who believes she is already dead.

The man racing across the First Court of St John's College, on the other hand, is very much alive, because in the human animal nothing affirms life quite like terror. Detective Inspector Mark Joesbury, of the branch of the Metropolitan Police that sends its officers into the most dangerous situations, has never been quite this scared in his life before.

Up on the tower, it's cold. The January

chill comes drifting over the Fens and wraps itself across the city like a paedophile's hand round that of a small, unresisting child. The woman isn't dressed for winter but seems to be unaware of the cold. She blinks and suddenly those dead eyes have tears in them.

DI Joesbury has reached the door to the chapel tower and finds it unlocked. It slams back against the stone wall and his left shoulder, which will always be the weaker of the two, registers the shock of pain. At the first corner, Joesbury spots a shoe, a narrow, low-heeled blue leather shoe, with a pointed toe and a high polish. He almost stops to pick it up and then realizes he can't bear to. Once before he held a woman's shoe in his hand and thought he'd lost her. He carries on, up the steps, counting them as he goes. Not because he has the faintest idea how many there are, but because he needs to be marking progress in his head. When he reaches the second flight, he hears footsteps behind him. Someone is following him up.

He feels the cold air just as he sees the door at the top. He's out on the roof before he has any idea what he's going to do if he's too late and she's already jumped. Or what the hell he'll do if she hasn't.

'Lacey,' he yells. 'No!'

1

Friday 11 January (eleven days earlier)

All Bar One near Waterloo Station was busy, with nearly a hundred people shouting to make themselves heard above the music. Smoking has been banned in the UK's public places for years but something seemed to be hovering around these folk, thickening the air, turning the scene around me into an out-of-focus photograph taken on a cheap camera.

I knew instinctively he wasn't there.

No need to look at my watch to know I was sixteen minutes late. I'd timed it to the second. Too late would look rude, or as if I were trying to make a point; too close to the agreed time would seem eager. Calm and professional, that's what I was going to be. A little distant. Being a bit late was part of that. Except now he was the one who was late.

At the bar, I ordered my usual drink-for-difficult-occasions and stretched up on to a vacant bar stool. Sipping the colourless liquid, I could see my reflection in the mirrors behind the bar. I'd come straight from work. Somehow, I'd resisted the temptation to leave early and spend the better part of two hours showering, blow-drying my hair, putting on make-up and choosing clothes. I'd been determined not to look nice for Mark Joesbury.

I fished my laptop out of my bag and put it down on the bar — not actually planning to work, just to make it look that way — and opened a presentation on the UK's laws on pornography that I was due to give the following week to a group of new recruits at Hendon. I opened a slide at random — the Criminal Justice and Immigration Act. The recruits would be surprised to learn, because most people were, that possession of all non-child pornography was perfectly legal in the UK until the 2008 Act outlawed extreme pornographic images. Naturally, they'd want to know what qualified as extreme. Hence the main content of the slide I was looking at.

An extreme pornographic image depicts a sexual act that:

- threatens, or appears to threaten, a person's life.
- results in serous injury to sexual organs.
- involves a human corpse.
- involves an animal

I changed a spelling mistake in the second bullet point and added a full stop to the fourth.

Joesbury hadn't arrived. Not that I'd looked round. I would know the minute he walked through the door.

Twenty-four hours earlier I'd had a five-minute briefing with my DI at Southwark Police Station. SCD10, still colloquially known by everyone as SO10, the special crimes directorate of the Metropolitan Police that deals with covert operations, had requested my help with a case. Not just any young female detective constable but me specifically, and the lead officer on the case, DI Mark Joesbury, would meet me the following evening. 'What case?' I'd asked. DI Joesbury would fill me in, I was told. My DI had been tight-lipped and grumpy, probably on account of having his staff filched without being told why.

I checked my watch again. He was twenty-three minutes late, my drink was disappearing too quickly and at half past I was going home.

I couldn't even remember what he looked like, I realized. Oh, I had a vague idea of height, build and colouring, and I remembered those turquoise eyes, but I couldn't conjure up a picture of his face. Which was odd, really, given that he was never out of my head for a second.

'Lacey Flint, as I live and breathe,' said a voice directly behind me.

I took a deep breath and turned round slowly, to see Mark Joesbury, maybe just a fraction over six feet tall, strongly built, suntanned skin even in January, bright turquoise eyes. Wearing a thick, untidy, ginger wig.

'I'm undercover,' he said. And then he winked at me.

2

The disabled parking space outside Dr Evi Oliver's house was empty for a change. Even with the prominent Private Parking sign on the old brick wall it wasn't unusual, especially at weekends, for Evi to arrive home and find that a tourist with a bad leg had claimed it for his own. Tonight she was in luck.

She steeled herself to the inevitable pain and got out of the car. She was thirty minutes overdue with her medication and it just wasn't handling the pain the way it used to. Unfolding the stick, she tucked it under her left arm and, a little steadier now, found her briefcase. As usual, the effort left her slightly out of breath. As usual, being alone in the dark didn't help.

Wanting to get inside as soon as she could, Evi made herself take a moment to look round and listen. The house where she'd lived for the last five and a half months was at the end of a cul de sac and surrounded by walled college gardens and the river Cam. It was probably one of the quietest streets in Cambridge.

There was no one in sight, and nothing to hear but traffic in the next street and the wind in the nearby trees.

It was late. Nine o'clock on a Friday evening and it simply hadn't been possible to stay at work any longer. Her new colleagues had already written her off as a sad, semi-crippled spinster, old before her time, with no life of her own outside work. They wouldn't exactly be wrong about that. But what really kept Evi at her desk until security closed down the building wasn't the emptiness of the rest of her life. It was fear.

3

I was aware of sniggers around us, a few curious glances. I half heard Joesbury tell the bloke behind the bar that he'd have a pint of IPA and the lady would have a refill. When I finally got my breath and had wiped my eyes, Joesbury was looking puzzled.

'I don't think I've ever seen you laugh before,' he said. Shaking his head softly, as though it was me who was nuts, he was watching the barman pour my drink. Bombay Sapphire over lots of ice in a tall glass. He slid it to me, eyebrows high.

'You drink neat gin?' he asked me.

'No. I drink it with ice and lemon,' I replied, as I realized the man at the bar, and several others near by, were watching us. What the hell was Joesbury playing at?

'What the hell are you playing at?' I asked him. 'Are you planning on wearing that thing all night?'

'Nah, it makes my head itch.' He pulled

the wig off, dropped it on to the bar and picked up his glass. The discarded hairpiece lay in front of him like roadkill as he scratched behind his left ear. 'I can put it back on later, though,' he said. 'If you want.'

His hair had grown since I'd last seen him, just touching his collar at the back. It was darker brown than I remembered, with just the faintest kink in it. The longer style suited him, softening the lines of his skull and lengthening his cheekbones, making him infinitely better-looking. The soft light of the bar made the scar around his right eye barely visible. The muscles in my jaw were aching. All this time I'd been grinning at him.

'And again I ask, what are you playing at?' If I sounded grumpy, he might not realize how ridiculously pleased I was to see him. 'Aren't you supposed to be low-profile man?'

'I thought it might break the ice,' he replied, wiping beer foam off his upper lip. 'Things were a bit tense last time I saw you.'

Last time I'd seen Joesbury, he'd been minutes away from bleeding to death. So had I, come to that. I guess 'a bit tense' just about covered it.

'How are you?' I asked him, although I already had a pretty good idea. For the last couple of months I'd shamelessly begged updates from mutual acquaintances. I knew the gunshot he'd taken that night had torn a good chunk of lung tissue that surgeons, and time, had managed to repair. I knew he'd spent four weeks in hospital, that he would be on light duties for another three months, but fine to return to full duties after that.

'I might give the London marathon a miss this year,' he said, stretching out one hand and taking hold of mine, causing tightly stretched guitar strings to start twanging in my stomach. 'Otherwise fine.' He turned my wrist to see its underside and looked for a second at the heavy-duty plaster I still wore, more because I didn't like looking at the scar beneath than because it needed to be covered. Three months on, it had healed as much as it ever would. Which would never be enough.

'I thought you might come and see me,' he went on. 'Those hospital-issue pyjamas were quite fetching.'

'I sent a teddy,' I replied. 'I expect it got lost in the post.'

We both knew I was lying. What I'd never tell him was that I'd spent nearly an hour gazing at pictures on the Steiff of Germany website, picking out the exact teddy I would have sent, if such a thing were possible. The one I'd finally settled on was similar to the one he'd once given me, just bigger and cheekier. Last time I checked the site it had been marked *unavailable.* Couldn't have put it better myself. He was looking at my face now, specifically at my newly modelled nose. It had been reset a month ago following a break and the post-op bruising had just about disappeared.

'Nice work,' he said. 'Tiny bit longer than it was?'

'I thought it made me look intellectual.'

He was still holding my wrist and I'd made no attempt to pull away. 'I hear they've got you working on porn,' he said. 'Enjoying it?'

'They've got me doing research and briefings,' I snapped, because I never like to hear men even half joking about porn. 'They seem to think I'm good at detail.'

Joesbury let go of me and I could see his mood changing. He turned away and his eyes settled on a table by the window.

'Well, if we've got the social pleasantries out of the way, we should sit down,' he said. Without waiting for me to agree, he tucked the wig under his arm, picked up both drinks and made his way through the bar. I followed, telling myself I had no right to be disappointed. This wasn't a date.

Joesbury had been carrying a rucksack. He pulled a slim brown case file out of it and put it down, unopened, on the table between us.

'I've got clearance from your guvnors at Southwark to request your help on a case,' he said, and he might have been any senior officer briefing any junior one. 'We need a woman. One who can pass for early twenties at most. There's no one in the division available. I thought of you.'

'I'm touched,' I said, playing for time. Cases referred to SO10 involved officers being sent undercover into difficult and dangerous situations. I wasn't sure I was ready for another of those.

'Do well and it'll look good on your record,' he said.

'The opposite, of course, also being the case.'

Joesbury smiled. 'I'm under orders to tell you that the decision is entirely yours,' he said. 'I'm further instructed by Dana to inform you that I'm an irresponsible fool, that it's far too soon after the Ripper business to even think about putting you on a case like this and that you should tell me to go to hell.'

'Tell her I said hi,' I replied. Dana was DI

Dana Tulloch, who headed up the Major Investigation Team that I'd worked with last autumn. She was also Joesbury's best mate. I liked Dana, but couldn't help resenting her closeness to Joesbury.

'On the other hand,' he was saying, 'the case largely came to our attention through Dana. She was contacted on an informal basis by an old university friend of hers, now head of student counselling at Cambridge University.'

'What's the case?' I asked.

Joesbury opened the file. 'That stomach of yours still pretty strong?' I nodded, although it hadn't exactly been put to the test much lately. He took out a small stack of photographs and slid them along the table towards me. I looked briefly at the one on the top and had to close my eyes for a second. There are some things that it really is better never to see.

4

Evi ran her eyes along the brick wall that surrounded her garden, around the nearby buildings, into dark areas under trees, wondering if fear was going to overshadow the rest of her life.

Fear of being alone. Fear of shadows that became substance. Of whispers that came scurrying out of the darkness. Of a beautiful face that was nothing more than a mask. Fear of the few short steps between the safety of her car and her house.

Had to be done sometime. She locked the car and set off towards her front gate. The wrought ironwork was old but had been resprung so that a light touch would send it swinging open.

The easterly wind coming off the Fens was strong tonight and the leaves on the two bay trees rustled together like old paper. Even the tiny leaves of the box hedging were dancing little jigs. Lavender bushes flanked each side of the path. In June the scent would welcome her home like the smile on a loved one's face. For now, the unclipped stalks were bare.

The Queen Anne house, built nearly three hundred years ago for the master of one of the older Cambridge colleges, was the last place Evi had expected to be offered as living accommodation when she'd accepted her new job. A large house of soft warm brickwork, with blond limestone detailing, it was one of the most prestigious homes in the university's gift. Its previous occupant, an internationally renowned professor of physics who'd narrowly missed the Nobel Prize twice, had lived in it for nearly thirty years. After meningitis robbed him of his lower limbs, the university had converted the house into disabled-living accommodation.

The professor had died nine months ago and when Evi was offered the post of head of student counselling, with part-time teaching and tutoring responsibilities, the university had seen a chance to recoup some of its investment.

The flagstone path was short. Just five yards through the centre of the knot garden and she'd be at the elaborate front porch. Carriage-style lanterns either side of the door lit the full length of the path. Usually she was glad of them. Tonight she wasn't so sure.

Because without them, she probably wouldn't have seen the trail of fir cones leading from the gate to the door.

5

'You're looking at Bryony Carter,' Joesbury told me. 'Nineteen years old. First-year medical student.'

'What happened?'

'She set fire to herself,' he replied. 'On the night of her college Christmas ball a few weeks ago. Maybe she was pissed off not to be invited, but dinner was just coming to an end when she staggered in like a human torch.'

I risked a glance at the figure enveloped in flames. 'Grim,' I said, which didn't seem enough. Choosing to die at your own hand was one thing. To do it by fire was another entirely. 'And people saw this happen?'

Joesbury gave a single, short nod. 'Not only did they see it, several took photographs on their iPhones. I ask you, kids!'

I started to look through the rest of the photographs. The burning girl had thrown her head back and it wasn't possible to see her face. One thing to be grateful for. More of a problem were small, vague shapes visible through the flames that looked like chunks of flesh melting away from her body. And her left hand, outstretched towards the camera, had turned black. It looked more like a chicken's claw than anything you might see on a human body.

The fifth photograph in the stack showed the girl on the floor. A long-haired man wearing a dinner jacket and a shocked expression was standing closest to her, a fire extinguisher in his arms. An upturned ice bucket lay nearby. A girl in a blue dress had a water jug in one hand.

'She was pretty high on some new-fangled hallucinogenic drug at the time,' said Joesbury. 'You have to hope she didn't know too much about what was going on.'

'What has it got to do with SO10?' I asked.

'First question I asked,' he replied. 'Local CID aren't unduly concerned. They've done the classic three-tick-box check to determine a suicide and found nothing to suggest anything sinister.'

I took a moment to wonder how many acts would be considered more sinister than setting fire to yourself. 'I'm not familiar with that,' I said. 'What you just said about tick-boxes.'

'Means, Motive, Intent,' said Joesbury. 'First thing to check with a possible suicide is whether the means of death was readily to hand. Pistol close by the shooting hand, noose round the neck and something to stand on, that sort of thing. In Bryony's case, the petrol can was found outside the dining hall. And the investigating officer found a receipt for it in her room. He also found traces of the drug she'd been using for Dutch courage.'

Someone leaned over to put an empty glass on the table and caught sight of the photograph. Without looking up, I slid the pictures under the file.

'Next box is motive,' Joesbury went on. 'Bryony had been depressed for some time. She was a bright girl but she was struggling to keep up with the coursework. Complained about never being able to sleep.'

'What about intent?' I asked.

Joesbury nodded. 'She left a note to her mother. Short and very sad, I'm told. The report prepared by the first officer on the scene and the SOCs report on the state of her room are in the file,' he went on. 'No evidence of staging that they could see.'

Staging refers to tricks sometimes used by killers to make a murder look like suicide. Placing a gun near to a victim's hand would be a classic example. The absence of the victim's fingerprints on the gun would indicate staging.

'And a couple of hundred people saw her do it,' I said.

'They certainly saw her in flames,' said Joesbury. 'And it's the third suicide at the university this academic year. Does the name Jackie King ring any bells?'

I thought for a moment and shook my head.

'Killed herself in November. Made a few of the national papers.'

'I must have missed it.' Since the case we'd both worked on last autumn, I'd made a point of avoiding the papers and the national news. I would never be comfortable seeing my own name in the spotlight, and constant reminders of what the team had been through were not, as the therapists would say, going to help the healing process.

'I still don't get it,' I went on. 'Why are SO10 interested in a college suicide?'

Joesbury pulled another file out of his bag. Asking him not to open it didn't really seem like an option so I sat and waited while he pulled out another set of photographs. Not that multiples were strictly necessary. I got the idea clearly enough from the one on the top. A girl, obviously dead, with wet hair and clothes. And a rope tied tight around her ankles.

'This was a suicide?' I asked.

'Apparently so,' he replied. 'Certainly no obvious evidence otherwise. This was Jackie in her better days.'

Joesbury had pulled the last of the photographs to the top of the pile. Jackie King looked the outdoor type. She was wearing a sailing-style sweatshirt, her hair was long, fair, shiny and straight. Young, healthy, bright and attractive, surely she'd had everything to live for?

'Poor girl,' I said, and waited for him to go on.

'Three suicides this year, three last, four the year before,' he said. 'Cambridge is developing a very unhealthy record when it comes to young people taking their own lives.'

6

Evi stopped, willing the wind to soften so that she could hear the snigger, the scuffle of feet that would tell her someone was watching. Because someone had to be watching. There was no way these cones had blown on to the path. There were twelve in all, one in the exact centre of each flagstone, forming a straight line right up to the front door.

Three nights in a row this had happened. Last night and the night before it had been possible to explain away. The cones had been scattered the first time she'd seen them, as though blown by the wind. Last night, there'd been a pile of them just inside the gate. This was much more deliberate.

Who could possibly know how much she hated fir cones?

She turned on the spot, using the stick for balance. Too much noise from the wind to hear anything. Too many shadows to be sure she was alone. She should get indoors. Walking as quickly up the path as she was able, she reached the front door and stepped inside.

Another cone, larger than the rest, lay on the mat.

Evi kept her indoor wheelchair to one side of the front door. Without taking her eyes off the cone, she pushed the door shut and sat down in it. She was in the grip of an old, irrational fear, one she acknowledged but was powerless to do anything about, dating back to when, as a chubby, inquisitive four-year-old, she'd picked up a large fir cone from beneath a tree.

She'd been on holiday in the north of Italy with her family. The pine trees in the forest had been massive, stretching up to the heavens, or so it had seemed to the tiny girl. The cone was huge too, easily dwarfing her little plump hands. She'd picked it up, turned to her mother in delight and felt a tickle on her left wrist.

When she looked down, her hands and the lower parts of her arms were covered in crawling insects. She remembered howling and one of her parents brushing the insects away. But some had got inside her clothes and they'd had to undress her in the forest. Years later, the memory of delight turning to revulsion still had the power to disturb her.

No one could know that. Even her parents hadn't mentioned the incident in decades. A weird joke, nothing more, probably nothing to do with her. Maybe a child had been playing here earlier, had left a trail of cones and popped one through her letter box. Evi wheeled herself towards the kitchen. She got as far as the doorway.

Heaped on the kitchen table, which several hours ago she'd left completely clear, was a pile of large fir cones.

7

'Young people committing suicide is hardly uncommon, though,' I said, thinking as I spoke. 'The suicide rate is higher among the student body than the rest of the population, isn't it? Wasn't there a case in Wales a few years ago?'

'You're thinking about Bridgend,' said Joesbury. 'Although technically, that didn't involve a university. Cluster suicides do happen. But they're rare. And Dana's mate isn't the only one who's worried. The media attention is getting the governing body very edgy too. Outlandish public suicides don't look good for one of the world's leading academic institutions.'

'But no suggestion of foul play?' I asked.

'On the contrary. Both Bryony and Jackie had a psychiatric history,' said Joesbury. 'Jackie in the past, Bryony more recently.'

'Bryony was receiving counselling?'

'She was,' said Joesbury. 'Not by Dana's

friend herself, what's her name . . .' He pulled a stack of paper from the file and flicked through it. 'Oliver,' he said, after a moment, 'Dr Evi Oliver . . . not with her but with one of her colleagues. There's a team of counsellors dedicated to the university and Dr Oliver heads it up.'

'What about the other girl?' I said.

Joesbury nodded. 'Jackie had her problems too, according to her friends,' he said. 'So did the young lad who hanged himself in his third week.' Joesbury glanced down at his notes. 'Jake Hammond. Nineteen-year-old English student.'

'How many cases are we talking about?'

'Nineteen in five years, including Bryony Carter,' said Joesbury.

'Well, I can see why the authorities are worried,' I said. 'But I don't get why SO10 are involved.'

Joesbury leaned back in his chair and put his hands behind his head. He looked thinner than I remembered. He'd lost muscle definition from his chest and shoulders. 'Old girls' network,' he said. 'Dr Oliver contacts her old Cambridge buddy Dana, who in turn gets in touch with her old mentor on the force, another Cambridge alumna.'

'Who is?'

'Sonia Hammond.'

Joesbury waited for the name to register. It didn't.

'Commander Sonia Hammond,' he prompted. 'Currently head of the covert operations directorate at Scotland Yard.'

I'd got it. 'Your boss,' I said. 'I didn't know you reported to a woman.'

Joesbury raised one eyebrow. I'd forgotten he could do that. 'Story of my life,' he said. 'Commander Hammond has a daughter at Cambridge, so she has an added interest.'

'Even so,' I said. 'What on earth do they think an undercover operation in the city of dreaming spires will achieve?'

'I think the city of dreaming spires is Oxford,' said Joesbury. 'Dr Oliver has this theory that the suicides aren't coincidence. She thinks there is something decidedly sinister going on.'

8

After Evi had thanked the young WPC, she locked and bolted the front door, still more shaken than she wanted to admit. The policewoman had been polite, searching the house thoroughly and stressing that Evi should call immediately if anything else happened. Otherwise, though, she clearly wasn't planning any action other than a report. There had been no evidence of a break-in, she'd explained, and fir cones were hardly threatening.

The woman had a point, of course. Evi wasn't even the only one with keys to her house. Her cleaning company let themselves in every Tuesday. The building was owned by the university and it wasn't impossible that there'd been some unscheduled, emergency visit by maintenance. Why fir cones should have been brought into the house by a maintenance team was another matter, but not one the young officer was going to spend any time worrying about.

Evi crossed the kitchen and filled the kettle. She'd just switched it on when something scraped along the kitchen window. She jumped so high in the air she almost fell over.

'Just the tree,' she told herself, realizing she still hadn't taken her painkillers. 'Just that blessed tree again.'

Evi's kitchen overlooked the rear walled garden, which led down to the river bank. A massive cedar tree grew just beyond the house and its lower branches had a habit of scratching against the ground-floor windows when the wind was strong.

Evi took her painkillers, waited a few minutes for the effect to kick in and then ate as much as she could manage. She cleared the plates and pushed herself through to the bedroom, only stopping to pick up the fir cone from the mat. She pushed it back through the letter box without so much as a shudder. The ones from her kitchen table were outside in the rubbish bin.

She turned on the bathroom taps and started to undress. On her bedside table was an opened letter. It had arrived a few days ago in a thick padded envelope. She'd shaken it over the bed and watched shells,

pebbles, dried seaweed and, finally, a snap-
shot of a family fall out. The photograph lay
face up on the table. Mum, dad, young
children. They'd been patients of hers the
previous year and had turned into friends.
They'd just bought a semi-derelict bunga-
low on the coast road of Lytham St Annes
in Lancashire and come the spring, the
mother had written, planned to demolish
the house and build their new dream home.
It would be their second attempt; their first
hadn't worked out too well. Evi was welcome, the letter insisted, to visit any time.
There had been no mention of Harry.

Knowing she shouldn't, Evi opened the
drawer of the bedside table and pulled out
a newspaper article that she'd found on an
internet archive. She didn't bother reading
the words, she knew them off by heart. She
just needed to look at his face.

The bath would be filling up. Just one
more second to look at hair that was somewhere between strawberry blond and honey,
at light brown eyes, square jaw and lips that
always seemed to be curved in a smile, even
when he was trying, as in the picture, to
look serious. Just one more second to
wonder when the good days, the ones when
she could push him to the back of her mind
like old memories, would outnumber the

bad ones, when he was hammering at the front, so vivid she could almost smell the lime and ginger fragrance of his skin. Just one more second to wonder when the pain was going to go away.

By the time the water began to go cold, Evi was almost asleep. She pressed the button that would activate the lift and bring her out of the bath. She managed to stand unaided for long enough to dry herself and rub body lotion into her skin. *You have such soft skin,* he'd whispered to her once. As she left the bathroom, there were tears in her eyes and she didn't even bother telling herself that it was just the pain, so much worse at night lately, that was making her cry.

She hadn't seen the message on the bathroom mirror, which only the steam from the hot water had made visible.

I can see you, it said.

9

'Sinister how?' I asked Joesbury.

'Dr Oliver believes there is — and I'm reading directly from notes now — a subversive subculture of glamorizing the suicidal act,' said Joesbury. 'She thinks these kids, backed up by an online network, are egging each other on.'

'People said that about Bridgend,' I said.

'Always very difficult to prove,' said Joesbury. 'But there are documented cases of suicide pacts, of people meeting, usually online, and deciding to end it all together. They give each other the courage to go through with it.'

I nodded. I'd read about such cases from time to time.

'More disturbing,' Joesbury went on, 'is a trend of what I can only call bottom-feeders accessing websites and chat rooms specifically to find depressed and vulnerable people. They strike up friendships, pretend to be concerned, but all the while they're pushing them towards topping themselves. And there are websites where suicidal people go to talk to like-minded others, discuss which methods are most effective, get a bit of courage together for when they finally take the plunge.' Joesbury looked down at his notes again. 'Dr Oliver calls it negative reinforcement,' he said, 'sometimes deliberate and malicious, of self-destructive urges.'

'She sounds a laugh a minute,' I said.

'Dana tells me she's a bit of a babe,' said Joesbury, with a smile I could cheerfully have slapped off him.

'So assuming I agree,' I said, 'what exactly will I be investigating?'

'You won't be investigating as such,' said Joesbury. 'At this stage it doesn't merit a full investigation. Your job will be to spend some time with this Dr Oliver, let her know we're taking her seriously.'

'So I'm a token gesture to keep her happy?' I interrupted.

'Not entirely. We also need you to immerse yourself in student life and report back on anything out of the ordinary. You'll pay particular attention to the online websites and chat rooms that fly around the Fenland ether. You'll be our eyes on the inside.'

I was silent for a second or two.

'We need you to be the sort of student who might be thinking about suicide,' Joesbury went on. 'Needy, a bit vulnerable, prone to depression. We also want you to get yourself noticed, so you need to step it up a bit with the appearance. Good-looking fruitcake. That's what we want.'

'So, absolutely nothing suspicious came up at Bryony's postmortem?' I asked, more because I was playing for time than because I needed to know right there and then.

'There hasn't been one.'

I waited while Joesbury flicked through the stack of photographs, pulled one out and turned it to face me. It showed a figure lying on a hospital bed, beneath a transparent tent, grotesquely swollen and so completely enveloped in dressings it resembled an Egyptian mummy. Both arms were stretched out from her body at right angles. A spaghetti-like mass of wires and tubes seemed to be growing out of her.

'She's still alive?' I said, without the faintest idea why that should be so much worse, only knowing that it was.

'This was taken twenty-four hours after she was admitted,' said Joesbury. 'Nobody really expected her to survive. Three weeks on, she's managed to fight off infection, avoid going into shock and hasn't suffered respiratory collapse. She may even recover. How much she'll be able to tell us though is a moot point. Her tongue was burned away.'

Not a lot you can say to that. 'What do you want me to do?'

'Read the file,' he replied. 'Think about it. Dana wants you to call her. She'll be trying to talk you out of it.'

I looked up. 'Will you be going?' I asked. 'To Cambridge, I mean.'

Turquoise eyes narrowed. 'Not necessary at this stage,' he said. 'I'll be popping in and out to keep an eye on you, but 90 per cent of the fieldwork will be down to you.'

It was how SO10 worked. Junior officers were sent into situations first, often for a year or more, to gather intelligence and report back. As a clearer picture emerged, the heavier guns got deployed.

'Can you see me as an eccentric don?' Joesbury was saying. 'Bow tie and tweeds? Long flowing gown? Untidy wig?'

With his muscular frame and scarred face, Joesbury always reminded me of a half-tamed thug. He was smiling at me again. It was always the smile that was hardest to deal with. Better by far just not to look at it. Better to leave now. Business was done.

On the table, the file had been closed, its contents hidden from view. The orange wig was a few inches away from me.

'It's very soft,' said Joesbury. 'Want to stroke it?'

I raised my eyes. 'What are we talking about exactly?'

His grin got even wider. 'God, I've missed you,' he said.

Silence. Still staring at each other across the table. I really had to go.

'Want to get some dinner?' he asked me.

So now it could be a date.

'Actually, I have plans.' I looked at my watch. 'I should get going.'

Joesbury leaned back on his chair, his grin gone. His right hand reached up and he began to rub the scar at his temple. 'Would the plans include a trip across town to Camden, by any chance?'

When I'd first met Joesbury, Camden had been where I'd gone most Friday evenings. To meet men. I hadn't been near the place since a certain night last October. And my plans for the evening were a Chinese take-away and an early night with a Lee Child paperback.

'Something like that.' I got to my feet. 'I'll get back to you over the weekend.'

He watched me pick up my bag and slip

the file into it. I let my eyes fall to the right side of his chest, to the exact spot that, last time I'd seen him, had been soaked in blood.

'I'm glad you're OK,' I said. And left.

10

Half an hour later I was home, eating Singapore noodles from the takeaway carton and opening the Bryony Carter case file. The photographs I pushed firmly to one side, except the only one taken of Bryony before the fire. It showed an exceptionally pretty girl with strawberry blonde hair, pale skin and bright blue eyes.

First I read the CID report. It was dated three days after the incident and seemed thorough enough. At 9.45 p.m., just as coffee was being served in the great hall of St John's College, a figure covered in flames had staggered in. A quick-thinking man called Scott Thornton, whom the report described as a senior member of the college, had grabbed the closest fire extinguisher. When it was empty, and Bryony was lying on the floor, he'd ordered the other guests to bring water. From jugs, bottles, ice buckets, even glasses, he'd encouraged everyone in the room to tip water over poor, prostrate Bryony while he summoned an ambulance on his mobile. Scott Thornton had almost certainly saved Bryony's life. Whether she'd thank him for it was another matter.

After the seriously injured girl had been taken away, uniformed police had conducted a thorough search of the college and its grounds. A petrol can had been found in a shadowed area of a space called Second Court and the ground around it was soaked in petrol. Bryony's fingerprints, and hers alone, were on the can.

Her room a few hundred yards away was neat and orderly. She'd done her laundry that day and returned several books to the library. A typewritten note to her mother was on her bedside table. The receipt for the petrol can was found amongst various other receipts in the pencil tray of her desk drawer. On her bedroom floor were the pipe, mesh screen and funnel bowl she'd used to inhale the fumes of a powerful hallucinogenic drug.

Her room-mate, a girl called Talaith Robinson, had said in interview that Bryony had been unhappy and unsettled for a while, but that she really hadn't anticipated her taking such a drastic step. The report had been prepared by a detective sergeant and signed off by his senior officer, a DI John Castell.

It's become customary, I learned as I read, to conduct an in-depth investigation into the state of mind of suicide victims. As Bryony's recovery was still very much in doubt, CID had requested a psychological report be prepared in her case too. Dr Oliver, as the psychiatrist with overall responsibility for Bryony's mental health, had produced it.

Dr Oliver's summary note at the front told me that Bryony Carter was a young woman who felt a strong need to be loved and taken care of, who wanted to surrender responsibility for her own life to another, kinder and stronger partner — a soulmate who would take care of her. The report talked about a strained relationship with both parents. The father, who had a time-consuming job, was rarely around and the mother never seemed particularly interested in Bryony, the youngest of her four children. Bryony had grown up believing herself to be the family nuisance.

The insecure, unhappy child had grown into a passive woman, aching for love and attention. Although bright and pretty, Bryony was clingy and vulnerable in relation-

51

ships, even friendships. At Cambridge, she suffered from insomnia and bad dreams. Towards the end of term, she'd been missing most of her classes. She'd been prescribed the antidepressant citalopram by her GP, a Dr Bell.

The summary was followed by several pages of notes made during individual counselling sessions. I got up, took the empty carton to the sink and poured myself another glass of wine.

I skimmed through the medical report on Bryony's condition, mainly because most of the technical detail meant nothing to me. A brief reference to the drug that had been found in her system caught my eye. Dimethyltryptamine, or DMT. I'd never heard of it but a quick Google search told me it was just about the most powerful psychedelic drug known to mankind. A class-A drug in the UK, the substance is normally inhaled and produces short but very intense experiences in which perceptions of reality can significantly alter. Users reported seeing fairies, elves, angels, even God.

The more I read, the more I couldn't help a sense of irritation. Bryony had a family, a good education, an opportunity to study at one of the world's most highly regarded universities. She had an awful lot more than me and I'd never been tempted to ruin a perfectly good Christmas party by getting high and setting fire to myself.

On the other hand, if Dr Oliver was right, this vulnerable, needy girl had fallen victim to a group of people who got their kicks from the emotional damage and ultimate destruction of others. Who believed they were clever enough to cause pain without even getting their hands dirty.

11

Evi woke with a start, convinced someone was tapping on her bedroom window. She lay still for several seconds. Nothing. Just a dream, one of the bad ones, the ones that started with a strange, misshapen creature banging on the window. She had to get back to sleep before she started thinking, because otherwise she'd be awake all night. She turned over in bed, just as the tapping noise began again. She raised her head from the pillow to listen properly.

Fully awake now, she knew it wasn't coming from the window. The cedar tree didn't even reach this side of the house. It was coming from right above her head. From the room upstairs. She reached out, found the light and sat up.

Tap, tap, tap. There was a phone beside her bed. The police, or university security, could be here in minutes. If she told them she thought someone was upstairs they wouldn't waste time. On the other hand, she'd feel a proper fool if she called out several hulking men in uniform to investigate a squirrel infestation.

She sat still in the bed, unable to make up her mind.

Did squirrels make that insistent, shrill tapping noise? The beak of a trapped bird might. The sound stopped. A second later it started again. Tap, tap, tap for a few more seconds and then silence. Only two choices really. Call help and risk looking ridiculous or investigate herself. Evi got up, tucked her stick under her arm and left the room.

The house had been fitted with a stairlift but Evi hated using anything that made her feel both elderly and disabled, so she slept downstairs, using a guest bedroom and bathroom. She sat now on the chair and pressed the button that would take her to the top. When the mechanism halted, there was nothing but silence in the house. Evi realized she hadn't brought a phone with her. If anything happened, she'd be trapped on the upper floor with no means of calling help.

The room directly above where she slept was at the end of the corridor. She could hear nothing. The door was closed. She pushed it open and switched on the light.

The room was empty. No en suite bathroom. Curtains drawn back. Nothing to hide behind. No sign of anything out of the ordinary, except stray ash and twigs around the fireplace. Knowing that a trapped bird or rodent could probably explain the sound she'd heard, Evi felt a small measure of relief. It would be a nuisance, getting the chimney swept, but hardly a big deal. She was halfway across the room when the tapping began again.

This close, there was no mistaking exactly where it was coming from. Not the chimney after all, but one of the beautiful fitted oak wardrobes to either side of the fireplace. The one to her right. Evi stepped closer. The sound was tiny, tinny. There was nothing to be afraid of, surely, from something that sounded so small?

Evi put her hand on the wardrobe door handle, knowing she was very afraid. Knowing also she didn't have a choice. She pulled open the door.

For a second she didn't see it. She'd been looking directly ahead, half flinching, expecting something to fly out at her. Then she looked down and saw the bone man.

12

Bryony's first session with the counsellor had been in the third week of term. Even that early in the academic year, she'd been struggling to cope, finding the rough and tumble of student life, the banter, the frequent practical jokes, difficult to deal with.

I finished my second glass of wine and wasn't sure I could stay awake much longer. Then I got to the notes of Bryony's third session with her counsellor and suddenly sleep seemed a very long way away.

During this session, Bryony had brought up her fear that someone was coming into her room at night and touching her while she was asleep. There were no transcripts of the sessions, so I couldn't judge exactly how the counsellor had reacted to Bryony's suspicions, but I had a sense, from her notes, that she wasn't taking the girl too seriously.

On her fourth and fifth meetings with her counsellor, Bryony referred again to her fears, her belief that she wasn't quite safe in her room. She'd suffered increasingly from sleeplessness and bad dreams, needing to catch up on her rest during the day. As she'd become more and more tired, her coursework had suffered. She'd gone on a downward spiral of exhaustion and anxiety.

In her notes, the counsellor used the word *delusion* more than once.

On her sixth session, Bryony had said she thought her night-time intruder had progressed beyond touching her, possibly even to having full-blown sex with her. She'd talked about being able to smell a man's sweat, and his aftershave, on her bedclothes. She'd found scratch marks on her body, even the trace of a small bite on one shoulder. All of which, the therapist had noted, could easily have been self-inflicted.

I got to the end of the file and sat back to think. According to Joesbury, I was going to Cambridge to keep a lookout for any unhealthy subculture that might be unduly influencing young people. It was to be a routine, low-key operation, not really expected to unearth anything. He hadn't actually said it was being done to placate the head of SO10 but I was pretty certain that's what he thought. Now, it seemed there might be more to it.

13

No, not a bone man, it couldn't be a bone man. Bone men were a silly, rural custom, in a place she'd left behind, hundreds of miles from here. This was nothing more than a child's toy. A six-inch-high skeleton with a wind-up mechanism like clockwork. Just a simple, common toy, the sort that was popular around Halloween. Wind the key and let the toy go. It would walk across a hard surface until the mechanism ran out or it hit an obstacle.

Hardly knowing whether she was still frightened or not, Evi picked it up. A small piece of Blu-tack was stuck to one half of the key. It looked as though the toy had been wound up tight, then stuck to the inside of the wardrobe with the Blu-tack. When the mechanical force of the key trying to turn had become too great, the toy had broken free of its sticky blue handcuffs.

There had been a child here today, it was

the only explanation. The cleaner, who had come on the wrong day, had brought a child. Maybe a child too sick for school and with no one else to take care of him. He'd played in the house, left a toy upstairs, put the fir cones along the path, left a heap of them on the kitchen table.

Evi looked through the rest of the upstairs rooms, found nothing, and let the lift take her back down. She left the skeleton toy on the hall table and made her way into the kitchen, knowing that even she didn't believe her sick-child theory and wondering what on earth she was going to do about it.

If she'd switched on the light straight away, she almost certainly wouldn't have seen the black-clad figure perched on one of the lower branches of the cedar tree, staring in through the kitchen's uncurtained windows. Even with the kitchen in darkness, she might not have noticed the crouching form, so still it was almost melting into the shadows. She might never have known it was there, had it not been for the mask.

The mask was black too but with fluorescent paint picking out the contours of the human skull. There was just enough light for Evi to be absolutely sure that a bone man was less than two yards from her kitchen window, watching her.

14

West Wales, twenty-three years earlier
'Humpty Dumpty sat on a wall.'

The boy flopped down the stairs, scratching his head, his armpit, his arse, in the usual way of teenage boys fresh out of bed.

'Humpty Dumpty had a great fall.'

His overlong jeans slapped on the polished wooden boards of the downstairs hall. The tall old clock by the front door told him it was somewhere between half past eleven and twenty to twelve in the morning. It couldn't be relied upon any more accurately than that. He vaguely remembered Mum saying something about going on to campus for a meeting; Dad would be in his study. His three-year-old sister was somewhere close, if the warbling was anything to go by. She'd want him to play fairies again. The latest craze. To dance round the garden and build fairy dens under trees.

'Humpty Dumpty fell off the wall.'

She hadn't quite got it yet.

The boy stopped outside Dad's study door and sniffed the air. Stale coffee? Normal. Well-done toast? Normal. The loo his sister had forgotten to flush? Normal. Gunpowder? No, not normal.

A year ago, when he was twelve, his father had started taking him out shooting and his mother always complained that they brought the harsh cordite smell indoors with them. Not cordite, Dad had corrected her, cordite hasn't been used since the Second World War. Gunpowder is what we smell of.

But Dad hadn't used his guns for six months now. 'I don't want your father taking you shooting until he feels better,' Mum had said. And so the guns were locked away in a secure cabinet in the study and the boy had no idea where the key was kept. 'Guns and teenage boys don't mix,' his mother reminded him regularly.

'All the king's horses and all the king's men.'

His sister was in the study. The boy pushed open the door, stepped inside and saw what was left of his father.

15

Saturday 12 January (ten days earlier)
'It's two o'clock in the morning, Flint.'
'Were you busy?'

There was the sound of someone stifling a yawn. 'Just dreaming about you as usual,' Joesbury said.

I ignored that. 'Why didn't you tell me she'd been raped?' I asked.

'No evidence to suggest she had been. You won't be investigating a rape, Flint, or any aspect of Bryony Carter's attempted suicide. Your job will be . . .'

'. . . to experience Cambridge student life for myself. Find out if there's any substance to Dr Oliver's subculture bollocks theory. Will I actually be studying something?'

'Psychology,' Joesbury replied. 'Dr Oliver's subject. That way we make it as easy as possible for the two of you to spend time together.'

'How long will I be expected to be there?'

'If you've absolutely nothing to report back on after three months, we'll pull you out.'

I could hear bedsprings creaking and Joesbury making a very soft grunt in the back of his throat as, presumably, he pushed himself upright on the bed. And suddenly there were pictures in my head I could do without. 'Who do I report to?' I asked.

'Me. Mainly by email. You won't be expected to do any academic work, I'm sure you'll be relieved to know. So when your room-mate is hammering out her essays, you can write me nice long reports.'

'Room-mate?' I was nearly twenty-eight. I wanted to spend the next three months sharing a room with a teenager like I wanted to spend the next three months emailing Joesbury on a nightly basis.

'Just a living space. Separate sleeping accommodation,' replied Joesbury. 'And the girl you'll be sharing with was Bryony Carter's room-mate. She'll know as well as anyone if anything dodgy is going on.'

Silence for a moment.

'It's worth repeating that you will not be an investigating officer, just there to observe and report back. The psychiatrist, Dr Oliver, will be the only person at the university who knows who you are,' continued Joesbury. 'Local CID will know nothing about the operation, so won't be available as backup. Not that you should need it.'

'How soon do you want me there?' I said.

Seconds more ticked by. 'Are you sure?' he asked.

'My spider sense is tingling,' I said. 'And it's not like I have anything to keep me in London.'

A few more seconds, then: 'I appreciate it, Flint,' he said, in a voice that had chilled down a degree or two. 'Term's only just started so you've only missed a week. We can get you there by Monday evening, if you're up for it.'

I agreed that I was up for it and, after arranging to meet on Sunday for a detailed briefing, Joesbury wished me good night and hung up. I walked through my small flat to the conservatory at the rear.

Over the Christmas break I'd put solar lights around the small lawn, and even in January they gave off a faint glow throughout the night. There was frost gathering on the leaves, turning their various shades of green into intricate white lacework. The grass looked like frosting on a Christmas cake.

I'd never been to Cambridge. I'd grown up in and out of foster care and children's homes. I hadn't struggled at school — I was bright enough — but I'd never really taken academia seriously. The UK's premier universities hadn't been an option for someone like me, but now I was going to be a student at one of them, amongst people who, intellectually, could wipe the floor with me.

Jesus, what was I thinking? I had no idea how to be an undercover officer. SO10 trained its officers rigorously. The programme was tough and not everyone who applied made it through. Whilst it wasn't unusual for run-of-the-mill detectives to go undercover, they were rarely sent into situations that would last any amount of time. Besides, I'd joined the Met to work on serious crimes against women. If I spent the next few months off the grid, I could miss the chance to transfer to one of the specialist units. Why had I agreed?

Like I needed the answer to that one. I was doing it for Joesbury.

16

Mark Joesbury switched on the light and pushed back the bedcovers. The room was cold: he slept with the window open summer and winter alike. And it was full of light. His bedroom wasn't directly overlooked and he rarely bothered pulling down the blinds. When he couldn't sleep, most nights these days, he liked to watch the moonlight playing around the room, listen to the traffic outside, see the shadows ebb and flow around the walls.

He got up, used the loo and ran a glass of water. As he drank, he realized the usual headache had kicked in already. He'd developed a constant, niggling cough from the bottom of his chest that his doctor told him was a sure sign he was drinking too much. He'd stop, no problem, once he got back to work properly. Once he got over this stupid obsession with Lacey Flint.

And he'd made a good start on that last

one, what with dragging her into his latest case.

The computer in his tiny spare bedroom was never switched off. He tapped the space bar to restore the screen and typed out a quick email. Two words.

You awake?

The answer came back in seconds.

Yup.

Joesbury picked up his phone and pressed speed dial 4. Speed dial 3 got him Dana Tulloch's mobile, speed dial 2 the house where his eight-year-old son lived with his ex-wife. The man on the end of speed dial 4 answered quickly.

'What's up?' he said.

'She'll do it,' Joesbury replied.

'Good stuff.' Soft noises in the background, as if someone was eating.

'I'm not happy,' said Joesbury.

'We've discussed this.' A low-pitched moan.

'We shouldn't keep her in the dark.'

'She knows as much as she needs to. Decision made. You been on YouPorn lately?'

Joesbury's skin was starting to goose-pimple. 'Can't say I have,' he told his boss.

'Check out *Dirty Brunette Finds New Use For Her Tongue*.'

'You need to get a life, guv. And a

girlfriend.'

'Could say the same about you, buddy. See you in the morning.'

Joesbury put the phone down and walked back to his bedroom. Yeah, he needed a life. And a nice uncomplicated girlfriend. Someone like a nurse, or an air stewardess. What he wanted was Lacey. He was still carrying his phone. His finger hovered over speed dial 1. They'd spoken fewer than ten minutes ago. She'd be awake. He got into bed and pulled the quilt round his shoulders. The phone lay beside him on the pillow.

He knew he wasn't going to call.

17

Sunday 13 January (nine days earlier)
The girl at the wheel of the Mini Convertible was staring straight ahead along an empty road. The trees on either side were very tall and thin, like long, skeletal fingers reaching to the sky. The few remaining leaves were still as stone. Wind that had earlier been racing across the Fens like a possessed soul seemed, at last, to have exhausted itself and the girl could hear nothing.

Except the voice in her head.

A sudden vibrating movement told her the car engine was running again. Her left hand reached down. The handbrake was off. This was it then.

Something, it could even have been her own foot, was pressing down on the accelerator. Tentative at first, and then with increasing pressure. More and more, until the pedal reached the floor of the car.

71

When the rope that had been firmly tied round a beech tree at one end and the girl's neck at the other reached its full length there came a sound a little like that of a firework spluttering its last.

The Mini continued to speed forward for some seconds after the girl was no longer actively working the pedals. It stopped only when it collided with a food-delivery van heading the opposite way. The driver wasn't injured, although what he saw in the driver's seat of the Mini would feature in his nightmares for quite some time to come.

The girl's severed head broke free of the rope, bounced a little way along the road, and came to rest amidst some nettle stumps.

18

Monday 14 January (eight days earlier)
'And this is second court, Miss Farrow,' said
the porter, using the name that would be
mine for the next few months. For the
foreseeable future, I was to be Laura Farrow.

'It's beautiful,' I said, knowing something
was expected of me. What I really wanted to
say was, it's overwhelming.

I was finding the whole city of Cambridge
overwhelming. The grandeur of the ancient
buildings, the secret gardens and the name-
dropping wall plaques; the boys on bicycles,
college scarves wrapped carelessly round
their throats, and the clear-skinned, plump-
faced girls with their long limbs and intelligent eyes. Everything spoke of a world I
would never truly understand, that I
couldn't even think of belonging to. And
the red, navy and pale-blue college scarf I
wore round my neck felt as though I'd

stolen it.

With every step I took through these cloistered, medieval buildings, I could feel myself shrinking. It wasn't going to be hard, pretending to be a vulnerable student, out of her depth in a new environment.

Minutes earlier, I'd presented myself at the main gate of the college I was to join. St John's, one of the oldest and most prestigious in the university. The porter on duty, a middle-aged man with neatly combed hair and an impeccable uniform, who'd introduced himself as George, had been expecting me.

'Most students don't face this trek,' he was saying as we passed through what looked like a castle gatehouse but was simply a passageway from one court to the next. 'At the start of every term we have a drop-off system but it was easier just to help you carry your bags.'

I glanced behind to smile at a younger man who was carrying two of my bags. One of them, loaded up with books, was pretty heavy. The other contained my new student wardrobe. I was carrying the bag with my new Scotland Yard-issue laptop, plus personal effects and stationery supplies. George had insisted on carrying my gym bag.

'There are a lot of porters,' I said, as

74

another man, as slick in his uniform as George himself, passed us and greeted George by name.

'Lot of students,' countered George. 'We're one of the biggest colleges in the university.'

I already knew that. Late the previous evening, DI Dana Tulloch had pitched up at Scotland Yard. After glaring at Joesbury, she'd attempted to explain the relationship between the university and the colleges, and how the Cambridge system differed from most other UK universities.

'The university is like the umbrella,' she'd explained. 'It provides the teaching, mainly in the form of lectures, administers the examinations and awards the degrees. It also provides other communal facilities such as sports fields, the main library and so on.'

I'd nodded. So far, so good.

'The colleges, on the other hand, are like homes,' Tulloch had continued. 'There are thirty-one of them. Each has a chapel, to take care of your spiritual needs, a dining hall for the physical, a library for knowledge, common rooms for recreation, big rooms for the dons and the fellows, little rooms for the undergraduates.'

'Dons and fellows,' I'd repeated, wondering if I should be making notes.

'The colleges provide each student with a tutor, who acts almost in loco parentis,' said Dana. 'Your tutor oversees your studies, but also takes care of your well-being. Your tutor, for the sake of this exercise, will be my friend Evi.'

I'd yet to meet Evi. 'Have you worked here long?' I asked George.

'Library on your right,' he said, as we entered some buildings on the western side of the court. We passed through and stepped out on to a covered bridge of stone. The river was beneath us. 'I'm the newest member of staff,' he went on. 'I'm just covering for one of the senior porters who's had to take some sick leave. And now we're in New Court, completed in 1831 in the Gothic style.'

Until that moment, I couldn't have said what the Gothic style was, but looking around New Court I gathered that Gothic meant over-the-top elaborate, turrets from fairy tales, intricate carving that seemed more suited to a wedding cake than a structure of stone. We passed through another gateway and found ourselves facing much newer buildings.

'This is where most of the undergraduates live,' said George, as we headed for an awning at the entrance to the new block.

'What do we say, Tom?' He turned back to the man who was following us with my bags.

'Start them at the back,' replied Tom, a man in his mid-thirties with dark hair and kind brown eyes. 'Let them move forward in their second year, then into First Court for their final year. They're right by the main door then and it's easier to kick 'em out.'

I gave the smile I knew was expected of me.

We entered the new building, climbing stairs and walking along a corridor that reminded me of a hospital, or a large police station. When we were almost at the end of it, George unlocked a door and stepped back to let me go inside first.

'Your key is here,' he said, putting it on a desk that ran the length of one wall. 'We keep a spare in the porters' lodge and your room-mate will have one. Nice girl, though we don't see much of her. Now, no noise between eleven p.m. and seven a.m., parties need your tutor's approval and your maid will report anything untoward to us.'

The room was some four yards square. Two desks ran along opposite walls. There were two easy chairs, two desk chairs, two wall-mounted bookcases. Two doors led off from the main room. One of them was ajar and I could see a small bedroom beyond it.

George had been watching me look round. 'Everyone finds it strange at first,' he said, 'but you'll soon get used to it. You've got an hour till dinner.'

I blinked hard. There had been tears in my eyes and George had seen them.

'Good to have you at St John's, Miss Farrow,' he said. 'You know where we are if you need us.'

I listened to their footsteps fade away down the corridor, thinking that their kindness had made me feel even more of a fraud.

'Better get used to it,' I told myself, and set about unpacking.

An hour later, I knew I'd never get used to it. I was trapped in a bubble of noise, of confident voices and the incessant chink of silverware. Surrounding me were pale faces above black robes, candles and floral arrangements, crystal goblets like raindrops along the starched linen, and all in a centuries-old dining hall in which Wordsworth and Wilberforce weren't characters from history but alumni.

'I think those flowers are expected to last most of the week,' said the thin-faced, ginger-haired boy across from me. I looked down at the petals I'd unknowingly pulled from a yellow daisy, then back up at the boy, who could boast eighteen years and the kind of self-assured ease I'd never know.

'Lady's first time in Hall, cut her some slack,' said the second-year physics student on my right. He'd taken pity on me earlier as I'd stood at the painted-arched doorway, feeling like an extra in a Harry Potter movie in my borrowed gown. He'd steered me inside, found me a seat and done his best to make conversation. After twenty minutes he'd given up. I was so nervous I couldn't remember any of my cover story and I'd answered every question he'd asked me in monosyllables. I'd been hungry but faced with a three-course waitress-served dinner found I couldn't eat. I needed a drink but didn't dare pick up the impossibly thin crystal goblet. I knew I had to get to know these people and I couldn't think of a single thing to say.

I was failing. Everyone who set eyes on me would know I didn't belong here. Joesbury had made a massive mistake sending me, I'd made an even bigger one agreeing to come. I was so far out of my element I might as well be on Mars. And this was Monday evening, for God's sake, when I normally work late, stop by the gym and shove a Tesco ready meal in the microwave.

When coffee was finally cleared away and

people began to leave the room, I got up and slipped quickly through the crowd. I'd phone him, tell him it really wasn't going to work.

'Laura!' A hand fell on my shoulder. I turned to see that the physics student had followed me out. 'Good to meet you,' he said. 'And don't worry. This place is weird, you just get used to it.'

As I tottered back to my room on borrowed heels, it occurred to me that, personal misgivings aside, the stage show that was needy, insecure Laura Farrow might just have pulled off a pretty impressive first act.

19

Tuesday 15 January (seven days earlier)
'It isn't true that the rate of suicides at universities is higher than among the rest of the population. I know a lot of people believe it to be the case, but it isn't.'

Dr Evi Oliver, the only person at Cambridge University who knew I was an undercover police officer, sipped from a glass of water on her desk. She'd been doing it a lot since I'd arrived, bringing the glass up to her mouth, sipping nervously and then putting it down again. The rest of the time, she was fiddling with a paper clip or rearranging papers. I didn't need to be a psychiatrist to spot that she was as much on edge as I was. Mind you, given the news of the latest Cambridge suicide, the second-year student who'd decapitated herself early Sunday morning, it was hardly surprising. Something had gone seriously out of kilter in this city.

'But it is prevalent among the young,' I said, trying not to get distracted by the steady flow of students milling around a paved area immediately outside. The student counselling service that Dr Oliver led was in the town, a little way from most of the academic buildings. I could see Regency houses, office blocks in the distance, the corner of a shopping centre. We were on the upper floor, but Dr Oliver's large, bright corner office had floor-to-ceiling windows. 'Young people get things out of proportion,' I went on. 'I think I read somewhere that they see suicide as a grand gesture. They don't necessarily equate it with being dead for ever.'

I'd spent a fair amount of time, the last couple of days, reading up on suicide. One thing I knew was that the suicide rate in the UK was around sixteen per 100,000 people per year. In a city the size of Cambridge, with a population of nearly 110,000, you would expect between sixteen and eighteen people to take their own lives each year. In that context, some four or five dead students didn't seem too alarming.

Dr Oliver leaned back and pulled a cord that closed the window blinds, effectively cutting off the view. 'The sun gets quite intense at this time of day,' she told me, and

I couldn't help feeling I'd been told off for not paying attention. Still, if she wanted my full attention, she could have it.

Evi Oliver looked like a Russian doll. Her chin-length hair was almost black and shone like patent leather. Her skin was the sort that would tan to a soft dusky rose but in January was creamy pale. She wore a lavender sweater that suited her well. She was younger and prettier than I'd expected. Mid-thirties at the most and, as Joesbury had said, a bit of a babe. She was also, as both wheelchair and aluminium stick told me, semi-crippled.

Catching me staring, she blinked at me. She had long black eyelashes, heavy with mascara, surrounding eyes so deep a blue they were almost indigo. 'Suicide is the second most common cause of death in young adults,' she said. 'And the incidence is rising, especially among young men. But the idea that student populations are particularly vulnerable is based on several inaccurate studies and, frankly, is wrong.'

I leaned back in my chair. 'Go on,' I said.

'There was a study done on suicides here in Cambridge between 1970 and 1996,' said Dr Oliver. 'It showed that statistically there are likely to be two suicides in the university each year. Yet we've had twenty in the last five years. Double what you might expect.'

'These cases were all investigated by the local CID?' I asked, although I already knew the answer.

Evi nodded. 'Yes, they were. And this is where my argument starts to look a bit weak, because they were all textbook cases.'

'How so?'

'Half were being treated for depression or similar conditions. Another five had a history of depression, anxiety or stress-related problems.'

'And depression is a common factor among suicides,' I said. 'At this point, your case isn't weak, it's verging on non-existent.'

I'd meant it as a joke. I think I'd half hoped to make her smile and chill a bit. God knows, her being so uptight was hardly helping me relax. 'What about Nicole Holt? The latest?' I asked, when I'd given up on getting a smile out of her.

'She wasn't one of our patients,' said Evi. 'So far, I know very little about her.'

'The post-mortem's been done?' I asked.

Evi nodded. 'Some time today, I believe. But the results won't be made public until the coroner's inquest and that could be months away.'

'She was a pretty girl,' I said, remembering the photograph I'd seen on various news websites. Nicole had been tall and slim, with long dark hair and big eyes. Bryony had been attractive too. 'Are pretty women more susceptible to suicidal acts?'

'Not to my knowledge,' said Evi. 'I'd have considered it a factor against, wouldn't you?'

'Bryony Carter thought she was being raped,' I said. 'Any thoughts on that?'

Evi glanced down at her notes, lips pursed, as though thinking hard. There was something compellingly graceful about the way her head moved. She reminded me of a ballerina. 'Bryony didn't feel safe in her room at night,' she said. 'Several times, she says, she had unusual, violent dreams of a sexual nature, and when she woke up the next day she felt as though someone had had sex with her.'

'Your colleague didn't believe her,' I said.

Evi looked down again. 'She certainly shouldn't have given any hint that she didn't believe her,' she said. 'Maintaining trust is extremely important in any doctor–patient relationship. But judging from what was written in her notes I think you might be right.'

'What do you think is happening here?' I asked.

Evi thought for a moment and seemed to slump in her chair. 'I hardly know,' she said.

'But things are bothering me. The first is that, of twenty suicides in the last five years, women outnumber the men by something like five to one.'

'Statistically, it should be the other way round,' I said.

'Exactly. The second thing that worries me is the . . .' She stopped and frowned, thought for a moment. 'Well,' she went on, 'the sheer originality and variety of the methods involved. We've got jumping off high buildings, self-immolation, self-stabbing, self-decapitation. It's as if they're competing to see who can come up with the most bizarre exit strategy. I shouldn't be surprised if there's a website somewhere giving them marks out of ten.'

So now she was joking to relieve the tension. She was as nervous about this as I.

'And the methods just aren't typical,' Evi went on. 'When women die by suicide, they choose the least violent methods. Overdose is the most common. Not the most reliable, of course, which is why women have a history of failed suicide attempts, but still women shy away from extreme violence. Cutting wrists in a hot bath is another one, but still . . .'

Her eyes fell to my wrist, the ugly scar still covered by a plaster. I waited for the question that didn't come.

'Self-immolation,' she said, shaking her head. 'It's almost unheard of in our culture. And that poor girl on Sunday morning. Who on earth would come up with such an idea?'

A pretty disturbed mind, I thought. And I'd met a few in my time.

'You mentioned a website,' I said. 'I was told you think there might be a subculture that's encouraging destructive behaviour.'

'These suicide websites vary from the well meaning but misguided to the downright ghoulish,' said Evi. 'I'm afraid something like that is going on here. I just can't find any evidence of it.'

'You've looked?'

'Repeatedly. There are internet sites and intranet sites and blogs, and chat rooms and tweets ad infinitum, all relating to life at Cambridge. There's practically a virtual town and university floating above the real one. All the ones I can find, though, are pretty harmless. My IT skills aren't great but I can't help thinking there's something going on that I haven't been able to access. I was told your IT knowledge is pretty good.'

'Not bad,' I said.

Evi glanced at her watch and then at the computer screen. 'I have a patient waiting,' she said, before turning back to me. 'OK, you're a mature student of twenty-three who started an undergraduate degree two years ago but had to leave halfway through because of health problems,' she said, recapping my cover story. 'You've suffered from depression and anxieties in the past and been on medication for eighteen months. It's all on my system on your personal file. I've agreed to let you join my psychology programme because I've seen great promise in your previous coursework. I'm also employing you, informally, on a part-time basis to help me with some research. That way, no one will question our spending time together. You have my various numbers if you need to contact me at any time?'

I thanked her and agreed that I had.

She frowned at me. 'Laura Farrow,' she said. 'That's not your real name, is it?'

I shook my head.

'Are you allowed to tell me what is?' she asked.

I couldn't help but smile. I never told anyone that. Lacey Flint was no more my real name than Laura Farrow was. 'Better not,' I said, as I'd been told to. 'It helps prevent mistakes.'

As I stood, she nodded, vaguely, and I had the feeling she didn't really care one way or the other. For her, I was a means to an end. Then she surprised me.

'Dana tells me you're exceptional,' she said.

I waited, halfway between her desk and the door, not really sure what to say to that. I'd never been called exceptional before. 'She also tells me you've had a difficult six months,' she went on, her eyes not leaving the desk. 'I have a habit of asking too much of people, Laura. Don't let me do that to you.'

20

The partridge may have seen the shadow of the predator hovering overhead. It may have felt the rush of wind as the falcon dived. It may even have had a split second to look death in the eyes and say how-do-you-do before strong talons crushed the life out of it. The falconer doubted it. He'd rarely seen a swifter kill.

The two birds, hunter and prey, fell from sight behind a hedge and the falconer stepped up his pace. Merry, the older and more reliable of his two pointers, trotted ahead, leading him right to the spot where the falcon's strong, curved beak was already tearing the partridge apart. The man bent and lifted the falcon before taking out a knife and cutting the partridge's head off. He gave it to the victor.

Whilst the falcon ate, the man who was sometimes foolish enough to tell himself that he owned the bird looked at the swirling grey sky, the upper clouds just turning the rich, deep peach of winter sunsets. The weak January sun was little more than an echo on the horizon and there was less than an hour of light left. As he fastened the falcon back on to the perch he ran his hand over its head, whispering praise.

The partridge joined the others in his bag and the falconer walked on. When his phone rang he cursed softly but pulled it from deep inside his oilskin coat.

'Nick Bell,' he said. Then, after a second, 'How bad do they say she is?'

A few more seconds passed while he listened. 'OK,' he said. 'I'll head over there now.'

21

'So how have you been this week, Jessica?'

'Fine.'

Evi smiled. There couldn't be more than five years between the girl sitting in the chair opposite and the policewoman who'd just vacated it, but Evi couldn't imagine two more different faces. The police officer had been close to classically beautiful, but with a face as silent as stone. She gave nothing away. This girl, on the other hand, with her large brown eyes and coffee-coloured skin, couldn't hide a thing. Flickering eyelashes, the gleam of a tear, eyes unable to maintain contact and so fidgety she could have just rolled in itching powder. This girl might say she was fine; her body language said she was anything but.

'I'm glad you came today,' said Evi. 'I was worried last week, when we didn't hear from you.'

Jessica Calloway looked down at the hands

in her lap, then up again, to the large window. She raised one hand and rubbed the side of her face. 'Sorry,' she said. 'I phoned, the next day. Maybe a couple of days later.'

'Yes, you did, thank you,' said Evi. 'The message I got was that you'd been ill, is that right?'

Jessica nodded. She pushed a finger into her hair and started twisting a tight blonde curl around it.

'Nothing serious, I hope,' said Evi. She already knew Jessica hadn't been to her GP. If she had, Evi's clinic would have been notified.

'Just a bug, I think,' said Jessica. 'To be honest, I can't remember much about it. I just crashed. Slept through a day, a night and another day. Woke up feeling like shit. Sorry.'

'No problem. I feel like that myself sometimes,' said Evi. 'How's your appetite?'

Jessica sighed, like a teenager whose mother was on her case again. 'OK,' she said. 'Pretty good.'

Evi let her eyes travel down Jessica's body to the fur-lined boots that swamped her lower legs. Jessica's jeans were loose on her and the shoulder seam of her top dropped halfway down her upper arms. She looked as though she'd lost even more weight in the two weeks since Evi had seen her.

'Have you had any more trouble with practical jokes?' Evi asked.

The glint in the girl's eyes became brighter.

'Anything you can tell me about?' Evi pressed.

Jessica shook her head. 'I don't know what goes on in some people's heads,' she said. 'What have I ever done to anyone?'

'Nothing,' said Evi firmly. 'We both know that what's happening is not your fault. Some people see gentleness and sensitivity and they don't have the intelligence to understand what they're looking at. So they register it as weakness and they prey upon it. Those people have a serious problem and I can't help them with it. I can help you, though.'

'Do you know what they did this time?' A hint of anger there now, which was good. Anger was better than acceptance. Evi waited.

'They came on to our corridor, where the airing cupboards are, and found my clothes. They took my underwear.'

'They stole your underwear?'

'Yeah, but that wasn't the worst. They replaced it with enormous stuff. Granny pants and massive great support bras. Like they were saying, who are you kidding, this is what you really need to wear.'

Evi took a moment to hide her annoyance. Most people would dismiss such a prank as a laugh. Jessica, who'd suffered from eating disorders since she was twelve and who had been hospitalized twice as a teenager when her weight had dropped to under six stone, would find it anything but amusing.

'Did you report the theft?' Evi asked.

'I did. One of the other girls told me I should and went with me to the police. They said they couldn't get involved in a student prank.'

'Anywhere else it would be burglary and intimidation,' said Evi. 'In a Cambridge college, it's a prank.'

'Do you remember that website I told you about? The one that had the photographs of me?'

'Yes,' said Evi. 'I tried to find it. None of the search engines I used could locate it.'

Jessica bent down and pulled a laptop from her bag. 'I'll show you,' she said. She opened the computer and switched it on. After a few seconds she tapped her fingers over the keys, waited a while longer, then turned the screen to face Evi.

Evi reached forward and picked it up, tilting the angle so that she could see it clearly. It was a Facebook spoof. Facefeeders, it was called. *Who's been eating the pies this week?* ran the subheading, directly above several photographs of Jessica herself.

Except they weren't Jessica. Jessica was an exceptionally lovely girl whose size ranged from model slim when she was well and happy to painfully thin when she wasn't. In the photographs someone had digitally altered Jessica's tiny frame to make it enormous. All the photographs were nude. All were Rubenesque in their proportions, with swollen bellies, rounded dimpled buttocks and great pendulous breasts. They'd even managed to make Jessica's face look fatter.

Oddly, the photographs weren't unattractive, but to Jessica it would be like seeing herself turned into a monster. And these were on a website, for the world to see.

'Remind me how you found this site?' Evi asked. 'Did someone tell you about it?'

'It popped up when I was working one night,' said Jessica. 'I clicked on it without thinking.'

Evi made a note on her pad to alert the detective to the website. 'Do you have any idea who might be doing it?' she asked.

Jessica shook her head. 'No,' she said.

'Everyone I've told thinks they're appalling.'

'I agree,' said Evi. 'Not that the photographs are appalling in themselves, because even if you were as large as the girl in these pictures is supposed to be you would still be beautiful — I know you don't believe that, but you would. They are appalling because they've been created to cause you distress.'

Tears were running down Jessica's cheeks.

'I feel like everybody's seen them,' she said. 'If I go to a lecture or a tutorial, even a bar or the dining room, I feel like everybody's whispering about how fat I am. I can even hear them in my sleep.'

'You're still not sleeping well?'

Jessica shook her head. 'You remember I told you about that night my mobile kept ringing, every half hour until I turned it off?'

'I remember,' said Evi. 'You never found out who it was?'

'No,' said Jessica. 'And now, although I always switch it off when I go to bed, I can still hear it ringing.'

'I don't understand.'

'I wake up several times every night, thinking I've heard my phone. But I haven't because it's switched off. I dream that it's waking me up and so it does.'

'How long has this been going on?'

The girl shook her head. 'A couple of weeks,' she said. 'But if it's not the phone, it's the voices.'

'Voices?'

'In my dreams. Whispering about how fat I'm getting.'

'Jessica, when did you last get a good night's sleep?'

The girl couldn't respond. She was trying too hard not to cry.

'Jessica, you need to sleep. I can give you something that will help. Just for a couple of weeks, just to break this cycle, does that sound like a . . . What? What's the matter?'

The girl looked terrified. 'I can't,' she said. 'I can't take sleeping pills.'

'It's understandable to be wary,' said Evi, 'but we're very careful to guard against addiction.'

'It's not that,' said Jessica. 'You don't understand.'

'No, I don't. Please try and explain to me.'

'The interruptions, the imaginary phone calls and the voices, I think they're my brain's way of protecting me, of stopping me falling into too deep a sleep.'

'Why would your subconscious do that?'

'Because of the real dreams, the ones I have when I'm so deeply asleep I can't wake up.'

'And what are those like?'
'Unimaginable. Like I'm in hell.'

22

I didn't go back to my room after leaving
Dr Oliver. I'd found the box-like space,
stripped of all traces of its previous occupant, oddly depressing. So, instead of
returning to college, I headed for my car
and drove to the hospital on the edge of
town where I knew I'd find Bryony Carter.

The nurse in the burns unit indicated a
private room about three-quarters of the
way down the corridor. I paused for a
second at the open door. I'd seen the
photographs. I knew what to expect.

So much worse than I'd expected. I
couldn't go into that room, I just couldn't.

I'd imagined something clinical: clean,
neat, white and sterile. I hadn't realized
there would be blood and other fluids seeping through the dark-stained bandages. I
hadn't expected that the skin covering her
face and her hairless head would be open to
the air and would look like something I'd

only ever seen before on corpses. I didn't know that her left arm had been amputated just above the elbow.

The room was so hot. And the smell . . . oh, Christ, I couldn't do it.

'She's not in any pain. She's very heavily sedated right now.'

I'd been transfixed by the sight of the lifeless figure under the transparent tent. I hadn't noticed anyone else in the room. The man speaking to me was standing by the window, dressed for the outdoors in a thick blue woollen sweater and blue jeans.

'She had a bit of a setback earlier,' he went on. 'They've been weaning her off the ventilator over the last few days but her oxygen levels plummeted. They've put her back on it for twenty-four hours, just so she can stabilize again.'

I swallowed hard. The smell would be tolerable if I breathed through my mouth. I'd come across worse.

'Are you a friend?' he asked, and I looked at him properly for the first time. In his mid-thirties, he could have been a model in a country-living magazine: tall and slim with curly hair the colour of a wet fox. 'If you are, you're the first to make it through the door,' he went on.

Without noticing, I'd crossed the threshold. 'I've just moved into her old room,' I said, having cooked up a cover story on the way over. 'And I found this tucked under her bed.' I pulled the book from my bag. 'There's a page corner turned down. I think she must have been reading it before it happened.'

'*Jane Eyre,*' he read, looking down at the Penguin Classic paperback. 'Doesn't the hero get very badly burned?'

'I didn't think of that,' I admitted, feeling stupid. 'I should just take it away again.'

'Leave it,' he said. 'Let her parents decide, when they come back.'

I made myself take another look at the girl in the clear plastic tent. 'Why does her face look like that?' I asked. 'Her skin looks dead.'

'That's not her skin,' the man replied. 'And it is dead. That's cadaver skin covering her face. Tell you what, I was just about to get a coffee and you look like you need one. Come on.'

23

'Can you tell me about the dreams?' Evi asked.

Jessica had left her chair and was at the window. Two weeks ago, she'd been a young girl with a history of anxiety and eating disorders who'd been struggling to cope with being away from home for the first time and the rigorous academic demands of the university. Now she seemed a seriously disturbed young woman, exhibiting behaviour that was making Evi think about hospitalization.

'We all have bad dreams, Jessica,' she said, when her patient didn't reply. 'I'm not going to get all Freudian on you, but I do think they can point towards what's worrying us.'

'Do you?' asked Jessica, without turning round. 'Have bad dreams?'

The question caught Evi by surprise and she answered without thinking. 'You have no idea,' she said.

Jessica had turned on the spot and was looking Evi full in the face now. 'What do you dream about?' she said.

'Something that happened to me just over a year ago,' said Evi. 'I can't give you details, because other people were involved, other patients, but it was a very difficult time. It became a very frightening time. And although it's over now, I still dream about it often.'

'Do you ever want to talk to someone about it?' asked Jessica.

'I do talk to someone about it,' replied Evi. 'And you have very cleverly turned this conversation into one about me. I'm going to turn it back again, if that's all right with you.'

The girl seemed calmer now. She sat down again, her hands rubbing her upper arms, as though for warmth. She really was horribly thin. Evi waited.

'I'm scared of clowns,' said Jessica, after a moment.

'A lot of people are,' replied Evi. 'It's a very common phobia.'

'But really scared,' said Jessica. 'I can't see a picture of one without feeling cold.'

'And are clowns what you dream about?'

'I think so.'

Evi waited. Nothing. She raised her eyebrows. Still nothing.

'You think so?' she prompted.

'I can't really remember,' said Jessica. 'That's the weirdest thing. I know I'm in a fairground. I can remember the lights spinning and the music. I was lost in a fairground, you see, when I was about four. I just got separated from my parents in the crowd. When they found me I was beside one of those mechanical laughing clowns in a big Perspex box. I didn't speak for a week.'

'That would have been a terrifying experience for a four-year-old,' said Evi. 'Being lost in an unfamiliar place that was noisy and crowded, and then coming face to face with a clown. And, you know, coming to university is putting you in an unfamiliar place, away from your parents for the first time. It's not surprising that your mind is harking back to a scary experience you had as a child.'

'You're probably right,' said Jessica. 'It's just . . . not knowing what happens in the dreams is the worst thing.'

'How do you mean?'

'I remember lights, music, laughing and bright colours. Swirling things like those horses on poles . . . but nothing else.'

'Perhaps that's all you can remember from

what happened to you as a child.'

'So why do I wake up exhausted?' said Jessica. 'And sore, like I've been beaten up in the night. Why do I wake up screaming?'

24

I walked ahead of the man with rust-coloured hair, out of Bryony's hospital room and into the corridor. He indicated a coffee machine close to the ward's reception desk. When the foul-smelling liquid had been poured, we sat down on nearby chairs.

'You OK?' he asked me.

I nodded. 'Sorry,' I said. 'I just wasn't expecting . . .'

'No one ever is. I'm Nick Bell, by the way. Bryony's GP.'

Nick Bell smelled of the outdoors, of wet mud and woodland in winter. Compared to the chemical smell of the hospital corridors and the putrid stench of the burns unit, being close to him felt like striding home through crisp winter air.

'Is she likely to recover?' I asked, after I'd told him the name that was still feeling odd on my tongue.

He shrugged. 'Bryony is one of the most

serious cases they've had here for some time,' he said. 'She has a mixture of first, second, third and even fourth degree burns over nearly 80 per cent of her body,' he replied. 'At 90 per cent, it's nearly always fatal.'

From my reading over the weekend, I knew that first degree burns were superficial, like sunburn, that second degree went deeper and damaged the underlying, dermal layer of skin, and that third degree burns, the ones I'd believed to be the most serious, invaded the fat and muscle layers beneath the skin. 'What are fourth degree burns?' I asked.

'Fourth degree burns damage the bone,' he told me. 'The surgeons couldn't save her left arm.'

I bent down to put my coffee on the floor and found I didn't want to straighten up again. So I stayed there, elbows on knees, looking at the floor tiles. Then a hand touched down lightly on my shoulder.

'Laura, given the severity of her injuries, she's not doing too badly.' The hand lifted away again. 'The flames were extinguished pretty quickly, which meant the damage to her respiratory system wasn't great. She should be breathing on her own again quite soon. The biggest challenges now are getting her wounds to heal.'

'Will they?' I asked, spotting a beautiful tortoiseshell-coloured feather on the sleeve of his sweater.

'The more superficial burns should heal by themselves,' he said. 'The epidermis is pretty clever at replenishing itself. The deeper ones will require a skin graft from a donor site elsewhere on the body. Are you sure you want to hear all this?'

I nodded. Strangely, it was helping.

Bell was drinking coffee as though it wasn't scalding hot and foul. 'The difficulty is that because so much of Bryony's skin was damaged, there isn't much they can harvest to use as grafts,' he said. 'They've created a donor site on the small of her back and they've used it to graft over the worst wounds, which were on her left shoulder. So far, they're taking quite well.'

'So that's good news,' I said.

'It is. But they have to wait now until the donor site replenishes itself before they can harvest it again. It's a long and painful process and there's no getting round it, I'm afraid.'

'One small area on her back has to grow enough skin to cover her whole body?' I said.

'Exactly.' Bell nodded at me, as if I were a

student who'd just grasped some important principle. 'In the meantime,' he went on, 'the cadaver skin is keeping her wounds covered, reducing the pain that exposure to the air would cause and helping to guard against fluid loss and infection. And, although it's from a corpse, technically it's still alive, meaning blood vessels from the wound can grow into it. Surgeons have been using it for thousands of years. It's called an allograft.'

He put his coffee on the floor and ran a hand through his hair. It was still damp from the rain outside. I looked back at the closed hospital door, to where the sedated girl lay, kept alive by a dead person's skin.

'Do you think she'll ever be able to tell us why?' I asked.

I sensed, rather than saw, Nick Bell shake his head at my side. 'Even if she survives, she'll probably remember very little about it,' he said. 'We'll probably never know what happened to her.'

25

'Meg, I thought he was going to come through the kitchen window,' said Evi. 'That he would just spring from the tree branch, straight through the glass, and that would be it.'

'Do you want to rest for a while?'

The two women had reached a wooden seat beneath a rose arbour. Evi put the brake on her chair and her companion, fellow psychiatrist and Cambridge alumna Megan Prince, sat beside her. When Evi had felt the need of someone to talk to about the events of the past year, Megan, who'd been just two years ahead of her at university, had been the obvious choice; known and trusted but not too close a friend. Evi had been seeing Megan weekly for three months. She wasn't feeling a huge improvement but, as she knew better than most, these things took time.

As always, Megan smelled of patchouli

and Marlboro Lights, a fragrance from her student days that she seemed unable to leave behind.

'I think I broke in here one night,' said Evi, looking round at the perfect formation of beds, box hedges and grassed walkways. After a day of weak winter sun, frost still gleamed on the thin branches around them and the thorns looked as sharp as steel. 'With cannabis and cider.'

'On your own?'

'Almost certainly not.' Evi smiled. 'But names and faces escape mc.'

'Cider and cannabis can do that.'

Silence fell as both women looked at the six-foot-high brick wall around the garden that Evi wouldn't have a hope of climbing now.

'Did you call the police?' asked Megan quickly, as though anxious to get the conversation back on track. 'On Friday night, I mean.'

Evi turned back. There was no point dwelling on the past, but avoiding it wasn't always easy because Megan looked as skinny and as young and dishevelled as she had in the old days. 'From a locked bedroom,' she replied. 'Of course, by the time they arrived there was no sign of him.'

Megan drew the lapels of her jacket a little

closer round her neck and clenched her jaw, as though trying not to shudder. She still never wore enough clothes in cold weather. 'Him?' she asked.

Evi shrugged. She had no idea whether the masked figure in her garden had been male or female.

'The police came pretty quickly?' Megan asked.

'Yes. Some uniformed constables arrived first, then a detective sergeant a few minutes later.' Directly in front of her a robin had landed on the stem of a rose bush. It paused and seemed to look directly at her.

'Did they take it seriously?'

The robin took flight and Evi looked back up again. 'Of course,' she said. 'Why wouldn't they?'

Megan glanced down for a second and squirmed, as though the seat were cold, or damp. 'What did they find?' she asked.

'Nothing,' said Evi. 'No sign of a break-in. No footprints in the garden. No recent fingerprints inside other than mine.'

A moment of silence, then the moment stretched. When Evi was in the counsellor's chair, she waited the silences out.

'There's something you want to say, isn't there?' said Megan.

'You won't like me for doing so.'

'Go for it.'

Evi braced herself. 'Is there any possibility someone could have accessed the notes you've made during our sessions?' she asked.

Megan tucked a loose coil of hair behind one ear. Then, 'You think someone has hacked into my records?' she asked. 'And then that someone broke into your house and used his inside knowledge to scare you witless?'

Evi pulled her face into an apologetic smile. 'Doesn't sound too likely, does it?' she admitted. 'But those pranks just seemed so personal. I haven't discussed what happened last year with anyone but you. No one but you would know I have a phobia about fir cones. Do you remember we talked about it in one of our early sessions?'

'It's not just unlikely, it's impossible,' said Megan. 'Our systems at the practice are completely secure. They have to be, to protect all our patients' confidentiality. Even my colleagues couldn't access my files without my passwords and most of them, frankly, have trouble switching their computers on in the morning.'

'I'm sorry,' said Evi. 'I was on edge and then scared on Friday night. It just felt like someone had got inside my head.'

'A bone man,' said Megan, her forehead creased with frown lines. 'But from what you've told me, the bone men were more like bonfire-night Guys. Built around a frame stuffed with rubbish and wearing clothes. They weren't skeletal. You're sure the figure in the tree was meant to be a bone man?'

Evi felt some of the tension draining out of her. 'You're right,' she said, after a few seconds. 'There were people, in that place I told you about, who dressed as skeletons but they weren't the bone men. The skeletons carried the bone men to the fire.'

Megan's thin, pencilled eyebrows disappeared into the coils of her fringe.

'It was an odd town,' said Evi.

'Remind me to give it a miss next time I'm walking the Pennines.'

Neither spoke for a moment.

'Rag week can't be very far away,' said Megan. 'Dressing up seems pretty much compulsory then. And fir cones are very common this time of year.'

'True,' said Evi. 'But it doesn't alter the fact that someone was in my house.'

'You mean the fir cones on the table? What did the police say about that?'

'They didn't think it was too sinister,' said Evi. 'But they advised I get the locks changed. Which I have done. The university's maintenance department did it yesterday.'

The two women fell quiet for a moment, as Megan looked at her scarlet fingernails and Evi watched a dried leaf fall from the stem of a rose bush.

'Are you thinking about Harry as much?' asked Megan.

As if she ever stopped thinking about Harry. He was there, in her head, like an unspoken awareness of her own self. Didn't mean she wanted to talk about him. And the college porter would be locking the garden gates soon.

'Are you still worried about the suicides?' asked Megan. 'Did you talk to CID again?'

Evi felt her eyes drop to the ground. She couldn't tell Megan about the undercover investigation she'd instigated. About the girl she'd installed in her faculty. So now she was hiding things from her counsellor. She shook her head.

'CID believe the suicides are exactly that,' she said. 'Suicides. There's no evidence of coercion or third party involvement. They've respectfully suggested I concentrate on being accessible to vulnerable members of the university community and leave them to policing Cambridgeshire.'

'Well, I guess we never hesitate to tell the police how to do their jobs when we see fit,' replied Megan with a smile. Then the smile faded. 'Wasn't there a spate of suicides when we were here?' she asked. 'Or was that before your time?'

Evi thought for a moment and then shook her head. 'From what I can gather, the suicide rate here has been bang on normal until five years ago,' she said. She looked at her watch again. 'Time's up,' she said. 'Is Nick around this afternoon, do you know?'

'I think he got called to the hospital. Do you want me to leave him a message?'

'It's OK. I'll call him at home.'

The two women left the walled garden and made their way the short distance down the street to the GPs' surgery where Megan was based two days a week.

As they turned the corner, Evi saw that an expensive-looking Japanese saloon was blocking her own car in. When he spotted them coming, the driver, a man she knew she'd seen before, got out. He was tall, late thirties, with short dark hair, square jaw and a muscular build. His dark suit looked expensive and fitted him well. Evi watched his dark eyes focus on Meg immediately behind her. As a slow, confident smile softened his jawline, she turned to see Meg smiling back at him.

'Hey,' he said to Meg, his left eye just hinting at a wink, before turning back to Evi. 'Detective Inspector Castell, Cambridgeshire Police.'

'John Castell?' asked Evi, her eyes flicking from him to Meg.

Meg nodded, still smiling. 'Yes, this is John,' she said. 'John, this is Evi. Do you remember her now?'

Castell smiled properly as he held out his hand. The wide grin gave his otherwise plain face a considerable dollop of charm. 'I think so,' he said. 'I was at Emmanuel. Read Law and Psychology. You do look a bit familiar.'

'Well, it's nice to meet you properly,' said Evi. 'Sorry if I've made Meg keep you waiting.'

'Actually, I came to find you,' he replied. 'Your secretary told me you were here. I've been asked to have a look at your report of an intruder on Friday night.'

'I'll leave you to it,' said Meg. She stretched up to kiss Castell on the cheek before disappearing inside the building.

'I wouldn't have thought Friday night merited a detective inspector,' Evi said. 'Do I get special attention because I'm Meg's friend?'

'Partly that,' said Castell. 'But I've been

keeping a watching brief on the suicides as well, so I've come across your name a couple of times before now. I wanted to have a chat with you about Friday, if that's all right.'

'Of course.'

Castell reached into his pocket and held out a small, thin sheet of paper in a clear plastic bag. Evi took it and looked down. The writing was very faint.

'What is it?' she asked.

'A receipt,' replied Castell. 'From a card and gift shop in town. Dated three weeks ago. It's for two greetings cards and a small wind-up toy.'

Evi screwed up her eyes to make out the faint lettering. 'It says skeleton toy,' she said.

'We took the toy you found in your house on Friday to the shop,' said Castell. 'They confirmed they'd had those toys in stock until a couple of weeks ago.'

'So where did you find the receipt?'

Castell seemed to lean a little closer towards her. 'Well, that's the problem, Evi,' he said. 'According to the officers who attended your house on Friday evening, it was found in your desk at home.'

26

The woman behind the hospital's main reception desk gazed at Nick Bell as if he were a rock star who'd just wandered in off the streets. Not that I could entirely blame her. I made a point of avoiding exceptionally good-looking men myself, they always behaved as though they were doing you a big favour, but there was something about Bell, about the way he seemed oblivious of his looks and gave you his full attention, that was flattering in spite of all the warnings you could give yourself.

We'd gone back in to see Bryony again but there had seemed little point staying with a patient who was deeply sedated. 'If she's awake I just sit and talk to her for a while,' Bell had told me in a low voice. 'Any old stuff about what's going on in the news, how the various university sports teams are doing. I imagine it must get quite bewildering for her otherwise, having no idea of the time, hearing nothing but nurses creeping around her and doctors muttering medical terminology.'

'What about her family?' I'd asked.

Nick's mouth had given a little twist but he avoided making eye contact. 'They've visited,' he said. 'Although not for a while. They live some way away. And she doesn't seem to have many friends. I don't know, maybe peace and quiet is what she needs. Maybe I'm just trying to salve my own conscience.'

We didn't talk on the way out of the hospital. Nick seemed genuinely upset by the condition Bryony was in. Outside, the air was so cold I felt as though my face had been slapped.

'It won't be easy for you,' he said, as we reached the car park. 'Joining a university partway through the academic year. Friendships are already formed. Everyone around you will appear to know exactly what they're doing. They'll be busy. Won't have time to look after a newcomer.'

'I expect I'll cope,' I replied, before remembering I wasn't self-reliant, cope-if-it-kills-me Lacey Flint any more. I was Laura Farrow, insecure and vulnerable. 'I know what you mean though,' I back-pedalled quickly. 'Everyone seems to have

121

formed tight little groups. I haven't even met my room-mate yet. She's never in.'

We'd reached my car. Bell glanced up at the clouds, which had taken on the colour of charcoal now the sun had gone in, then back down at me. 'It was kind of you to come and see Bryony,' he said. 'Take care.'

He turned, walked quickly over to an old Range Rover, climbed inside and drove away.

27

I drove back to college via the B road where Nicole Holt had died. Remains of police tape still clung to trees and petrol-station flowers had been left at the side of the road. I parked and got out of the car.

It was an eerie enough spot. A narrow road, just wide enough for two cars to pass, with tall trees on either side. There were no streetlights and no kerb. Not somewhere you'd want to break down if you were female and on your own at night. It struck me as a very lonely place to take your own life.

In my Sunday-afternoon briefing, I'd learned that Nicole had bought a strong nylon rope in a hardware shop three days before her death (the police had found the receipt in her room) and had tied it round the thick trunk of a beech tree. The other end had gone round her neck.

The tree in question, still with police tape

round its base, was on the left side of the road as I looked out of the city. It stood a good half-metre closer to the tarmac than most of its neighbours. By choosing this one, Nicole had minimized the chances of the rope's being tangled on other trees.

I'd brought a torch from the car and by this time I needed it. I shone its beam up and down the tree trunk. Just over a metre from the ground, some of the bark had been broken away, no doubt by the sudden tightening of the nylon rope as it reached its full length.

The Mini convertible goes from 0 to 60 miles per hour in 11.8 seconds, according to the CID report into Nicole's death. It wouldn't have had time to reach that speed on this short stretch of road, probably hadn't got to much more than thirty mph. Still fast enough to sever a slim neck.

I started to walk along the road, thinking that it would have required some planning, a suicide of this nature. You'd need to think about speed, distance, length of rope needed. Had the rope been too short, Nicole could be with Bryony right now, nursing a crippling neck injury. She'd been a history student. A suicide involving mathematical calculations didn't really seem her thing.

I figured I was reaching the point where the rope had stretched tight and Nicole's head had left her body. There would have been a lot of blood and I knew it hadn't rained in Cambridge since Saturday afternoon.

Fearful of discovering I was walking across pink-stained frost I took a quick look down. No blood, just a few half-rotten remains of beech nuts and conker shells. And fresh tyre tracks. I looked back and followed them for a few yards. When they disappeared I stopped and shone the torch around. At the point where I was standing, a vehicle had left the road and driven instead along the grass verge. A short distance ahead, it had swerved to avoid a bank of earth and then gone on for another sixty paces before rejoining the road.

OK, think. The tracks had to be fresh because the CID file had contained a weather report. It had rained on Saturday afternoon and both road and surrounding ground had been damp. It hadn't rained since, though, so any tracks or prints made after Saturday afternoon would still be here. Early Sunday morning, police tape had been stretched along the length of the road and, at each extremity, into the woods. It was still there.

So, sometime between late Saturday afternoon and early Sunday morning, a car had left the road and travelled about twenty yards along the verge.

I pulled out my phone and took close-up photographs of the tread. Then I turned back, following the tracks again. I stepped over the bank of earth just as a very cold, fine rain started to fall.

It couldn't have been the Mini that made these tracks. I would compare tyre prints to be certain but it was impossible. On the road I could see the chalk mark that the police had made to indicate the point at which the rope stretched tight and Nicole was killed. The car that left the road had been further out of town. Even if the Mini had swerved after Nicole was dead (in itself quite likely) it could not have steered itself around the bank of earth. There'd been another vehicle here.

28

Evi let herself in, using the new keys the university's maintenance department had provided. The house felt cold, even though the heating should have kicked in an hour ago. She checked the controls as she entered the kitchen. Both heating and hot water were switched off. She cursed softly and flicked both on. Getting cold always made the pain worse and she'd spent too much time outdoors today. She flicked the switch on the kettle and pulled open the fridge door. Cooked salmon, green vegetables, pasta. It was getting harder all the time to drum up any interest in food.

She left the room and went into her study.

DI Castell could not have been kinder. He'd stressed that if someone had been able to gain entry into her house to leave the fir cones and the skeleton toy behind, they could easily have left the receipt as well. It was being sent away for fingerprint analysis and it would make no difference to their treatment of the case. He'd done his best to reassure her.

Trouble was, after he'd left, Evi had checked back through her diary. On the date in question, she had been shopping in Cambridge. The receipt was from a shop she knew. She remembered buying two of the items — cards, one for a friend whose birthday was coming up, the other of Tuscan sunflowers, an all-purpose greeting card.

The receipt was for three items, two of which she definitely remembered buying. Was it remotely possible she'd bought the skeleton toy herself? Bought it, put it in the cupboard upstairs and forgotten all about it? Grief and depression played tricks with people's memories, she knew that perfectly well. She'd been depressed for a long time, even before what had happened last year. Losing Harry had been the final straw.

But to have done something so totally out of character and then to have forgotten about it completely. It wasn't possible.

Was it?

Dinner in the college refectory, otherwise known as the Buttery, was a whole lot easier than dining in Hall but still an experience.

I'd forgotten just how self-conscious young people can be. The students around me in the brightly lit, noisy dining room were all hair and limbs, brash loud accents and forced laughter. The girls fiddled with food on their plates and jewellery on their bodies; the boys scratched and yawned and used longer words than they seemed comfortable with.

Each kid around me appeared to have at least two conversations going, the first with their immediate neighbours, the second with some absent friend on the receiving end of text messages. The tinny beeping of texting was a constant backdrop to the buzz of conversation. Heads craned constantly to see who might have entered the room.

And this wasn't even the busiest time. I'd sat in my room earlier, waiting for the queue outside the building to get smaller. I'd used the time to get to know my new laptop. Standard-issue Met laptops are ruggedized, serious pieces of kit that will stand up to a great deal of physical and intellectual punishment. They are as secure as you could hope a piece of IT equipment could be. One of those babies would have been far too conspicuous in the possession of an undergraduate, so I'd been given instead an off-the-shelf model along with clear instructions to keep it with me at all times, make sure the password requirement kicked in after sixty seconds of inactivity and not accept any incoming mail from unknown sources.

There was nothing in my inbox apart from a welcome email from Student Counselling Services with a Freshers' questionnaire for me to fill in.

I'd glanced up. Still a queue. So I'd opened the Freshers' questionnaire. Strictly confidential, totally anonymous, purely in the interests of researching general trends, etc., etc. I glanced quickly down the list of questions and decided it was needy, self-indulgent nonsense. Right up Laura Farrow's street.

Did I find the experience of being at university for the first time overwhelming? Well, yes actually, I did. *Was I unsure of the demands that were being placed on me?* Yes, I could probably tick that one as well. *Did I experience feelings of isolation and loneliness?* Tell me about it.

I went down the questionnaire ticking boxes and half laughed when I realized I sounded a complete basket-case. I stopped when I realized 99 per cent of what I'd put was absolutely true. I closed the file and sent it back.

■ ■ ■ ■

When the Buttery started to clear I went
too. Around me kids were inviting each
other for coffee or making arrangements to
meet in various pubs or bars later. I even
heard someone talking about the library. It
was nearly half past seven and I wanted
nothing more than to go back to my room,
make my first report to Joesbury and curl
up with a book. No such luck. I had work
to do.

Back at her desk, Evi accessed her clinic's
files. The detective calling herself Laura Farrow had picked up on the reference in Bryony's notes to possible rapes. It had been
the only time during their conversation that
her self-control had seemed to be slipping.

Evi's clinic had a policy of attaching key
words to the summaries of patient consulta-
tions. Rape would almost certainly be one
of them. Evi keyed rape into the search
engine and waited.

Thirty-eight case files were found. The
most recent was the case of Bryony Carter.
The next on the list was that of a girl who'd
been raped by her uncle when she was
fourteen. Evi didn't bother with the details.

She closed the file down and moved on. There were several other cases that academic year, a few more in the previous year. None seemed relevant. Evi was starting to lose heart when she got to the case of Freya Robin, a plant sciences student. The computer files contained only summaries — the more detailed notes of meetings weren't usually typed up — but there were still sufficient similarities to Bryony's case for Evi to read carefully.

During the Lent term three years earlier, Freya had talked about bad dreams, problems sleeping and an unsubstantiated fear that someone was getting access to her room at night while she slept. One night she'd woken in the small hours, convinced she'd been raped. Her college friends, alarmed at the semi-hysterical state they'd found her in, had persuaded her to go to the police. No physical evidence had been found on her body, other than some scratches and minor bruising, and the rape test the police had carried out had proved inconclusive. With nothing to go on, the police had been unable to pursue the case.

Freya had drowned herself in a university swimming pool six weeks later.

Evi reached across the desk for the list of suicides. Freya Robin was on it.

Cross-checking the two lists, it didn't take Evi long to find the rest. Donna Leather, a 21-year-old medical student, had never used the word 'rape' in her counselling sessions, but like Freya and Bryony had talked about bad dreams, often of a sexual nature; of feeling hungover and sluggish in the morning, although she claimed she hadn't been drinking; of soreness in the genital region. 'Violated' was the word Donna had used to describe how she'd felt on certain mornings, but as though her own mind were doing the abusing. Donna hadn't gone to the police. She'd hanged herself within two months of first raising her concerns.

The same year, French-language student Jayne Pearson had reported her suspicions of ongoing rape to the police. They'd found substantial levels of ketamine in her blood, although she'd sworn she'd never taken it. Unfortunately for the case, no conclusive physical evidence of rape was found. Jayne had died later that year, after a gunshot wound to the head. The fourth and last similar case Evi found was that of Danielle Brown, a neurology student from Clare College. Danielle's claims were all too familiar by this stage. Bad dreams, trouble sleeping and vague recollections of sexual abuse whilst she'd been asleep. Danielle had hanged herself three days before the Christmas vacation but had been found before she'd suffocated.

The computer screen went into sleep mode but Evi didn't notice.

Including Bryony, it made five instances of possible rape in five years. Statistically, that wasn't remotely remarkable in itself. But when you factored in that all five women had attempted to take their own lives shortly afterwards, the coincidence was starting to feel stretched.

From: DC Lacey Flint
Subject: Field Report 1
Date: Tuesday 15 January, 22.22 GMT
To: DI Mark Joesbury, Scotland Yard

It's now ten thirty in the evening, Sir. I've drunk so much coffee I'm hyper and enough mineral water to keep me on the loo all night. I've been chatted up by nineteen-year-old nerds who stand five foot four in heels and drunken jocks who think manly sweat a powerful aphrodisiac. And a lesbian with peroxide blonde hair who was easily the best company of the lot. Many more evenings like this and I might just try batting for the other team.

I stopped typing. I was whingeing on my first night on a case but — good God above — less than an hour after leaving my room I could cheerfully have wrapped a nylon rope round Joesbury's neck and pulled it tight. The thought that I might have to keep this up for another three months was enough to give me suicidal thoughts. I'd wandered from library to TV room to coffee bar to pub. I'd been anywhere and everywhere I could find where students hung out. I'd made small talk all evening and learned nothing.

I leaned back in the chair, stretched and turned my head first one way then the other. A shiny blue jacket strung across the opposite desk and a faint floral scent reminded me of my room-mate's existence. OK . . .

Evi Oliver is very bright and certainly committed to her job but seems nervy and uptight. Has issues of her own, in my opinion, and could well be the type to overreact to a problem. I take it you've run a background check, Sir. Any chance of sharing?

What I can't ignore, though, are her concerns about the statistical anomalies in the suicide stats. Not only are there simply more of them than you would expect, but there is a disproportionate number of women on the list and the methods they're choosing are untypically violent.

Practically none of what I'd written so far was in language suitable for a senior officer and I should just scrub it and start again, pretend I was writing to Dana Tulloch, or my DI at Southwark nick. Someone who didn't rub me up the wrong way simply when I allowed myself to think about him.

I was too tired to start over. I went on to describe my visit to Bryony and her GP's opinion that she was being neglected by her friends and family. It was nearly eleven o'clock by this stage and I had no idea whether Joesbury would be at home, on the top floor of that white-painted house in Pimlico, or out somewhere having fun.

Bryony Carter's GP is exceptionally good looking and, whilst on the surface very nice, seems more involved with Bryony than I might expect a GP to be. Do you think I should try to get to know him a little better?

I finished by describing my visit to the site of Nicole Holt's death.

The presence of another car on the road that night needs further investigation, in my view. I've compared the tyre print at the site with the prints of several tyres commonly used on Mini Coopers and found no matches at all. Not even close. A different vehicle was on that stretch of road close to the time Nicole died yet no mention of this in the CID report.

It was well after eleven by the time I finally pressed Send and put the laptop into sleep mode. It felt like I was alone in the block. I undressed, locked my door and crossed the corridor to the communal bathroom. Inside, I turned the taps on full pelt.

Evi had turned on the bath taps and begun the slow and difficult process of getting undressed when the phone rang. The first thought in her head, as always, was Harry. It was never Harry, though. Harry had probably forgotten all about her by now.

'Hey, sweetie, it's me.'

'Hi, Mum.'

Her mother was so proud of her clever, brave daughter and was always such an effort to speak to because the need to seem fine was more important with her than with anyone.

'How was your day?'

'Pretty good,' lied Evi. 'Got lots done.'

Evi's mother had been with her on the skiing holiday when Evi had seriously damaged the sciatic nerve in her left leg. Evi's mother, the better skier of the two, had talked her daughter into taking a difficult black run. Evi had caught her ski on a rock, lost control and fallen into a crevasse. Any hint now that she was less than perfectly fine would be more than her mother could deal with.

By the time she said goodbye, Evi was getting anxious that the bath was overrunning. In the bathroom, the second thing she noticed was the message on the mirror above the bath. *I can see you,* it said. The first was that the bathtub was full of blood.

29

The noise level outside had picked up by the time I got back to my room. Sleep wasn't going to happen any time soon. And sharing a bathroom with six other women wouldn't be the least of the challenges I'd face for the next three months. At eighteen I could have coped — hell, there were times in my life when I'd have given anything to have access to a bathroom of any description — but over the last few years, it seemed, standards of hygiene had crept up on me unawares.

Two messages in my inbox. The first was from Student Counselling Services acknowledging receipt of the completed questionnaire. The second was from Joesbury.

From: DI Mark Joesbury, Scotland Yard
Subject: Field Report 1
Date: Tuesday 15 January, 23.16 GMT
To: DC Lacey Flint

You might want to learn the art of the precise, Flint. If I fancy a novel I'll visit Waterstones. I'll make discreet inquiries about the tyre prints, but I wouldn't get your knickers in a twist. The rain finished around four in the afternoon. Police attended the scene around three in the morning. That's eleven hours in which any number of inebriated, over-privileged, public-school tossers could take a detour off the road.

Does it bear repeating that you are not there to investigate Nicole Holt's death, or any of them for that matter, just to be a good-looking fruitcake and observe? Sweet dreams.

Five minutes went by and not a single word passed my lips that could be repeated in church. I was just about to email him back — which, given my mood, wouldn't have been wise — when the door opened. A purple-haired girl whose limbs looked too thin to hold her upright stood in the door-way.

'Laura?' she said, swaying on impossibly high heels. 'Thank God, a room-mate as old as me. God, I'm rat-arsed. Is there coffee in that mug?'

There was, it was steaming on my desk.

She stumbled over to me, picked it up and drank from it. She didn't seem to notice it was hot enough to scald her.

'Talaith?' I said. She was a little older than I'd expected. Maybe twenty-two or three.

'Toxic,' she said as a trickle of hot liquid ran down her chin. For a moment, it seemed as if she didn't much rate my coffee-making skills. 'Or Tox,' she went on. 'Only the vicar calls me Talaith.' Taking my coffee with her, she flicked the main door shut, staggered across the room, pushed open the door to her bedroom, put my mug on the floor and collapsed face down on the bed. She mumbled something in the pillow that I think was intended to express disbelief at how her evening had unfolded.

I stood up, not knowing whether I was amused or annoyed, and then the drumbeats started.

'It's not blood, Evi.'

Evi was sitting at her kitchen table, trying to make polite conversation with a young WPC. DI Castell stood in the doorway.

'What, then?' she asked.

Castell shrugged, looked apologetic. 'Our kit's not good enough to tell us that, I'm afraid,' he said. 'We'll have to send it off. Could be a couple of weeks before we know.

But definitely not blood. Some sort of dye or paint would be my best guess.'

'How did it get in my bath?'

'Now that we can tell you,' he said, stepping further into the room. 'Someone poured it into your header tank. We've run it all out and it's filled up clear again but you should probably get a plumber round to check it out tomorrow. Just to make sure there was nothing corrosive.'

'I had the locks changed,' said Evi. 'No one should be able to get in here.'

For a second, DI Castell just looked back at her. 'If people were working here today, it's possible that's when whoever it was got in,' he said. 'We'll check with university maintenance, see if anyone turned up claiming to need a look at the water system or anything.'

'Thank you,' said Evi.

'That message written in the steam. *I can see you.* Does that mean anything?'

Evi shook her head.

'Creepy sort of thing to write in a bathroom,' said the WPC.

'Right then,' said Castell. 'We've checked the entire house, upstairs and down. Nothing out of place and we'll get SOCs out here in the morning. Are you sure you don't want me to phone Meg? She can be here in ten minutes.'

Evi shook her head again and thanked him. She stood, found her stick and followed them to the door. Castell hesitated on the doorstep.

'You know where we are if you need us?' he said.

She nodded. He'd already given her his card with his direct line and mobile numbers. He'd been both kind and professional, but was she imagining it, or was he finding it difficult to make eye contact? What if he was reasoning that, if she'd bought the skeleton toy herself, maybe she'd put the dye in the tank too?

Ba ba ba boom, ba ba ba boom. Someone was beating out a rhythm on a large drum right outside the block. There were voices too, hardly audible above the drumbeats. Men's voices, urging each other on; girls' voices, squealing and screaming. Then something hit my bedroom window. A split second later it happened again. Talaith pushed herself up on the bed and staggered into the main room.

'They're not serious,' she said. 'Not again.'

'What's going on?' I asked her. She didn't reply, just muttered something about checking the front door was locked and ran from the room. The drumbeat went on. A bit like a heartbeat. Rather like my own heartbeat, which I could feel getting faster by the second. Stupid to be alarmed: students outside were just pissing about, the way students were supposed to do. They'd get bored and cold before long.

But there was something about that drumming that couldn't be ignored. It wasn't just the volume, there was something purposeful about it. Something instinctively intimidating. Not for nothing, I realized, did armies march into battle to the sound of a drum.

I leaned across my desk and opened the curtain a fraction. The lawn immediately below my window was full of people. Fifty students at least, and more appearing all the time. They were being summoned by the drum. I had a feeling they knew what to expect. Around the green, lights were on in every window and faces peered out. A couple of the braver ones jeered down at the crowd, getting abuse in return.

Talaith joined me at the window just as the crowd started to chant. Two words, over and over again.

'What's fresh wheat?' I asked Talaith.

'Fresh meat,' said Talaith. 'I think they mean you.'

A total surprise, that sudden stab of panic in my stomach. I let the curtain fall in place. This was for me?

'What the hell do you mean?' I asked the purple-haired, white-faced girl beside me.

'It's a stupid freshers' thing,' Talaith told me. 'They did it a lot last term.'

'Did what?'

'It's OK. I locked the front door.'

From the hall outside came the sound of banging and loud voices demanding to be let in. Then heavy footsteps.

'I think someone just unlocked it,' I said, still not quite believing this fuss had anything to do with me.

'Get keys, quick,' Talaith told me, striding towards the room's main door and pushing it shut. 'Mine are in my bag.'

She leaned against the door as I turned to find her bag. I had no idea where my own keys were. I'd picked up the small black leather rucksack when I saw the door slide inwards, Talaith's full weight of something like seven and a half stone proving no barrier at all to the force that was pushing it open. Giving up, she staggered out of the way as three tall figures stepped into the room.

Three men, all of them over six feet tall, all powerfully built. All three were stripped to the waist and their fashionable jeans sat low on their hips. The flesh of their torsos was shiny with oil and had been painted with weird red and gold symbols. Two of them had slicked their hair up with gel to form spikes around their faces. The third had long dark hair that rippled down to his shoulders. All wore simple cloth masks covering their eyes.

Oh, to have been able to laugh, to pull my warrant card from my back pocket and tell them to get the fuck out of my room or I'd have the three of them banged up. Not going to happen. My warrant card was back in my locker at Southwark nick. As was all the authority I'd taken for granted over the past four years. I wasn't a police officer in this place, just a student like thousands of others. And as the three of them came towards me, I felt something I'd hoped never to experience again, something that was verging on terror.

'What the hell are you lot supposed to be?' Talaith found her voice first. 'Ninja bloody turtles? Get out of — no, leave her alone!'

The long-haired one had grabbed hold of me by the upper arms, the rough skin on his hands scratching my bare shoulders. He spun me round as the second closed in. I took a deep breath, bracing myself to swing both legs up and kick number two in the chest, hopefully hard enough to send him flying. Then before number one realized what I'd done, I'd drive one elbow back into his solar plexus. If he didn't back off then, I'd go for his balls.

Except that, if I fought these guys with anything other than girly struggling and squealing, I might as well just announce who I really was. Emotionally damaged Laura Farrow would never get physical with three big guys. Shit, I would have to take what was coming with nothing more than a ladylike squirm and a few gasps. 'Touch me and you're fucking dead,' I said, to number two.

OK, maybe a bit of strong language too.

I might as well not have bothered. Number two bent down and grabbed my legs and I was lifted from the floor.

'Hit it,' said the one who had my shoulders and we began to move towards the door. I twisted to get free and the third stepped in and grabbed me round the waist.

'You wankers, it's freezing outside.'

Talaith's protests were fading away. By this time my arms were pinned to my side and my face pressed close to the bloke who'd picked me up. His chest hair was scratching my cheek and I could smell both shower gel and sweat. Number three had his arms around my hips and the second was holding my feet together to stop me kicking.

'Swing it,' said the long-haired man. We turned at the top of the stairway and began the descent and I had to bite my lip to keep myself from screaming.

The night air hit me like a slap. Another cheer went up as we appeared and the chanting got louder. *Fresh meat, fresh meat.* I was being carried through the crowd. Faces, pumpkin-orange in the lamplight, were staring at me. I could see eyes gleaming, heads twitching.

No, I could not scream. They were just kids messing around; it was nothing to be afraid of.

We'd reached a space in the middle of the green where the frosted grass was already brown with mud. A heavy chain lay around the central tree. At the front of the crowd I saw boys had formed a line and were passing along buckets from the nearest block. Water. They were going to throw water at me. That was all. It would be unpleasant and humiliating but I had no need to be afraid. I was on my feet, still held firmly from behind, as one of my captors bent down and grasped hold of my ankle. Then I felt something heavy and cold pulling down on it. They'd padlocked the chain round my leg.

The first bucket took me totally by surprise. Freezing cold water hit me full in the face, streaming into my mouth and nose. For a second blind panic hit me when I couldn't breathe. A moment later I was coughing hard.

'Ladies and gentlemen, welcome to the St John's wet T-shirt competition,' yelled a male voice as the contents of another bucket hit me. Another cheer went up and I looked down to see that the cotton running vest I nearly always wear in bed was soaked through. And that something like seventy people, standing in a circle around me, knew what my breasts looked like. One of the masked twats actually had a video camera, and for a second fury got the better of fear. This was sexual abuse, plain and simple. Where the hell were university security? Why was no one calling the police?

The bloke with the video camera was closer than the rest and at that moment I really didn't care if I blew my cover, I was going to land him one. Forgetting the chain, I ran at him. I got three feet and saw alarm in pale-blue eyes before a stabbing pain shot through my ankle. A split second later I found myself sprawled in the mud. More cheers. And voices rising from the crowd.

'I think that's enough now, guys. Come on, let her go.'

Whoever he was, they took no notice of him. Six more buckets of ice-cold water were thrown at me while I was on the ground. I'd like to think it was the need to maintain my Laura Farrow cover that kept me lying there, curled into a ball, hiding my head behind one arm, but I'm honestly not sure. I just wanted it to be over. I wanted it to be over before I started to howl. When I couldn't stop myself shaking I heard several voices shouting that that was enough. Then a warm hand was on my ankle and the cold chain was lifted away. Someone took hold of me under the arms and I was on my feet again.

'You all right, love?' said a northern accent. Not one of the masked boys. They'd disappeared into the night.

'Does she bloody well look all right, you effing moron?' A bright-yellow coat was wrapped around my shoulders and I was being steered by my tiny room-mate towards our block. I raised my head and pushed hair out of my eyes.

'Christ, the mud we're bringing in. Like that lot are going to clean it up. Come on, sweetie, let's get you in.' I let Talaith lead me inside. I was walking over linoleum, my feet squelching mud with every step. Talaith was guiding me towards the bathrooms at the end of the hallway. Doors were opening; girls who hadn't dared leave their rooms before were appearing in the hallway.

'Is she OK, Tox?'

'She doesn't look too good.'

'She'll be fine. She just needs to get warm. Can someone make tea?' We'd reached the door of the bathroom and Talaith ushered me inside. She reached over and turned on the shower. Steam began to rise. 'Go on, love,' she told me. 'You're filthy. Get yourself warm. I'll get you some towels. Can you manage? The front door's locked. They can't get in.'

She was still talking as the door closed and I was left alone. Without even bothering to take off my clothes I stepped under the hot water, telling myself I was OK, the front door was locked, they couldn't get in. I was OK.

At my feet mud swirled in the basin. Grass and pebbles were already clogging the drain. I was still shaking. Talaith was wrong. The door to our block was left open all the time. The girls who lived in it, their visitors, the cleaners, came and went continuously. They could get in any time they liked and I was a very long way from being OK.

30

Berkshire, nineteen years earlier
The mother started howling as the coffin sank.
The father, almost as green as the foliage on
the coffin lid, took hold of her more firmly and
a collective shudder ran through the mourners. This was always the moment when it hit
home. To put someone you loved so much
into the ground. To lose your only child. At
thirteen years old. How did you deal with that?

'The days of man are but as grass, for he
flourisheth as a flower of the field,' said the
minister. 'For as soon as the wind goeth over
it, it is gone.'

The seventeen-year-old boy, in the smart,
blazered uniform of a good public school,
looked at the perfect rectangle of the grave
and pictured the still, cold face of the boy
inside. I did this, he said to himself. There
were thunderclouds overhead and he wondered perhaps if guilt would hit him hard and
hot, like a strike from a lightning bolt.

Since the news that young Foster had hanged himself one Saturday morning in the dorm while the rest of the school were watching an inter-house cricket match, he'd been waiting for the guilt. He'd seen the horror-struck faces of his co-conspirators, the ones who'd helped him make Nathan Foster's life a misery for the past twelve months, but, unlike him, had never really expected it to come to this. They were feeling it already, it was written all over their faces. Shame and contrition that would eat away at them like a parasite in their guts for the rest of their lives.

Any time now it was coming for him too and it was going to hurt. Like a physical pain, he imagined it, a vicious cramp squeezing in on his heart, or maybe like maggots nibbling away at his brain. He knew, from the faces of those who were almost as guilty as he, that guilt was going to be bad.

'Forasmuch as it has pleased Almighty God of his great mercy to take unto himself the soul of our dear brother here departed, we therefore commit his body to the ground.'

Good God above, his English teacher was snivelling. Who'd have thought old Cartwright had a shred of compassion in him? Around the grave, mourners were throwing handfuls of earth on to the coffin like they didn't have two perfectly good sextons with ruddy great shovels less than a hundred yards away. One of the undertaker's staff was standing directly in front of him, holding out the box of soil. No choice but to dip in his hand, take hold of stuff that felt damp and slimy, and step forward for one last look. I did this, he said to himself, as he opened his hand and the soil fell directly on to one perfect white rose.

Shadows were spreading fast around the crematorium garden. The day was getting colder and those with umbrellas were glancing down at them, as though to check they were still there. Maybe guilt would be like a heavy downpour from above, the first drops hardly noticeable, but gradually seeping through him until his entire being was drenched in it. Maybe guilt was slow to begin but relentless, building a momentum of its own once it got going. The boy took a deep breath and waited.

'In sure and certain hope of the resurrection to eternal life, through our Lord Jesus Christ. Amen.'

The service was done and the caterwauling mother being led away. There'd be questions to face, now that the funeral was over, but he had it covered. They'd had time to sort out their stories and he'd been careful to cover his back from the start. There'd be no repercussions, he'd made sure of that. Just the guilt to be dealt with.

'Come along, Iestyn.' A warm hand was on his shoulder. Cartwright was touching him again, with the same hand he'd just used to wipe snot away from his dribbling nose. 'Dreadful business, lad. We're all feeling it.'

'Thank you, Sir.' The boy turned and stepped a little way to the side so that the teacher's hand fell away.

'Think we might be lucky with the weather after all,' said Cartwright, as they walked across the short, grassed area to follow the other mourners back to the car park.

Overhead, there was a sudden break in the clouds and the summer's day became warm again. Ahead of Iestyn and his teacher, sunshine was streaming down upon the small, black-clad procession that made its way up the hill. Iestyn watched and saw sadness and confusion drifting behind them like the smoke from a tar boiler.

I did this, he said to himself, as the warmth from the sun washed through him, making him feel alive, happy, even blessed. And he smiled.

31

Wednesday 16 January (six days earlier)
By the time Joesbury got back to the Cripps
building, Lacey was being led back to her
block by a group of young women. Her wet
clothes clung to her body and her hair
streamed down her back. She was gritting
her teeth, he could tell from the way her
jaw was set, and seemed determined not to
make eye contact with anyone around her,
keeping her gaze up and ahead.

Joesbury, on the edge of the crowd, was
wearing dark, plain clothes. The collar of
his jacket was pulled up and a black woollen cap covered most of his head. He was
standing in the shadows, little more than a
shadow himself. Wouldn't make any difference. She'd know him. Joesbury stood still
as stone, knowing that if she looked in his
direction now, movement could give him
away.

He'd seen the three masked figures slip

away into the night minutes earlier and had given chase. He'd seen the vehicle they'd driven away in, memorized the make and registration number and already called it in. Not that he held out much hope. It would almost certainly be a stolen car they'd abandon after tonight. In ordinary circumstances he might have sprinted to his own car, taking a chance on the direction they'd take and finding them again. Ordinary circumstances when he didn't have a damaged lung, and when Lacey wasn't in the hands of irresponsible twats. Instead, he'd jogged back to the green.

Almost at the door of the building, she tottered and Joesbury took an involuntary step forward.

Biggest fucking mistake of his career, allowing himself to be talked into bringing her here. He simply could not function properly where she was concerned.

And now that the fun was over, several of the students still on the green were starting to notice him. A few long-legged strides and he was gone.

'Hello?'

No background noise. She'd be in that tiny room, the one with the impossibly narrow bed pushed against the window wall.

'Did I wake you up?' He knew he hadn't. There hadn't been time for her to shower, drink tea, agree with the rest of the girls on the corridor what pillocks men could be, say goodnight and fall asleep.

'No.'

Silence. He couldn't ask her if she was OK. Couldn't tell her what it had cost him to watch her go through that and not put someone in hospital for it. His scar was hurting again. He reached up, pressed fingers against the skin just below his right temple.

'Thanks for the report,' he said. 'Very thorough.'

A moment passed, whilst she thought of something sarcastic to say back.

'Pleasure,' she said. 'Where are you?'

Joesbury took a step closer to the window. From the third floor of the hotel he could see the tower and some of the taller buildings of St John's. He was looking in the exact direction of her room.

'Thames Embankment,' he said. 'On my way home. Long day.'

The tiniest sigh that could almost have been a crackle on the line. Or, if he didn't know her better, the start of a sob. 'Pity,' she said.

'Why?' he asked, before he could stop

himself.

An intake of breath. Then a gulp. 'Oh, nothing. I could just use a drink and some grown-up conversation right now.'

Joesbury turned back to his room, to the neatly made double bed with its dark-red throw, and saw Lacey's head on the crimson silk, her arms outstretched, hair trailing to the carpet.

'Are you OK?' he asked.

'Fine, just tired. I should let you go too. Thanks for checking in. Goodnight, Sir.'

'Lacey, be careful.' Idiot. Shouldn't have said that.

'Why? What's up?' Alert again.

'Just do what you're told for once,' he said. 'Keep your wits about you. I'll see you soon.'

32

It's surprising how a spot of medieval-style humiliation can give you an appetite. I woke early and went straight up to the Buttery, where I helped myself to scrambled eggs and bacon that were surprisingly good. As the hall filled I became increasingly aware of the sideways glances directed my way, and the muttered conversations that were just out of earshot.

Instinct told me to hold my head high and thump anyone who stepped out of line. Common sense made me keep my body language submissive, to avoid eye contact. I was Laura, nervous and needy. Laura would not fight back.

By the time I left, the room was largely full and a small queue had formed outside. I was about to leave the building when something made me stop. The crowd outside the entrance weren't queuing, they were looking at something on the notice board. Something I was pretty certain hadn't been there when I arrived. I walked over.

Two large pieces of white card covered most of the board. The card, in turn, was filled with photographs. Of me.

The pictures told the story. They started with the arrival of the three boys at the door of my block, then showed me being carried out and across the lawn. As I'd become increasingly drenched, the photographer had moved in closer. One shot was of little more than my breasts, all too visible beneath a soaking wet vest. Two shots from the end, I disappeared from view, ushered by Talaith and the girls back into my block. The last two were of the three boys, posing triumphantly for the camera. One was a pretty good close-up of their masked faces.

'Oh, I think we can do without this crap,' muttered a voice beside me.

I turned. The boy wasn't much bigger than me, pale and flabby from too much time indoors. He reached up, slid his fingernails behind the drawing pins and began pulling them out. In seconds, the card and photographs fell to the floor.

'Want me to get rid of them?' he offered.

'Thank you,' I said.

He was leaving the building when I called

162

him back. I found the picture of the three masked men and ripped it from the card. Thanking him again, I slipped the photograph in my pocket and went back to my block.

'Thanks for seeing me so early.'

The two women made their way along the towpath. Most of the narrowboats moored along this stretch had been closed up for the winter months. Only the occasional one they passed showed signs of recent occupancy. The taller, thinner woman pushing the wheelchair looked down at the dark-haired one sitting in it. 'You've never let me push you before,' she said.

'Not sure I have the energy,' replied Evi in a dull voice.

'I thought you looked tired,' said Megan. 'Didn't you sleep? After they'd gone?'

'Would you have done?' asked Evi, without turning her head.

They slowed as they approached the lock, to allow three female students to wind their way round them on the path. When they'd moved out of earshot, Megan said, '*I can see you?* It's creepy, but does it have any special significance?'

Evi nodded. 'I think so,' she said. 'When I was working with that little boy last year, the thing that struck me most was his belief that the family were being watched all the time. Even before I knew he was telling the truth, it used to creep me out. Just the idea of someone always watching.'

'Not pleasant,' Megan agreed. 'And the blood in the bath?'

Evi nodded again. 'The woman I was treating, do you remember me telling you, the case I seriously screwed up? She was found in a bath full of blood.'

The women moved on, drawing level with a navy-blue narrow-boat with a row of potted plants on its flat roof. An elderly man, huddled in oilskins against the cold, pulled weeds from a pot directly above the main cabin. As Evi watched, a duck landed on the bow of the boat.

'Did John say who they think is doing it?' asked Megan after a moment.

Me, thought Evi. They think I'm doing it. Out loud she said, 'They have no idea. No sign of a break-in. The locks were changed recently. No fingerprints that they can find. Nothing.'

The chair's wheels crunched over the rough path; from the river came the sound of waterfowl fighting over scraps and the soft plash, plash of a sculling boat passing by.

'Evi,' said Megan, 'did you talk to Nick about increasing your medication?'

Evi nodded. 'A couple of weeks ago,' she admitted. 'He put me on gabapentin and OxyContin. Amitriptyline to help me sleep. It helped for a few days but it's just got steadily worse since.'

'What does he say?'

A pile of blown leaves lay across the path. Some of them became caught on the chair's wheels, altering the sound it made as it was pushed along.

'He's sympathetic,' said Evi, 'but we both know pain management is all he can do for me.'

'Are you in much pain?'

Evi took a deep breath, her special way, since being a child, of fighting back tears. 'It never goes,' she said. 'All day long, it hurts. When I wake in the night, the pain is the first thing I think about. But if I take anything stronger I'll be like a zombie. I'm only thirty-four, Meg. How can I get through the next forty years?'

Megan stopped pushing and came round to crouch in front of Evi. She took her hands, forcing Evi to look directly at her. A couple approaching didn't bother to hide their stares.

'Evi, you need to take some time off,'

Megan said. 'You're not fit to be working.'

Megan's face had become blurred. 'I'm doing practically no clinical care at the moment,' Evi said. 'You don't need to worry about my patients.'

She felt her hands being squeezed. 'It's you I'm worried about,' Megan told her.

'I know. But if I stop work now, I might never start again.'

Megan stood up and walked to the back of the chair.

'I hear voices too, did I mention that?' Evi went on, as Megan turned the chair on the spot and headed back towards St John's. 'Voices in the night when I'm half asleep, half awake.'

'What do they say?'

'They say, *Evi fall.*'

The chair slowed for a second then picked up pace again. 'Evi fall?' Megan repeated.

'It's what scares me the most. Falling. Falling is how I became like this in the first place. Then last year I had another fall that nearly killed me. It's how I imagine my death, falling from a great height. Meg, what's happening to me?'

The chair stopped in its tracks again and a deep sigh came from behind her. 'Evi, I want your permission to talk to Nick about you. I can't . . .'

'Do you know what it feels like?' said Evi, turning round in the chair to face Megan. 'It feels as if someone's been in my head, rummaging around there, finding all the things that I'm most scared of and using that knowledge to drive me nuts.'

No response. Just a sad, worried look on her psychiatrist's face.

'Except,' said Evi, 'the only person inside my head is me.'

33

That day I became a psychology student in earnest. I went to a lecture. I sat at the very back of a large theatre, listening to a man in red corduroy trousers talking about something called the Hawthorne Effect and pretending to type up notes on my laptop. In reality, I was surfing. Dr Oliver had talked about the destructive subculture that was manifest largely on the internet; a virtual world that legitimized and even glamorized the act of suicide. That's what I was looking for.

It didn't take me long. Type phrases like *Suicide Websites, Online Suicide* or *Suicide Pacts* into any search engine and you'll be awash with results. I started reading through news coverage. I wanted to know a little more about the particular incidence of suicide among people new to the university environment, especially those considered to be the world's top academic institutions.

Most of the online sites of the national papers had something to say on the subject and I read accounts of students for whom years of planning, effort and achievement had brought them only to a place where the future was more than they could face. These bright young things talked of continual over-achievement as the pressure inside slowly and relentlessly built up. They talked about blind panic overwhelming them as they got ready to go away to Oxford or Cambridge for the first time.

I'd experienced something of that myself, I realized, even though my presence here was largely a sham. I'd felt something of the pressure of finding myself amongst an elite.

When I moved on to cyber suicide, though, the net widened way beyond academia. Anyone computer literate, it seemed, could find themselves drawn in.

A particularly disturbing case was that of the 42-year-old from Shropshire who'd hanged himself in front of a webcam, watched by dozens of cyber pals, after being goaded in a so-called 'insult' chat room. *'Fucking do it. Get with it,'* one viewer was reported to have yelled down his microphone as the father of two slipped a noose over his neck and slowly choked to death.

Families of those who died had been

scathing about the sites. 'They tell them how to do it,' said one grieving mother. 'They tell them how many pills to take, how putting a plastic bag over your head will make the pills work faster. And they give them advice on trying to hide it from their families. They tell them to keep their room tidy, to keep washing their hair, to keep up the front. They help them maintain the façade.'

When I'd gone through the news coverage, I started on the websites themselves, moving from one to the next. There was something relentless about the pain I found that morning. 'I feel so alone,' said a woman on one site. 'Is there nobody out there?' 'I don't think I can go on much longer,' said another. 'I dream constantly about the failures of my life, I wake up drenched and stinking of sweat. Is there nowhere I can find peace?'

I learned of the existence of cults who believe the world is overpopulated, that suicide is a responsible and selfless act, and offer advice on the most effective ways of taking one's own life. They cite the cruelty and distress of botched methods as their justification.

When I didn't think it could get much worse, I discovered the trolls.

Wherever there is human misery, it seems to me, there are those who will feed on it. These so-called trolls are gatecrashers who access suicide sites to join and manipulate the online discussions for their own entertainment. Put bluntly, they're getting off on other people's despair. There were more cases than I wanted to think about of trolls actively goading people into acts of self-destruction, all the while keeping up a caring and helpful façade.

I sat back in my chair too suddenly and caught the lecturer's eye. Not good. I looked down quickly. A boy in the same row as me glanced my way with what looked like a smirk on his face. He'd probably been in the crowd last night at my initiation ceremony. That made me remember the photograph of the three boys in my pocket. I wanted to know who those bozos were. Student prank or not, it went totally against every bone in my copper's body that someone could do that to me and get away with it. Somehow, though, I didn't think Joesbury was going to be too helpful with a personal vendetta. On this one I was on my own.

And it was hardly a priority. Twenty dead kids were my priority. Or was it nineteen? Bryony wasn't exactly dead. Either way, it didn't feel right that they were still just numbers for me. How could I investigate anything if I didn't even know who my victims were? And I knew what Joesbury's answer to that would be. You are not investigating anything, Flint. You are a pair of eyes and ears. Not a brain.

Well, they should have sent somebody else. Twenty dead kids, nineteen, strictly, was too many for me. Now there was a thought. Was my invisible list actually complete? What if there were other Bryonys out there? Other students who'd attempted suicide but failed? They belonged on this list too. I sent a quick email to Evi, asking her for details of failed suicide attempts over the last few years. That wasn't giving me a good feeling. If I added failed attempts, my suicide list could get a whole lot bigger.

34

'Nick, it's Evi.'

Nick Bell pushed his phone against his ear, held it in place with his shoulder and beeped open his car. 'Hi, Evi,' he said. 'You OK?'

'Fine, thanks. Is this a good time?'

'I'm just getting into my car,' said Nick, as he did exactly that. One dog on the rear seat looked up and waved its tail in greeting. The other didn't even open its eyes. 'I have to set off in five minutes so unless you want to be responsible for me committing an illegal act, that's how long you've got.'

'You can get hands-free systems now, you know,' Evi told him.

'Had one. Dog ate it. What can I do for you?'

'How would you feel about releasing information on suicide attempts over the last five years?'

Nick slipped the key into the ignition. 'You

mean amongst patients at the practice?' he asked.

'I know you can't give me names, but numbers of cases and a rough idea of the dates would help.'

'It's still bothering you, then?'

'It is, yes.'

'Let me run it past the partners. I'll get back to you. Now are you sure you're OK? You don't sound too . . .'

'I'm fine, thanks, Nick. Talk to you later.'

35

Wednesday afternoon at most UK universities is set aside for sports and Cambridge was no exception. After lunch, students emerged from their residential blocks and courts dressed in sports kit of various kinds and went off to be athletic. I spent the first couple of hours in a quiet corner of St John's library. Slowly, the invisible list of twenty students was beginning to assume substance.

I'd run a Google search of student suicides at Cambridge and had found news coverage of several. I knew about law student Kate George, who'd dropped a plugged-in hairdryer into her bath, and about Nina Hatton, who'd been studying zoology until she'd slashed her femoral artery. Photographs accompanying the stories showed attractive, happy girls.

Peter Roberts had found the demands of his mathematics course too much to deal with and had hanged himself in 2005. That same year the grieving mother of another student suicide, Helen Stott, told reporters that she had had no hint of her daughter's despair. Along with Nicole, Bryony, Jackie and Jake I now had eight names, twelve blanks remaining.

At three o'clock I'd had enough. So far I'd worked non-stop on the case; now I was going to find time for a small personal vendetta. I got my coat, hat, scarf and gloves and went out in search of the Ninja turtles.

Oh, I knew I was being unprofessional, allowing my focus to be distracted away from my main reason for being here, but what had happened the previous night had knocked me for six. Most would see it as an unpleasant but harmless prank. To me it had been one of the worst things I could imagine.

There was an incident when I was younger (which even now I can't bear to think about) that pretty much shaped who I am. Being set upon, finding myself helpless in the hands of an adrenalin-fuelled gang, had brought it all back. If I was going to function here, I had to wrestle back some sense of control and that meant I had to know who those boys were.

All three had been big blokes. As they'd

been half naked, I'd got a pretty good look at their physiques. None had had the wide-shouldered, slim-hipped build of swimmers, or the lean strength of soccer players. They certainly weren't track and field athletes. If I'd had to put money on it, I'd have said rugby. One of them had a mass of black curly hair. He'd be the easiest to spot.

I asked George the porter where I was most likely to find rugby matches and he directed me to three different sports fields. I went on my bike and was at the first pitch in minutes. Concentrating on the Cambridge squad, I figured perhaps there were two possibilities. I took photographs of both men then cycled to the next pitch.

This game took longer because it was an inter-college match: Magdalene versus King's. By the time I'd finished I had three possibilities. I took photographs and moved on.

The game on the third pitch was just finishing when I arrived and it wasn't so easy to get a good look at the players. By the time they started walking back to the changing rooms I'd spotted four vague possibilities, but taking photos would have made me very conspicuous.

It would be Saturday before I got another chance to stake out any more matches, and if the temperature continued to fall the pitches were likely to be too frozen for play. Ah well, they do say revenge is a dish best served cold.

I took the long way home, following the trail of one of the more popular walks in Cambridge. Once over the Cam I turned south to make my way around the Backs. The sun sank lower in the sky and the taller of the old buildings to my left began to gleam as though lit from within.

The Backs is the land between the Queen's Road and the riverside colleges: St John's, Trinity, Clare, Trinity Hall, King's and Queens'. Some of it is laid out to elegant lawns or formal parkland, some is grazing land for cattle, other stretches are wildflower meadows.

Pushing the bike now, I walked on, relishing the quiet but getting lonelier by the second. Three days here and already my sense of well-being, not especially robust at the best of times, had sunk. The case Joesbury and I had worked on just a few months ago had been as bad as they come. A serial killer had struck London fast and hard, barely giving us time to blink before each new victim was found. That would have been bad enough, but as the crimes multiplied they seemed to be getting closer, until it looked as though I was the fat, juicy fly the intricate and bloody web was being spun around.

It was over, the killer caught and locked away, but as any officer who deals with violent crime will tell you, emotional closure doesn't happen overnight.

I'd thought I was coping. The truth was I'd kept myself so busy I hadn't had time to think of it. I'd been staying up late, only risking sleep when I was exhausted; I'd been exercising hard because being in control of my body had given me the illusion of being in control of my life. Now, the support structure of routine and familiarity had been stripped away and I was drifting in a sea of vague concerns and half-formed problems. I was getting too much time with no company but the contents of my own head.

I was starting to get seriously cold by this time and decided to head back. I turned round and stared, almost in awe.

The day had been cold and the sky clear, and the sunset was the dark orange of ripe fruit, an unbroken wash of colour that stretched as far as I could see. The river in front of me shimmered like light on a polished old sovereign. Breaking the two swathes of gold were the silhouettes of the trees on the far bank, layer upon layer of deep brown, glossy black and soft charcoal. Beyond the trees and directly ahead of me, like a castle from a fairy tale, were the four pinnacles of King's College Chapel.

As I watched, a boat drew up alongside me; a long, narrow sheaf of fibreglass that couldn't possibly be strong enough to support the two men perched on top of it but somehow was managing to do so. The oarsmen — they had two oars each so I guess, strictly, they were scullers — slowed the boat and then, with the grace and precision of a ballerina, turned it on the spot. They barely disturbed the water.

And I remembered. Rough, calloused hands on my bare shoulders. *Hit it,* he'd said, meaning let's go and then *swing it,* meaning we've come to a bend and have to turn. Both were rowing terms. The long-haired bloke from last night was an oarsman.

I'd have to hurry. I cycled back towards college and found my car. Ten minutes later I was making my way on foot down to the St John's boathouse. Only one crew, the women's coxed fours, had returned.

The men's coxed fours came back next, glowing pink with the cold and the exertion. They drifted to the bank, climbed out

180

and lifted the boat from the river. None of them was the man I was looking for.

The women's eight came back and then the men's appeared from round the river's bend. They came at a fast pace, only letting up at the last second, and the boat struck the bank hard. One by one they climbed out, visibly tired, hair dank with sweat. I got up and slipped away to the front of the boathouse where I knew that, eventually, after showering and changing, they'd emerge.

I'd found him. The hair, even slick with sweat and river water, was unmissable. He'd rowed in stroke position, at the front of the boat, the team member who was traditionally the strongest and who set the pace for the entire boat.

Twenty minutes later, when I'd spent so much time clenched up and shivering I was in pain, he came out. He was wearing jeans, suede boots and a thick hooded sweater. His hair was dry now and looked exactly how I remembered. What I hadn't realized the previous night was that he almost certainly wasn't an undergraduate student. This man was in his mid to late thirties, a post-graduate, possibly, more likely a tutor or a lecturer. I watched him walk up the road, climb inside a red Saab convertible and drive away.

I followed, allowing at least two cars to stay between us. In the city, I had to concentrate hard to keep up with him but once we left town it became easier.

Would a lecturer really dress up like Zorro, break into student accommodation and assault a young female just for fun? Somehow, that didn't strike me as too likely.

We were heading east out of Cambridge along an A road and I was just starting to wonder how long I could reasonably tail him when he indicated left and turned off the main road. I followed and, a few minutes later, saw the red Saab turn into the main road of an industrial estate.

It was early evening by now and I pulled over by a large sign listing the various units housed on the estate. A quick count told me there were around fifty or so. The Saab had turned into a smaller side road a couple of hundred yards ahead.

Most of the units I could see around me had been constructed in the last ten years. They were warehouse-type spaces mainly, with corrugated steel walls and gently sloping apex roofs. Most had massive cargo doors. Several had windows at second-storey level, indicating office space or pos-

182

sibly showrooms. Some of the units were brick-built, shabby and obviously much older. Peeling paintwork and faded fascia signs told me a few were probably vacant.

I set off again, turned into the side road and slowed to a crawl. The Saab was parked at the far end. I watched the long-haired oarsman stride the few steps to the front door of the unit and let himself inside. I turned the car and drove back to the sign at the estate's entrance. My quarry had gone into Unit 33, JST Vision.

There was a small cul de sac just a few yards away, one used for turning lorries, I guessed. I reversed my car into it and was almost hidden from the bigger road by some overhanging trees. Behind me was a sign leading to a riverside public footpath. I waited thirty minutes and decided, personal vendetta or not, I couldn't really justify spending my evening in the car. So I pulled out my phone.

'DC Stenning,' said the voice that could always bring a smile to my face.

'Pete, it's Lacey.'

'Good God, Flint, what are you doing? We were told you'd gone deep, deep, deep.'

'I am,' I said. 'I need a favour. No questions asked. Can you help?'

'Go on,' he drawled and I knew he wasn't

sure. The case we'd worked on last autumn had got me the reputation of something of a wild card. Pete Stenning, on the other hand, was as straight as they came. I could practically hear him wondering what I was getting him into.

'Romeo Echo Five Nine,' I said. 'Golf Tango Lima. Red Saab convertible. I need to find out who it's registered to and where he lives.'

Silence for a second, just as I'd expected. The system records all such enquiries. If Stenning traced any vehicle without good reason, he could find himself in trouble.

'Do it with my details,' I said, giving him my log-in name and password.

'It'll cost you.'

'Are we talking beer or sexual favours?'

'Oh, like I'm going to mess with Joesbury,' came back Stenning. 'How is he, by the way?'

'On sick leave as far as I know,' I said. 'Will you do it?'

'Hold on, system's a bit slow today. OK, here we go. Nice car, by the way. Registered to a Scott Thornton. 108 St Clement's Road, Cambridge. You're in Cambridge?'

'If you tell anyone we had this conversation, it'll be shit that I'm deep in, Pete.'

'I won't. Now, whatever you're up to, be bloody careful.'

36

Twenty-two minutes after getting home from work, Evi could no longer resist the temptation that had been nagging away at her for days. She opened up Facebook, typed Harry Laycock into the search engine and waited. The system churned and . . . of course he was on Facebook, anyone as hip as Harry was bound to be.

Harry Laycock, Anglican minister, with 207 friends. His birthday was 7 April. She hadn't known that. The photograph was one she hadn't seen before: outdoor clothes, mountains in the background. The system invited her to send him a message. Evi closed the page down.

She opened up her mail account and the email message she'd received earlier from the policewoman. She wanted details of students who'd attempted suicide in the last five years. Easier said than done. Nick hadn't exactly been encouraging that afternoon. And his was one of twenty GP surgeries in Cambridge, each of which was likely to have a number of the 22,000 student population on its patient base. Each surgery operated independently. Data was rarely shared and patient confidentiality was sacrosanct. Anything she did find, she couldn't pass on to the policewoman without risking her entire career.

The phone on her desk was ringing. Evi reached out and put it to her ear. 'Evi Oliver,' she announced. To silence. 'Hello,' she tried. No response. She put the phone down.

The girl with the fake name, Laura Farrow, talked tough but looked brittle. The way she held her face when she wasn't speaking had made Evi think of glass blown almost to breaking point. The way it hovers, fragile and beautiful, a split second before it shatters. The phone was ringing again.

'Evi Oliver.'

No response.

'Hello.' Not even trying to sound patient this time.

Evi put the phone down, telling herself not to overreact. It could simply be a genuine caller with line problems. It was ringing again. She picked it up and put it to her ear without speaking. Silence on the

187

line. Not even the sound of breathing. Very strong, the temptation to say something. She resisted, just put the phone softly down.

It rang again immediately.

OK, this wasn't going to scare her. This was going to piss her off. She picked up the receiver and put it softly down on her desk. A few seconds later, her mobile began ringing. She reached into her bag and pulled it out. Number withheld. Evi answered the call.

'Hello.'

Just empty air. Five seconds later it was ringing again. Evi switched the mobile off, replaced the receiver on the desk phone and unplugged it at the wall. Then she got up and walked round the ground floor. There were three more handsets to be unplugged.

She wasn't going to overreact. It would be someone pissing about. They'd get bored and move on to someone else. When she got back to her desk she had a new email. She clicked it open.

I can see you, it said.

I stood just inside the front door of my block, taking in the chaos. 'So did the boys with the buckets come back?' I asked a slim girl with dark curly hair who'd made me tea the previous night.

The girl with the mop gave me a quick smile. 'Plumbing problems,' she said. 'Sounds a bit gynaecological, doesn't it? Second time this year. Your room's a bit of a mess, I'm afraid. I think it might have been your pipe that burst. Maintenance are still in there.'

The day was just getting better. I opened my door to find no sign of Talaith, plenty of water on the floor and a man in my bedroom. A tall man, with dark hair and kind eyes.

'Hello, Tom,' I called to him, before turning back to the corridor. 'Yell when you've finished with the mop,' I told the girl with black curls. Then I squelched my way across to my bedroom.

'What happened?' I asked, pausing in the doorway. There wasn't really room for two people in these tiny rooms, unless you wanted to get very cosy.

Tom looked up from whatever he'd been doing under the sink. 'Frost damage,' he told me. 'This is the fourth we've had this year. You know, we hardly ever have problems in the old buildings. There's pipes in there hundreds of years old and they just keep going. Crap in the new blocks hardly lasts five minutes.'

'Guess they don't make poisonous lead

piping like they used to,' I said, looking round. There was no damage to speak of, just a damp and muddy floor and small piles of dust where Tom had been drilling. The cupboard beneath the basin had seen plumbing activity, as had the pipes that ran round the mirror. A fairly complicated metal junction looked new.

'Chipped your mirror,' I'm afraid,' Tom said to me, nodding to where a tiny fraction of the glass was missing. 'I'll report it, should be able to get it replaced without much trouble.'

I thanked him and went to find the cleaning cupboard.

Evi's hands were shaking but if anything she felt better. She hadn't been phoning herself for the past half hour, nor had she sent herself the email. Which almost certainly meant she hadn't poured red dye into her header tank and she probably hadn't bought the skeleton toy either. She wasn't losing her marbles, she was being stalked. By someone who had had access to her house. Thank God she'd had the locks changed.

And emails could be traced. Even if it had been sent from somewhere anonymous like an internet café or a public library, there would still be a record of it on her computer. She resisted the temptation to reply to it and carried on working.

Another email had arrived in her inbox. Great, more evidence. Evi flicked it open.

Purple makes you look sallow. Try another colour.

Evi stood up and walked as quickly as she could to the window. The curtains were drawn, no gaps through which anyone could see, but she pulled them a little closer all the same. She didn't need to look down at what she was wearing. The cashmere sweater, the colour of lavender in bud, had belonged to her grandmother. Keep it from moths and cashmere lasts for ever, Granny had told her. It wasn't quite true. It was looking worn and bobbly in places and she only ever wore it at home. She'd changed after the police had left. No one could have known that she was wearing purple right now.

Cracks in the mullioned windows might have been made by stray arrows, centuries ago, and the enclosed stone staircase looked old enough to have ivy growing on the inside. As I climbed, I left behind the smell of woodsmoke and cooked food, to have it replaced by that of fresh laundry and used towels, cosmetics and damp sports equipment. It was the smell of youth, with feminine undertones.

After speaking to Stenning, I'd accessed the university website and typed Scott Thornton into the search facility, realizing as I did so that there was something a bit familiar about the name. I found out that he was part of the medical faculty and a member of St John's. He was also a Cambridge alumnus, having studied medicine here some fifteen years ago. It was probably all I needed to know for now. I still couldn't remember where I'd heard the name before, but if it was important it would come to me. A more urgent priority was finding out a little more about Nicole Holt's last days. The second set of tyre tracks I'd found near where she'd died was bothering me.

The room guide at the base of the stairwell had told me that Nicole lived in room 27. A single flower, pink and daisy-like, pinned opposite her name suggested that might not be strictly true any more.

I spotted Nicole's room the minute I pushed open the door to the corridor. Cones of cellophane with flowers somewhere in their midst had been propped against the wall outside. Cards had been pinned to the door, addressed to Nicole, occasionally Nicky. Sometime in the next few days, I guessed, her parents might take them down, even read them if they could bear to.

At the end of the corridor I could hear female voices. In the communal kitchen four girls, caught in the act of making coffee, were passing a milk bottle between them. I stood in the doorway, waiting for one of them to notice me.

'Hi,' I said, a second later. 'I'm really sorry to intrude.'

'No worries,' replied one. 'You lost?'

'No,' I said. 'Actually I came about Nicole.' This was the tricky bit. This was where I had to feign emotion for a dead girl I'd never met, in front of bright young women who might just have been her genuine friends. I dropped my eyes, brought my hand up to cover my nose, as though to conceal tears. Tears that weren't actually there. I was obviously getting better at this acting lark because two of the girls had stepped forward. One of them had a hand on my shoulder, the other was steering me to a chair. I sniffed and realized the tears were there after all. My eyes had been watering in the cold most of the way over and now they were just flowing.

'It's OK,' said a third girl, whose own eyes were damp now. 'We're all upset. Are you from the history department?'

I shook my head. 'I knew her from the Blue,' I said. 'You know, the pub where she worked.'

They were nodding their heads. Nicole had worked two nights a week and one lunchtime in the Cambridge Blue, a pub on Gwydir Street. There had been photographs and a number of references to it on Facebook. 'I just came to see if there was going to be some sort of memorial service for her,' I said. 'I know she went to church from time to time.' Something else I'd discovered on Facebook.

The girls were looking at each other, faces puzzled, shoulders shrugging. It was far too soon for a memorial service.

'Also, there was something she asked me to get for her,' I went on, lifting my bag up from the floor. Its contents chinked softly together. 'I've got a contact in the wine trade and I can get it quite cheap. She said somebody called Flick had a birthday coming up and she wanted to surprise her.'

I'd already spotted Flick, a gorgeous Amazon of a girl, nearly six feet tall, with an athlete's build and long Nordic blonde hair. She looked like Eowyn from *The Lord of the Rings* and she had her hand to her mouth.

'It's nothing special,' I said, pressing home my advantage. I'd learned all about Flick, her imminent twentieth birthday and her love of all drinks sparkling on Nicole's Facebook pages. 'Just Prosecco, but quite a good one.'

I pulled three bottles of sparkling Italian wine from my bag. I'd bought them in a supermarket on the way over, making sure they were chilled. 'If you could see Flick gets them, that would be great,' I said, going in for the kill. 'I'll leave you in peace now. Sorry to be so pathetic. I'm still in shock, I guess.'

'Would you like a coffee?' one of the girls asked me. I feigned surprise and opened my mouth to accept.

'I've got a better idea,' said Flick. 'Who's got some glasses?'

Evi put the phone down, half expecting it to start ringing again any second. The sergeant she'd spoken to had been polite but distant. He'd told her to make a note of the number and times of the calls and to forward the emails on to him. He hadn't suggested sending anyone round.

She stood up and went into the kitchen. If someone was watching her from outside, the back garden was where he'd be. She crossed to the door, double-checking that it was locked. She really needed to get blinds put on these windows.

'I've seen you wear purple more than once, Dr Oliver,' the sergeant had said to her. 'Bit of a favourite of yours, isn't it? Could be just a lucky guess. Send me the emails and we'll have a look at them. I wouldn't hold out much hope, though. If they were sent from a public building using an anonymous Gmail account, there won't be a lot we can do.'

Evi sat down in her stairlift and pressed the button. The police weren't coming and someone had to check her top floor. She'd never sleep otherwise.

Ten minutes later the phone was ringing again. She almost didn't answer.

'John Castell here, Evi,' the deep voice with its faint Norfolk accent said. 'The duty sergeant just called me at home to tell me about your emails. Are you planning to send them through tonight?'

'I sent them fifteen minutes ago,' said Evi.

'Really? I checked with him not two minutes ago. Hang on, let me check again. The line will go dead for a few seconds.'

A short pause while Evi walked back to her desk.

'Nope, nothing,' said Castell. 'Can you try sending them direct to me?'

'Let me try.' Evi opened her inbox and ran the cursor to the top of the list. The two emails weren't there. She flicked open Junk Mail, Personal Messages and Deleted Items, in case she'd accidentally binned them or filed them away. Nothing. Finally, she clicked on Sent Mail. Nothing at all.

The two emails had disappeared from her system.

Two bottles of Prosecco later, we'd moved from the kitchen into Flick's room. It was a study bedroom, with a large desk and a narrow bed. A crimson creeper was poking its way in through the open window. Flick had offered me the one chair; two more were brought from rooms nearby. Flick and a girl called Sarah lay on the bed.

'I know it's normal to wish there was more you could have done,' I was saying as sympathetic faces nodded around me. 'The last time I saw Nicole I knew something wasn't right but I was in a hurry. I figured we could talk it through properly when I saw her again.'

'We always think we have more time,' said Flick.

'I just knew, though,' I went on. 'I knew something wasn't right. Did she say anything to any of you?'

'What sort of not right?' asked Sarah.

'I didn't give her chance,' I admitted. 'But a couple of times she mentioned to me that she thought someone was coming into her room at night when it was locked.'

One big thing bothering me, apart from the second set of tyre tracks on the B road, was Bryony's reported insistence that she was being abused by mysterious night-time assailants. I was just a little less willing to write her off as delusional than everyone else seemed to be.

Around the room the four girls looked interested but puzzled.

'Coming into her room?' asked a dark-skinned girl called Jasmine.

I nodded. 'To be honest, I wasn't sure what to make of it,' I said. 'She seemed pretty worried about it, though.'

Still puzzled. Shrugs. Hair tossing.

'She did have quite noisy bad dreams but she never mentioned that,' said Flick.

'Coming in and doing what?' asked a thin, pale girl called Lynsey.

I squirmed a bit on my chair, tried to look

as though what I was about to say was making me feel uncomfortable. 'Well, touching her,' I said. 'While she was asleep. To be honest, she made it sound pretty creepy.'

Three of them were very interested now. A few bottles of wine and some spooky stories. Not a bad way to spend an evening. The fourth girl, Lynsey, looked worried. 'She never said anything to me,' she said. 'But she got very odd towards the end.' She looked at the others. 'Do you remember?'

A couple of heads were nodding. 'It started in October, didn't it?' said Flick. 'When she disappeared.'

Someone was banging on her door. Evi still hadn't got used to how loud the round brass doorknocker was. The disabled physics professor had probably been half deaf as well.

'Hi,' said the tall man on her doorstep. The last person she'd have guessed.

'Nick?'

Nick Bell gave an apologetic smile. 'Sorry to pounce on you like this, Evi. I can come back another time.'

'It's fine, really,' said Evi, stepping back to release the chain and open the door. Nick stepped inside, bringing a scent of cold January air with him. He was in his usual jeans and oiled-wool blue sweater, the only clothes she'd ever seen him wear when he wasn't at work. She was pretty certain she remembered the sweater from their student days. Men who looked like Nick didn't need to make an effort and, as far as she could remember, he never had. 'I won't keep you,' he said. 'I just didn't want to do this over the phone.'

'Now I'm intrigued,' said Evi. 'Coffee? Glass of wine?'

'Thank you.'

Evi made her way to the kitchen, hearing his footsteps following behind. He took the glass of red wine she held out and she leaned back against the counter, wondering if he was going to tell her off for drinking alcohol. It really wasn't a good idea with the combination of painkillers she took.

'I ran your request past the other partners,' Nick said. 'Megan was pretty relaxed but I didn't get a particularly encouraging response from the others, I'm afraid.'

Evi shrugged. 'Don't worry,' she said. 'I didn't really expect you to.'

'They want you to put it in writing, at the very least,' Nick went on. 'They also want to know if you have Ethics Board approval. If you get anything out of us, officially, it'll be months down the line.'

Evi nodded. Exactly what she'd expected. 'Thanks for trying,' she said.

She waited. Nick hadn't touched his wine yet. He looked as though he had more to tell her. 'Let's go and sit down,' she said.

'Beautiful house,' Nick said, as he followed her into the room. 'You were lucky to get it.'

'I never thought of it that way,' she said, crossing to the chair at her desk. 'I assumed I got it because I'm disabled.'

Nick stopped in mid-stride. 'Open mouth, insert foot,' he said, shaking his head. 'You should see my bedside manner.'

Evi couldn't help a tiny smile. He saw it the same second he realized what he'd said. 'You see, I just can't help myself,' he went on. 'I knew I should have gone into research.'

Evi indicated an easy chair close by. He sat, cradling his wine glass in both hands.

'You could have told me on the phone about the partners,' she said.

He raised the glass to his lips then put it softly down on a side table. 'True,' he said. 'But I was curious enough to have a look at the records myself. And something occurred to me.'

Evi pursed her lips and raised her eye-brows.

'A patient of ours who self-harmed would invariably be recommended a period of counselling,' Nick told her. 'They don't all take up the offer, of course, and there's a pretty high drop-out rate, but it's rare for them to refuse the initial referral.'

'That makes sense,' said Evi. 'Self-harm is often a cry for attention. Counselling pro-vides that.'

Nick nodded his head at her. 'If a student patient of ours self-harmed, we'd invariably refer them to you and your team,' he said. 'I rang round a few other GPs in the area, just to find out what their policy is. It's the same. So, I think it fairly safe to assume that a student in the city who attempted suicide would be referred to you.'

'We'll have them on record,' said Evi. 'We'll have the information I was looking for ourselves. Why didn't I think of that?'

'If your database will allow you to search according to reasons for initial referral, you can probably find them very quickly.'

He was right. When she had time, she'd be bloody annoyed with herself for not thinking of it first.

'Give me a sec,' she said, turning to face her screen and typing in the login name and password that would access the Counselling Services database. A few more seconds and she'd typed *Episodes of Self-Harm* into the search facility.

'Here they are,' she said, scanning through the entries. 'Nine in the last five years. Seven of them women.'

37

From: DC Lacey Flint
Subject: Field Report 2
Date: Wednesday 16 January, 21.17
   GMT
To: DI Mark Joesbury, Scotland Yard

Greetings from Starbucks, DI Joe. (Oops. Sorry, Sir, spent the last hour breathing in Prosecco bubbles and they've quite gone to my head.)

Anyway, here's the big news. Nicole Holt disappeared late last October for four days. According to the girls on her corridor, she went off to lectures on Friday and didn't come back all weekend. They're pretty certain about the time because they remember she missed the Halloween party. Her friends weren't too worried at first, they just assumed she'd gone to stay with her boyfriend in Peterhouse, but then on Sunday evening he turned up and he hadn't seen her all weekend either.

You're going to ask if they reported it, aren't you? They didn't. Bloody numpties! It was difficult, apparently. They didn't want to make a big fuss and risk embarrassing her if she'd just gone off with someone. They phoned round a few of her friends but no one had heard anything. Then, at two o'clock in the morning, when they were starting to think that perhaps they should report it — *what do you reckon, gals, do we involve those nice chaps in uniform yet?* — two girls from the ground floor found her in the stairwell.

'In the stairwell?' says me, in astonishment.

'Yes, indeed, the stairwell,' they reply. 'Obviously she couldn't have been there all evening or someone would have seen her. She was half asleep. Really dopey.' (Not the only one, I'd suggest!)

So, my new best mates, Winkin, Blinkin and Nod, found a drugged-up, semi-conscious girl on the stairwell, couldn't get any sense out of her, and were just about to call an ambulance when she came round. She was still a bit woozy, apparently, but basically seemed OK.

So, where had our friend Nicole been, you'll be asking. So was I. So were they, surprisingly enough. Trouble was, Nicole had no idea. She didn't know what day it was. Couldn't tell them where she'd been, what she'd been doing or with whom. And she was exhausted. She just wanted to go to bed. The next day they tried to talk her into going to the police but she refused. They all assumed she'd been with another bloke and didn't want to tell them about him. Her boyfriend jumped to the same conclusion and dumped her.

Don't you just love men?

After that, not surprisingly, she got a bit depressed or, to use their words, 'well weird'. What they seem to mean by that is she became jumpy and nervous, keeping to her room most of the time, not really talking to anyone, stopped going to lectures, complained about not being able to sleep and bad dreams.

And she developed a pretty bad rat fixation. Yes, you read it right, rats. Seemed convinced the building was overrun with rodents. Nobody else noticed but she heard them all the time, day and night. She even found a dead one under her bed one time. She went absolutely mental and, yes, I am quoting my new best friends again, because once they got started on rats there was no stopping them. Seems Nicole was the butt of a few practical jokes on the subject of rats. Someone set off a mechanical one in Hall one day and she nearly lost it, someone else broke into her room and covered the walls with photographs of them.

So, to summarize (and I heard you mutter 'about time too', by the way), Nicole sounds like a classic suicide case to me: depressed, not sleeping, bad dreams when she did sleep, not keeping up with coursework, dropping out of social life. On the other hand, she was picked on by some fellow students with a rather warped sense of humour and, most alarmingly, disappeared for several days shortly before she died.

Should we be worried about that, do you think?

Right, this is me signing off now, my coffee's going cold and there's just one more thing I want to check out before I stumble Lethe-wards. You see, all this academic bollocks is starting to rub off. Hope London's a bit warmer than this place. Snow is forecast any day now but luckily I brought some boots.

Sleep well.

Joesbury got up and walked to the window. She'd sent him the email just five minutes ago. She'd be leaving Starbucks, probably the one on Market Street, pulling her coat up round her shoulders, wrapping that stupid college scarf round her neck, stepping outside. He turned and looked at the street map of Cambridge on his desk. If she was going back to St John's she'd walk along St Mary's Street. If. He had to be in King's Parade in ten and could well walk straight into her. The case was turning into a farce. 'Enter Brian Rix, stage left, with his trousers round his ankles,' he muttered, as he found his coat, grabbed his wallet and left the room.

38

'Four out of the nine were patients of ours,' said Nick.

'Did you know them personally?' asked Evi.

He shook his head and a faint tinge of pink spread across his upper cheeks. 'As far as possible we put the young women under the care of the other partners,' he said. 'Probably being over-cautious but there you go, better safe than sorry. I get the men and the women over forty.'

'I'm registered with you,' Evi reminded him. 'And I'm a few years off forty.'

'We assumed familiarity would have bred contempt in your case.'

Evi smiled. Women had been falling head over heels for Nick for as long as she'd known him. She looked down at the spreadsheet on her desk.

'I have a list here of nineteen students who took their own lives in the last five years,' she said. 'Bryony Carter would have made twenty. Now we have another nine attempted suicides.'

'I'm not getting a good feeling about this,' said Nick.

'Join the club.'

The night outside had got even colder. I pulled my collar up, wrapped my new college scarf around my face and set off. I was heading for the site of the first suicide this academic year. In late October, Jackie King had drowned herself beneath a bridge belonging to Clare College. She'd been a third-year English student.

The bridge was of pale stone, with three arches to let the boat traffic pass below. By the time I reached it I was having serious misgivings about my email to Joesbury. I probably shouldn't have been so familiar. It was just easier, somehow, to talk to him when he wasn't close.

The whole bridge was shiny with frost. I stayed close to the stone balustrade on the left-hand side and stopped in the exact centre, just as Jackie had done. Only she'd brought a length of washing line with her. She'd tied one end to a baluster. The other she'd fastened securely round both her ankles. The exact length of the rope had been important. She must have worked it out beforehand, cutting it carefully. I have no idea what happened to her during the next few seconds. I can only guess.

So here's my guess. I think she must have sat on the stone rail and swung her legs over the side. She'd have looked down, just as I was doing now, seen the water black and slow-moving beneath her. She would have been cold. It was late in the year. It was also around four a.m.: she was caught on a CCTV camera making her way over here. She must have looked down at the water and asked herself what on earth she thought she was doing. She must have seriously considered giving it up and going home. She hadn't. She'd jumped.

Jackie, Bryony and Nicole. Three young women who'd chosen to end their lives in what Evi Oliver called very untypical ways. She was right. Each death, or near death in Bryony's case, had been complicated, considered and violent. So what was happening to women in this city?

'Twenty-nine students, twenty-three of them women, either killed themselves or tried to in the last five years,' said Evi, leaning back against the chair and trying not to let the pain show.

211

'Friggin' hell, it doesn't look good, does it?' said Nick.

'No,' said Evi.

Silence for a second.

'I saw Meg yesterday,' said Evi. 'She mentioned a spate of suicides when we were here. Ring any bells with you?'

'Can't say it does. There was that chap who jumped off Great St Mary's around exam time, but other than that . . .'

'No, he's the only one I can remember.'

'And you've already spoken to the police?'

Evi nodded, then gave a small half-shrug.

'What?'

'I'm think I'm beginning to have credibility issues with the local CID,' she said.

Nick frowned at her. Evi finished her wine and told him about her intruder, about the tricks that had been played on her, and the phone calls and messages from earlier.

'And these emails have just vanished from your computer?' he asked her. 'I know nothing about IT. Is that even possible?'

Evi pulled a face.

'Are you worried?'

'A bit.'

'Want to come and stay at my house tonight?' he asked her. 'Any number of spare bedrooms.'

Evi shook her head. 'Kind thought, but I

think I might die of exposure in the night.'

He laughed. 'I could lend you a dog to cuddle, but you're probably right. Look, why don't I talk to my partners, show them this list? If I can get them on side, CID will have to listen to five of us.'

She thought about it for a second. 'It can't hurt,' she said.

'I need to get going. I'll see you on Friday, right?'

Evi agreed that he would. 'Actually, I thought I might bring someone with me after all,' she said. 'No, not a date. A new mature student who's helping me out with some research. She needs to meet a few people. Would that be OK?'

'Course. Now, want me to check the house for you?'

Evi opened her mouth to say she'd done it herself earlier.

'Yes please,' was what came out.

I looked at my watch. Nine o'clock. I headed back to college, let myself into the library and checked emails.

Nothing from Joesbury. One from Evi, reporting modest progress. Her words, not mine. She'd found nine cases of students attempting suicide by various means. Medical confidentiality prevented her from giving me their names but it meant my list was approaching thirty.

Now I'd learned that Nicole had disappeared for a few days. Had any of the others done the same? And this pathological fear of rats? Was that remotely relevant?

I was about to close the laptop when a box popped up in one corner of the screen. *Got the Cambridge Blues?* said the text. The photograph was of a boy, in a college scarf, leaning against one of the bridges. I find it kind of spooky the way that happens. You'll be searching the net for, say, party shoes, and suddenly all kinds of ads and boxes advertising shoes start appearing on your screen. I'd run several Google searches for information on suicides and, somewhere out in cyberspace, I'd been put on a mailing list for depressives. Curious, though, I clicked the box open and found myself in a blog about life in Cambridge, with an attached chat room. The Cambridge Blues, it was called, the survivor's guide to the ultimate in academia.

The site was well designed and quite appealing, and I began flicking through. Here was a community of people who felt as disaffected by Cambridge as I did, albeit for very different reasons. They were writing about their experiences with eloquence and compassion for others. Sometimes very movingly. To my surprise I found myself clicking on the button that would take me into the chat room.

Quite a few people were online. I registered as Laura and began typing:

Almost found myself in tears today down by the river. Difficult to imagine being anywhere more beautiful. So why did it make me sad?

Within seconds I had a reply.

Beauty never fails to move us. If we're happy, great beauty makes us more so, if we're sad it can be what tips us over the edge.

I'm finding it difficult to imagine anything worse than being somewhere you don't belong. (Me again.) *Surrounded by people who will never know you. Never have the faintest clue who you really are.*

The people you need are out there, Laura. You just have to keep looking.

OK, enough was enough. I came out of the chat room feeling guilty. If Joesbury knew what I'd just done, he'd tell me I'd taken the needy-fruitcake act that was Laura Farrow a bit far. Trouble was, I had a feeling it hadn't been only Laura in the chat room just now. That had been Lacey, too.

39

Jessica Calloway regained consciousness slowly. Her mouth was dry and her eyes were sore. She swallowed and the back of her throat felt like the skin had been scraped away. Behind her eyelids she was aware of murky grey light in the room. Morning then. Her eyes opened before she had a chance to ask herself whether it was a good idea. Oh, thank God.

She sat upright, letting the duvet fall down around her waist. She was wearing a tight yellow camisole and yellow striped pyjama trousers. What she always wore to bed. She pushed the duvet aside and swung her legs round to touch the cold linoleum of her bedroom floor. She sat there for a whole minute, not quite believing it.

She was in her room in college. Her body was sore and stiff, but seemed otherwise OK. The back of her skull felt tense, as though a serious headache might be threatening but nothing a couple of aspirins wouldn't sort out. On the table by her bedside was her clock radio. Nearly seven thirty in the morning. In just a few seconds it would be . . . it clicked on. Heart Radio, what she always woke up to, even on the morning after the worst nightmare imaginable.

The curtains of her room were drawn tight but outside she could hear the usual early-morning sounds of St Catharine's College. The odd jogger running past. A cyclist. A delivery van on the road outside.

Everything was exactly as it should be. The horrible, scratching things that had crawled towards her in the dark had been the result of something slipped into her drink. The shapeless forms that had banged on the inside of the wardrobe door to be let out had existed only in her own head. The cold, claw-like hands that had stroked . . . Jesus, she needed a shower.

Jessica got up, on legs that weren't too steady. She felt weak, as though she hadn't eaten for some time, and a little nauseous. There was a bruise on her forearm she didn't remember from the evening before. She reached for the gown on the back of the chair. Her work was where she'd left it on her desk. Her laptop was switched off but still open, her books on the bookshelf, her bag from the night before under the desk, spilling half its contents over the floor. Everything normal.

Except that all the books on the shelf were upside down.

Jessica reached out to the books, just to make sure they were real. They felt very real. So who had turned them all the wrong way round? Nearly fifty books. Why would someone do that? The song on the radio was speeding up. Like an old-fashioned vinyl record being played at the wrong speed. Jessica looked back at the radio, suddenly afraid. The song stopped. There was a second of silence and then a new tune began to play. Fairground music.

No.

Jessica half ran, half fell to the door of her room. It was locked, of course, she always locked it at night, but the key was right there, in the lock, all she had to do was turn it, take hold of the handle and pull the door open. The lock turned, the handle was slick with sweat and the door would not open.

She tried again, checked the key — it looked the same — pulled on the handle, even banged on the door a couple of times. Then she turned and ran to the window.

She half fell across her desk and pulled at the curtains.

The window wasn't there. In its place was a photograph of the head and torso of a circus clown, large enough to fill the entire frame. Jessica had always been scared of clowns, but even she had never imagined one like this. The huge red nose, red and white cone-shaped hat and royal-blue ruff could, at a pinch, have belonged to a clown who wouldn't scare a child to death. But no parent would ever expose her child to a clown with a face that long, bony, yellow and old, with a grinning mouth so huge, so full of yellowing teeth, with opaque white eyes, rimmed in black and scarlet. No child could see this clown and keep its sanity. Jessica thought she was probably about to lose hers when she heard a soft tapping sound behind her.

Still half lying across her desk, she turned. The door to her wardrobe creaked and swung open. Standing inside was another clown. This one was worse, far worse. This one wore a mask that was white as a winter coat, with a huge, animal-like mouth and hooked red nose. Only the eyes looked human.

40

To my surprise, Talaith was in our living room when I got back, her tiny bottom perched on the chair, feet up on the desk in front of her. She was dressed for bed and, judging from the relatively steady way she was painting her toenails black, was sober. Her hair wasn't quite the shade of purple I remembered from the previous evening. More red, less blue, bit more of a plum shade. She waved a mug at me. 'Coffee?' she offered. 'It's instant shit but I'm broke as usual.'

'Thanks,' I said. 'I'll do it, though. You'll smudge.'

While I filled the kettle, found a couple of mugs and put instant coffee in them, Talaith finished her artwork, raised her feet off the desk and waggled her toes in the air, supporting herself entirely by stomach muscles. She had to be sober. No drunk could manage that.

'Someone asked me about Bryony today,' I said, when we'd exchanged the usual social pleasantries about the sort of day we'd had and how I was settling in. 'That must have been really grim for you.'

'Worse for her,' said Talaith. I inclined my head. Difficult to argue with that one.

'Do you know how she is?' I asked.

'Better today,' said Talaith. 'I visited. I think she knew me. The nurse who came in said they thought she might pull through.'

Something on Talaith's face made me think that wasn't necessarily good news.

'She's going to be very badly disfigured,' I tried.

Talaith shook her head. 'She won't cope. She was gorgeous before and she couldn't cope. Take looks away from someone like Bryony and she'll have nothing left.'

'Sounds a bit harsh,' I said.

'Realistic,' Talaith insisted. 'You wouldn't believe the hours she'd spend on her appearance. Or the money, come to that. She was paranoid about wrinkles. At her age, most girls are just grateful they've outgrown zits.'

'Not sure I have yet.'

'All the photographs she had around the place were of her,' Talaith went on. 'Not family, mates, boyfriends, just her. And they were all those arty-farty studio shots, you know, soft focus, tons of make-up. Sometimes I'd catch her just staring at herself in the mirror.'

'Sounds like you didn't get on too well,' I said.

Talaith shrugged and drank coffee. Mine was still too hot to touch. 'She wasn't too bad when she first got here,' she said. 'Bit highly strung, nervy. Easily bruised flower is what my mum would say, but to be honest, a lot of people here are.'

'Really?'

'God yes. When you think about the pressure we're all under to get a place at any decent university, let alone here, it's a wonder we're not all basket cases by the time we arrive. Bryony was bright enough, but she was no rocket scientist. I think she'd been coached and hot-housed and pushed all her life. Not too bad, though, no worse than a lot.'

'So what went wrong?' I asked.

Plum-coloured hair danced around as Talaith shook her head. 'I don't know. I wasn't around too much. I was having a good time and it was obvious we weren't going to be soulmates. She got a bit freaky, though, towards the end.'

Freaky? Nicole had got freaky too, according to her college-mates. Or what was the phrase they'd used? Well weird.

'Freaky how?' I asked.

Talaith looked as though she wasn't sure how much to say. 'She had bad dreams,' she opted for.

That didn't sound too bad, until I remembered that Nicole Holt had also had bad dreams shortly before she killed herself. 'Naked-in-public bad dreams or blue-lizards-crawling-out-of-the-walls   bad dreams?'

'Well, that's just it, she couldn't really tell me. When I was here — and you've probably noticed, I'm not here that much — she'd wake me up moaning and screaming. One time I found her in the room here.' She nodded towards a spot on the floor. 'Very early in the morning. She was stark naked, huddled up, crying and yelping. Woke the whole block up. It was like one of those night terrors you hear about kids having.'

'Was she taking something?' I asked.

'Well, that's what we thought, to be honest, which is why we didn't call an ambulance. One of the boys sleeping over was a third-year medical student. He checked her heart rate, her pupils and everything and we put her back to bed. I sat in the doorway until I could see she was more settled.'

'And in the morning?'

'She felt like shit, couldn't remember a thing. That was the worst episode, but I'm not sure she was getting any real sleep towards the end. Kept talking about noise in the night, people talking, phone calls waking her up. Have to say, it never bothered me.'

'I heard the police found evidence she'd been smoking something pretty powerful the night of the accident. Did she do that a lot?'

Talaith looked down at her toes for a second, then reached out and rubbed away an imaginary smudge. 'Not that I saw,' she said. 'But she was pretty jumpy about people going into her room, so she could well have had something to hide.'

'Who would go into her room?' I asked.

Talaith shrugged. 'She thought I was coming in at night, while she was asleep,' she said. 'She talked about how things were being moved round. How she'd go to bed leaving things in a certain way and when she woke up they were different.'

I figured I'd pushed as far as I could for now. My room-mate was a long way from stupid. I sat back in my chair, finished my coffee and stretched my arms behind my head.

'So why does everyone but the vicar call you Tox or Toxic?' I asked.

'Family nickname,' she replied. 'My older brother gave it to me on account of my unusual flatulence as a kid.'

'Oh?'

'Don't panic. I outgrew it.'

'So what are you studying?' I asked her, expecting something like psychology or sociology. Talaith (Tox) had shown a pretty thorough grasp of the human psyche.

'Aeronautical engineering,' she told me, then laughed at the look on my face. 'I am a rocket scientist.'

I laughed and we said goodnight.

That was the night I started having dreams.

41

Thursday 17 January (five days earlier)
I woke up late, feeling like I'd aged a decade overnight. I got out of bed and my body told me to get back in right now. Couldn't be done. I had a lecture at nine and I'd have to hurry to make breakfast.

Tox was just getting back from the Buttery when I opened the block's front door, wondering how long it would take me to get used to walking through freezing January air to get hold of a bowl of cornflakes. She held eye contact for just a second longer than seemed natural. 'Hi,' she said. 'How you doing?'

'Good,' I replied. 'You OK?'

'Oh, I'm fine,' she replied, emphasizing the *I*. At that moment, another girl left the block in a hurry and Tox stepped inside. I made my way to the Buttery, pushed open the door to the main building and joined the straggling remnants of the queue, wondering if getting out of bed had been the right decision after all. My mouth was dry, my throat felt as though I'd swallowed wire wool and my eyes could barely stay open. I hadn't drunk alcohol last night but this felt like the worst hangover ever.

Then the room went dark and the floor seemed to fall from beneath me.

'You all right? Can you hear me?'

'Can someone get a chair?'

I was on the floor of the Buttery serving area with no memory of having reached the front of the queue. A boy and a girl were crouched next to me; behind the counter several kitchen staff looked more interested than concerned. Nothing they hadn't seen before.

A chair appeared and I let them lift me up and put me on it. 'I'm fine, thank you,' I said to the pale-faced girl with scarlet glasses who'd helped lift me. 'Don't miss your breakfast. I'll just stay here for a bit.'

Gradually, they left me alone. An older, kind-looking woman behind the counter offered me a drink. After a few minutes I felt better.

I caught Tox just as she was about to leave.

'Sorry about last night,' I said. 'Did I scare you?'

She shook her head, but didn't quite meet my eyes. I'd scared her. 'It must have been talking about what happened to Bryony,' I said. 'It must have been playing on my mind. I don't normally dream at all.'

She glanced at her watch. It was ten minutes to nine. She'd have to rush to make nine o'clock lectures. 'Bryony could never remember anything in the morning,' she said.

'I didn't at first,' I said. 'I just felt rough, like I'd drunk too much and slept too little. It started coming back to me just now.'

'What?' she said.

'I was awake,' I said. 'In my dream, I mean. But I couldn't move. I knew exactly where I was, I just couldn't move a muscle or open my eyes. And someone was standing over me, watching me. Was I noisy?'

'Not as bad as Bryony could be,' Tox replied.

But bad enough, judging by the look on her face.

'I remembered something about Bryony's dreams,' Tox said. 'There was this one time when she was sobbing that someone had cut her face to ribbons, that blood was pouring out of her. It wasn't, of course, she was perfectly fine. Just freaking out.'

At that moment my phone buzzed. A text from Evi wondering if I could see her at noon, in her rooms. There was something she needed to talk to me about.

'I'll see a doctor this morning,' I said. 'I'm sure it's just being in a new place, talking about what happened to Bryony and that business with the boys on Tuesday night. But if it happens again, I'll move out.'

At that, Tox looked a little ashamed of herself. Which was exactly what I'd planned. 'You don't need to do that,' she said.

'You should go,' I said. 'Thanks for being so sweet. I'll catch you later.'

42

'Nice room,' said Laura Farrow, standing just a pace or two inside it, looking round at the walls of pale, uncovered stone and arched stone-framed windows.

'My official room in college,' said Evi. 'Where I see my students, as opposed to my patients.'

'Who's the stiff?' asked the detective, her eyes rising to the oil painting above the hearth.

'Some twit in a black gown and curled wig,' replied Evi, as a spark jumped out of the fire and landed on the worn rug. Before Evi could even move, Laura had stepped forward and crushed it under foot. Then she almost lost her balance, stumbled and recovered.

'There's a hook behind the door,' said Evi. 'Have a seat. You might need a notebook.'

Laura took off her jacket, gloves and scarf, sat on the winged chair opposite Evi's own and took a student pad and pencil from her bag. When she looked up, her pupils were too large.

'Are you OK?' Evi asked.

'Of course,' said Laura, a little too quickly. 'Don't I look it?'

Evi took her time. Natural poise aside, Laura really didn't look well. Her make-up seemed to sit on her pale face, rather than blending in naturally.

'I didn't sleep well,' Laura added. 'The student blocks can be quite noisy at night.' Then she seemed to force a smile. 'And the truth is I'm not nearly as young as I'm pretending to be.'

Evi decided to let it go. She picked up a file from a small table by her side and opened it. 'I found something that worried me,' she began, flicking through the first few pages. 'Shortly after we met on Tuesday. I didn't mention it straight away because I wanted to think about it and I certainly didn't want to put it in an email.'

Looking up, she saw a tiny flake of mascara high on Laura's left cheek. Oddly, it suited her, like an old-fashioned, painted beauty spot.

'You have to understand this is very difficult for me,' Evi went on. 'Patient confidentiality is sacrosanct in the medical profession. At least it should be. Talking to you at all without clearing it with — well, with the world and his wife, frankly — is putting my career at risk.'

'I understand,' said Laura.

'You picked up on Bryony's fear that she'd been raped,' Evi said after a moment. 'Bryony is a very troubled young woman with all sorts of problems. I just wondered why that, of everything in her case notes, struck you.'

Laura dropped her eyes. 'It's an interest of mine,' she said. 'I joined the police to work on violent crime against women. So it's natural it would strike a chord.'

Evi half considered asking if violent crime was something of which the detective had personal experience. Bad idea. She was letting her interest in Laura Farrow herself get in the way of the job both of them were trying to do. She nodded at Laura to go on.

'But it was more than that,' Laura said. 'Everything else going on in Bryony's life, the problems sleeping, the stress over workload, her feelings of worthlessness, they were all of her own making, if you know what I mean. I'm not trying to minimize her problems, far from it, I'm just trying to say that they were . . . oh, help me out here, you're the psychiatrist.'

'Of an internal origin?' suggested Evi.

'Exactly. Rape, though, is quite the opposite. Rape is inflicted upon you by an external aggressor.'

'If the rape was real,' Evi reminded her, and saw a flash of annoyance in the girl's hazel-blue eyes. 'As opposed to something Bryony either imagined or invented. Are you sure you're OK, Laura? Your hands are shaking.'

'I'm fine,' said Laura, a bit faster than was strictly polite. 'Thank you. I know the counsellor on your team wasn't convinced by Bryony's story, but my instinct when a woman says she's been raped is to give her the benefit of the doubt.'

This young woman had been abused, possibly even raped, herself. Evi was now sure of it. She wondered if her superiors in the police service were aware of her history.

'Good for you,' she said. 'So if I told you that four other students claimed to have been raped, in a manner very similar to that which Bryony reported, in the months leading up to their taking their own lives, you'd consider that significant?'

Evi watched Laura nod her head slowly, saw the spark leap into her eyes.

'We're talking a period of five years,' Evi went on. 'No proof in any case. Nothing to corroborate the women's stories.'

'Tell me about them.'

'I can't,' said Evi. 'That's the problem.'

'They're dead,' Laura argued.

Evi shook her head. 'Doesn't matter.'

'Then how on earth do you expect me —'

Evi held up a hand. 'Three years ago,' she said, 'a patient of the clinic, we'll call her Patient A —'

'Just give me first names,' said Laura.

'If I give you first names, you'll be able to identify them from newspaper reports.'

'OK, tell me what happened to Patient A,' said Laura, who was almost certainly thinking she could probably do that anyway.

'Patient A reported bad dreams, problems sleeping, and a fear of someone entering her room at night,' Evi said. 'One night, convinced she'd been raped, she went to the police. There was no physical evidence at all. She killed herself six weeks later.'

Laura wrote in her notebook.

'A few months before that, Patient B, a medical student, reported similar fears,' said Evi. 'Bad dreams of a sexual nature, waking up feeling hungover and sluggish, even though she claimed she hadn't been drinking or taken anything. Patient B never used the word rape. She felt as though she was being violated repeatedly, but she thought it was her own mind that was doing the damage.'

'That's creepy,' said Laura. 'She killed herself too?'

Evi nodded. 'At the start of that same year, another girl, Patient C, reported her fears of ongoing rape to the police,' she said. 'Excessive levels of ketamine were found in her bloodstream that she swore she hadn't taken. Other than that, though, no evidence. The police were sympathetic but had nothing to go on.'

'You said four,' Laura reminded her.

'Patient D attempted to kill herself five years ago,' Evi said. 'Similar history. Bad dreams, trouble sleeping, vague recollections of sexual abuse.'

'Attempted? You mean she's still alive?'

Evi said nothing. After a moment, Laura stood up and crossed to the window. 'Since you found the figures on suicide attempts,' she said, over her shoulder, 'our list has gone up to twenty-nine.'

'That's true,' agreed Evi.

Laura turned back to look at her. 'You know who they all are?' she asked.

Evi nodded.

'But you won't tell me?'

'I'm not ready to be struck off just yet,' Evi told her. 'Besides, there are other ways you can get the information. There'll be coroner's reports on the actual suicides. The police can access those, as long as you prove to the coroner you have good reason.'

Laura didn't look convinced. Her lips pursed and her eyes fell to the floor. Then she seemed to think of something. She looked up and forced a polite smile on to her face.

'I do understand,' she told Evi. 'Thank you for telling me what you have. I'll discuss it with my senior officers. If they think it important, I'm sure they'll take it further.'

Laura Farrow was up to something she shouldn't be. There was a glint of excitement behind those eyes now. And she was looking at the back of the door where her jacket was hanging.

'Let me know if anything comes up, won't you?' Evi asked her.

Laura agreed that she would but she was already mentally somewhere else. She crossed the room, pulled down her jacket and put it on. A second later she was gone.

43

Visiting time had just started but there was no one in the small, private room with its tropical microclimate except Bryony herself. As I approached the protective tent, I could see that the cadaver's face had been fastened to Bryony's own flesh with centimetre-long steel staples. They ran around her eyes and her mouth, along the top of her head. Frankenstein, I couldn't help thinking. Frankenstein stitched dead people together to make a living creature.

Bryony's ventilator had been removed again. All that was left was a small length of plastic pipe attached to her throat in case the staff needed to hook her up again quickly. For the moment, she was breathing unaided.

I would rather be dead. I would a million times rather be dead than spend a single day looking like this.

The door closed behind me and, at the

faint swishing sound it made, Bryony's eyes opened. She looked at me and blinked.

'Hello,' I said.

Her eyes were bright blue. Beautiful eyes, hardly touched by the fire, but seeing them move beneath dead skin was like watching an animated corpse. I pulled the bedside chair a little way from the bed and sat down. I think I'd been hoping I'd no longer have to see her eyes. It didn't work. She turned her head and those eyes were fixed on me again.

How could I ever have thought this was a good idea?

'You're probably wondering who I am,' I said, making myself look directly at her. 'And the truth is, I'm not sure what to tell you.'

Her lashless eyelids closed briefly, then opened again. I had no means of knowing what, if anything, she was taking in. She might be awake but her pain medication would still be very strong.

'I can't even tell you my name,' I went on, 'because I'm not allowed to tell you my real one. And I don't want to lie to you.'

Something in those eyes. It could have been curiosity. It could have been fear. I really didn't want to frighten her.

'If you want me to leave,' I said, 'I will. I

don't know whether you can talk but if you blink your eyes at me very rapidly, I'll take that as a signal to go. OK?'

I didn't really expect a response, but Bryony moved her head up and down.

'I'm living in your old room,' I said. 'Sharing with Talaith. But I'm not a student. I'm pretending to be one, but I'm not.'

What on earth was I doing? If Bryony had any way of communicating with people, I'd just blown it. I'd destroyed my cover, wrecked the case and was probably on the verge of jeopardizing this girl's recovery.

'I'm here,' I went on, knowing I was committed, 'because people are concerned. They think someone might be harming students. Maybe not directly, maybe it's all quite subtle, but it's dangerous all the same.'

Bryony raised her right hand from the bed. It was heavily bandaged. She pressed her forefinger and thumb close together and waved her hand around in the air.

'What is it?' I said. 'Can I get you something? Do you need the nurse?'

She let her hand fall back to the bed. Her breathing had quickened, her chest rising and falling beneath the bedclothes. In spite of what Nick had told me the other day about sedatives, she seemed to be in pain.

'I'm sorry,' I said. 'I really don't want to

upset you and I'll go the minute you ask me to.'

I stopped, looking for the rapid blinking that would be my signal to beat it. I was half hoping to see it. She just looked at me. Waiting.

'OK, here's the thing,' I said, just wanting to get it over with now. 'I've read your case notes and I know what you think was happening to you in your room at night. I also know that at least four other women students have reported very similar things happening to them.'

Her eyes seemed to widen.

'Four young women talked about bad dreams, of someone coming into their rooms at night. They talked about being raped. All the things that happened to you.'

Her eyes didn't leave mine for a second.

'Bryony,' I said, 'do you have any idea who it was that was coming into your room?'

Bryony closed her eyes and moved her head from side to side. She didn't know. It was several seconds before she opened her eyes again. I was tiring her.

'Thank you,' I said. 'I'll let you get some rest now.'

Her right arm was off the bedclothes again. Thumb and forefinger clenched together, she was waving her hand around.

'I'll get the nurse,' I said.

Heading for the door I was stopped in my tracks by urgent sounds coming from the bed behind me. The sort of sounds you make when you can't speak but you really want to make a noise. I turned back. Bryony had half raised herself from the bedclothes. She was still making that odd, jerky movement with her hand. Then, exhaustion getting the better of her, she collapsed back on the bed and moaned softly. I walked round to the right side of the tent, to the vents the nurses used to get close to her. Dangling from beneath the one closest to her hand was a small, rectangular piece of white plastic and a fibre-tipped pen.

'Bryony,' I said to her, 'can you write?'

A short, sharp nod of the head answered me. I pulled a sterile glove from a box by the bedside and, as gently as I could, slid the pen between her thumb and forefinger. Then I held the plastic up to meet her hand.

Holding the pen and moving it around was a huge effort, I could tell from the way her eyes narrowed and little gasps escaped from her throat. Feeling hopeful and guilty at the same time, I watched as she traced out a letter.

W

It took her a long time but at last her hand

fell to the bed again and there were two words on the pad.

WATCHING ME

Movement outside. The handle of Bryony's door started to turn then stopped again. Footsteps walked away. I looked back down to see Bryony had written something else.

SCARED

'What are you scared of?' I asked, in a voice I'm not sure she could have heard, then leaned closer to read the final word she'd written. Her hand fell back on the bed covers. She'd written *BELL*.

What kind of bell? Why on earth would a bell scare her? I had to bite back a dozen questions. Bryony had had enough. Even I could see that. I made myself smile at her, took a step towards the door, and remembered the last time I'd been in this room.

There'd been a bell here then. Nick Bell. And he'd been watching her.

44

Sad. Hopeless. Despair. These were the sorts of words you expected from a young woman who'd attempted suicide. Not *Watching me.* Not *Scared.* What on earth had been going on in Bryony's life to lead her to such a drastic step? If she wasn't either delusional or making it up for attention, this was a whole different ball game. And where did *Bell* fit in?

All the way back to my room, I desperately wanted someone to talk to. I'd always thought of myself as a solitary creature, not given to sharing. How wrong I'd been. In the police there was always someone to report back to, to bounce ideas off. For the first time in years I had too much going on in my head and no one to turn to.

Bell didn't necessarily mean Nick Bell. It wasn't a common name, but even so I would not let that particular cat out of the bag just yet. There had to be other Bells in

Cambridge. I opened up my laptop and started searching the university websites for someone else called Bell, looking first through the list of undergraduates, then post-graduates, then research fellows, fellows, honorary fellows, masters and staff. In a community of over twenty thousand people I found three others, two of them women. The third was a man called Harold whose brief biographical details told me he'd been retired for some time.

Someone in the town, maybe. Someone in a bar, restaurant, bookshop? Talaith could probably help me with the places where Bryony had hung out.

And yes, I knew exactly what I was doing. I didn't want Nick Bell to be involved in whatever was going on here. I'd liked him.

When I'd drawn a complete blank with Bell, I turned to my other self-appointed task. Finding the names of the women Evi had half told me about that morning, the suicides who'd suspected they'd been raped.

Three academic years earlier, five young women and one man had taken their own lives, making it one of the worst years on record for student suicides. I spent some time searching through the university newspapers and journals and the more general Cambridge-based ones, and eventually found six names. Without Joesbury's help, though, there was no way of knowing which one Evi had been talking about.

The previous year was an even harder task, with seven self-inflicted student deaths. I couldn't even find all the names, so had no way of knowing who Evi's two had been. The year before that, though, I struck lucky. The woman Evi had referred to as Patient D hadn't died and I found her quite quickly. Danielle Brown, a twenty-year-old neurology student from Clare College, had tried to hang herself in woods just outside the city. She'd been spotted by some kids who'd cut her down and saved her life.

Danielle Brown. Still alive.

By three o'clock, I knew I couldn't stay indoors much longer. For one thing, I was still feeling groggy, making it pretty difficult to concentrate. For another, I was getting less and less comfortable in my room. Maybe it was just the recollection of what Bryony had gone through, but something was making me edgy.

And with every hour that went by, my feeling of frustration was growing. I'd spent the better part of three days doing exactly what I'd been told to — immersing myself in university life, watching and observing. I'd spent several hours of each day just surfing, looking for evidence of Evi's theory that some virtual subculture was damaging the collective mental health of the university. There was plenty on the net about suicide websites, but nothing I could find that was Cambridge-specific.

By quarter past three I was on the verge of going nuts. Normally, feeling like this I'd try to shake off the sluggishness with sixty or more lengths, but I hadn't discovered the pool or begun to work out the timetable. I decided I was well enough to risk a run.

I changed, took a look at the map and was about to head for the river when I remembered my trip to the industrial estate the previous day and the riverside public footpath I'd noticed. Another quick check of the map told me it was a four-mile circular walk close to one of the Cam's tributaries. As good a place as any for a late-afternoon run.

At first it was hard work, maybe for half a mile I struggled, but I soon found a rhythm. It's all in the breathing, running any distance. Get your breathing under control and you can more or less keep going till your strength gives up. For someone of my age with my fitness, that can be several hours. And as I ran I couldn't help but think about

Bryony's strange scribbled message.

Someone was watching her. Someone was scaring her. Real fears or just the imaginings of someone semi-delusional? She wouldn't be the first disturbed young woman to invent a stalker as a cry for attention. And was I right or wrong to suspect Nick Bell? Was it normal for GPs to visit patients in hospital? Once, maybe, but on the regular basis that Bell himself had admitted to? Somehow I didn't think so.

Once I left the buildings behind, the landscape blanched. Grass crackled beneath my feet, iced-over puddles shattered like glass and trees sprinkled tiny ice-flakes over me like confetti as I passed beneath them.

I ran on, as the sun got lower in the sky, through ploughed fields and over stiles. For a mile or so I followed a small river that wound its way, serpent-like, through the meadows. Willow trees grew on either side and the water was lined with rushes that, as the sun cast out its colour, seemed to be made of polished copper.

After thirty minutes, I crossed the tiniest of footbridges and knew I was heading back. I'd covered the better part of a mile when, some distance ahead, I thought I could see the large, corrugated roofs of industrial-type buildings. I was approaching the estate again from the opposite side from where I'd parked. As I climbed the wooden stile into the next field, I saw it was closer than I'd thought. Maybe another half-mile. From this direction I could see a much older brick building. It looked Victorian, and derelict. Like an old factory, or possibly a foundry.

Then it happened. Quite literally out of the blue, the very last thing I'd have expected. One second I was running along, conscious that my pace had slowed and that sweat was trickling down between my shoulder blades. The next, a high-pitched screeching took me completely by surprise. Some instinct made me look up. About a hundred yards ahead, flying low and heading my way, was a large bird.

I wasn't too alarmed at first, but as the bird drew closer, screaming all the time, I found myself slowing down, as though putting off the moment when we'd reach each other. I looked up, just as it passed directly overhead, low enough for me to make out dappled brown breast feathers, estimate that its wingspan was about three feet, and see yellow scaled talons.

I turned, fully expecting to see the bird flying away. It was, but not for long. It was harder to see now because it was coming directly from the sun but there really wasn't much doubt it had turned and was coming back.

OK, what do you do? You're a couple of miles from shelter, there's no one else around and a large bird of prey attacks you. Any terms of reference for that? Because I hadn't. Knowing the stupidity of trying to outrun a bird, especially a big one, that's exactly what I did. I felt the rush of wind that could even have been physical contact as the bird passed overhead again.

What the hell was going on here? Birds didn't attack people. Had I fallen asleep at my desk and woken up in a Hitchcock movie? I glanced up. OK, I needed a plan. Fast. To my left was a wired fence, about four feet high, with woodland on the other side. The bird would almost certainly find it harder to attack me around trees than in open countryside.

It was coming back, lower, heading straight for my face. I turned and sprinted for the fence. The bird rose higher in the air, hovering above me, screeching like a banshee all the while. The trees were tall but slender. Luckily for me, they grew very close together and I really didn't think the bird could fly down here.

It couldn't and it didn't try. But it wasn't giving up easily. I could still hear it above the tree canopy, screeching, probably accusing me of all sorts of cowardice in birdspeak.

I made my way through the woods, ducking to avoid a low-hanging branch, and after about five minutes came into a small clearing. In the centre were the remains of a campfire. Kids sneaking out to drink cheap booze and smoke dodgy cigarettes was my first assumption. Except there were no obvious signs that teenagers had been here. Teenagers are messy; they don't party and go home via the recycling bins. Yet there was nothing here but the blackened remains of a fire.

On the other side of the clearing was a narrow track and I made for it with relief. To my surprise, I found the path was lit. To either side of it, at five-yard intervals, alternating from the left side to the right, were small lamps. In brighter light I'd hardly have noticed them, but as the daylight got weaker they began to glow. They were solar powered, not dissimilar to the ones I had at home. Which meant they had to be wired up to panels. I walked to the tree nearest the lamp I was standing by. Sure enough, a thin covered wire ran up the trunk, going up higher than I could see.

Installing solar lights in a wood in the

middle of nowhere was an expensive operation. And why would you light up a path leading to a clearing?

It was difficult to be sure in the growing gloom but I had a feeling I was coming to the end of the woodland. Through the trees ahead of me and to my left, I caught glimpses of large buildings. To my right was the field where the footpath lay and that was the obvious way home, but I was willing to bet the hawk from hell would have better night vision than I had. Better to get among the buildings, keep close to shelter and make my way back to the car.

I was still pretty jumpy by this stage so when something sounded behind me I spun round like I'd been shot. Nothing I could see, but woodlands are full of tiny creatures. Branches fall from trees, sometimes things just crack for no reason. No need to be alarmed, and walking backwards through a thick tangle of brambles, nettles and tough ground elder probably wasn't a great idea. I turned back to face the way I was going.

And thought I might die of fright.

Directly in front of me, not ten yards away, a human figure hung by the neck from a tree. A split second later I realized it wasn't a real person. It was just a large rag doll.

I moved closer. The doll was about three feet high. Its arms and legs seemed to have been made from a creamy-coloured cotton. It wore a yellow dress, stained by rain, mildew and bird droppings. Matching fabric had been sewn around its feet to simulate shoes. Its hands had been painted. Its hair was made from orange wool, twisted either side of its face in two plaits. Both were tied with large yellow bows. Its face was grotesque. A huge, grinning, misshapen mouth, heavy brows and fierce black eyes. A massive scar ran down the right cheek. This was no child's toy: this had been made to scare. And it worked.

I made my way round the tree, giving the hanging figure a wide birth, suddenly feeling that a second encounter with a territorial bird might not be such a bad idea. Definitely not a bad idea, because the rag doll wasn't the only thing hanging by the neck in these woods. Directly in front of me was an animal, swinging gently as though someone had given it a playful tap not moments before.

The fox was real. There was blood around its neck, which meant it had probably been alive when it was strung up here. On another tree, about five yards away, I could see another hanging figure. I was too far away to be sure it wasn't human so I had to go closer. Too small to be adult, only about three or four feet high. I was close enough. Another hideously painted cotton face. Red hair this time, tied with blue ribbon.

Oh, this felt very wrong.

'These woods are private.'

I'd had no idea anyone was near by and yet the small, silver-haired man had crept up close enough to touch. He was in country clothes, brown corduroy trousers and an oilskin coat.

'What's going on here?' I asked without thinking, indicating the nearest doll. 'What is this?'

I had to half admire the way a man hardly more than five foot seven could look down his nose at me. 'Did you hear what I said?' he asked. 'Do you understand the word private?'

Oh, to have had my warrant card. 'Sorry,' I said, through gritted teeth.

'That's your quickest way out,' he said, pointing to the field on my right, the one I'd been running through when the bird attacked. 'I suggest you take it.'

I looked towards the industrial estate. 'I'll go that way,' I said. 'It's a bit dark to be running through fields.'

His outstretched right arm didn't budge.

'That way,' he said.

A bit annoyed now, I wished him a good evening and stepped to the side, meaning to go round him and head towards the buildings. He mirrored me, effectively blocking my path.

'What do you think you're doing?' I asked him, sounding bolshie enough but just beginning to be a tiny bit afraid of him. He was in his early sixties and, whilst not a big man by any means, would probably outmatch me in strength. And there was something in his eyes that didn't look quite reasonable.

'My land,' he said. 'I can do what I like.'

'No you can't,' I told him. 'Get out of my way.'

He didn't move. Except to point more emphatically with his right hand. 'That is your way.'

'What's your name?' I asked.

'What's yours?' he replied.

Well, he had me there. Laura Farrow could not get into a public argument with a local landowner. If the regional police got involved, they'd find out soon enough that Laura Farrow didn't exist. It could blow the whole undercover operation.

'Have a nice evening, sir,' I told him, which, on reflection, probably wasn't wise.

Wishing someone a pleasant evening and calling them sir was a decidedly copper-ish thing to do. I turned and walked quickly to the edge of the woodland. Once more over the fence and I was in the field. When I turned back, he was still watching me.

I started running. Didn't stop till I got to my car.

I got home to an email message from Evi, asking if I might be free to join her at a supper party the following night. It would be a chance for me to meet more people, she said, and might give the two of us time to talk if anything had come up.

It would also, I realized, give me a chance to ask her about Nick Bell, whether she knew him, what she thought of him. I sent her a quick message back saying I'd be happy to join her and she replied instantly with the address. A farmhouse just outside Cambridge. We'd meet there at eight.

I spent the evening cruising the net again, looking for sites that might be inciting vulnerable people like Bryony, Nicole and Jackie to take their own lives. If they were out there, they were elusive. I was getting increasingly convinced that Evi's theory wasn't right. When I felt as if my eyes were in danger of falling out of their sockets,

I sent my report to Joesbury and went to bed.

45

Joesbury let out the breath he hadn't even realized he'd been holding. For the love of . . . What part of *you are not there to investigate* was the woman struggling with? He leaned back, stretched, rubbed his eyes and read the paragraph again.

This isn't date rape, remember, Sir. These four women, five including Bryony, didn't go home with someone they met in a bar. They all believed someone came into their room at night, while they slept, and abused them. Most girls in college-type environments lock their rooms at night, which means someone gained entry through locked doors. Most women would wake up and scream the place down if a stranger started touching them in the middle of the night.

Except you, Lacey, Joesbury was thinking,

as he walked to the window. A stranger touching you in the middle of the night is an entirely normal occurrence. Jesus, he needed to be off this case. No, he needed her off this case. He simply could not think straight when . . . and he was starting to feel like a caged animal in this hotel bedroom. He'd go for a walk except he knew where he'd end up. On the green outside the residential block of St John's.

Instead, he turned back and looked at the blue file next to his laptop on the narrow hotel desk. He knew exactly who the four women were. Freya Robin, Donna Leather, Jayne Pearson and Danielle Brown. He was starting to recite their names — and those of all the others — in his sleep. He sighed again and went back to the report.

Christ, only Lacey Flint could be attacked by a rabid kestrel, find dead animals hanging from trees and be ordered off private land by a psychotic farmer all in one afternoon. When she finally finished rabbiting on about how she spent her leisure time, she went back to her previous point.

Seems to me there's a pattern developing. Bad dreams, possible disappearances, recreational drug use, unproven sexual abuse and even rape, then death.

I know you said I'm not investigating, Sir, but with the attempted suicides there are potentially twenty-nine cases of something very sinister going on here. Evi won't give me names, some patient-confidentiality bollocks, but I found a few of them, including Danielle Brown, one of the possible rape victims, in newspaper archives. I know you can get the rest from CID files. It would be really helpful to know who they are. I've got plenty of time on my hands here. I can just sit at a computer and go through the facts. See if anything jumps out. I'm good at detail, did I mention that? Another thing that would be really useful is to track down Danielle Brown and go and talk to her. If she tells us her actions were influenced by online pressure, that's a major step forward, isn't it? I might just work on that tomorrow.

She wrote in a way she never spoke to him. Much less formal, even friendly. When they were face to face she was always guarded, as though measuring every word that came out of her mouth. Except when she lost her temper. When he'd first got to know her, he'd made a point of winding her up in a way that was completely unprofessional, just to get a reaction out of her that seemed real.

OK, here's the really serious bit. I went to see Bryony Carter again today and I discovered something. She can't talk but she can write. Only the odd word at a time because she doesn't seem to have much control over her muscles. She told me someone was watching her. Which really doesn't fit with Evi's online bullying theory. For someone to be watching, it all sounds more focused and deliberate. She also said that she was scared and then wrote down the word *Bell*. Mean anything to you? Bryony's GP is called Nick Bell and he was in her room (watching her?) the day I met him, but to be honest I can't see it. He seems nice. No one else of that name at the university who seems likely. I'm going to go and see her again. I don't want to push it, though, she's in a very delicate condition.

OK, I think that's all for today. I can barely keep my eyes open and there's a young gentleman reclining on my pillow who is looking decidedly neglected. I'm talking about the teddy, by the way. I call him Joe, did I mention that? Blimey,

I'm tired. Good night. Sleep tight. Don't let the bedbugs . . . I'm really going now. Zzzzz . . .

Joesbury stood up, crossed the room and let his head fall against the cool wood of the door. After five minutes he sighed and reached for the phone.

46

Cambridge, fifteen years earlier

'No one has to do this,' said the young man who'd stolen the key and opened the door at the top of the church tower. He was tall and lean and at twenty-one his body was as close to perfect as the male form usually gets. His hair, grown longer since he'd left his strict boarding school behind, flew out around his head like a pagan crown. 'I know we've talked, but until we got here, none of us knew how we'd feel. If anyone changes his mind, that's OK.'

The first of his two companions to step on to the roof was wearing the navy, red and yellow scarf of one of the more famous Cambridge colleges. He shook his head. 'I won't change mine,' he said. 'You've no idea how much clearer it's all been since we decided. Like a massive weight just gone.' He turned to look back at the stairs. 'I can't go back down there,' he said, and there was the gleam of tears in his eyes. 'I just can't.'

'Got to, one way or another,' said the third boy. Then he glanced anxiously at each of the other two. 'Sorry,' he said. His pupils were enormous in his pale face and seemed to have lost their ability to focus. His hands were shaking. He was smaller and thinner than his two companions, a boy bred for indoors.

The long-haired boy rested a hand on the smaller one's shoulder. 'It's OK,' he said. 'We deal with it how we can.'

'So how do we do this?' asked the third boy, speaking faster than seemed natural. 'Hold hands and count to three?'

'Let's just go look,' suggested the boy with long hair. 'I want everyone to be sure.'

'I'm sure,' said the one wearing the Trinity scarf. 'Thanks for being with me, guys. Whether you come with me all the way or you don't, I couldn't have made it this far without you. You've been good friends.'

He held out his arms and, in turn, the other two stepped into them. The hugs were brief, blokesy, little more than mutual back-patting.

Together they walked across the roof to the parapet. A yard or two away, the third boy held back. The first two either didn't notice or pretended not to. They reached the stone edging and sat down on it. Not taking their eyes from each other, they swung their legs over the edge until two pairs of shoes were dangling.

'Good luck, mate,' said the first.

'Love you, man,' his companion replied.

A strangled scream from behind. The third boy was running at them, his mouth open, fists pumping. He reached them, sprang up on to the parapet and leaped.

Silence for three, maybe four seconds. Then a crunch. Silence again.

Both boys on the parapet had leaned forward to watch the moment of impact. Moving as one, they straightened up and turned to each other.

'You know, Iestyn, even if he hadn't, a bloody good push would have done it,' said the long-haired boy.

The one wearing the Trinity scarf, Iestyn, shook his head. 'No good,' he said. 'Trust me, takes all the fun out of it.'

Still moving as one, they smiled, raised their right hands and slapped a noisy high five.

47

Friday 18 January (four days earlier)
'You're late.'

The denim-clad bottom wiggled itself into a comfortable position on the leather passenger seat and its owner ostentatiously raised her left wrist.

'Your watch is fast,' she said, without looking at him. 'I'm bang on time.' Joesbury released the handbrake, checked the rear mirror and pulled out, just as Chris Evans announced that they were listening to the Friday show and that it was nine thirty-two on Radio 2.

'Guess the BBC's watch is fast too,' he said.

'How was the traffic?'

'Not bad, considering,' he told her, which pretty accurately described the five-minute trip from the central multi-storey car park to the spot on the Queen's Road, some way down from the college, where he'd agreed to pick her up. Because of the email he'd sent at the crack of dawn she thought he'd driven up from London.

She was looking round, into the back seat, up at the ceiling. 'This isn't your car,' she announced as he turned on to the Huntingdon Road. Heading north out of Cambridge the traffic was busy but moving steadily. On the radio, a James Brown track started.

'Isn't it?'

Now she was in it the car smelled gorgeous; like sweet oranges and tiny white flowers on a tropical evening, and what the fuck was he now, a poet?

'When I knew you last autumn you had a poncy green convertible. A real ladies-who-lunch wagon.'

'Sweet of you to remember.' There were lights ahead and Joesbury eased his foot off the accelerator. If they came to a standstill, he could look at her. Otherwise, it really wasn't responsible. He pursed his lips to keep the smile at bay, wondering if there was a penalty for driving under the influence of Lacey.

'Mind you, when I knew you last autumn you had a right lung that hadn't been ripped open by a bullet. I guess life moves on.'

'Ouch,' said Joesbury. Nope, he was not going to look.

'Does it hurt?'

That didn't sound like concern in her voice — more like hope — but it was hard to tell without looking at her.

'No, it's actually a pretty comfortable drive.'

The lights stayed on green, the suburbs started to fade away and the speed of the traffic picked up. Out of the corner of his eye he could see she was looking directly at him. He glanced round before he could stop himself and his stomach did a little flip-flop. She hardly ever wore make-up. For a moment, he found himself grinning inside at the thought she'd dressed up for him. Then he remembered she was undercover. As the glamorous albeit drippy-as-an-old-tap Laura Farrow.

'I still own the ladies-who-lunch wagon,' he told her, as they neared the dual carriageway. 'This vehicle is registered to a company in Essex that ceased trading two years ago.'

'Wow, a real spy car.'

He faked a sigh. 'Flint, are you taking this a hundred per cent seriously?'

She wiggled a bit in the seat, like an overexcited child on an outing. 'Too right I am,' she said. 'I missed two lectures to come out on a jaunt with you, you know. So where are we going?'

'Lincoln,' he said, pulling into the outside lane and picking up speed. The instrument panel told him the temperature outside had fallen to zero degrees. 'To meet Danielle Brown.'

Silence for a second and then, 'Why?'

'Because she's a former Cambridge student who attempted suicide and who, prior to that, claimed sexual abuse by assailants unknown.'

She ran a hand through her hair. 'I know that,' she said. 'I told you that last night. I mean, why are we going to see her? Sounds an awful lot like investigating to me and I'm not here to investigate. You were very clear about that.'

'Are you going to keep this up the whole trip?' he said.

'Probably. And the way back too. And why get you involved? I thought you were on light duties. You know, making tea for important people at the Yard.'

'I guess the important people at the Yard thought driving you a hundred miles and watching you interview a nice young lady counted as light duties. They clearly don't know you like I do.'

When he glanced across again, she was smiling. An unfamiliar ache in his cheekbones told him he was too.

Megan had been right. Fifteen years ago, when Evi Oliver had been a first-year medical student at St John's College, shiny-haired and sound of limb, five students had taken their own lives.

Evi, in her consulting room at the SCS offices, sat back, her left hand going automatically down to her thigh to try to massage away some of the ache there. She remembered one of them, the one Nick had mentioned on Wednesday evening, a boy who'd jumped off the tower of one of the older churches. The area at its base had been closed off for over twenty-four hours and then strewn with cheap flowers for days afterwards. And now she'd learned about four others, none of whom she could remember. Maybe such things had been hushed up in those days. She went back to the stats on the screen.

Nothing else remarkable at all. One suicide in a year, two suicides, none at all some years. Absolutely what you might expect. Except for the blip when she'd been an undergraduate and what was happening now, Cambridge's record on student deaths was bang on normal.

With one eye on the clock, knowing she

had a departmental meeting in fifteen minutes, Evi accessed the archived site of the university newspaper. She entered suicide into the search facility and a few moments later had details of the five young people who'd died in her first year.

Four boys, one girl. One jumper, one wrist-slasher, three overdosers. Three of them had been medical students, one in his second year (jumper) and two in their first (wrist-slasher and overdoser). Evi looked at the clock again and picked up the phone.

'I ran a check on your friend Nick Bell,' said Joesbury, as they reached the A1.

'Anything?' asked Lacey, her head flicking in his direction just a fraction faster than he would have liked.

'Clean as a whistle, but we'll keep an eye on him.'

'I could accidentally bump into him. Try to get to know him a bit better?'

She was winding him up. At least he hoped she was. 'Keep your mind on the job, Flint. You can resume your unusual love life when we pull you off the case.'

She didn't reply. When he glanced over she was staring straight ahead, pink-painted lips pursed just a fraction. Sulking. He hadn't realized how plump her lower lip was.

'We can also get someone into the practice he works for to check out his computers,' Joesbury said, bringing his eyes firmly back on to the road. 'If he's been on any dodgy internet sites we'll soon know about it.' She was still staring at the dashboard. 'It'll take a week or so to sort out.'

'How?' She'd turned to look at him again. 'You can't just turn up on someone's door-step and ask to inspect their hard drive.'

On the radio, Michael Bublé began to sing about how it was a new dawn and a new day. Not his favourite cover but a good song. Joesbury reached forward to turn the volume up a tad. And was he going to let that last one go? Probably better if he did.

'First of all we send 'em a hard-to-trace virus,' he said. 'Just enough to toss a few gremlins into the system. Then we reroute their telephone calls out of the building to pick up the one to their IT support when they call for help. We send someone along that afternoon.'

'That's sneaky.'

'You did look up the dictionary definition of covert operations before you took this job, didn't you, Flint?'

She gave a soft exhalation that might even

have been something approaching a giggle and he was getting that feeling again. The one he always had when he was with her, even when the biggest load of shit ever was being fanned in all directions. The one that told him there was nowhere else in the whole world he'd rather be.

'Meg, did I wake you?'

Silence on the other end of the line. Then the sound of fabric moving together. Something creaking, and, possibly, a yawn. Meg was still in bed.

'Nope, wide awake,' she replied, in her usual gravelly early-morning smoker's voice. 'Just not completely alert. It's my day off and I've not had my caffeine fix yet. What's up, Evi?'

'Sorry, I didn't realize. I can call you next week.'

More sounds of sliding fabric, a tiny grunt. 'No, go on.'

Evi named the year both women had been students at St John's, Evi in her first year, Megan in her third. 'Five suicides,' she said. 'Only time other than the last five years when anything out of the ordinary in that respect has happened here. You mentioned it the other day. How much do you remember?'

272

Silence for a second, while Megan was thinking, and pushing herself up in the bed.

'Not a lot, to be honest,' she said after a moment. 'But Evi, fifteen years ago, it was very early days for the internet. The sort of online bullying and goading you've been talking about wouldn't have had a chance to get going. I don't see how it can be relevant.'

She had a point. 'That's true.'

A small sigh. 'Look, Evi, I'm really not sure this is what should be occupying your head right now. You're far from well yourself. Let me pass this on to John. His team can follow it up if they think it's important.'

Something in Megan's voice suggested she found that last idea amusing. 'Is he there?' asked Evi.

Pause. 'Might be,' said Meg, with a definite smile in her voice.

'OK, OK, I'm out of your hair. Enjoy the rest of your day, Meg.'

'I'll let you ladies chat,' said Joesbury, walking to a dining table at the far side of the room and pulling out one of the chairs. Earlier he'd bought a copy of the *Daily Mirror.* He turned to the sports pages and dropped his head into his fingers. Now he had a good view of the two women, and would look like he was reading.

Danielle Brown was a mess. No other way of putting it, really. At twenty-five, she could have been a decade older. She was about four stone overweight, riddled with acne and scratched herself constantly. An hour and a half earlier, he and Flint had arrived at the small solicitors' office where she worked as a legal clerk. They'd introduced themselves and asked to talk to her during her lunch break. She'd agreed willingly enough, almost seemed to welcome the unexpected attention. At one p.m., they'd driven her to the house on the outskirts of town where she lived with her parents.

The house was a big 1930s semi, with large rooms, high ceilings and art deco-style windows. The massive open-plan living room (two rooms knocked through) was full of photographs of Danielle as a schoolgirl and a young student. She'd been slim and athletic, with long, glossy brown hair. The hair was short now, cut for ease of care rather than to flatter. She could have been a different woman.

'I read about that girl,' she was saying to Lacey as she picked at some dry skin on the inside of her wrist. 'The one who self-immolated at the end of Michaelmas. Is she dead?'

'She was very badly hurt,' said Lacey. 'Her recovery isn't certain.'

'And the one this week. The papers didn't give any details. What happened to her?'

'We suspect she may have deliberately crashed her car,' said Lacey. 'Danielle, I'm going to ask you some questions that you might find difficult to answer. I'm truly sorry to cause you distress but I wouldn't ask if it wasn't important. Is that OK?'

Out of the corner of his eye, Joesbury saw Danielle nodding her head, looking wary but also, he thought, intrigued. He looked down again, waiting for the inevitable question about the alleged sexual abuse.

'Danielle,' said Lacey, 'when you were at Cambridge, were you ever scared?'

Joesbury realized he hadn't turned a page in twenty minutes. Danielle was getting a whole load of free therapy from Lacey, who'd clearly missed her vocation in life as a student counsellor, but otherwise they'd made little progress.

He'd known before they arrived, because he'd been through Danielle's file in some detail, that she'd struggled to cope with life at Cambridge. She'd missed assignments, forgotten to attend lectures and tutorials, frequently overslept. Her work had suffered to the point where the authorities were considering taking action. He'd already seen the files from the Student Counselling Services and knew about Danielle's unsubstantiated claims of sexual abuse in her room at night. What he hadn't known, in fairness, was what Lacey had unearthed. The fact that, before hanging herself from an oak tree, Danielle had been scared.

'One of the lines we're pursuing,' Lacey was saying, 'is that vulnerable students are being encouraged to harm themselves by some sort of online bullying. Did you ever visit any sort of suicide website or chat room while you were at Cambridge?'

Danielle nodded her head. Joesbury sat further back in his chair and watched her. From where the two women were sitting, Lacey could see him, Danielle couldn't.

'I just needed to know there were other people out there who felt as bad as I did,' Danielle said.

'Did anyone tell you about these sites?'

Blank look.

'Did these sites find you, in any way? Did you get any emails, or did they pop up in your search engines, or anything like that? How did you know about them?'

'I Googled *suicide*,' said Danielle, with a faintly contemptuous tone to her voice. 'It wasn't hard.'

'Were any of the sites Cambridge-specific?'

Again, Danielle shook her head. 'Most of them seemed to be based in the United States from what I can remember,' she said.

Quietly, Joesbury stood up and walked to the window. The garden outside was mature and well cared for. Even in winter it was attractive, with grasses and evergreen shrubs gleaming with frost. He'd give them ten more minutes then bring it to a close. There was still time for lunch, maybe a chance to talk about something that wasn't police work. Had they ever actually done that before?

Over on the sofas Lacey and Danielle were talking about the event itself, the morning Danielle had ridden her bike to some nearby woods, thrown a rope over a branch and hanged herself.

'How did you reach the branch?' Lacey was asking. 'If it was high enough for you to hang yourself, it must have been too high to reach from the ground.'

'It's all a bit fuzzy,' said Danielle. 'Even the next day I couldn't remember it too clearly. The police said I'd had the rope ready looped and just thrown it over.'

'You must be good with knots,' said Lacey. 'I'm hopeless. Can never sort out my reefs from my bowlines.'

No response.

'So how do you make a loop in a rope?' asked Lacey. 'And then, how do you get the knot round your neck right? So that it tightens as it should? I wouldn't have a clue.'

Joesbury gave up all pretence of admiring the garden. He turned round to face the two women.

'I don't remember,' said Danielle. 'I'd taken something, according to the doctors. It's all just a blur.'

'What had you taken?'

A shrug. The girl's face had stiffened. Defences were coming down.

'What did you usually take?'

'Nothing. I didn't take drugs.'

'Just on the morning you tried to kill yourself?'

'DC Flint,' said Joesbury, stepping forward.

She looked up, half defiant, half guilty. Then, with a tiny purse of the lips, she turned back to Danielle. 'What did you stand on?'

'DC Flint . . .' Joesbury raised his voice.

'To die by hanging, you need to raise yourself off the ground, tighten the rope and then jump. What did you stand on?'

'According to the CID report, Miss Brown

balanced on the pedals of her bicycle for long enough to tie the rope,' said Joesbury. 'And if we don't take her back now, she'll be late for work.'

'Bull — *shit!*'

Joesbury glanced along the road and pulled out of the small car park. 'Don't mince words, Flint, say what you think.'

'Double bullshit. What was she, a trick cyclist? She balanced on bicycle pedals for long enough to tie a noose round her neck and the other end round a tree. Bullshit in triplicate!'

It was kind of nice, in a way, seeing her composure slip.

'Yeah, I get the point,' he said. 'You hungry?'

'She couldn't have done that by herself. You heard her, she didn't know her knots from her knitting. She had help.'

'Possibly. Pub grub do you?'

'What the hell do you mean, possibly?'

'Danielle didn't die because someone found her and cut her down,' said Joesbury. 'They phoned for help and then legged it. CID never found them. It's possible it was some sort of black joke that went a bit too far.'

'She couldn't identify them?'

Joesbury shook his head. 'Unconscious when they found her. The important point to take away from today is that websites don't seem to have unduly influenced her.'

'She visited them.'

Up ahead was a pub. The sign outside said it served food all day. It also said it offered overnight accommodation. Oh, if only. Steak pie and chips, a bottle of good claret and then upstairs for the rest of the afternoon.

'Of course she did,' he said. 'Anyone semi-computer literate contemplating any major step Googles it first these days. What we don't have is any indication that what she found online made a significant difference.'

Make that the rest of the week.

'Guess not,' agreed Lacey.

Joesbury indicated left and pulled into the pub car park. 'So, you've had a day out of school and done some proper detective work,' he said, as he switched off the engine. 'Now, can you get on with the brief you were given or do I have to replace you with an officer who understands the meaning of the phrase do what you're told?'

For a second, maybe two, they stared at each other. She'd kissed him once, last October, at around four in the morning, had pulled him gently towards her bed. And he really could have done without remembering that right now.

'Is it a disciplinary offence to call a senior officer a patronizing bastard?' she asked him.

She might never know what it had cost him to say no. What every second in her presence cost him when he couldn't touch her.

'Pay for lunch, Flint,' he said, 'and you can call me what you like.'

48

The supper party at which I'd been invited to be Evi's guest was in the middle of nowhere. Or, if you want to be picky, a tiny hamlet called Endicott, between two villages called Burwell and Waterbeach, some eight miles north-east of Cambridge. I was well and truly in the Fens now. I had a feeling that, had it been a clear night, the view would have been uninterrupted until the North Sea. I've spent my life in cities and I was finding the vastness of the East Anglian landscape disturbing. There was just too much of it somehow, too much emptiness. No place to hide.

Mind you, the sunset that evening as Joes-bury and I had driven back had been awe-inspiring. There had been plenty of cloud cover all afternoon, and as the sun went down the wind picked up and the heavens began to swirl with endless shades of orange, crimson and gold. If someone had told me the sky was on fire, I might just have believed it.

The awesome skyscape seemed to have affected Joesbury too. He was silent for most of the journey back and dropped me off with barely a goodbye. Now, colour had largely fled the world and just a few ribbons of gold broke up the unrelenting blackness. Like memories of a day I really hadn't wanted to end.

I spotted the gap in the hedgerow Evi had told me to watch out for and turned off the road. A few yards down the lane I switched off the Black Eyed Peas album I'd been listening to. There was something about the farm track, stretching for what seemed like miles ahead of me before disappearing into a black void, that made hip-hop seem entirely out of place.

The surface wasn't great and I had to go slowly, rocking and lurching from one rut to another. I seemed to have left civilization behind, my headlights the only break in the darkness for miles. Nor could I rely on anything astral. Someone had taken a vacuum and cleaned the sky of stars, and if the moon had come up at all this evening, it had changed its mind and gone in again.

On a whim, I slowed right down and switched off the headlights, just to see. The night seemed to solidify. It leaped closer, surrounding the car. I swear I could hear the metal of the bodywork groaning under the pressure. Completely freaky! I switched my headlights back on quickly. I'd had no idea that night-time could be so intense.

I carried on past farm buildings on the right-hand side of the track and what could even have been a house. No lights though. No parked cars. Nothing to indicate a gathering. I think I was almost considering giving up when I passed through two tall stone columns and saw the farmhouse ahead. Several vehicles were parked at the front and there were lights on in the downstairs windows. I parked and got out. The email Evi had sent me earlier had warned against wearing heels. Easy now to see why. This wasn't even a rough gravel drive. This was rock-spattered earth.

The house was two storey, square built, of stone construction. It looked like a haunted house in a children's story book: carved window ledges, elaborate crest over the front door and those nasty imp-like statues that leer down at you, tongues dangling, from the roof edge. There was a large iron ring centrally placed on the door. I lifted it, was about to let it fall.

'That door hasn't been opened since the

old Queen died,' said a voice from the side of the house. I turned to see Nick Bell heading towards me, lit cigarette in one hand.

'This is your house?' I asked when he was closer, cursing my stupidity for not asking Evi whose party she was inviting me to.

'I rather think it owns me,' he replied. 'Laura, isn't it? Evi told me you were coming. Good to see you again.'

He bent lower and kissed me on one cheek. The skin of his face was cold and his breath smelled of smoke and red wine. I couldn't help a shudder as his lips made contact.

'So did the old Queen die here?' I asked, more to cover my confusion than because I have any interest in deceased royalty. The house looked old enough for any number of dead queens to be associated with it.

'Quite possibly,' he replied. He was wearing jeans and the same blue and brown flecked woollen sweater I'd seen him in at the hospital. 'Her rotting corpse could still be in one of the attic bedrooms,' he was saying. 'We get some very odd smells from time to time.'

I followed Nick round the side of the house, past smokers huddled around a firepit and in through a boot room that smelled of dogs. On a counter I saw what looked like a cardboard box of fluffy yellow chicks. I leaned closer. Chicks all right. Dead ones. I was about to ask Nick why he kept dead poultry in his boot room when he ushered me into the kitchen. A slim woman in her early fifties with shoulder-length dark hair claimed his attention and a couple of pointers grabbed mine.

I have very little experience of dogs but it's difficult to resist creatures that are so unashamedly pleased to see you. Both were predominantly white with speckled markings. The smaller and slimmer of the two had a chocolate-brown face with ears so active they almost seemed to be talking at me. The other, with red-brown face and markings, looked older, its big cocoa-coloured eyes both wise and friendly. The name tag on the older one said Merry. The younger was Pippin.

In my experience, people who are very keen on *The Lord of the Rings* can be a bit odd. On the other hand, I was quite a Tolkien fan myself.

Nick was searching around in a kitchen drawer. I put down a bottle of wine and poured myself an orange juice.

'Wonderful house,' I said, when Nick had emptied the drawer of cutlery and I had his attention again.

'Belonged to my parents,' he replied. 'I inherited a few years ago. I'm going to sell it to someone who can afford to renovate it just as soon as I can get it safe enough to show estate agents round. The place is falling apart.'

Someone else came over to speak to Nick and I took myself through to an oak-panelled dining room awash with old Toby jugs and willow-patterned plates. The fireplace was massive. A second later I realized it needed to be. There was practically a breeze running through the room from ill-fitting windows on opposite walls. I counted two buckets and a bowl on the stone-flagged floor to catch the rain. And this was the ground floor.

There were around a dozen people in the room and not much space for more. I carried on walking into another stone-flagged room with easy chairs, a shiny black grand piano, an even larger fireplace and, cliché though it was, the decapitated head of a large mammal on one wall. Evi was perched on a window seat at the far end. An older man was sitting next to her, leaning rather closer than would have felt comfortable had I been in her position. Evi was dressed in bright scarlet this evening: red sweater that came down to mid-thigh, black jeans tucked into red boots. Her hair had been gathered up and was held in place by a red clip. Tiny, sparkly red earrings. She had a long neck, I noticed, and she held her head high.

She caught my eye and gave me a smile. I was about to cross the room and join her when someone spoke to me.

'Dried off, have you?' asked a boy I thought I recognized. He looked a little older than the average student, his skin a little more papery, deeper lines around the eyes. He was about five foot seven and thin. Pinched around the face. Runty was a word I might have used, had I been feeling mean.

'Is it raining out?' I replied, although I knew exactly what he meant. He saw the look in my eye and almost turned away. I was being Lacey.

'I take it you were on the green on Tuesday night,' I said, grabbing a nearby bowl and offering it to him. He glanced down and a confused look took hold of his face. Well, I was offering him pot pourri. Curled wood-shavings and dried leaves, to be specific. Lacey would have put one in her mouth just to prove a point. Laura put them back down on the piano and looked sheepish.

'I'm Laura,' I said.

'Will,' he told me. 'What are you reading?'

I bit back the temptation to say Dan

Brown. 'Psychology,' I replied. 'You?'

'I'm doing part three of the mathematical tripos,' he told me and I nodded, as though it meant something.

'Who were those boys?' I asked him. 'The ones on the green the other night wearing masks?' Scott Thornton I already knew about. Wouldn't hurt to put names on the others.

He smirked and his eyes fell to my chest. 'Why, are you planning revenge?' he said.

'Just want to know which shins I have to kick when I see them in daylight,' I said, before I could stop myself. There was something about this guy that was really bringing out the Lacey in me.

'To be honest I've not seen that lot before,' he said. 'A lot of freshers get dunked in the first few weeks but not usually by Lone Ranger lookalikes. So did you enjoy the experience of being chained up?'

God, this bloke was a twat. Fortunately, at that moment, people began appearing with loaded dinner plates.

'I'm starving,' I muttered. 'Catch you later.'

Evi had been abandoned by her admirer. 'Can I get you something to eat?' I offered. She started to shake her head, then seemed to change her mind.

'That would be great,' she said.

Back in the kitchen I joined the small queue. The curry I could smell was a mildly spiced pheasant casserole served with roasted root vegetables. People were still tucking into the first course, though, which was some sort of pâté.

I cut Evi a slice of pâté, found some bread and a knife and carried it back through, meaning to ask her how long she'd known Nick Bell and, if I could do it discreetly, what she thought of him. It probably wouldn't hurt to find out how good his IT skills were.

It wasn't to be. Two men were talking to her now. She was beautiful and fragile, like a princess in a fairy tale. They just couldn't help themselves. I reached around one of them to hand over the plate.

'Thanks, Laura,' she said. 'Can we catch up later?'

I left her to her admirers and went back to the food. The pâté was great, then the dark-haired woman started serving the casserole. I made polite conversation about nothing with people near by and was just wondering whether second helpings were acceptable when my host reappeared.

'How you doing?' he asked me.

'Bursting out of my jeans but otherwise

fine,' I told him. 'Fabulous food.'

'Liz and I have an arrangement,' he said, nodding towards the dark-haired woman. She caught her name being mentioned and gave him the sort of look a son gets from a mother who is just a little too fond of him. 'I kill it, she cooks it,' he went on. 'What we don't eat she sells at the Third Tuesday Farmers' Market.'

I was not in Kansas any more.

'When you say kill it, you're speaking figuratively, right?' I said. 'You mean you pop down to Waitrose, stalk the aisles in a predatory fashion and wrestle the last piece of frozen chicken from a single mum with toddler twins.'

'You're in the country now,' said Liz, who'd crept closer. 'Jim wouldn't eat a piece of meat that's seen the inside of a supermarket.' She nodded towards a wiry, silver-haired man by the window and Lacey had an urge to ask if Jim were her husband or her brother, or both. Laura, though, gave her a tight-lipped smile. Without returning it, Liz picked up a stack of dirty plates and left the room.

'So you're a killer?' I asked Nick, looking into his eyes, trying to see if there was anything not quite right in there. They looked steadily back, a rich golden brown.

Beautiful eyes. With a light in them that I couldn't interpret.

'Got a problem with that?' he asked.

'Depends what you kill,' I said. 'And, I guess, on how you do it.' Oh, I had to be careful. Lacey was standing on tiptoe, arms out-stretched, desperate to be out of her box, and if this man had anything to hide I was probably putting him on maximum alert.

He was a cool customer, I had to admit. He gave me a very wide grin and took my empty plate from me. 'Come on,' he said. 'I'll show you my lethal weapons.'

Jessica Calloway opened her eyes to find she was no longer in her room at college, the scene of so many dreadful nightmares lately. She was in a forest. She got to her feet slowly. She could see stars shining down through impossibly tall trees. The ground was covered with a soft sprinkling of frost that gleamed silver in the starlight.

'Jessica,' called a voice from somewhere among the trees. A high-pitched, tinny voice that didn't sound quite human. This was just another bad dream. She'd wake up soon, trembling and sweating and scream-ing, but awake and safe.

She was standing on a rough path that had

been formed by the constant passage of footsteps. Every few yards or so a small light was half hidden amidst the undergrowth, each giving off a soft glow. The lights seemed to invite her on, deeper into the woods.

A movement above her head made her jump. She looked up to see a creature, a very large bat, swooping down from the trees towards her. Jessica started, then stared at it in astonishment. The bat was the palest shade of blue and it left behind a trail like a silver moonbeam. As Jessica watched, the bat disappeared and the trail shimmered away to nothing.

In the boot room, Nick was holding out an oilskin coat for me. I slipped my arms into it and we stepped outside to find that snow was falling. I felt a flurry of nerves and told myself to chill. We were surrounded by people. This was his home. Nothing was going to happen.

'I didn't bring a torch,' he said. 'Stay close.'

We followed a flagstone path that led away from the main house towards a row of outbuildings. Some of them looked like stables. As we drew closer the long, pale face of a horse appeared.

'This is Shadowfax,' Nick said, stopping to stroke the horse's nose.

'You really are a *Lord of the Rings* fan,' I muttered, as he pulled keys from his jeans pocket and slid one of them into the door of the next building.

'They'll be asleep,' he said. 'Keep your voice low.'

Inside the shed was darkness, a strong smell of animal waste and an odd, expectant silence. Then a flapping just over my left shoulder. Light began to grow. I could see Nick's hand in the corner of the room, adjusting a dimmer switch. I was being watched by ten pairs of soft, black eyes.

I'd stepped back against the door. Too quickly. I'd startled them. They jumped, squawked, flapped and grumbled.

'Are you OK?' asked Nick, frowning at me. 'Sorry, should I have warned you?'

'What are they?' I asked, my eyes flicking from one creature to the next, taking in that they were all tethered to their perches. I still wasn't moving from the door.

'Peregrine falcons,' Nick replied, approaching the nearest bird. The creature bent its head towards Nick's outstretched hand, as though it would nuzzle against him. Or bite. Nick pulled out of reach before either could happen.

The birds differed slightly in size but were identical in colouring. The feathers on their backs and upper wings were the colour of rain-drenched slate. Those on their breasts were cream and cinnamon, dappled with black. 'Fastest creatures on the planet,' said Nick. 'Haldir, this is Laura.'

The falcon looked at me. Its eyes were black, rimmed with yellow. I'd seen people with less intelligence in their eyes.

'I thought that was the cheetah,' I said. The falcon hadn't taken its eyes off me.

'Cheetah, shmeetah,' said Nick, lifting his fingers towards the bird again, pulling them out of reach as the bird ducked its head. 'The cheetah can run at seventy miles an hour for a couple of minutes. Peregrines have been recorded diving at two hundred miles per hour.'

At the far end of the shed, on a separate, raised perch, a bird that I was pretty certain was an owl jumped and spread its wings, as though clamouring for attention.

'Well, I would be impressed, but isn't that just the same as falling?' I said. 'If you're high enough, don't you just gather speed ad infinitum?'

Nick held out his arm and the falcon stepped on to it. 'The essential difference between freefall and a controlled dive is that a peregrine can pull himself out of a dive in two seconds.'

I took a step closer to them both. 'Will he let me touch him?' I asked. The bird looked at me as if to say, *Try it, sweetheart.*

'He's a bit jumpy,' said Nick. 'Even I have to watch myself. Leah will, though.' He put his arm back to the perch and the falcon graciously stepped down.

'Put this on.' Nick was holding out a long leather glove. I pulled it on over my right hand. It stretched halfway up my arm. Then Nick raised my arm until it was horizontal and led me further into the shed until we were both surrounded by intense black eyes. He lifted the owl from her perch and put her gently down on my outstretched arm. She was almost entirely white except that the feathers on her back and wings were the colour you might see if a tortoiseshell cat was turning slowly to gold.

'She weighs nothing,' I said, lifting my arm a fraction. She gave a little jump and shook her wing feathers.

'She's really just a pet,' Nick replied. 'A barn owl. Owls aren't much good for hunting. I fly her sometimes, just for fun.'

'And these birds hunt for you?' I asked. 'They actually catch food that you eat?'

'More than I can eat. That's why Liz

comes in handy. You should come out with me one day.'

'Do you fly them every day?'

'In the season, yes.'

'How do you find time to work?' I asked.

'I'm a GP,' he said. 'We work part time and get paid a fortune. Don't you read the papers?'

Leah turned her head to look directly at me. There was something a bit eerie about the way her head could move independently of her body. Nick reached out and ran his hand lightly over her crown. As his hand left her, she seemed to stretch up towards him.

'Never thought I'd hear one of you admit it,' I said.

'Oh, I'm always honest about the small things,' he said. 'That way the big lies tend to go unnoticed. You weren't too sure when you came in, were you?'

'Not really,' I said. 'A bird very like these attacked me yesterday.'

'Where?'

'A couple of miles from here. Not far out of town. I was out running. I thought I might lose my eyes at one point. It was a bit freaky.'

'Describe it for me,' he said.

As best I could, from memory, I described

the bird that had flown at me the day before. I gave a rough idea of its wingspan, the colour of its feathers. 'Bigger than these,' I finished, looking carefully at the falcons. 'And with different feathers underneath.'

'Sounds like a buzzard,' said Nick.

'Are they known for rowdy behaviour?'

'Well, funnily enough, it's not unheard of,' he replied. 'Especially in the summer when they've got young in the nests. This time of year, though, it is unusual. I can only imagine it had been kept in captivity at some point and became used to humans providing food.'

The birds sensed the commotion before we heard it. One second they were relaxed, getting used to our presence, maybe even enjoying the unexpected company, the next there was a massive ruffling of feathers, excited jumping around and frantic squawking. Nick gave the door a worried glance before reaching out to take Leah from me. He put her back on her perch, spoke softly to the others and led me to the door.

'You there, Nick?' called a man's voice. I stayed in the shed. I'd recognized that voice.

'We're here,' called Nick. 'What's up?'

'There's a dog in with the yows down at Tydes End,' said the voice I knew. 'Causing fuckin' mayhem, according to Sam.'

Nick sucked in a deep breath. 'Shit,' he said. 'It's too bloody dark. We'll need lights.'

'Got 'em. John's taken the truck down. I said we'd follow.'

Nick turned to me. I had no choice but to step outside. Two men had approached. One was a tall dark-haired man in his late forties who looked as though he ate too much red meat. The other was smaller and slimmer, with silver hair and narrow-set eyes. He was the man called Jim whom Liz had pointed out earlier. He was also the farmer-bully who'd turned me out of the scary woods the previous day.

'Laura, can you make your way back to the house?' Nick said. 'I'll be back as soon as I can.'

I sensed Jim hadn't recognized me. The day before, I'd been in jogging clothes, my hair pulled back and dark with sweat, no make-up. Dressed for a party I looked very different. 'Of course,' I replied. 'Everything all right?'

'There's a dog worrying the sheep a couple of fields along,' said Nick. 'They're all in lamb so it's pretty serious. Half the flock could miscarry if we don't get it out of there. Back soon.'

He patted my shoulder and was off, stopping only to unlock the last shed in the row and pull something that looked a lot like a shotgun out of it. Then he and the other two men disappeared over a fence and across the field.

Jessica walked on, further into the forest, and gradually became aware that the light was changing. The trees were no longer black and silver in the moonlight but a pale shade of gold. They were gleaming all around her, glowing brightly as though reflecting back sunshine. She looked up. As each tree reached the midnight-blue sky, the gold trunks splintered into a glittering cobweb of branches. And tiny pieces of gold were drifting down from above. At first Jessica thought they were falling leaves, but as one landed on her outstretched arm she realized it was snowing.

The snowflake, nearly three centimetres in diameter, stayed on her wrist. She could see its intricate pattern, like the inside of a kaleidoscope, against her pale skin. She watched it melt and others take its place. Golden snowflakes were falling all around her, landing on her arms, her legs, her hair, and covering the ground like a carpet of silk.

Jessica stood up. She had never seen anything so beautiful in her life as this golden wood, in which the trees seemed almost to be growing before her eyes. She could see them breathing, their long, strong trunks swelling as they took in air, then relaxing as they breathed out again. She'd always known that trees breathed, all plants did, but had never thought she'd actually see it happening.

With each breath they grew a little taller. And were they singing? They were. The trees were singing to her, a soft, high-pitched, almost tuneless song, like the sound whales make when they call to each other across hundreds of miles of ocean. It was the sort of music you might hear among the stars.

Jessica turned on the spot, listening to the trees call to each other, knowing that if she stood here and listened hard, she might actually start to understand what they were saying. She realized she wasn't afraid any more. There was nothing to be afraid of in a wood so beautiful. She took a step closer to the nearest tree and reached out. It was warm and soft, like the skin on a warm-blooded animal. She stroked it and felt the tree purr in response like a great cat.

From behind her came a low-pitched chuckle.

Jessica jumped round, her back against the cat-like tree. Someone was watching her.

Inching her way round the tree, she began to back away. She'd long since left the path behind. She had only the light from the golden trees to guide her, and the soft iridescence of the snow at her feet. She backed up against another tree and worked her way round it. She almost stumbled but managed to get her balance in time.

Still watching her. And getting closer. She couldn't see them but she could hear them breathing, smell the bitter, stale male odour.

A twig snapped behind her and Jessica began to run. She didn't dare look back, just kept on running, over rough ground, dodging undergrowth, finding narrow paths through the trees. She saw the lights and the thought flashed into her head that this might be fresh danger. She didn't process it in time. She'd reached the clearing, had stumbled among them, before she saw the clowns.

I was in no hurry to get back to polite conversation with strangers, but when I reached the back garden I saw the fire-pit was still lit. Two men and a girl were gathered on fold-up chairs around it. Maybe I'd join them. I'd heard people say smokers were the best fun at a social gathering. I was just drawing close when Evi appeared at the back door wearing a blue woollen coat speckled with snowflakes.

'There you are, Laura,' she said. 'Any chance of you walking me to my car?'

Evi didn't strike me as the sort of woman who'd need walking to her car, disabled or not, so I figured she wanted to talk to me.

'You're leaving early,' I said. 'Or is it over? Does everybody have to get up for milking?'

'No, it's just me,' she said. 'I don't really do late nights.'

Evi's car was parked next to mine. I held the door open for her and she looked around, as though checking we were alone.

'Are you OK?' I asked.

She didn't reply for a moment, letting her eyes fall to the steering wheel then raising them back to me again. In the dim light they looked black. Then, 'Do you know much about IT, Laura?' she said. 'From a forensic point of view?'

'A bit,' I replied. 'What's happened?'

Other people were leaving too and drawing closer. I walked round and climbed into the passenger seat of Evi's car.

'There's another track twenty yards down the lane,' I said, as she turned to me in surprise. 'You can drop me off there.'

We drove for a second or two and then she pulled over. The car behind passed us.

'I didn't realize you knew Nick,' Evi said.

'I met him a few days ago at the hospital,' I replied. 'Do you know him well?'

'We both studied medicine here,' she told me. 'Nick was a couple of years ahead of me.' Her face relaxed into a smile. 'He came to see me yesterday. He's worried about the suicides too. He was quite relieved to know someone is doing something.'

Worried about the suicides? Or worried that Evi might be on to him?

'You didn't tell him about me?' I asked.

Her eyes opened wider. 'No, of course not,' she said. 'I just thought you might have done.'

I shook my head firmly. 'No, I haven't. He can't know.' If there was one thing Joesbury and the others had impressed upon me it was that no one could know who I was. Trust no one.

'So your IT problem,' I said. 'What's that all about?'

She turned away again, tapped her fingers on the steering wheel, glanced into the mirror. There was nothing behind us, just dark shapes all around. 'I may have a stalker,' she said eventually. 'But the police don't take me terribly seriously. They think I'm a bit . . . hysterical.'

Hysterical wasn't a word I'd use to describe Evi Oliver. Anxious maybe, suffering from poor health certainly, but otherwise very considered in everything she said and did.

'What sort of stalker?' I asked.

'I had a couple of threatening emails the other night,' she told me. 'But when I tried to forward them on to the detective I've been speaking to, they disappeared from my system completely. Now he doubts whether they ever existed in the first place and I'm beginning to think the same thing myself.'

'They vanished when you forwarded them on?'

'Yes. Is that possible?'

'Perfectly,' I said. 'They'll have had some sort of malware built into them that activated when you tried to forward, save or print them. They'll still be on your computer somewhere. We have forensic computer analysts in the Met. They'd find them in a jiffy.'

'I'm not sure it merits the attention of the Metropolitan Police,' said Evi. 'But it's good to know I might not be losing it completely.'

'You and I probably shouldn't exchange any more emails until we know your system's secure,' I said.

She sighed and looked worried.

'Is that it?' I asked, pretty certain it wasn't.

She shook her head. 'There were phone calls too,' she said. 'A lot of them, one after the other on my mobile and my home phone. Nobody there. Number withheld.'

'When?' I asked again.

'Two nights ago,' she said. 'Wednesday was when they started. There were more last night and tonight before I came out. I switched both phones off in the end. Which doesn't really work given that I have to be on call next week.'

'It's a real pain,' I said. 'But it happens, sadly. You may have to change your numbers and hope they give up. It's probably not personal.'

Evi said nothing. She didn't have to. The way she tucked both thumbs into her mouth in a desperate, childlike gesture spoke volumes. I waited, counting in my head. At thirty, she looked at me again.

'That's just it,' she said. 'It's very personal.'

Three clowns were sitting around a slatted wooden crate that served as a tea table. A teapot, white with coloured spots, and three matching cups and saucers stood on the crate. There was a plate of cupcakes and another of sandwiches. One clown, dressed in a patchwork jumpsuit, was being mother.

It had huge, white, skeletal hands that shook as it raised the pot and poured. All three clowns giggled when the steaming liquid spilled on to the ground. The clown with the teapot had three tufts of scarlet hair that bounced up and down as he laughed. The lower third of his white face was all teeth.

The clown who took the outstretched teacup wore the red and yellow checked suit of an eccentric English country squire. His face seemed twice the normal length, tapering into a sharp point that reached almost to his breastbone. His hair was long, wild and a lurid green.

The third clown seemed enormous. It wore layer after layer of multicoloured ruff round its neck and red and white striped trousers. Its belly and bottom were massive. So were its feet, in the clown's traditional enormous shoes. This clown's face, like the others, was mostly grinning yellow teeth.

'Hello, Jessica,' it said.

Ten minutes later I watched the tail lights of Evi's car disappear, then turned back to the house, wondering if I'd done the right thing telling her not to worry and that I'd see her on Tuesday.

Creepy toys. Masked figures in the garden. Blood — albeit fake — in the bath. Those

307

were the actions of a seriously disturbed mind. And a clever one at that.

Two more cars passed me in the lane and I could hear more cars starting up. Country folk obviously did keep earlier hours. I really had to go myself. Evi's story had worried me. I also wanted to think about Nick Bell and whether I really suspected him. And if he was involved, involved with what? Then there was Scott Thornton, a senior member of my college who, together with a couple of mates, had dressed up like Zorro and borrowed a well-established college ritual in order to scare and humiliate a new student.

Then all thoughts of Bell and Thornton fled, to be replaced by the most hideous sound. Several short guttural sounds, in fact. Like someone trying to scream and having the breath choked out of them at each attempt.

Run! The voice in my head told me. *Hide!*

Telling myself the sounds had been faint, that whatever had made them was almost certainly some distance away, and that they'd been carried to me on the wind, I nevertheless stepped into the lane, not wanting to be too close to the hedge. Or to anything that might be hiding. The night had fallen silent again.

What on earth had I heard? A woman

308

screaming in distress had been my first thought, but we were miles from anywhere out here. I looked back towards the house, wondering how long it would take me to sprint there, in the dark and over uneven ground.

There was something moving in the hedge. Something large, breathing heavily. I stepped back, a second from running for my life, at the same time not daring to take my eyes from what was coming at me. A creature, on four powerful legs, teeth gleaming as though they were lit from within. It bounded up to me with a speed I couldn't hope to match. Then stopped, just a little too well mannered to spring.

'Hello,' I said, with a voice that didn't sound too steady. 'Where did you come from?'

The dog was soaking wet. It poked its long white nose towards the pockets of my borrowed oilskin. Its tail was wagging and its ears were back and it simply knew that my fingers were made to tickle the backs of its ears. When I stopped it stood upright on its hind legs, putting its front paws on my chest. It wasn't far off my height. Could a dog, this dog, have made the noise I'd just heard? I didn't think so.

Oh, having my face licked was a compliment I could do without.

Then I heard shouting from the field immediately on the other side of the hedge. I recognized Nick's voice and the thin, reedy tones of silver-haired Jim. This had to be the dog from the sheep field. If so, they were hot on its trail. They'd be with us any second.

'Come on,' I whispered to the dog. Obedient in the way only dogs are, it followed me to my car.

'In you get.' It jumped inside and settled itself down on my back seat.

'Keep your head down,' I told it, before heading back towards the house. By the time I'd found my coat, Nick and the others were back.

'Any luck?' Liz asked Nick, completely ignoring Jim. He shook his head and turned to me.

'Are we losing you?'

'Early start,' I lied. 'Thanks for having me over.'

'I'll walk you to your car,' he offered.

'No, really. You should see to your guests.'

'You are my guest.'

We were out of the door, heading across the side courtyard.

'Have you registered with a GP yet?' he asked me, when we were ten yards from the car and I was sure I could see eyes gleaming at me from the back seat.

'Why, are you touting for business?' I asked, catching the flick of a white tail. Oh, I was so busted.

'On the contrary, I was going to ask you not to register with us,' he said.

'Why?' I said, which wasn't too bright, I grant you, but there was a white paw on each of the front seats and a long white nose was pointing right at me. Any second now . . .

'Because if you're my patient, I can't ask you to have din— What the bugger?'

Dog and man were eyeballing each other on either side of the passenger window. Given that one had tried to shoot the other minutes earlier, the other was looking remarkably pleased to see the one.

'Please tell me this isn't . . .' He stopped and just looked at me. I had to admit, he was cute. Joesbury's height, but not quite so bulky. Not that I'd ever really gone for the body-builder type.

'Well, I'd like to,' I began. 'I've just never been a particularly good liar.' Which in itself, I suppose, was a lie. I've long been an excellent liar.

'Do you know how many thousands of pounds of damage a dog can cause in a field of pregnant ewes?' he asked me.

'He didn't though, did he?' I said. 'There wasn't a speck of blood on him. That dog hasn't killed anything.'

He opened his mouth, closed it, looked round, opened it again. I think he might have been the only man in the world to make such a gormless act look appealing.

'Do you also know that I, and several other men in that house, are quite within our rights to shoot it right there in your car?' he said.

'You'll have to get the keys off me first,' I said. 'And no, you're not.'

He blinked and ran one hand through his hair, making it stand upright on his head. 'Excuse me?' he said.

'If a dog is attacking livestock, and the only way to make it desist is to shoot it, you have a defence in law if the dog's owner takes issue with you,' I said. 'You do not have any right to put down an animal without the owner's permission. Only a judge has the authority to make that happen.'

'What the hell are you, a lawyer?'

OK, I was on dangerous ground now. Not only was I being Lacey again, I was demonstrating knowledge that Lacey, not Laura, would have.

'An animal lover,' I said, which was another lie. There's hardly been time for animals in my life. 'Oh, look, I'm sure he didn't kill any sheep.'

'The entire bloody field could miscarry during the night.'

I looked down, then peered up at him again through my eyelashes. I think I even dropped my head to one side.

'Well, aren't you more likely to get compensation from the owner if the dog is delivered home safe and well?' I said. 'I'll take it to the nearest dog shelter in the morning. I'll also report it to the dog warden. Sorry, I'm just a bit soppy about dogs.'

'And if it's a stray?'

I shrugged. Pouted a bit. 'It'll be in the dog shelter,' I said. 'Can't get up to much in there.'

He looked as though he were about to argue again and then shook his head. 'I give up,' he said, but he was close to smiling now. 'If I agree to say no more about it, will you have dinner with me tomorrow night?'

Joesbury would kill me. Or might not give a toss. Either way. 'Seems churlish to refuse,' I said.

'I'll pick you up at eight,' he said, properly smiling by this time.

I waved cheerfully at Nick in the rear-view mirror as I drove away. Well, they do say to keep your enemies close.

49

On the Queen's Road Joesbury found an empty parking space and opened his laptop. He connected to Scotland Yard's central computer system and typed in a six-digit code. A few seconds later he was looking at a map of Cambridge. A red dot travelling along the A1303 told him his quarry was getting close.

He pushed the seat further back and closed his eyes for a second. He should have left for London half an hour ago. People were expecting him and God knows he was tired. He'd go, just as soon as he'd seen her.

When he opened his eyes again the red dot was very close. He could see her headlights approaching from behind. He watched, half hoping she'd see the reflection of his eyes in the mirror and stop. She didn't. She drove on before reversing into a space just five yards or so from his. He heard the engine die, saw the headlights disappear and felt a moment's exasperation. What the hell was she thinking of, parking this far away from the buildings? Any old low-life could be hanging round.

Joesbury smiled to himself. Any old low-life was probably exactly how she'd describe him.

The driver's door opened and she got out. She was wearing tight jeans tucked into flat-heeled boots and a bottle green military coat. He knew, because he'd seen the receipts she'd submitted, that the coat had cost twenty-five quid in one of the bigger supermarkets. Even in daylight it wouldn't look cheap on her. Nothing ever did.

She'd opened the rear door and was leaning inside, as though talking to someone on the back seat, and if she'd brought some half-drunk kid home for a quick shag he might just blow his cover and land the git one.

She'd got a dog.

A dog, the size and shape of a greyhound, but with the white markings on its legs, face and tail that gave away its collie parentage, had jumped from the car and was wagging its tail as if it had been reunited with its owner after years of separation. She'd fastened something round its collar to act as a lead and was bending into the car again.

Joesbury rubbed his eyes. He'd been on some stakeouts in his time.

She was out of the car again and the dog was beside itself with excitement. Joesbury watched as Lacey bent down and pulled a small square Styrofoam box from a large paper bag. She opened it, picked something out with her finger and thumb and popped it into her mouth. The rest she put on the ground and let the dog help itself.

Three minutes later, when the dog was licking the grease off the empty box, Lacey reached into the car again and brought out a half litre of bottled water. She poured some into the carton and let the dog lap it up. When it had done, she walked it up and down the small patch of grass until nature took its course and the dog stopped and squatted.

OK, that was it. If she left it there he was arresting her for allowing her dog to foul a public space and to hell if it blew both their covers. She didn't. She bent, scooped the shit up into the takeaway carton, and dumped it in the nearest bin before disappearing with the dog into the college buildings.

Perfect excuse to follow her, ask her what the hell she thought she was doing sneaking livestock into a Cambridge college. He'd invent some reason for still being in town. She'd offer coffee, try to talk him round. They'd be alone. Joesbury's hand was on the door, the ignition key in his hand, when he came to his senses.

He replaced the key and started the engine.

50

Smuggling a large, over-excited dog into a college bedroom wasn't the easiest challenge of my career but I managed it. I bumped into three boys at the foot of the stairs but none of them looked sober. 'Mascot,' I said to them, when they stared at the dog. None of them thought of an answer in the time it took us to run up the stairs and disappear along the top corridor.

Joesbury, it went without saying, would be livid if he knew what I'd done. He'd argue that drawing attention to myself without good reason was stupidly compromising my cover. I could always counter, of course, that students were known for doing daft things, and if anything it could even cement my cover. Whatever, I really didn't care. I just didn't want the dog to be shot. The following morning, I'd report it to the dog warden and drop it off at the local dog rescue centre.

Talaith wasn't in our room, no surprise there, and the dog spent ten minutes exploring the various smells before turning on the spot three times and settling down on the rug in front of my desk. I made myself tea and spent an hour updating Joesbury on everything that had happened that evening and, in particular, my worries about Evi. Then, more because I wanted to show willing than because I believed I'd find anything, I started my daily trawl around the Cambridge websites. Someone called Jessica hadn't been back to her room for the past two nights and her friends, Belinda and Sarah, were wondering if they should let her tutor know. Otherwise, nothing.

All the time I was working, the dog didn't once take his soft brown eyes off me, as though he found every movement of my fingers on the keyboard completely fascinating. Oddly, it was comforting to have him there.

When I'd been on every website I knew of, I sat back to think some more about Danielle Brown. As soon as I'd prompted her to use the word scared, it seemed she couldn't stop. Danielle had spent her last weeks at Cambridge afraid. Scared of failing, she'd told me, of letting down her parents who'd been so proud that she'd got into Cambridge. Scared of not keeping up with the others. Of being proved not good enough. Ironically, it seemed, the more scared she became, the more her work suffered and it all became a self-fulfilling prophecy.

Not really thinking what I was doing, I typed *Danielle Brown* and *Cambridge* into Google and pressed Return just to see what would happen. Several references came up, some of which were from newspaper archives I'd seen before. One was about her being part of a winning sailing team in her first year. One reference was on YouTube. Not really expecting anything I clicked on it.

This footage has been removed as it breached YouTube's publishing code.

Mildly intrigued, I typed *Danielle Brown* and *YouTube* into Google and pressed Return again. I found one chat-room discussion, mainly about YouTube's policy on removing offensive material, with a brief reference to the case of video footage, taken on someone's mobile phone, of the attempted suicide of Cambridge student Danielle Brown.

Earlier, Joesbury had speculated that Danielle's suicide might have been a practical joke that went too far. That the kids who'd cut her down and phoned for help might actually have helped string her up in the first place. So had they filmed her dangling before stepping in? I sent another quick email to Joesbury asking him if he was aware that Danielle's attempted death had been filmed.

At half past midnight I brushed my teeth, took my make-up off and went to bed. Sniffy-Dog followed me into my room, gave everything a good checking out with his nostrils and then settled down on the rug next to the bed. Realizing I was actually quite glad of the company, I let him stay.

Shortly before I dropped off, someone screamed outside. It was followed by giggles, a yell and running footsteps. Youthful high spirits, nothing more, and certainly nothing like the scream I thought I'd heard earlier at Nick's farm, but it meant that, as I fell asleep, the sound of a woman screaming for help was uppermost in my mind.

Just after one o'clock in the morning, Joesbury walked into his office in Scotland Yard. Not entirely to his surprise, the room wasn't empty. Two of his colleagues, currently assigned to other cases, worked quietly at their desks, a third was on the phone. His boss, DCI Pete Phillips, whom everyone called

PP, but only behind his back, was in his glass-walled room in the corner. He glanced up as Joesbury settled himself at his desk and held up one hand, fingers splayed. He was asking for five minutes. Joesbury opened his laptop.

Four cheerful pings as emails arrived. The first from the accounts department, the second from his younger brother. The third to arrive was from DC Flint. Joesbury clicked it open and blinked at the sheer amount of text in the message. She'd sent it just forty minutes ago, which meant she'd gone straight back to her room and started work on it immediately. He began reading.

The most ordinary of sounds can twist themselves round when they enter your dreams, or so I'm told. Not being a dreamer, I have little experience of such things, but I've heard, for example, that the sound of milk bottles being put down gently on a doorstep can, in the dreams of the sleeper upstairs, take the form of bones rattling; that the gentle rat-a-tat of the postman can sound like a troll trying to break its way into the house.

It was the opposite for me that night. The sound I heard in my dream wasn't threatening. It was quite pleasant in its way, but when I woke and heard it properly I knew immediately it wasn't raindrops that I could hear running down the window pane. It was fingernails, scratching against the glass.

I lay there, my heartbeat getting faster, telling myself it would be a joke, just another student prank. All I had to do was sit up, open the window and shove the bozo off his ladder.

Except I couldn't move.

Halfway through Lacey's account of the academic soirée at that tosser Bell's country pad, Joesbury's smile had disappeared. He got up, crossed to the coffee machine and pressed the button for double-strength espresso, knowing she was trying to wind him up and knowing also that it was working.

'We expected you an hour ago,' said the boss's voice behind him.

Joesbury muttered something about an accident on the M1. 'Car came up zilch,' he added quickly, referring to the car Lacey's three assailants had escaped in three nights ago. 'Registered to a canteen worker in her late fifties. Didn't even know it had been "borrowed".'

'Student prank then?'

'Almost certainly. Soaking barely clad

young women happens a lot, from what I can gather. And they'd never have targeted her this quickly.'

Phillips circled his forefingers on his temples as though easing a nagging headache. 'Well, it's a long shot they target her at all,' he said.

Joesbury said nothing. He'd argued that himself more than once.

The coffee was poured and both men moved away from the machine.

'You know, guv, if we go public, it ends. Once the authorities and the students themselves know what's been going on there, it can't go on.'

'If we go public, we'll never catch them. They'll move to another town and start the whole thing again. There's too much money involved for them to give up. And that's not to mention the unholy row we'd have with local CID if we accuse them of missing umpteen unlawful deaths but haven't a dicky bird to back it up.'

'Ever occur to you that local CID might be involved?' said Joesbury. 'Every so-called suicide neatly wrapped up, all the supporting evidence in place, every box ticked. What are the chances of that in the real world?'

Phillips was silent for a moment. 'Well,

that would widen the goalposts a bit,' he said.

'Width of the whole fucking field,' said Joesbury.

For several minutes I thought my room was darker than usual. Then I realized I just couldn't open my eyes. A little way to the right of my head, where the window ledge served as a bedside table, I could hear the scratching sound. In my head I could see thin, bony fingers, long, yellow fingernails, the hand clenched like a claw as it was drawn down the glass once more. In reality I could see nothing. My eyes just would not open.

I tried to make a sound. Just the smallest noise in the back of my throat to prove I was still in control of my body. I could hear nothing except the relentless scratching. Then the sound of scratching stopped. It was replaced by that of the window catch being forced from outside. Then that of the window opening.

I could feel cold air on my face, then something else that could have been the curtains being blown against me. Then, worst of all, a creaking of metal, the friction squeak glass makes when it's touched, then a soft bump. The sounds of something climbing in through the window.

'I'll have someone look into it. See if any of the locals have form. Or if any of them are flashing cash around.'

Phillips returned to his office and Joesbury to Flint's report. Oh, for fuck's sake, white horses and falcons! Who did the twat think he was? Robin Hood?

Joesbury sighed. It might take him fifteen more minutes to finish the latest episode of *War and Peace* and type a quick response, and then he could go. He was due to see his son the following day for the first time in three weeks. Spending any time at all with Huck these days was getting increasingly difficult. Which was ironic really, given that his supposed neglect of their child was one of the reasons why his wife had left him.

Joesbury read through to the end and realized he wasn't going anywhere in a hurry. He highlighted a chunk of text and forwarded it, marked urgent, to his boss. When he saw PP slip his reading glasses on to see the screen, he stood up and crossed the room. He opened the door without being invited in. PP glanced up.

'She's getting too close,' said Joesbury.

No response. PP looked down at the screen again.

'We should pull her out,' Joesbury tried.

'Give me a sec,' said PP.

Joesbury gave him two. 'She knows about the video of Danielle Brown on YouTube. She'll have it figured out in days,' he said.

'Days might be all we need,' PP replied. 'This Dr Oliver's a worry, though.'

Joesbury stepped forward and leaned on the desk. 'Well, exactly,' he said. 'I really don't have a good feeling about these practical jokes and disappearing emails. If Oliver's getting dodgy emails, someone could have infiltrated her system. If they know she's been feeding us information, she could be at risk.'

The other man leaned back in his chair and rubbed a hand over his eyes. 'If someone's accessing Oliver's files and if there are emails from Flint among them, the whole op could go belly up.'

'We should get her out of there.'

Phillips's eyes narrowed. 'Who?' he asked. 'DC Flint or Dr Oliver?'

'Both. Dr Oliver can take a couple of weeks off sick. Laura Farrow can quietly disappear.'

PP leaned back in his chair. 'Christ,' he said. 'Nearly nine months' work and these two bloody women could blow the whole thing apart.'

'No disrespect, guv, but I didn't want to send her there in the first place.'

'Let me think about it. Go home. I'll call you in the morning.'

The thing was inches above me, choosing its moment. I couldn't see it but I knew it was there. Like a bad smell, like the howling in the wind, like the fingertips on the back of your neck, there was no denying it. I reached up, my hand claw-like, scratching and tearing. Except I touched nothing. My hand hadn't moved from where it lay on the bed. I could not move.

The silence was broken by howling. Howling like wolves, like banshees, like demons. It rang through the night until I thought my head would burst. Then a sound like thunder. Relentless hammering, over and over again. I was lifted up, high into the air, and flung across the room. I landed hard and knew it would hurt if I lived through the next few seconds.

The thing above me lowered its head and I felt hot breath against my face. I knew teeth were a split second away.

'Tox! Laura! What the hell's going on?'

Voices I knew. I could see again. The nightmare took a pace back. I was in the study room that Tox and I shared, crouched on all fours like a toddler that had given up on the whole gravity business. The dog, shaking, but holding it together a whole lot better than I, was licking my face. And the hammering of thunder had been the sound of the other girls banging on the door, wondering why on earth they'd been woken by a barking and snarling dog.

51

When the knock sounded Evi almost didn't get up. She'd had too little sleep the night before, finally dropping off a couple of hours before dawn. The pain she'd woken to had been the worst in years and her medication, so far, wasn't helping. She'd spent the last hour in an armchair by the garden window. The patch of sunlight was soothing, the warmth helped the pain and she was beginning to feel she might doze off again. Now there was someone at the door.

The banging began again. Not a hesitant, trying-its-luck sort of sound. This was the knock of someone determined to have attention. Evi got to her feet.

Laura Farrow, the undercover police officer, was on her doorstep and Evi's first thought was that she looked dreadful. There were dark circles beneath eyes that seemed to have shrunk in her face. Her mouth was paler and smaller. It was the first time Evi had seen her without make-up or so plainly dressed. Normally, Laura made an effort with her appearance. This morning, she'd just thrown on jogging clothes and trainers.

The second thing she noticed was that Laura hadn't come alone. Wrapped around her right hand was what looked like the belt from a dressing gown. Attached to the other end of the belt was a dog collar. With a dog in it.

The dog's white-tipped tail was waving like a flag and excitement shone out of its big brown eyes. Considering they hadn't met before, it was looking remarkably pleased to see Evi.

'We need to talk,' Laura said.

'You have a dog,' replied Evi, not moving from her spot just inside the front door.

The detective glanced down, as though only just remembering the dog was there. It looked like a greyhound, sleek and slim, with a long, thin nose. Its black coat had white markings. It turned its head from Evi to look at Laura, ears perked. It almost seemed to be waiting for her to speak. Then it looked back at Evi. The movement of its white-tipped tail slowed.

'Yes,' Laura said. 'Do you mind? I tried to

leave him in the car. Twice. He starts howling every time I walk away. I think he's house-trained.'

In the greater scheme of things . . . Evi stepped back and led Laura and her dog to the sitting room. Evi took the armchair she'd just vacated and nodded to Laura to take the other. The dog began to explore the room, sniffing under chairs, in corners, behind the TV.

'If he cocks a leg I'll be mortified,' said Laura, watching its progress nervously.

'You and me both,' said Evi.

It didn't. It completed its tour of the room and found the patch of sunlight at Evi's feet. One ear up, the other down, sighing deeply, it settled down, lying like a sheepdog, with legs tucked beneath it, its attention shifting from one woman to the other, as though waiting for an instruction. Or for a ball to be thrown.

'How come you have a dog?' asked Evi.

'Long story,' said Laura. 'I know we're not supposed to meet today but things are worrying me. You don't look too good, by the way, sorry to be blunt. Has something else happened?'

Evi held back from telling Laura she didn't look great either. When she'd taken the lead off the dog, her hands had been shaking. And her pupils were unusually large and bright.

'No, nothing new,' Evi said. 'I rely on painkillers most of the time. A skiing injury some years ago. Sometimes they take a while to kick in. So, what's worrying you?'

Laura tapped the first finger of her left hand with the first on her right. She had a list. 'First of all what you told me last night,' she said. 'About all the weird stuff that's been happening to you. Seems to me there are two possibilities. The first is that you're nuts.'

Evi didn't like the small stab of something that felt a bit like guilt and a whole lot more like vindication that poked her in the stomach. 'That term's considered a bit old-fashioned in professional circles these days,' she said, trying for a relaxed smile and knowing she just looked prim.

'I think you have issues,' said Laura, 'which is probably not a technical term either. I think you're edgy and jumpy and I think you're verging on a serious depression, which could be a result of living with too much pain, but I don't think you're nuts.'

Not sure whether to be annoyed or amused, Evi looked the other woman full in the face. Laura held eye contact but her hands were still unsteady. And her breathing seemed accelerated, as though she'd run to get here. 'Well, that's good to know,' said Evi. 'So the other possibility?'

'Is that you have a real and extremely sophisticated stalker,' said Laura. 'Someone with exceptional IT skills, for one thing. I did some research before I went to bed last night. That thing I talked about, loading up an email so that it disappeared completely when you activated it. It's possible but it's not easy. The chances are someone's broken in here and used a USB stick to boot your machine and install the malware directly. They could have set any number of booby traps we have no way of knowing about without getting the machine checked out. For the time being, I'm afraid, you really can't trust your computer.'

'Who would do that?' said Evi.

'No idea. But it seems safe to say whoever it is has found out a great deal about you. Do you keep a diary or journal on the computer?'

'Nothing like that,' said Evi. 'Yet that's the really disturbing thing. It's like they've been inside my head.'

'Twisted people can be clever,' said Laura. 'And devious in ways we normal types don't think of. That's how they keep us guessing.

But if you think about it, it's obvious what's happened.'

'It is?'

'That business in Lancashire last year was in lots of papers,' said Laura. 'It was even on the national news. I Googled you last night and found loads of stuff. The little girls and weird rituals and that patient of yours who died in a bath of blood. I reckon someone has found all this stuff exactly how I did and now they're using it to mess with your head.'

Evi sat back in her chair to think about it. A hot stream of pain shot up her left leg but for once she hardly noticed it. What Laura was saying made sense. She should have thought of it herself. It would almost make her feel better to know there was an explanation. Except . . .

'Why?' she said. 'Why would anyone do that?'

'Well, it could be a revenge thing,' said Laura. 'From what I can gather you were instrumental in uncovering what was going on up there. It could be someone you pissed off getting their own back. But I don't think so.'

'What do you think?'

'I think it's connected to what's going on here. Sorry to be rude, but do you mind if I make a cup of tea?'

'Of course,' said Evi. 'Do you need me to . . .'

'I'll be fine,' replied Laura, already on her way out of the room. 'I can instinctively find my way round a kitchen. Which is interesting in its way, because I'm a lousy cook.'

Evi watched Laura stumble in the doorway, her hand shooting up to the doorframe for balance. Then she'd gone. The dog at Evi's feet stood and looked towards the hall. Then it approached Evi and looked her directly in the eyes. The tip of its right ear was missing.

'Hi,' mouthed Evi. The dog stepped forward and laid its head on Evi's lap, not for a second taking its round brown eyes from hers. As Evi reached out and ran her hand gently along its nose and over its brow, it gave a heavy and contented sigh. Its fur was smooth and warm, its ears like velvet.

Evi's hand had returned to her lap. The dog raised its head and lifted one front paw. It nudged her, tapping lightly on the side of her leg. Evi began stroking and scratching its ears again, until Laura came back with two steaming mugs of tea. Her hands were still shaking.

Not wanting to risk scalding it with hot tea, Evi gave the dog a gentle shove away. It went back to the patch of sunshine and lay down, not once taking its eyes off her. Evi turned to Laura, who was clutching her mug as though it couldn't cool down quickly enough.

'Right, first of all, tell me what's wrong with you,' said Evi. 'If I didn't know better, I'd say you'd taken something.'

Laura shook her head. 'I had a bad night too,' she said. 'I might be coming down with a bug. Or I could have eaten something last night that didn't really agree with me. Lord knows I'm more used to burgers and Chinese takeaways than game casserole.'

'Do you need anything?' said Evi. 'Paracetamol?'

'Had the maximum dose an hour ago, thanks,' said Laura. She risked sipping from the mug and tears sprang into her eyes. 'So, your stalker is really bothering me,' she went on. 'You've stirred up a hornet's nest here. You've got the university authorities and the police twitchy about sinister goings-on and suddenly someone is trying to scare you and undermine your professional credibility at the same time. I think someone's trying to warn you off.'

'Warn me off what? Laura, what we have here, if anything, is some sort of dangerous but completely intangible culture of encouraging and feeding upon . . .'

'No, I really don't think so,' said Laura, as the dog sighed heavily and rolled over on to its back.

'You don't?'

'That's the second thing that's worrying me,' said Laura. 'This theory you have. You know, the subversive online subculture business? I haven't been able to find any of it. And I've been looking hard. I've been on every Cambridge-based site there is, weeping and wailing and gnashing my teeth, pretending to be depressed and anxious and suicidal. All I've had back is sympathy. The online community around here is actually pretty supportive.'

Evi waited. She hadn't the heart to argue and, besides, Laura was only coming to the same conclusion she had herself.

'So, my inclination at the moment is to say that if these suicides are linked in some way, it's not necessarily the case that they're being goaded into it by some sort of suicidal group-think.'

Evi felt her eyebrows lifting.

'I've spent a week attending psychology lectures,' Laura said. 'The odd technical term was going to rub off.'

Fair point. Group-think referred to the phenomenon of people being induced, through the influence of those around them, into behaviour that they wouldn't normally contemplate. 'So, I'm wrong,' Evi said. 'I always knew that was a possibility. I'm still grateful to you for looking into it.'

'Oh, I'm not done yet,' said Laura. 'I think what we've got here could be much worse.'

Outside, a squirrel ran across the lawn, stopping to examine some fallen beech leaves. The dog jumped to its feet and trotted over to the window.

'Worse than goading people into taking their own lives?' said Evi.

Laura had been watching the squirrel too. She glanced back. 'Yes,' she said. 'These chat rooms and websites all operate at a distance. That's why it's always so difficult to prove any sort of crime has taken place. The victims and the perpetrators never meet. There's no hard physical evidence.'

Evi waited.

'Here, though, there's a lot of physical stuff going on. Your stalker, for one.'

'Which could be completely unconnected,' said Evi.

'Yep, could be coincidence. Then there are the rapes you told me about. Five of them.'

'By person or persons unknown, with absolutely no proof in any case and just five over five years,' Evi reminded her.

'Then you have the disappearances,' said Laura.

'The what?'

'Nicole Holt disappeared for several days shortly before her death. I spoke to friends at her college. She came back seriously under the influence of something, claiming to have no recollection of where she'd been or what had happened to her. Her bozo college friends didn't get her checked out so we have no proof. But now another student's disappeared. Did you know that?'

At the window, the dog was whining at the squirrel. The hackles on the back of its neck were erect. Evi shook her head.

'Jessica someone. A few of the websites refer to it. And Facebook. Her friends are getting worried. And Nicole wasn't alone when she died. I examined the scene. A bit more thoroughly than the local CID did because I found tyre tracks that couldn't have been Nicole's. I think there was another car there.'

Evi put her mug down on the table. 'Laura, you're going too fast. Jessica who?'

'Sorry, they didn't mention a second name. Why?'

Evi thought for a moment then shook her

head. 'Probably nothing,' she said. 'Anything else?'

'Five years ago a woman tried to hang herself and was filmed in the process. The footage ended up on YouTube with nearly a million hits before it was taken off. This stuff isn't happening by itself, Evi. Someone is orchestrating it.'

52

For several seconds Evi didn't speak. An expression crossed her face that made me think she was going to ask me to leave, to say that it was all too much for her to deal with. God knows I had been a bit full on. But four days in this place and I knew I couldn't be a disinterested observer any more.

The scream had done it, I realized, the scream I'd heard up at Nick's farm. It didn't matter if it had been a hunting barn owl or a fox disembowelling a rabbit, it had sounded enough like a scream to drive home to me that women in this city were afraid. Something had scared Danielle, Nicole and Bryony, something was scaring Evi, and women who got scared in Cambridge had a habit of ending up dead.

And then, right before my eyes, I saw the fragile, nervous Evi Oliver come to exactly the same conclusion. She pursed her lips, widened her eyes and leaned towards me.

'What do we do?' she said.

No time for the sigh of relief. 'I'm glad you asked,' I said. 'Because, first, we have to stop working blind. I need to know who the victims were. I need names.'

As I'd expected, she shook her head. 'Laura, that's confidential information,' she began. 'I can't . . .'

I wasn't letting her get a head of steam. 'I need names, ages, colleges, courses, hobbies and interests,' I went on. 'I need to know what they looked like. Who their friends were. What medication they were on, who their GP was. Once I can get my SO interested, I can probably get it all inputted into the police major incident inquiry system. It will spot connections, links between the victims, in seconds. Far faster than we can. In the meantime, we'll have to do our best.'

A deep line had formed between Evi's eyebrows.

'Isn't there a rule that says that if you suspect people are at risk, that if they may harm themselves or others, you're not just allowed to break confidentiality, you're expected to?' Anticipating Evi's response, I'd done a bit of Googling myself that morning.

344

She didn't reply and I knew I'd struck a chord.

'Most of the people I'm interested in are dead,' I said. 'I know confidentiality doesn't disappear but it will be a mitigating circumstance.'

Evi looked seriously troubled. The dog sidled up to her and glared at me. At that moment, a beeping on my phone told me I had a text message. I excused myself and stepped into the hall. It was from Joesbury.

I'll be in London for a couple of days. Call me if it's urgent, otherwise no electronic communication. I'll manage without *Book at Bedtime* for a night or two. Very important you do not phone or email Evi Oliver and keep contact to a minimum. Her computer files may have been compromised. In fact, do not phone, text or email anyone on official business. Wait for me to be in touch.

I closed the text. Well, I hadn't phoned or emailed Evi and I'd already guessed her computer had been compromised. As for keeping contact to a minimum, it was a bit late for that. Given the breakthrough I'd just made with her, I wasn't going anywhere. I put my phone away and went back into the sitting room. Evi didn't appear to have moved.

'Nineteen students are dead,' I said. 'I'm a police officer, conducting an official inquiry. And you have a responsibility to those who may be next in line to tell me what you know.'

Silence for a moment. I gave her time. Then,

'Tell me again what you need,' she said.

53

An hour later, Evi's study resembled a police incident room. On one daffodil-yellow wall Laura had stuck endless pieces of paper, names of students written in thick felt pen, typewritten notes showing names of colleges, courses, ages, psychiatric history, photographs drawn from newspapers, student records and even Facebook. Any newspaper coverage they'd found of the suicides had been included. For the first time, it brought home to Evi the full scale of the problem.

Staring down at her were twenty-nine Cambridge students who'd attempted to take their own lives in the last five years. Most had succeeded. Only ten of them, starting with Danielle Brown five years earlier down to Bryony Carter just a few weeks ago, were still alive. Five of the women on the list had suspected they were being raped, several had reported bad dreams of a sexual nature.

'Too many women,' muttered Evi. 'It's flying in the face of all the statistics.'

On Laura's laptop computer was a spreadsheet with exactly the same information and the two women had tried endless calculations in an attempt to discover a link between the victims.

'There's no link,' said Laura. 'The colleges they belonged to, the courses they did, they're all random. They come from all over the country, a couple of them from overseas. They're not all members of the sailing club, or the young Tories. There's nothing that connects them.'

'Seventy per cent had a history of psychiatric problems,' said Evi. 'But you'd expect that anyway with a group of self-harmers.'

'HOLMES might have more success,' said Laura. 'That's the police computer system I was telling you about. If they all had their ears pierced at the age of nine, it'll spot it.'

'Well, that's not impossible,' said Evi. 'A lot of good-looking girls up there. Such a dreadful shame.'

Laura had stepped back to give herself a better look at the entire wall.

'Not that it's any less sad when a plain girl kills herself,' Evi added quickly.

'Hello,' muttered Laura.

'What?'

Laura had stepped closer to the wall again, was walking from one photograph to the next.

'I think you've found a link,' she said. 'Look.' She pulled a photograph off the wall and held it out to Evi. 'Olivia Cutler,' she said. 'Second-year chemistry student. Churchill College.'

Evi looked down at a photograph of an overweight girl with lank hair. Laura had taken two more photographs down. 'Anita Hunt,' she said. 'First-year Russian student. Bit horsey, wouldn't you say? And Helen Stott, linguistics. Needed a serious skin-care regime.'

'Laura, what . . . ?'

'Rebecca Graham, the classics student, was no oil painting either,' Laura continued. 'That's the four uglies out of the way. Now, look at the rest. Hang on, let me just get rid of the boys. Look at the rest of the girls.'

There were nineteen photographs left. Judith Creasey, a striking blonde engineering student from Churchill College who'd self-asphyxiated; Kate George, from Peterhouse, with black shiny hair and sparkling eyes who'd lain down in a bath and dropped a hairdryer into it; Sarah Treen, of Magdalene, a beautiful black girl with glossy skin and braided hair who'd thrown herself on to a train track. Every photograph still on the wall was of a slim, attractive young woman.

'I think he likes them pretty,' said Laura.

54

'He?' said Evi. 'We have a he?'

'Just think about it,' I said. 'If your first theory was right, that there are websites out there where the dangerously disturbed make contact with the seriously depressed, and then goad them into self-harm just for the fun of it, what are the chances of nearly 70 per cent of them being very pretty women?'

'Well, slim,' admitted Evi. 'You think these girls were targeted?'

'Not slim,' I said. 'Verging on non-existent. What I'm struggling with is how far are they going? If the victim won't jump, does she get pushed?'

'Laura, slow down. CID investigated all these deaths,' said Evi. 'If there was any suggestion that they were anything other than suicides, surely they'd have found it.'

'You'd hope so,' I said, thinking about the second set of car tracks at the site of Nicole's death.

'Your senior officers,' said Evi. 'The ones who sent you here. Did they hint that we might not be looking at suicides?'

'Not for a second,' I said.

'Nearly two hundred people saw Bryony set fire to herself,' said Evi.

'No, they saw her stagger into the hall in flames,' I said.

Evi's creamy face visibly paled. 'Oh, good God. Laura, you can't think . . .'

'I don't know what to think right now. But even if she did strike the match, she was high on some powerful hallucinogen.'

Evi went behind her desk, pulled open a drawer and took out a file. 'You're right. Extremely high levels of dimethyltryptamine in Bryony's system,' she said after a few moments of searching. 'Her blood and urine were tested shortly after she was admitted. Standard procedure.'

'I know very little about hallucinogenic drugs,' I said. 'Can they make you do things you wouldn't normally?' I'd done basic courses on the most common street drugs as part of my training, all police officers do, but since I'd never worked for the drug squad my knowledge of the different drugs available and their effects was pretty weak.

Evi was nodding her head. I only had half her attention. She was still reading through

Bryony's notes.

'There's nothing about recreational drug use in her counselling notes,' she said. 'We always ask whether students have any sort of drug history.'

'The paraphernalia for smoking it were found in her bedroom,' I said.

Evi looked up and blinked. 'She smoked it?'

'According to the CID report,' I said. 'It's the usual way, from what I've read.'

'I was never shown the CID report,' said Evi, her eyes going back down again. 'That's worrying.'

'What?'

'Well, two things, the first being that this is a very high concentration to have come from inhalation. I'd expect this sort of level to be administered intravenously.'

'CID found a smoking bowl and pipe, not a hypodermic,' I said.

We both thought about that for a moment. I didn't want to say the word 'staging', but it was right up there on the end of my tongue. Maybe someone had wanted to make it look as though Bryony had voluntarily taken drugs, only not quite got the detail right.

'If there'd been a post-mortem, would that discrepancy have been picked up?' I asked.

Evi nodded. 'Almost certainly,' she said.

'What else?' I asked. 'You said two things were worrying you.'

'Bryony was taking an SSRI,' she said. 'That's an antidepressant, in the same class as Prozac. There's no way Nick would have prescribed that if he'd known she was using hallucinogens. So she must have lied to him and been pretty convincing.'

Or he'd known exactly what he was doing.

'Because . . .' I said.

'Hallucinogens react badly with certain antidepressants,' she said. 'Taken together they've been known to create a dissociative fugue state.'

'Come again?'

She looked up at me. 'A state of temporary amnesia,' she said. 'When the sufferer forgets completely who he or she is and goes wandering, sometimes lost and frightened, sometimes imagining they're someone else entirely. It can last for hours, or weeks.'

'Nicole Holt disappeared for several days before she died,' I reminded her. 'She turned up in quite a state, with no recollection of where she'd been or what she'd been doing.'

Evi looked at me. When Bryony had tried to kill herself, she'd been taking a combination of drugs that could have wiped out huge chunks of her memory. A few weeks later, another girl with a history of memory loss had taken her own life.

'If there was DMT in Nicole's bloodstream too, that can't be coincidence,' I said. 'Her post-mortem was done this week, wasn't it?'

Evi nodded at me. 'Tuesday, I think,' she said. 'Nicole disappeared, you say?'

'I need to get hold of that report,' I said. 'Can you access it?'

Evi shook her head. 'She wasn't my patient,' she said. 'If Nicole had been taking drugs, or if there were any excess levels of alcohol in her system, it'll all come out at the inquest. Until then . . .'

I breathed out heavily. The normal course of events was for an inquest to be opened and then immediately adjourned. The full inquest could be six months away. 'Do you know the local coroner?' I asked.

Evi waved her head around in a completely non-committal way. 'I've met him,' she said. 'At one of the college dinners. We talked for a while.'

'What sort of age?'

She shrugged. 'Late fifties.'

'Married?'

'Bachelor, I thought. What has this . . .'

'Gay or straight?'

'I didn't ask.'

'Oh, like you'd need to. Gay or straight?'

'Straight,' said Evi. 'Quite flirtatious, if you must know.'

'Couldn't be better,' I said. 'We need to see him. Do you have his home phone number?'

Evi held up one hand. 'Hang on a sec. You said a girl had disappeared. Did you say her name was Jessica?'

I nodded. 'Yes, why?'

Instead of answering, she picked up her desk phone and dialled a number.

'Hello,' she said after a moment. 'Could you try Jessica Calloway's room for me?'

We waited. I was trying to remember what I'd seen on various websites the night before about the girl who was missing.

'Hello, may I speak to Jessica, please?' said Evi a second later. 'This is Dr Oliver.' The frown line on her forehead deepened. 'I see,' she went on after a moment. 'And have you spoken to her family at all?'

She looked up at me. For the first time, I thought she looked scared. 'OK, thank you,' she said, before putting the phone down.

'Jessica Calloway,' she said to me. 'I've been seeing her for a few months now. She has a history of depression and eating disorders. I saw her on Tuesday and was seriously concerned. I was starting to think about hospitalization. Now she hasn't been seen since that evening. I need to go and talk to the people in her block, her tutor.'

'I'll go,' I said. 'You're taking the local coroner out to lunch.'

55

It wasn't far from Evi's house to St Catharine's. When I reached the candy-striped canopies of the open-air market, I got off the bike and pushed it through the stalls. The early sunshine had all but disappeared by this time and the sky had clouded over. It had a yellow, heavy look that suggested snow wasn't so far away. I wove my way in and out of the shoppers, past bread stalls, flower stalls, fruit and veg stalls, and everywhere I turned there was an almost visible sense of urgency. People wanted to get their shopping done and get home before the snow came down. I picked up speed again and was soon at the college.

I made my way up to the third floor slowly, praying I wasn't coming down with something serious. The last thing I needed was to be laid up in bed for days. At the top, I stopped to get my breath, then found Jessica's room.

She would have a view of Main Court from her window. I knocked and waited. At the sound of a lavatory being flushed I turned to see another young woman coming out of a communal bathroom.

'Hi,' I said, before she had time to speak. 'I wonder if you can help me. I'm here about Jessica.'

'Nineteen dead women,' said Evi. 'It could be twenty by the end of the weekend. One of my patients hasn't been seen since Tuesday evening.'

Dr Francis Warrener, the coroner for the city of Cambridge, lifted the corner of his napkin and dabbed his mouth. He'd been amenable enough to Evi's suggestion that they meet for lunch and had sounded intrigued when she'd admitted she needed a favour. Now he was clearly regretting agreeing to see her. Well, tough.

'It's only a matter of time before the national press run with the story, asking very pertinent questions about what we've allowed to go on here. And before some parents start to get litigious,' she said. 'I don't know about you, Francis, but when that happens I want to know all my boxes are ticked.'

Francis Warrener was small and slim and

359

slick. All his movements were neat and precise. He had dark brown eyes, features that might have been pretty on a woman and very white teeth. He spoke little, but every word he uttered was precise and to the point. He'd stopped speaking a couple of minutes earlier.

'You know the first question always asked in cases like these?' said Evi. 'Could anything have been done sooner? When I'm asked that, I don't want to have to say, well, yes, actually, I was a bit worried, but I didn't want to rock any professional boats.'

Warrener picked up his fork, speared a pea and put it carefully into his mouth. Most of his food was still on the plate, cooling rapidly. 'If you've reported your concerns to the police,' he said, 'then surely you've done all you can.'

'Yes, that might just save my career,' said Evi. 'And if it's not enough by itself, then the fact that I met you, spelled out my concerns and asked you to look into it further will also help. Having both you and the police tell me to mind my own business will, at a pinch, exonerate me.'

'And pass the buck firmly into my court,' said Warrener.

'I think you just mixed a couple of metaphors but, basically, yes,' said Evi, forcing her cheek muscles into a smile. She waited, while Warrener pushed the remains of his chicken breast to the side of his plate and then put both knife and fork neatly down in the exact centre of it.

'Why don't you just look,' suggested Evi, feeling sorry for him, but not enough to back down. 'If you go through the reports and there's nothing to substantiate what I'm saying, just tell me. I'll accept your word for it. Then no confidences will be broken and no professional rules breached.'

'And if I do find something?' he asked.

'Then you'll be very glad you looked,' said Evi, knowing he was going to do it. 'And if you think that's even a possibility, we shouldn't be wasting any time.'

Nearly an hour later I'd learned nothing new. Except that it's possible to feel seriously concerned about someone you've never met. I'd explained I worked for Jessica's counsellor, and her friends had been happy to talk. After thirty minutes I felt like I'd known her myself. She was a girl with problems, that had been obvious from the day she'd arrived at the college. She was unnaturally obsessive about her appearance, in particular her weight, and hadn't put anything in her mouth without carefully weighing up its calorific value. Sensing her vulnerability, people had begun picking on her.

'Which people?' I'd asked.

The girls had looked at each other for inspiration.

'We never found out,' said the one with cropped blonde hair. 'Most people round here just don't seem the type. Everyone's pretty nice. A lot of it was on websites, you know, that sort of thing. Those things are completely anonymous.'

'But there were practical jokes played on her too,' I said. Evi had given me a quick summary before I left.

'Yeah, but we never saw who was doing it,' said the one with brown pigtails wrapped, Princess Leia style, above her ears. 'During the day this floor is pretty quiet. Anyone could come and go and never be seen.'

As the term had gone on, Jessica had become more and more withdrawn, sometimes not leaving her room for whole days at a time.

'Do you think she might have been on drugs?' I asked.

Around the room, eyes became evasive.

'If she's in trouble, you won't help her by keeping quiet,' I said.

'I'm sure she was,' said the cropped blonde. 'You just had to look into her eyes some mornings.'

'We don't know that for certain, though,' said the one with the yellow and purple scarf wrapped round her neck. 'You're just guessing.'

'There were days when she could barely get out of bed and I never saw her drinking much alcohol,' said the blonde. 'She was on drugs.'

'Do you know where she was getting them from?' I asked. 'Did you see anyone dodgy hanging around? Was there anyone she met, anywhere she went on a regular basis?'

They looked at each other, thought some more and shook their heads.

'Did she have money problems?' I asked. Drugs were invariably expensive.

'She never seemed to,' replied Princess Leia. 'She spent quite a lot on clothes and make-up.'

'Did you notice scars on her arms?' I asked. 'Or a constant sniff? Did you smell anything odd in her room?'

More blank looks, more head shakes. Jessica wasn't coming across as a classic drug addict. Neither had Bryony. I thanked them for their time, made sure they had my number and Evi's in case anything happened and told them I was sure Jessica would be fine. I was lying. I was becoming more and more convinced that by the end of the weekend, Jessica would be dead.

Leaving the building I had a text from Evi to say she was on her way to the coroner's office. He'd agreed to look through his files. She asked me to meet her back at her house in a couple of hours.

So I had time to kill. What I wanted to do was speak to Joesbury. Or at least let him know what I'd found out. It was still little more than a theory, though, and he'd been very clear about not contacting him unless it was an emergency. Couple of hours. I decided to check on Bryony.

Evi looked at her watch. The dog had been alone now for three hours. It could have peed on the carpet, chewed the furniture, howled a hole in the roof. And had Laura actually fed it that day? Had it been walked?

'Evi.'

Evi looked up to see Warrener in the doorway. He had a single sheet of paper in his right hand.

'Anything?' she asked.

Warrener glanced down at the sheet of paper and then back up at Evi.

'I checked eleven post-mortem reports,'

he said. 'Starting with the most recent, that of Nicole Holt.'

Evi nodded. When she and Laura had taken out the boys, the less attractive girls and the girls whose suicides had failed, the list had numbered eleven. She'd asked Francis to check if any of the women had been under the influence of drugs when they'd taken their own lives.

He handed over the sheet of paper. 'I'll be emailing this to the chief constable on Monday morning,' he said. 'What he makes of it is anyone's guess.'

Bryony was just as I'd left her two days earlier, staring up at the roof of the tent that kept her free from infection. She heard the door and her head turned slowly in my direction.

Her resemblance to an animated corpse was strengthening. The skin covering her face looked waxier than it had, and there were patches of discoloration. It looked as though the process of rejection by Bryony's body was beginning.

'Hi,' I said.

She watched me approach the bed.

'Same rules,' I said. 'The minute you want me to go, just blink a few times and I'm out of here.'

I waited for the blinking to start. It didn't. I pulled the chair forward and sat down.

'Had a bit of an adventure after I saw you the other day,' I said. 'Got attacked by a buzzard.' I told her the story of disturbing the bird, of it swooping down on me and how I'd run for cover in the adjoining woods. There were things I wanted to ask her but I didn't want to agitate her too soon and, besides, I had a feeling she had very little company. I was just about to tell her about the woods and the scary farmer when a nurse came in to check her blood pressure and oxygen levels.

By the time the nurse had gone it was getting late and I knew I had to be back at Evi's before the end of the afternoon. The spooky woods story would wait another day.

'Bryony,' I said as the door closed. 'There's something I want to ask you. It won't be easy for you, but it's important. Is that OK?'

I waited for Bryony to incline her head down towards her chin and then lift it again. Oh, Lord, I'd been half hoping she'd say no, because what I was about to ask seemed horribly cruel, but Evi's comment earlier about two hundred people seeing Bryony set fire to herself had struck home. Because they hadn't. Two hundred people had seen her in flames.

Someone else had been present when Nicole had decapitated herself. Danielle hadn't been alone when she'd hung from that tree. Maybe Bryony hadn't acted alone either.

'Bryony, what I need to ask is whether anyone was with you when you set fire to yourself.'

Maybe all three of them had had help.

'What I need to know, Bryony, is whether someone was helping you.'

Maybe these weren't suicides at all.

'Whether anyone else did that to you?'

Bryony's hand was moving across the bed, had taken hold of the pen. She was moving it slowly across the pad. At that moment, the door opened and an orderly came in. He nodded at me and walked to the waste bin.

'So there I am, half naked, soaking wet, chained by my ankle and with a video camera pushed into my face,' I said, in as cheerful a voice as I could muster. 'Talaith said they did it a lot last term.'

As I'd been talking, I'd leaned over the bed to see what Bryony was writing. The orderly was emptying the bin into a large plastic sack he'd brought with him.

ME, she'd written. *I DID IT*

367

I gave her a little nod, to show I understood, and a half smile to thank her. Giving me a dark look, the orderly left the room.

'I'm going to leave you in peace now,' I went on. 'To be honest, I'm pretty whacked myself. Had some weird dreams last night. Must be something to do with that room.'

Bryony's eyes had opened wide with alarm.

'Sorry,' I said. 'It's just that Talaith happened to mention that when you and she were sharing a room, you had bad dreams too.'

She started writing again. *NO,* she wrote, and then *NOT DREAMS.*

Not dreams? What did that mean?

Her pen was still moving across the pad. *BELL,* she wrote again.

'I know, you said,' I told her. 'Bryony, do you mean Nick Bell, your GP?'

Instant agitation. She started tapping the pen on the plastic. First above the word *Bell* then above *Not dreams.* The pencil slipped from her fingers but she carried on as though it was terribly important that I understood. *Bell.* And *Not dreams.*

Behind me, the door opened and a nurse stood in the doorway.

'I think she needs some sleep now,' she

told me in a voice that brooked no argument.

Evi looked down. Toxicology screens were carried out on suicides as a matter of course and any unusual substances found in blood, saliva or urine would be noted on the post-mortem report. Warrener had lifted the toxicology reports from each of the eleven victims. Nina Hatton, the zoology student who'd died five years earlier after cutting open her femoral artery, had temazepam, a reasonably common sedative, and psilocybin, a hallucinogen, in her system. Jayne Pearson, the French student who'd stolen a family gun and shot herself seven months later, showed traces of another sedative called flunitrazepam. Its trade name was Rohypnol. That same academic year, the post-mortems of Kate George and Donna Leather showed traces of LSD and mescaline respectively. Both had also used the sedative drugs benzodiazepines. The following year, Bella Hardy and Freya Robin had died after taking ibogaine and DMT. Evi made her way down the list until she found the results of the post-mortem on Nicole Holt. She'd taken LSD before she died.

'Other than the combination of hallucinogens and sedatives, there's no real pattern here,' Evi said, looking up at the coroner.

'There isn't,' agreed Francis. 'And there is nothing unusual in finding traces of drugs in the body of a suicide.'

'No,' said Evi. Claire McGann, fourteen months earlier, had taken mandrake, a rare herbal-derived hallucinogenic drug. Shortly afterwards, Miranda Harman had died after taking Benadryl.

'I'm referring this to the chief constable,' continued Francis, 'and, against my better judgement, showing it to you, for two reasons.'

'Some of these drugs are very unusual,' said Evi.

'They are,' he agreed. 'Not at all what you would expect the average university student to get hold of by themselves. My other concern is that by far the most common drug we would normally find in the system of a suicide is alcohol.'

Evi glanced down at the list again.

'None of them,' she said. 'Traces in Kate and Freya but only what would be consistent with a single glass of wine some time earlier. None of them had drunk to excess.'

'Exactly. And it may just be me being fanciful,' Francis said, 'but it strikes me that, of all the incapacitating drugs, substantial quantities of alcohol would be the hardest to administer to someone else.'

Evi looked down at the list again. 'It strikes me,' she said, 'that if there's foul play going on, someone really knows his drugs.'

'Are we done now, Evi?' asked Warrener, and from the look on his face there was little doubt what he wanted her answer to be.

'Not quite,' Evi replied.

56

'So they are acting alone,' said Evi. 'Whatever might be leading up to it, in the end the decision to die is theirs.'

'That would appear to be the case with Bryony,' I agreed. 'Danielle was very hazy about details but I'm sure she'd remember being lynched. Difficult to ask the others, of course.'

'And not dreams?' said Evi. 'You're sure that's what she meant?'

'Not completely, but it fits,' I said. 'Bryony herself never talked about bad dreams, remember, she talked about someone coming into her room at night and touching her. It was her room-mate, Talaith, who mentioned that Bryony used to scream in her sleep.'

'Jessica was very clear,' said Evi. 'She was having very bad dreams. Although she was vague about the detail.'

'With Nicole, it was her friends again,' I

said. 'They heard her yelling at night.'

We were sitting in Evi's kitchen, a lovely large room at the back of the house that overlooked the garden. A huge cedar tree stood in the centre of the lawn, with other smaller trees and bushes around the outer beds. A low brick wall with a centrally placed iron gate formed the boundary at the lower edge. Beyond it, I could see heavily pollarded willows. The sky outside seemed to have fallen lower, and had taken on the colour of clotted cream.

'If these so-called dreams are actually vague memories of real abuse, why aren't the girls waking up and screaming their heads off the minute the bedroom door opens?'

'I'd guess they're sedated,' said Evi, indicating the coroner's list. 'Whoever's doing this has a pretty good grasp of sedative drugs. We've got Rohypnol, ketamine. Get enough of either in your system and you're going to be pretty submissive, with only the vaguest recollection or none at all the next day.'

'Fits so far,' I said. 'But sometimes they do wake up screaming. Is whatever's happening to them so bad it's overriding the effect of the sedative?'

'Unless there was actual pain involved,

that's unlikely,' said Evi. 'And these girls aren't physically harmed, remember. I'd say there was something else going on as well.'

As if what we had already wasn't enough. 'Something else?' I said.

'There are a lot of hallucinogens on this list,' she said. 'Several of the victims had traces of psychedelic drugs in their systems.'

I must have looked blank because Evi gave a heavy sigh. 'OK,' she said. 'You're aware that hallucinogenic drugs induce experiences that are different from those of ordinary consciousness?'

'You mean not real?'

She nodded her head. 'Yes, you could say experiences that aren't real. But under that umbrella there is a huge range of possibilities, depending upon the type of drug taken and the circumstances of the user.'

The dog had followed us from the sitting room but had transferred his allegiance completely to Evi. He was lying at her feet now, on the hard tiled floor, gazing up at her adoringly. Which says something about the loyalty of dogs, it seems to me. I'd rescued him from a bullet, fed him, offered him shelter and now he'd fallen in love with the prettier face.

'Go on,' I said.

'Hallucinogenic drugs are grouped into

three basic types,' said Evi. 'First of all you have the psychedelic drugs. These don't induce hallucinations in the true sense, they just alter the user's perception of reality. Someone under the influence might see unusually bright colours, or inanimate objects move in some way. Often senses get mixed up, people talk about hearing colours and seeing sounds.'

'Far out,' I said.

Evi didn't smile. 'Psychedelic isn't a hippy term, by the way, it's from the ancient Greek,' she said. 'Psyche meaning mind or soul and delos meaning reveal or manifest. LSD is a psychedelic drug, so are DMT and mescaline. And what they do is to bring some hidden part of you to the surface.'

'Hidden but real?' I said.

'Exactly. There were medical experiments in the late 1960s, the theory being that use of psychedelic drugs could bring to the forefront of a person's mind whatever they were keeping hidden. Risky, of course, because when people are keeping memories tucked away it's usually for a good reason. Artificially forcing them into the open could be very dangerous.'

'If someone had a dark secret, psychedelics could root it out?' I asked, feeling a chill that had nothing to do with the temperature.

I had a few secrets of my own that I wanted to keep firmly in the closet.

'Yes. Then you have the dissociative drugs,' Evi said. 'They induce a perception of the outside world's being dream-like or false. You're aware of what's going on around you but you feel detached. People have reported a sense of watching themselves from a distance, even of seeing the world like a giant cinema screen. Are you with me?'

'Yes, of course,' I said. 'And typical dissociative drugs might be?'

'PCP, ketamine again. Both initially developed as anaesthetics for surgery. Both on this list.'

'And the third group,' I prompted.

'Possibly the most dangerous, the deliriants,' said Evi. 'These can cause hallucinations in the true sense. Users have conversations with people who aren't there, see things that have no basis in reality.'

'And these things they see, are they likely to be scary?' I asked.

'Depends,' said Evi. 'Someone in a good frame of mind, in a situation in which they feel safe, would be likely to have a good trip.'

'The converse being that someone depressed, anxious, in a situation where they feel vulnerable and scared, will have a bad one?'

'Someone in that position should never take hallucinogens,' said Evi. 'The consequences would be dire.'

'OK,' I said. 'So let's just say, for the sake of argument, that you're depressed, vulnerable and scared, you're then sedated and abused and, just for good measure, you're given a pretty powerful hallucinogenic. What would the effect be?'

I'd never seen Evi look so pale. 'It really doesn't bear thinking about,' she said.

I looked at the list of drugs Evi had brought back from the coroner's office. Some of them I didn't recognize.

'So are they taking this shit knowingly, or are they being slipped it without their knowledge?' I asked.

'Bryony insisted to her counsellor that she wasn't taking anything,' said Evi. 'And she must have had Nick convinced as well for him to prescribe the antidepressant he did.'

'Jessica's friends thought she was using,' I said. 'Although from how they described her behaviour, I wouldn't have said it was typical of an addict.'

'I don't think Jessica was a user,' said Evi. 'I would have noticed the signs. She wasn't displaying them when she came to see me.'

'What are the signs?' I asked.

'Pupil dilation, unusual pallor, rapid

respiration, sweating, trembling of the extremities,' said Evi. 'Pretty much the state you were in this morning.'

OK, that was a bit unexpected.

'And the other day,' she went on, before I could think of what to say. 'When you came to see me in college. I noticed then you didn't look well.'

'I've never taken a recreational drug in my life,' I said truthfully. 'I'm fighting off a cold, that's all.'

'Had any bad dreams?' Evi asked me.

I stood and walked over to where the dog had fallen fast asleep on a rug in front of the cooker. Its legs stuck out at angles from its body, displaying its undercarriage to the world.

'This dog's a bitch,' I said.

'I think she's quite sweet,' Evi replied.

'I've been referring to her as a he all day,' I said. I turned back to look at Evi again. 'Did you know?'

'Of course,' she said. 'I just assumed biology wasn't your strong point. And a dog's gender-confusion is the least of our worries. So, want to tell me about these dreams you've been having?'

Evi thought I . . . I shook my head. 'It's not possible.'

She didn't move, didn't speak.

'I dreamed that someone was trying to break into my room,' I admitted. 'That I heard them coming in and couldn't move. It was pretty scary. When I woke up, I was in the main room, cuddling the dog. Door locked, window closed, no sign of a break-in, several pissed-off girls on the corridor.'

'When you left the party last night, where did you go?' asked Evi.

'I drove to a burger bar to get Sniffy-Dog something to eat, then back to college,' I told her. 'My room-mate was out. I made a cup of tea, did some work and went to bed.'

'It must have been at the party,' said Evi. 'Which, I agree, seems unlikely.'

'It is,' I said. 'Don't these things act pretty quickly?'

Evi shrugged. 'Some do, some don't,' she said, not too helpfully.

'I was fine driving home. I worked for about an hour when I got in. I felt absolutely normal when I went to bed.'

'You made tea?'

'Hallucinogenic drugs via a teabag?' I said. 'No really, my bad dreams and the state I was in this morning were down to a combination of stress, tiredness, a disturbing late-night conversation — with you — and the possible onset of flu. I'm feeling a lot better now, honestly.'

Evi stared at me for a moment before getting up and fetching her medical bag from a closet in the hallway. 'How about we send off some samples?' she said, from the doorway. 'Just to make sure.'

I opened my mouth to refuse and realized it couldn't do any harm. I would know, surely, if I'd been drugged, but if it gave Evi peace of mind . . .

'So just going with your theory for a minute,' I said. 'How can drugs be administered to people without them knowing about it?' I watched her take needle, syringe, vials and a urine specimen jar from her bag. She ripped the packaging off the needle.

'Left arm, roll up your sleeve,' she told me, as she fitted the various pieces together. 'Well, there's a whole collection that can be slipped into drinks,' she went on, as I did what I was told. 'That's how the date-rape drugs work. But students tend to be quite wise to that these days.'

'Ouch,' I contributed, helpfully, as Evi bagged and labelled my blood and put it to one side on the table. 'It can be sent off first thing Monday morning,' she said.

Evi hadn't finished with me yet. When I got back from the loo and handed over my urine specimen, she dug into her bag again, then shone a light into my eyes, took my pulse and blood pressure and listened to my breathing with a stethoscope.

'You'll live,' she told me, in the end.

'Let's hope Jessica does,' I said. When she didn't reply, I regretted being flippant. Evi cared about her patients. She was genuinely worried about Jessica. So was I, come to that.

'Maybe you should sleep somewhere else for a few nights,' she said. 'There are several spare bedrooms here.'

I shook my head. 'Without clearing it with my SO, I can't make any major changes,' I said. 'And until those results come back, we don't know anything for sure. Don't worry, I'll be careful.'

Evi looked troubled but she didn't argue. 'The coroner is planning to send this list to the chief constable on Monday,' she said, picking up the printed sheet Francis Warrener had given her. 'What will he do, do you think?'

'Nothing in a hurry,' I said. 'Which won't help Jessica much. He'll most likely send it down to CID, ask them to have another look at the various cases and report back to him. As the girls are all dead anyway, it's unlikely to get a high priority. They'll get round to it in the next few weeks.'

The carriage clock in Evi's hallway struck

the quarter-hour and there didn't seem much more we could do for one day. 'I need to run,' I said, getting up and finding my bag. 'I'll call you tomorrow.'

'Laura,' Evi called after me, as I had my hand on the door and was about to step out. 'Haven't you forgotten something?'

I turned to see her holding up my improvised dog lead. 'Well, here's the thing,' I said. 'We don't know anyone's reported her missing yet but it's only a matter of time. In the meantime, I thought she should stay with you.'

Evi's eyebrows disappeared into her hair. 'And what gave you the idea that would be . . .'

'Well, she obviously likes you,' I said. 'And from what I can tell it's mutual.'

'I can't have a dog, Laura. How would I walk her?'

'I'll pop round in the morning to do that,' I said. 'Try her for tonight. I know she's soft as pig-shit but she's pretty big and when she barks she sounds like a Dobermann. And just in case the excitement of the last few hours has made you forget it, you have a stalker. If anyone's been breaking in here, they'll think twice now you've got Sniffy-Dog staying with you.'

'What on earth do I feed her?'

'Dog food,' I replied. 'There are twenty-four cans outside your front door. I bought them earlier. I'll just carry them in for you. She doesn't need a basket. She'll sleep on your bedroom carpet.'

'She won't get through twenty-four cans in one night,' grumbled Evi as I walked past her into the kitchen, two trays of dog food in my arms. Sniffy-Dog didn't even wake up as I left. She'd already decided where she was staying.

57

Cycling back to St John's I was trying to remember when I'd last been on a date. As I pushed my bike through the main gate, I realized I never had. As a teenager I'd had boyfriends, probably more than most girls — I was no angel — but I'd met them on street corners, on park benches, by climbing the railings of children's playgrounds after dark. We'd met, hung around, drunk cheap booze and smoked. The snogging and the petting had gone further and further, until by sixteen there wasn't much I didn't know about sex.

At seventeen I'd left home and had spent time living rough. I'd hit rock bottom and then discovered there are places even worse. Gradually, though, I'd pulled myself up and sorted myself out. I'd joined the RAF reserves, then the police, studied for a law degree and established a career. It hadn't left much time for socializing and, besides,

I'd decided long ago that I couldn't allow anyone to get close. Which pretty much ruled out boyfriends.

I certainly wasn't afraid of men. Until recently I'd had a pretty active sex life, I just didn't try to convince myself that the men who passed through my life were about anything other than sex. Now I was in my late twenties and on the verge of my first date. With a man who might just be a monster in human form. Well, they did say dating was a minefield.

I could hear heavy rock music from the other end of the corridor. I opened the door to a wall of sound and found Tox sitting in the middle of the rug. Her plum-coloured hair was twisted up on top of her head. It looked like she hadn't combed it in weeks and seemed to be held in place with a pair of chopsticks. She was wearing pink leggings with a hole in the bum. One leg, her right one, was twisted up and doubled back so that her ankle rested behind her head. The other leg was curved in front of her. Her hands were by her side for balance. Her eyes were closed. She didn't open them as I came in.

Shaking my head — kids! — I walked past her and into my own room. In spite of what I'd told Evi, I still didn't feel great. I had two hours to let paracetamol, strong coffee and hot water work their magic.

The music died. 'Hi, hon,' I heard Tox call from the main room, when my ears had stopped pounding. 'Can you give me a hand a sec?'

I walked back. Tox hadn't moved, except to shuffle round a bit on her bottom so that she could face me. 'I'm stuck,' she said. 'Can you just, like, unhook me?'

She was winding me up. 'You can't be stuck,' I said. 'Just bend your head forward.'

'Doesn't work,' she said, and in fairness, she was looking a bit red in the face. 'My leggings are caught on the back of my choker. I can't unfasten it. I've been fiddling and fiddling and I've just made it worse. There're some scissors in my top drawer.'

I bent to look. Sure enough, several strands of wool had got caught on the fastening of the thing she was wearing round her neck. I tried to release the choker, but the wool was wrapped round both sides of the fastener.

'It's not going to unfasten,' I said.

'Scissors,' said Tox. 'For God's sake, I've been like this for an hour.'

After I'd cut her free, she used both hands to unhook her leg from the back of her neck and lower it slowly. Then she stretched out and rolled over on to her stomach, her face pressed against the rug.

'Yoga?' I said, when she'd stopped groaning.

'Tantric,' she muttered to the carpet. 'Does wonders for your sex life.'

'I'll take your word for it,' I replied, glancing at her iPod on the floor beside her. 'And the Killers were to drown out your screams?'

She reached out and picked up the iPod. 'The Killers were to attract attention,' she said. 'I knew sooner or later someone would come and complain.' She reached back and started massaging the flesh of her right buttock. 'Oh, Christ, I'm in pain,' she said. 'I think I've pulled something.'

'I'll run you a bath,' I offered.

'I know you're laughing, you unsympathetic cow,' she called out to me as I walked down the corridor to the bathroom.

Nearly two hours later, I'd followed Tox into the bath and soaked until I was in danger of coming out wrinkled. Then I'd dosed myself up on codeine and paracetamol. I'd drunk another gallon of water and a couple of cups of very strong coffee. I was feeling better and probably as good as I was going to short of ten hours' sleep.

Tox, having hobbled up to the Buttery for food and back down again, was kneeling on one of the easy chairs, her buttocks presumably still too sore to sit down properly. 'Town or gown,' she called to me.

'Excuse me?'

'Your date. Town or gown?'

'Six stinky old fellows and a couple of moustached lesbians,' I replied, finding my jeans from the wardrobe. I'd told her I'd been invited to a departmental dinner. She hadn't looked convinced.

'You are shitting me,' she said, watching me wriggle into them. 'Those are fuck-me jeans. There is actually a hole at the crotch.'

'There is not,' I snapped, although, strictly, it was debatable. The jeans were a pair I'd bought a couple of years ago in Camden Market. They were made of old, distressed denim and would have been skintight had they not been more holes than jeans. All the way down each leg, the denim had been slashed in a series of horizontal tears. They were Lacey jeans, not at all the sort of thing Laura would wear, but if I was going to get through the evening I was going to have to let Lacey out of her box for a while.

'You are going to get frostbite,' my self-appointed mother-stand-in went on. 'Do you know it's actually snowing outside?'

She had a point. Sometime over the last couple of hours soft white powder had started to collect in the window corners. Not that I had time to rethink and change. I pulled my sweater over my head. Ten minutes to go. Was there any chance of getting rid of Tox before Nick arrived?

'Are you actually staying in tonight?' I asked her.

'Shit no,' she said. 'I'd be chewing the furniture by ten o'clock. Barney's team's been playing away, though. He's not back for another hour. That is a great colour on you.'

'Thanks,' I said. The sweater was powder blue, the fabric a poor-woman's cashmere. I was never entirely sure about it, always wondered if it was a bit . . .

'And I love the two styles screaming at each other. You know, rock-chick-slut and the postmistress's grandmother.'

'That's what I was going for,' I said, wondering if I did maybe have time to rethink and change.

'You know what, I have the perfect pair of earrings for that outfit.' Tox had climbed down off her perch and was hobbling to her own room.

'Actually, I don't really do earrings,' I

called after her. 'Earrings are a bit wasted when you have long hair.'

She was back, brandishing a pair of huge, dangly earrings as if she were presenting me with the Holy Grail. 'Absolutely perfect,' she said, holding them up against my sweater. 'You need something to get your hair out of the way though.'

She disappeared again. Each earring was several powder-blue feathers hanging from a miniature mirror ball. They looked like something that might tumble out of a cheap Christmas cracker. At that second there was a knock on the door. When I opened it, a man with snowflakes in his copper-coloured hair stood on the other side. Just nudging six foot, I judged, the perfect height for a man.

'Hi,' he said.

'Yowsa,' said Tox from behind me.

'This is Talaith,' I said without turning round. 'But unless you're about to take up holy orders, you have to call her Tox.'

'You can call me anything you like,' said Tox, as I stepped backwards to let Nick come in. From the corner of my eye I saw she had dropped the hobble and was slinking across the room like a cat teaching deportment class. She held out her hand to him as if she were the Queen Mother.

'Nick Bell,' he told her. A second later, he glanced down. She was still holding his hand.

'So do you want to reconsider?' she asked him, looking from him to me and then down at herself. 'Cos in the Cripps Building we like to offer a choice.'

'Get out of here, you tart,' I told her. 'And let go of his hand. You're scaring him.'

Tox stepped closer to Nick, still clinging on to him. 'She called you a stinky old fellow,' she said. 'She's not polite.'

'You're a scream,' he said, his smile faltering just a fraction.

'That would be blood-curdling,' I said, glaring at her. 'We should go. She'll only get worse.'

I turned for my coat as Tox finally dropped Nick's hand. 'Earrings!' she yelped.

She took them from me and, not without a few painful jabs, shoved them into my ears. Luckily, because she didn't check, they have been pierced.

'You can't see them,' she wailed and raced back into her room. I looked at Nick. He shrugged. Tox came back and started grabbing my hair by the handful. Five seconds later she pushed me in front of the mirror.

'There,' she said. 'Rock chick meets postmistress meets . . .'

'Deranged poultry keeper,' I finished for her. Powder-blue feathers hung from my ears. Half my hair had been twisted up and secured in place by combs, all with more powder-blue feathers. 'Thanks,' I said. 'I owe you.'

Tox waved us off, trilling like a real mother sending her baby girl off on a first date, wishing us a lovely evening and insisting Nick didn't keep me out too late.

'I'll take these out in a minute,' I said, as we walked down the stairs. I was acutely conscious of pieces of dead bird sticking out of my head at all angles.

'I kind of like them,' he replied. 'Makes you look less serious.'

'Know this place?' he asked me, as the waitress settled us down at a table on the mezzanine level, above the main room of a restaurant called the Galleria. We'd walked for ten minutes through the thickening snow to Bridge Street and to a brick building almost on the bridge itself. Outside the windows the river gleamed at us like oil against the snow-frosted banks.

I'd been in Cambridge less than a week. There had hardly been time for fine dining. I shook my head. 'No, but it looks lovely,' I said, thinking that was a suitably Laura thing to say.

The room was large and light, the table linen white, the cutlery and crystalware very simple. Diners who'd arrived in the last few minutes had left trails of melted snow across the wooden floors.

Nick put the wine list down. 'So what happened to the dog?' he asked me.

'Staying with a friend until its owner can be traced,' I said. 'Which reminds me. I heard the weirdest noise last night at your place. Just before Sniffy showed up.'

'What sort of noise?' he said. 'And Sniffy?'

'It's what she does,' I said. 'A very scary noise,' I went on, remembering how freaked I'd been. 'A bit like a scream and a bit like something being strangled. And a bit like a wild animal about to attack.'

Nick had been frowning. His face relaxed. 'Muntjac,' he said. 'Almost certainly. Most people get alarmed the first time they hear one.'

'And a muntjac is . . .'

'Small, stocky deer,' he said. 'Generally considered a bit of a pest in these parts.'

'Do you shoot them?'

'If they don't run too fast. What are you going to have?'

I picked up the menu. 'Do they do muntjac?' I asked.

'You should come out with me,' he said. 'Tomorrow afternoon, just before the light starts to fade. The duck in Chinese spices is excellent, by the way.'

A second date in as many days? This guy worked fast. Or did he have other reasons for wanting to get to know me better?

'Duck it is,' I said, closing the menu. 'And don't you want to see how the evening goes first?'

'Oh, I'm smitten already,' he replied. 'How do you get on with Evi?'

'Very well,' I said. 'Old friend of yours?'

'We studied medicine here together, although she was a couple of years behind me. I tipped her off when her current job came up.'

'She's worried about the number of student suicides the university has seen in the last couple of years,' I said, deciding to risk taking the conversation up a level.

He was nodding at me. 'Yeah,' he said. 'She's had a bee in her bonnet about it for a while now.'

'Do you think she's worrying unnecessarily?' If he tried to make light of Evi's fears, it could suggest he didn't want anyone else taking them seriously.

He shook his head. 'Sadly, no,' he said. 'I think she's probably right to be concerned.

Which makes it only a matter of time before the national press gets wind of what's going on and media attention will make it a dozen times worse.'

'She thinks there's an unduly influential subculture of glamorizing self-destructive behaviour,' I said, slightly smug at how easily I'd embraced psychobabble.

Our starters arrived, giant prawns in citrus butter for Nick, tomato and basil salad for me. 'And,' I went on, 'that someone could be feeding it.'

He looked puzzled, so I explained the websites I'd found where suicide wasn't just glorified but positively encouraged. Where people in despair were taunted, coaxed and cajoled into acts of self-destruction. All the time I was talking I was watching his eyes, for just a flicker that might tell me he was more involved than he should be. Nothing. Either he was genuine, or a very cool customer. I could probably push him a bit more.

'I'm supposed to know a thing or two about psychology,' I said. 'But the truth is, I don't get it. I don't get why people want to harm others that they don't even know.' I stopped and shrugged. There was a tiny patch of stubble on his right cheek where he hadn't shaved too carefully. And he had just a smattering of grey hairs an inch or so above each temple, so few I could probably count them.

'Well, there are any number of textbooks on the psychology of evil,' he said. 'But ultimately, I guess it all comes down to power. We do it because we can.' He broke off to pick up his bread roll. 'When I was studying here one of the other students told us a story about a kid whose father committed suicide when he was young. He shot himself in the head. The kid's three-year-old sister found their father's body. Traumatized both of them for years.'

'Well, it would,' I said, as the waitress took our starter plates away. 'So what happened to him?'

'Well, as I remember, at school he got in with a crowd of bullies. They plagued the life out of a classmate. One of the younger ones. Made his life an absolute misery until one day he hanged himself in his dorm with a ripped sheet.'

'Nasty story,' I said. 'And was that the end of it?'

'If only. The ringleader got a real buzz out of it, apparently. The feeling of power was like nothing he'd ever experienced. It made him want to do it again.'

A story of fifteen years ago, being told in

quite some detail. I found myself wondering if Nick had a sister.

'And this was somebody you were studying with? Someone who came here?'

He shook his head. 'The guy I studied with told the story,' he said. 'Supposedly about someone he'd once known.'

'Supposedly?'

Nick shrugged. 'He was an odd chap, to be honest. Thin, a bit geeky. Dropped out at the end of his third year, I think.'

'Remember his name?'

Nick sat back in his chair. 'Why?' he asked, and looked at me carefully through narrowed eyes.

Shit, I was close to blowing it. Why on earth would Laura want the name of a geeky Cambridge dropout who'd once told a good story about suicide?

'Evi told me a similar story,' I lied, making a mental note to tip her off the next day. 'Only she seemed convinced the guy was talking about himself. She mentioned a Scottish name, McLean or McLinnie or something.'

'Could well have been,' said Nick, shaking his head. 'Sorry, it's gone.'

By the time we finished dinner, I still had no idea whether my date for the evening was an exceptionally nice and seriously good-looking bloke, or a cold-blooded killer playing cat and mouse with me. And given my history with men, the chances seemed pretty evenly split.

We left the restaurant to find snow had covered the ground outside and Nick suggested we take a longer route home to enjoy what he described as the city with a coat of whitewash. Despite jeans that were more hole than fabric, I agreed, because I still hadn't worked this man out. Besides, there is something about snow, isn't there? About the way it softens harsh sound and brightens the darkness, hiding everything that's ugly and making the world look clean. As we walked through the town, students had left their buildings, even the pubs and cafés, to come outside and play. All around us were the sounds of fun: footsteps crunching at speed, high-pitched squealing and good-natured taunting.

For a few minutes we followed the river, watching flakes fall and melt on its slow-moving surface, then we turned across a stretch of field that Nick told me was Jesus Green. There was an epic snowball fight going on.

'That lot are Jesus, the others are Queens',' said Nick, as he gallantly put himself between me and the fight. 'Keep your head down and walk fast, they might not spot us.'

'How can you tell?' I asked.

'Jesus attracts an inordinate number of red-haired women,' he told me, 'whereas Queens' men are known for wearing their jeans very low down on their hips.'

I looked over at the skirmish. A girl with a Peruvian hat was rugby-tackled to the ground by a man wearing nothing warmer than a sleeveless vest. She didn't seem to mind too much. No red-haired women or low-slung jeans that I could see. I gave Nick my best quizzical look.

'Scarves,' he said. 'Jesus are red and black, Queens' are green and white.'

A stray snowball came our way and caught him on the side of the head.

'Serves you right,' I told him.

'Ouch,' he said. 'That is very cold down the back of my neck.'

We walked on, leaving the squeals behind us, and approached the town again. As we left the Green, I thought for a moment, and then took his arm. In front of us was a long, low house of honey-coloured stone, the ledges of its tiny paned windows frosted with snow. Over our heads a snowball soared through the air and exploded against

399

the stonework. We turned a corner and beautiful buildings, gleaming white and gold in the lamplight, rose up around us. It was like stepping into a fairy tale.

'I never tire of it,' Nick said, as we made our way along the pavement and snow covered our footsteps almost immediately. 'My parents both worked at the university. Their worst arguments when I was growing up were over which college I'd attend. My idea of teenage rebellion was threatening to apply to Oxford.'

My idea of teenage rebellion had been torching cars in the Cardiff docks. It didn't seem like the moment to mention it. 'So where did you end up?' I asked.

'Trinity,' he said. 'Dad's old college. He'd died by that stage and my mother thought it would be a kind of memorial to him if I went there.'

His father had died. How exactly? Natural causes or . . . we were in amongst the buildings now. Towers and turrets stretched up above us.

'It's at moments like these,' said Nick, who was looking up towards the rooftops, 'that I always hope I'll see a night climber.'

There was a tiny scar on the underside of his chin. This close, he smelled good. Something warm and rich. 'Sounds like a low-budget horror film,' I said.

'I think that's night crawlers,' he replied. 'Don't tell me you haven't heard of the night climbers.'

Careful now. This might be something every real student in Cambridge was expected to know.

'Rings a bell,' I said. 'I think I just assumed they were a myth.'

'Oh no, they're very real,' he said. 'Any amount of photographic evidence. Most years in December you'll see a Father Christmas hat on one of the pinnacles at King's. All of them on a good year.'

'So who are they exactly?'

He smiled down at me. 'No one knows, that's the whole point. There's no club or society you can join because it's all strictly against the rules. Get caught climbing and you'll be sent down. No argument.'

'And what do they climb?'

Nick raised his hand and gestured at the sky around us. 'Everything,' he said. 'Rooftops, chimneys, drainpipes, spires, turrets. It started in the old days when colleges were locked at ten o'clock. Men who stayed out late had to climb their way back in. Some of them got a taste for it.'

I looked at a nearby church spire. It looked pretty high off the ground to me.

'Do they ever fall?' I asked.

'Absolutely. A few years ago a chap got impaled on some railings. Story is he was so drunk they operated without anaesthetic.'

We'd reached the main gate of St John's. Cambridge is a small city. Nick greeted the porter on duty by name as we stepped through the small inner door into First Court. A group of third-year students were building a snowman.

'So, did you ever night-climb?'

'Ah, that's the thing,' he said. 'We never climb and tell.'

A cat watched us from a first-floor window ledge as we approached the main entrance to the Cripps Building and I could feel the beginnings of a nervous tickle. Nick would expect to be invited up.

We'd reached the door. He turned to face me, taking hold of the lapels of my coat to pull me closer, and I actually found myself considering it. He was the best-looking man I'd met in a long time and it wasn't uncommon for undercover officers to have sexual relationships with people they were investigating. It was all part of infiltration and establishing trust.

On the other hand, wasn't it turquoise eyes, not russet-brown ones, that I wanted looking down at me the next time I had sex?

'So tomorrow,' he said. 'Three o'clock. My house. Come out hawking with me?'

I could not have Joesbury. Not ever. He was the one man in the world I would never be able to keep at arm's length.

'OK,' I agreed, tilting my head back so the angle between his mouth and mine was perfect. All he had to do was lower his head. He smiled at me.

'See you then,' he said. Then he let go of my jacket, turned, and walked away.

58

Since the accident that had crippled her, Evi had dreamed many times that she could run. Occasionally, that she could fly. Only once had she dreamed that she could ski, and she'd woken trembling and sweating in the early hours. She had never dreamed that she could dance.

Until now.

Rock music. Springsteen's 'Dancing in the Dark'. A pounding, insistent rhythm, turned up loud to be heard above the wind. Her hair flying round her head, her neck cold in the November air, the heat of a man's body pressed against her. Harry. The priest who'd played in a rock band, who'd held her upright and moved them both around the bare rock of the Lancashire Tor. The night they'd fallen in love.

Harry back again. Harry in her arms. She could feel his breath against her forehead, knew the wonderful anticipation of a first kiss. They danced closer and closer to the edge of the Tor. He tucked her right hand against his chest, freeing his to gently tilt her chin up towards him. She saw brown eyes smiling down at her. This was it.

'Evi fall,' he said. And threw her off the Tor.

Evi was out of bed and the pain running the length of her body was all she could think of. She made herself take deep breaths. Just a dream. She hadn't fallen. Maybe out of bed, maybe that accounted for the sudden stabbing pain, but she was fine. She found the light. Sniffy looked up at her, blinking, from her place on the rug. Then she gave a lazy wag of her tail. Nothing to worry about. She'd take some more painkillers, maybe get a hot drink and go back to bed. Everything was fine.

Except Springsteen was still singing.

Somewhere in the house, music was playing. And not just any music. It was the tune that meant more to her than any other. The track she could never listen to, the one that had her switching off the car radio on the occasions it was played, because she simply couldn't hear it without crying.

Biting her lip, Evi made her way round the bed and towards the door. Then she turned back and called to the dog. Sniffy got up reluctantly, not remotely concerned about either the phantom music or the intruder who must have broken in to put the CD in the music system.

Evi's CD player was in the sitting room. The hallway was in darkness. She released her hold on Sniffy's collar and the dog stayed by her side. The door to the sitting room was closed. Evi turned the handle and reached in to find the light switch.

The music stopped. The room was empty.

'Go see,' she whispered. Sniffy looked at her. The only possible hiding place in the room was behind the curtains covering the large front windows. The dog would know, surely, if there was anyone there. There were no lights on the music system. It made a faint twanging noise when it was switched off: she would have heard it.

Now that she thought about it, she didn't even have the Springsteen CD.

Clutching tight to Sniffy's collar, Evi limped across the room and pulled back the curtains. No one there. Sniffy cocked her head, as if to say, *Now can we go back to bed?*

'I was dreaming, wasn't I?' said Evi. 'There was no music, was there?'

Sniffy's tail waved left and then right. One ear drooped, the other stayed pert.

Evi set off back again. She was halfway across the bedroom when she stopped. She knew, beyond any doubt, that someone was watching her. She turned on the spot. Curtains drawn, doors closed, she was completely alone. She'd reached the bed when she heard the voice directly behind.

'Evi fall,' it said.

59

Sunday 20 January (two days earlier)
Next morning I felt massively better. After several hours of completely dreamless sleep, whatever germs I'd been fighting off appeared to have thrown in the towel. There was certainly no sign of any surreptitiously administered illegal drugs. Evi had been right to be cautious; luckily she'd been wrong.

I'd also had an idea. Bryony might have struck the match that nearly killed her, but clear evidence that she'd bought the petrol herself would indicate intent like nothing else. Lighting a match under the influence of drugs was one thing. Getting yourself to a petrol station, filling a can and paying for it was another entirely. I doubled-checked the CID report into the investigation following Bryony's suicide attempt. As I remembered, the receipt for a can of petrol had been found in Bryony's desk. I found the name of the petrol station and the date and time of the can's purchase. Then I got dressed and went out.

The snow had put a lot of motorists off leaving their houses and the garage on Station Road was quiet. A thin trickle of people coming in to buy milk and papers was exactly what I needed. Enough custom to be distracting, but not so much the counter staff would feel stressed. A young Asian man behind the counter watched me walk the length of the shop. I gave him an appraising look, figuring he was just about good-looking enough to be taken in by it. Then I grinned. He grinned back.

'Hi,' I said, when I was close enough to lean on the counter and pout. 'I'm Laura. I've come to look at your CCTV footage.'

His smile faded just perceptibly. 'Sorry?' he said.

I dug into my pocket and pulled out my university ID. 'No, I'm sorry,' I said. 'Here are my credentials. So you know I'm not a villain or anything. I'm doing a research project into how petrol stations are taking over from corner shops. I arranged with Mr Watson to pop in for ten minutes this morning. Just to do a random viewing of your recorded CCTV footage.'

'First I've heard of it,' he said, bristling.

'Really?' I said. 'You know, I'm not surprised. I've had ten places to visit this week and in over half the message didn't get through. Trouble is, I have to submit the results tomorrow. Still, not your fault. Bye.'

I was almost at the door and thinking it hadn't worked when he called me back.

'Do you just need to look at some stored footage?' he asked me.

I nodded. 'I've got some random dates and times that our software programme generated. Shouldn't take more than an hour.'

Forty minutes later I left. I'd watched the footage twice to be sure. Bryony had not been in the petrol station anywhere close to the time the petrol can had been bought. The only possible candidate for the purchase had been a tall bloke, who'd kept his face hidden beneath a hooded sweatshirt the whole time he'd been in the shop. He'd also kept whatever he was buying very close to his chest — literally — but when he turned to leave the camera got a pretty good shot at the thing he was clutching. Looked a lot like a petrol can to me.

By three o'clock I was back at Nick's house, standing outside the falcons' shed, having some sort of harness fitted round my shoulders.

'You're sure you're OK to do this?' he asked me for the third time. 'I can take the second lot out later while you're catching up on the *EastEnders* omnibus.'

'I don't believe your house even has electricity,' I said.

Nick lowered a square wooden frame over my shoulders and fastened it to the harness. On it, I'd been informed, I would carry three falcons. Nick would do the same. He disappeared into the shed and brought out a bird with a medieval-style leather hood covering its head. It settled on the wooden frame in front of me, its talons tied with thin leather strips. It ruffled its feathers in response to the cold but otherwise seemed completely at ease.

Ten minutes later, accompanied by the two pointers, Nick and I were striding down the snow-covered farm track further into the Cambridgeshire countryside.

'Why are they hooded?' I asked, as we climbed a stile into a ploughed field. Nick leaped over it as though he didn't have a live cargo slung around his waist. I went slowly, terrified of falling into a snowdrift and hurting one of the tiny creatures.

'Stops them getting distracted,' he said. 'If

they weren't blind, the minute we see any game they'd all want to be off. It'd be chaos.'

'So they take it in turns?' I asked. 'What happens, do we let them off and see what they can find? How long do they get before we give up and let another one have a go? And what stops them flying away and not coming back?'

'Lot of questions at once,' he replied. 'It's not uncommon for birds to be lost. You just have to give them enough of an incentive to come back. This lot have been trained since they were infants to associate me with food. That's why they come back, usually. As far as the hunting is concerned, they don't find the game, they just catch it.'

'So who finds it?' I asked.

We passed through a gate and Nick closed it behind me.

'We're on Jim Notley's land now and he's happy for me to hunt here, so we can start,' he said. 'OK, this is how it works. The dogs find the game. Watch them now.'

At a signal from Nick, Merry and Pippin ran on ahead and started sniffing around. Pippin disappeared from sight into a drift, occasionally sending up fountains of snow. Merry stayed where we could see him, poking his nose into rabbit holes, beneath brambles, under logs.

'We'll fly Arwen first,' Nick said, reaching out and taking the hood off the bird to his right. Getting its vision back, the falcon flapped its wings and gave a little hop. The other birds seemed to sense something going on. A little collective shiver passed from one to the other. Both dogs had disappeared from view.

'What are they looking for?' I asked. 'Rabbits?'

'Peregrines won't take prey from the ground,' said Nick. 'Some birds will, owls for instance, and buzzards, but peregrines have too much speed. If they hit the ground at over a hundred miles an hour they wouldn't survive. They have to take their prey on the wing. Steady, sweetheart.'

Arwen wanted to be off. She was straining against the tether, pecking at Nick. Keeping a tight hold of the straps, he lifted her off and put her on his forearm. We walked on, Nick holding his arm at right angles like a medieval huntsman, and I felt a ridiculous sense of anticipation. If someone had told me two weeks ago I'd be out falconing!

Then everything happened at once. One of the dogs started barking and a mass of flapping grey feathers shot into the air. Then Arwen was soaring into the sky like a bullet, wings that had seemed so light and delicate on the perch pumping her upwards with incredible force.

'She's seen it,' said Nick. 'Keep your eye on her.'

I tried, but it was over so quickly. The partridge — I learned later that's what it was — didn't stand a chance. The peregrine saw it, accelerated, and a couple of seconds later the mid-air collision took place twenty feet above us. I thought I heard the captured bird screaming, or it could have been Arwen howling in triumph, then the two began to plummet. For a moment I thought something had gone wrong, then Arwen's wings stretched out to slow her down. They landed and Nick picked up his pace to reach them.

The dogs beat us to it but stood waiting politely. Nick lowered his framework of birds to the ground, lifted Arwen off the dead partridge, and tethered her back on the frame. Then he pulled out a knife, cut the partridge's head off and offered it to Arwen, who sat, alert and eager, on his gloved hand.

'Are you squeamish?' he asked, as she tore the head apart in seconds and tiny speckles of red began to stain the snow. Smelling blood, the other birds grumbled and pulled against their tethers.

'I have my moments,' I said.

We flew the birds one by one. When Nick's had all had their turn and his game bag was filling up, he let me try. The trick was in keeping the bird calm until the moment for it to fly, then releasing it quickly and smoothly. Clearly there was a knack to it because my birds weren't nearly as successful as Nick's. By the time the last bird had flown, ribbons of pink and gold were strung across the sky and my legs, working extra hard because of the snow, were starting to ache. A sudden cry overhead made me look up to see three swans flying above us.

'I think we're done,' Nick said. 'If we follow the fence at this point, we can pick up a short cut.'

I was happy with that, so we made our way round the outskirts of a small copse. As we turned away from the sunset, the vista opened up for us again. About a mile away was a collection of large, low buildings.

'What's that?' I asked.

'Industrial estate,' Nick replied. 'Couple of miles outside Cambridge. We've walked quite a way.'

Between us and the estate was a long, narrow wood of beech trees. I could see a line of quivering willow trees too, telling me a river was close.

'I think that's where I had my buzzard encounter,' I said. 'And where your friend Jim Notley ordered me off his land, incidentally.'

Nick gave me a surprised look. 'He never told me.'

'I don't think he recognized me. I was in running gear.'

'That's a footpath down there,' Nick said. 'He shouldn't have ordered you off that.'

'I wasn't on the path,' I admitted. 'I'd gone into the woods to escape the blood-sucking feathered fiend.'

'Ah, well, that explains it. Jim's very protective about that copse. He has a lot of nesting pheasants in there.'

'In January?' I asked, not entirely sure when the pheasant breeding season was but thinking midwinter seemed a bit unlikely.

'Maybe it was force of habit,' Nick said. 'The ground round here's riddled with rabbit holes. Take care.'

'There was something odd about those woods,' I said. 'There were effigies.'

Nick stopped walking. 'There were what?' he said.

'Stuffed figures, hanging from trees. It was a bit freaky.'

He frowned at me. 'Are you sure?'

'No,' I said. 'It's possible they were something else entirely. A bit of sphagnum moss hanging from the trees and I just mistook them for human figures. And the dead animals strung up could have been, I don't know, litter from the industrial units. Possibly balloons; maybe your friend Jim's planning a party.'

'Dead animals?'

I shrugged and he started walking again.

'Jim's a bit odd but I haven't heard of anything like that before,' he said. 'Unless some kids have been hanging around. Maybe that's why he was a bit jumpy with you.'

That certainly seemed reasonable but I wasn't sure Jim was ever going to be a bosom friend. There'd been something unhinged about him.

'What was that?' I asked, stopping in my tracks and making Nick jump to one side to avoid walking into me. The sound had been low-pitched, metallic, almost mournful.

'Ask not for whom the bell tolls,' Nick said, stepping closer to me. The wind, gentle for such a cold day, blew in our faces.

'There's a church near here?' I'd known it was a bell the second it had sounded up. It had just seemed so unlikely in the middle of the Cambridgeshire countryside.

'That's the foundry bell,' said Nick.

Bell, Bryony had written.

'Foundries don't have bells.'

'The whole estate is built on the site of an old Victorian bell foundry. Why do you think it's called Bell Foundries Industrial Estate?'

'I didn't know it was.' I'd assumed Bell was a person, that Nick Bell was probably the one Bryony was scared of. I'd never thought it would be an actual bell.

'What you can hear is an ancient iron bell hanging from the wall of the old factory building,' Nick said, taking my arm and steering me towards home. 'You can only hear it when the wind's in the right direction.'

Which it was now. As we headed for home I could hear the low, sonorous clanging, eerie, like the sound of a ghost ship about to materialize out of fog.

60

At three o'clock, when the sun was low in the sky, Evi and the dog that was already answering to Sniffy went outside. There were tracks in the snow from Sniffy's earlier explorations. And two none-too-fragrant little presents from previous calls of nature. As Sniffy padded round, poking her nose under shrubs and squatting periodically to leave pools of yellow in the snow, Evi walked the length of where she judged the path would be.

At the bottom of the garden was a low brick wall with an iron gate that led to the river bank and a tiny landing stage. Tied to a post and covered in tarpaulin was a small canoe. Evi had plans, when she was feeling better, to take up canoeing. Her arms were as strong as anyone's and there was no reason why she wouldn't make a reasonably good canoeist.

If she ever felt better again.

She'd spent most of the night huddled under the duvet, waiting for painkillers she shouldn't have taken to kick in or for the amitriptyline to knock her out. The dog had joined her on the bed and Evi hadn't the heart to push her off. Sniffy's presence soothed her somehow, even though it was the dog, more than anything, that was making Evi believe that Laura's first instinct might have been right after all. That she was nuts.

Because Sniffy had been completely unperturbed, either by the music or by the voice. There couldn't have been anyone in the house, playing music and speaking to her, because the dog would have heard, sensed or smelled them. The only conclusion left was that the music and the voice had been in Evi's head.

Excited by the snow, Sniffy was leaping around the garden now, digging with her front paws, hurling snow into the air with her nose. She raced down to the wall, turned and sped back again. She was very fast.

A few hours before dawn, Evi had fallen into an exhausted doze, only to be woken at seven when Sniffy needed to go out. Laura had called round mid-morning, as promised, to take her out for a run. They'd been gone for an hour and had returned drenched in sweat and trembling with exhaustion.

Exercise-induced weariness aside, Laura had been looking hugely better that morning. She'd slept well and thought she was managing to shake off whatever bug had been threatening. Her sleep hadn't been disturbed by a single dream.

Evi had said nothing about her own night.

After Laura had left, Evi had called Jessica's friends in St Catharine's to see if they'd heard from her. They hadn't. At six o'clock that evening, they told her, Jessica's tutor would contact the police. Evi sent a short email to the tutor stating that, in her opinion, Jessica was a vulnerable person who needed to be located as a matter of priority.

Evi fall.

Before coming out, Evi had wrapped her thickest coat round her shoulders. She'd pulled on gloves and a scarf. None of them stopped her shivering. Twice now, once on a mountain in Austria, once in a new house in Lancashire, she'd almost died after a fall. Sometimes she dreamed that she was falling. She never hit the ground in her dreams but in those few seconds it always felt as though this was how it was meant to be.

That Evi was destined to fall to her death.

No one could have learned that on the internet. No one could have Googled Evi Oliver and discovered that the song with the power to break her heart was Springsteen's 'Dancing in the Dark'. No one could have found out that she hated fir cones. Laura had been wrong. This wasn't someone bent on revenge, or even someone down here trying to stop her from rocking the boat. She was losing her grip on reality. Going nuts. It was as simple as that.

61

'You're very quiet,' said Nick, topping up my wine glass.

'I had a new experience today,' I said, managing a smile. 'That usually makes me thoughtful.'

Thoughtful didn't nearly cover it. Bryony had named a bell as something she was scared of. Scott Thornton, a man with unusual hobbies involving female humiliation, had visited an industrial estate named after an old bell foundry. Had I found a connection? And was it significant enough for me to break Joesbury's embargo on contact?

We were in the large old-fashioned kitchen of Nick's house. I'd helped him settle the birds in their shed and feed them; an interesting, if slightly gory experience, given that they ate dead chicks and pieces of the game we'd caught that wouldn't make the grade as human food. After the birds were sorted, Nick mixed up three buckets of horse feed and gave one to the grey gelding, Shadowfax. He usually rode him early in the morning, he told me, with the dogs going along for the exercise. I was beginning to feel as though I'd stepped into the pages of *Country Life.*

By the time we finished supper I knew I should really get back, phone Evi, check whether there was any news on Jessica and try once more to re-establish contact with the elusive Mark Joesbury.

'Anything you want to share?' Nick asked me.

On the other hand, they all had my mobile number. And I really needed to strike Nick off my list of prime suspects if I could. 'You know this thing Evi Oliver's been worried about,' I said. 'The suicides?'

Nick gave a theatrical sigh, but put his glass down and leaned back on his chair. 'Go on,' he said.

'You know she's been talking about suicide websites and online goading.'

He nodded.

'Well, let's just say that it's a bit more organized than that. What if someone is actually targeting vulnerable people, then making their lives as miserable as possible?'

'With the sole intent of driving them over

the edge?' said Nick, a tiny smile on his face that told me he thought I was being fanciful.

'Yes. Is it possible, in theory, to spot potential suicides?'

'That's really a question for Evi,' said Nick.

'You're right,' I said, putting both hands on the table in front of me, as though I were about to stand up. 'I'll go ask her.'

Beneath the table, first one long leg, and then the other, wrapped themselves around my ankle. I wasn't going anywhere.

'Anyone suffering severe emotional pain, for whatever reason, must be a potential suicide,' said Nick. 'But that's a lot of people. Very few of whom, fortunately, will take the ultimate step.'

'How do you find them, though? They don't wear badges.'

'It's not difficult to spot someone with problems. Anyone with half a brain can do it. You, for example.'

'Me?'

One hand reached out and covered mine. 'You're hiding a dark secret,' he said. 'Going to tell me what it is?'

Where would I start? 'So it's just a question of finding someone with issues and getting to know them better,' I said. 'Finding out what buttons to press?' I was thinking of what Evi had told me about Jessica, the girl with an eating disorder who'd been publicly teased about her weight. Nicole had been afraid of rats and had been teased about it.

'That would be the minimum, in my view. The survival instinct is pretty strong in most people.'

'So what else? If you were going to drive someone to suicide how would you do it?'

'Making them live in this house from December through February would be a start,' he said.

'Seriously.'

'Can we talk about something nice soon? Like the fact that the skin just below your collar bone looks like the perfect place to warm my cold nose.'

'You've been spending too much time with your dogs. Come on, how?'

'Seriously,' he said, 'I'd attack their body and their mind simultaneously. I'd find out what they were afraid of and then feed their fears.'

'How?' I said.

He gave his head a funny, sideways shake. 'Blimey, I don't know,' he said. 'Give me a minute to think about it. OK, let's say they're afraid of spiders. I'd fill their houses with them, every night. Get them permanently on edge.'

'And their bodies?'

'Sleep and food deprivation would work fastest, but quite how you do it without making it obvious I don't know. Pain would also be pretty effective. Dealing with severe pain on a regular basis is a lot for anyone to cope with. Lots of suicides have major pain issues.'

'If someone has found a way to do this, anonymously . . .'

Nick pushed himself back from the table. 'Laura, what are you getting into?' he asked me. 'You've only been here a week. You have a huge amount of catching up to do. If you end up blowing your chance here because Evi has dragged you into some hare-brained scheme . . .'

'Evi isn't an idiot,' I said, and I was actually a bit annoyed that he didn't seem to be taking me seriously.

'I know she's not. And, if you must know, I'm going to bring this up tomorrow morning at our partners' meeting. If I can get their support, we can make a joint approach to the university and the police. I also happen to know, because Evi called me this afternoon, that the coroner is concerned. These people between them will find anything there is to find and they'll deal with it. It's not your problem.'

Now he was starting to sound like Joesbury. Which probably went more towards convincing me he was genuine than anything I'd learned so far. 'You're right,' I said. 'Sorry, I get a bit intense at times.'

'I think Laura Farrow is probably the loveliest name I've ever come across,' he said.

Oh, this was getting a little beyond my comfort zone. If this man wasn't playing me, trying to find out what I knew, then it was starting to look as though he actually liked me. And I'd been going along with it, letting him think the two of us had a chance at a relationship. Loveliest name he'd ever . . . Laura Farrow didn't even exist.

'Do you realize that if you drink any more of that wine, you won't be able to drive home?' he asked me. 'And I can't leave the dogs at night to drive you. They panic.'

I looked down. The glass was large and it was my third of the evening. What Nick didn't know was that most of the previous two had been poured down the kitchen sink when he'd been out of the room. I may indulge in casual sex but I never do it drunk. As though it belonged to someone else, I watched my hand reach out towards the glass and raise it to my lips.

62

Monday 21 January (one day earlier)
I woke in darkness, with no idea where I was. Blue cotton sheets. A man's bed.

'Laura,' said a voice behind my head. I turned. Nick was in the doorway, a mug of steaming liquid in each hand. He was dressed in a shirt and tie, neatly creased black trousers, ready for work.

'I forgot to ask whether you drink tea or coffee in the morning,' he said. 'So I brought both.'

He put both mugs down on a bedside table that rocked dangerously under their weight. 'It's almost eight,' he said. 'I have surgery at nine and I expect you have lectures.'

It was Monday morning. 'The good news is that there's lots of hot water in the bathroom,' he said. 'The bad being that the rest of the house is freezing. See you downstairs.' He stood up and turned to the door. Then he stopped and came back to squat down beside the bed. He leaned forward and kissed me. 'Good morning,' he said.

'Morning,' I replied, conscious of smudged make-up and seriously bad breath.

'So for future reference,' he said, 'which is it? Tea or coffee?'

'Both,' I replied. He grinned at me and left the room.

I sat up. Oh boy, he hadn't been kidding. The room was so cold it felt as though my face and shoulders were being slapped. I took a deep breath and pulled the covers back, swinging my legs over the side before I could change my mind.

My clothes were scattered around the thick sheepskin rug in front of the fire. I knelt on the rug, hoping some warmth might have survived the night, and found underwear, socks and my sweater.

Last night the fire had blazed as Nick had kissed me. I'd watched bold, darting flames licking over the logs as he'd slowly unbuttoned my blouse. He'd pulled off his own shirt and then both his skin and mine had glowed in the firelight. Sparks had shot into the air like fireworks when the heat found a damp piece of wood. And I'd known I couldn't go through with it.

'I'm sorry,' I'd said, stepping back and bracing myself for a fight, even if just a verbal one. 'I guess I'm just not ready. I'll go.'

Looking round now, I found my jeans slung over an old-fashioned CD player. I hadn't been allowed to drive home. Nick still thought I'd drunk more than I really had and I could hardly disillusion him. Gallantly, he'd left me in his own room and taken himself off to a spare.

As the flames had died down and the embers began to gleam like fire opals, I'd fallen asleep. I'd dreamed of gently stroking hands, probing fingers, soft kisses running the length of my spine. And when, in my dream, I'd opened my eyes, the ones looking back into mine hadn't been russet brown.

My boots would be downstairs.

Pulling the bedcovers straight, I stepped out into the corridor. The first door I tried was locked. The second was the bathroom. The mirror told me my eye make-up had smudged but not appallingly so. My hair was a mess but I told myself in a sexy sort of way. The water was hot but I wasn't getting undressed again in this icebox Nick called home so I splashed some over my face and used the loo. I would sort myself out when I got back to St John's.

Sipping on the tea, holding the coffee in my other hand, I made my way downstairs. I'd never woken up in a man's bedroom before. It was more my style to go home with a man, have sex with him, say goodbye and leave. I had no idea how to handle a morning after. Could I just go? Dump the mugs down, slip out of the door and drive away without seeing him?

Apparently not. Because to do that I'd have to cross the kitchen and he was in it, slicing bread that smelled like it had been baked that morning. I could hear the gurgle of a coffee machine. This room, thank God, was pleasantly warm, most of the heat coming from an ancient-looking Aga against one wall. Both pointers were curled on a rug in front of it. They both looked up as I came in. One of them gave me a merry wag of the tail. The other sighed heavily and settled down again, uninterested. A woman in the house in the morning wasn't anything they hadn't seen before.

Nick had set the table for two. There was a glass of orange juice at the place that I guessed must be mine. As I sat down, he ran the bread knife through the brown loaf in the middle of the table again. The yeasty smell intensified. As did the feeling that I'd woken up on Mars.

'Were you up at five baking?' I asked.

'I was up at five mucking out the horse, walking the dogs and checking the birds,' he told me. 'The bread is courtesy of the bread machine. I set the timer before we went up.'

The butter practically sizzled when it made contact with the warm slice of bread he'd offered me. I didn't have to spread, it was just going to ooze its way across the surface.

'Liz Notley's hedgerow jam,' he said, pushing a jar of red stuff towards me. 'Excellent.'

'Do I want to know what's in hedgerow jam?' I took a bite by way of experiment and, in fairness, it was excellent.

'Mainly blackberries,' he replied. 'Some wild apples, sloes, hips and haws.'

Hips and haws? I wasn't going to ask. 'So, you're gorgeous, you're a GP and you bake your own bread,' I said. 'I guess the catch must be your embarrassing taste in music. Were we listening to Billy Joel last night?'

He made a sheepish face. 'You got me,' he said. 'We used to play it around the house a lot when I was a kid. I guess it reminds me of Mum. Another one?'

And he'd loved his mother! I let him cut

me another slice of bread. I felt as though I could eat the whole loaf if it was offered. If this was what mornings after were like — blimey, they were quite nice.

'Lucky for me you were snoring before Neil Diamond came on,' he said.

That took a second to register. 'I don't snore.'

'You do,' he said. 'I could hear you from the corridor. But only in a cute, snuffly, dormouse sort of way.' He raised his wrist and looked at the slim, elegant man's watch he wore. 'We have to hustle,' he said. 'Can I call you tonight?'

He found my coat and boots and ushered me out of the house and into my car. The two pointers went with him, jumping into the back of his Range Rover. He set off along the pothole-strewn path and I followed more slowly, not sure how much punishment my suspension could cope with, or how I was going to deal with the turn events had taken. I'd started this investigation with no real idea of what it had in store for me, but what I really hadn't expected was that I'd find myself with a boyfriend.

Or, at nearly twenty-eight years old, with the knowledge that I snore.

63

I drove back to St John's, parked the car and jumped out, knowing that if I didn't run I'd be late for my first lecture. All around me, people had the same idea. Bikes were speeding past, people hurrying through the rear gates. Just one solitary figure wasn't moving. A tall man, padded coat concealing his muscular build, woollen hat pulled down over his ears, was leaning against one of the gate's pillars.

I needed to touch base with Evi before I went out again, find out the latest on Jessica. I also wanted to check emails.

The man in the padded jacket straightened up when he saw me coming and stepped into my path. I slowed down.

Turquoise eyes were looking directly into mine. Don't give him a chance, I told myself. Get in there first. Ask him where the hell he's been, how he can just abandon you like that. I couldn't say a word. All I could do was to look into his eyes and wish something large and heavy would fall down from the old building and knock me into oblivion. I stopped three feet away and waited for him to start. It was going to be bad. He was going to say things I'd never be able to forget.

'Good morning,' Joesbury said. 'How are you?'

'Fine,' I replied, still bracing myself for the blow. 'You?'

He actually smiled. 'Couldn't be better,' he said. 'New orders for you, Flint. Go to your room, pack your bags and drive yourself back to London. Report to the Yard nine o'clock tomorrow for a debrief.'

It took me a second to take it in. 'I'm not sure I . . .'

'Don't contact your room-mate, Dr Oliver, or any of the people in college. Above all, don't attempt to contact Nick Bell. If you do, we'll know.'

I'd expected it to be bad. I hadn't expected this.

'What's going on?'

He sighed and looked at his watch. 'You're off the case,' he said. 'I want you out of Cambridge within the hour.'

'Oh, screw you, Joesbury.'

OK, that wasn't wise, I know that, but I

wasn't having him pulling rank on me when we both knew what this was about. He barely blinked. 'Excuse me?' he said.

'You can't kick me off the case because I spent the night with someone.'

And then he laughed. 'Get over yourself, Flint,' he said. 'The only interest I have in your boyfriend is that he's taken your mind off the job and seriously jeopardized your cover. The decision's made.'

'There's something I need to tell you,' I began.

He held up one hand. 'Save it for the Yard, Flint. That'll be soon enough.'

I wasn't going to win this. I had to turn and leave now if I wanted to retain any shred of dignity. But I took a step closer. I could smell coffee on his breath.

'I think you need a reality check,' I said. 'Students have sex. They're known for it. My room-mate never sleeps in her own bed.'

He leaned away as though I still had morning breath. I probably did. 'No, I'm giving you a reality check,' he said. 'Sending you here was a massive mistake. You've disobeyed orders from the moment you arrived. You've persistently run around like some sort of demented Nancy Drew, poking your nose in everywhere and threatening to jeopardize months of work. Your antics yesterday were the last straw.'

Three girls passing looked at us curiously. It was pretty obvious to everyone in the vicinity that we were rowing. I didn't care. Something he'd just said had made my ears prick up like a fox hound's.

'What do you mean, months of work?'

For the first time, he couldn't look me in the eye. 'You have nothing like the focus needed for this sort of operation,' he said to the snow at our feet. 'I want your bags packed in thirty minutes.'

'What do you mean, months of work? What the hell is going on here?'

He turned away, tried to walk off. I wasn't having it. I grabbed his arm and pulled him back.

He took a deep breath. 'Take your hands off me,' he said, 'or I'll stick you on.'

Stick me on meant make an official complaint. I was past caring. I stepped closer. 'What job have I taken my mind off?' I insisted. 'What exactly is the job here, Joesbury? Every time I send you information, you tell me to butt out, that I'm not investigating, that there's nothing to investigate, to keep my eyes open and my head down. Now you're telling me I've messed up months of work.'

Getting this close gave him the perfect opportunity to look down and sneer. 'How come every time we get close, you stink of another man?'

I was going to break his nose for that the second I had a chance. In the meantime . . .

'Women are being drugged and abused and raped,' I said. 'They're disappearing from college and turning up seriously fucked up. Then they're dying. Someone is doing this and you know it, don't you? But every time I try to help, you say the same thing. Don't interfere, don't ask questions, just keep up the good-looking fruitcake act . . . Wait a minute . . .'

As my hands released him, Joesbury stepped back. He dropped his eyes to the ground and ran a hand over his face.

'You set me up,' I said.

'Lacey . . .'

'I'm bait,' I said, and half of me was praying he'd deny it. 'That's it, isn't it? I can't believe you'd do that to me again.'

Even I knew enough about undercover work to know that officers were never sent into operations without being fully apprised of the facts. Joesbury had broken a major rule by keeping me in the dark. He turned his back on me and looked up at the sky. I watched his shoulders rise and fall and knew that I'd have done it anyway, if he'd asked. But to know he'd put me in danger without even . . .

'You put me in Bryony's room, made me as conspicuous as possible,' I said. 'You know what's going on here. You know why women are ending up dead. When would you have stepped in, sir? When my corpse came floating down the Cam?'

He turned back. The skin around his eyes was red. 'Lacey, I wanted to tell you,' he said. 'I have to obey orders too.'

I'd never heard Joesbury sound pathetic before. 'I'm next on the list, aren't I?' I said. 'Jessica will turn up dead sometime in the next couple of days and then it's my turn. I've already had the college hazing ritual and the weird hallucinogenic dreams. Evi thought I'd been drugged two days ago. I told her she was wrong. Looks like she wasn't.'

His face stiffened. 'What do you mean, you've been drugged?'

'Oh, like you didn't know. Apparently I was displaying all the symptoms of recreational drug use. As was Bryony, as were Nicole and Jessica. I have no idea how they do it, but you know, don't you? You know!'

Joesbury pulled himself together. He stepped closer, took my arm and started to frogmarch me down the path. 'OK, I need you to stop yelling now, Flint. They'd never have targeted you this quickly. If you really have been drugged, it means they know who you are. Who have you told?'

So now everything was my fault. 'No one, you prat. Evi knows, that's all.'

'What about your boyfriend?'

'Thinks I'm Laura Farrow.'

'This is serious. You're leaving now.' He half walked, half dragged me back to where I'd left the car and waited while I opened it up.

'Go to the Yard now,' he told me. 'Report to DCI Phillips. I'll meet you there later.'

'What about my room?' I said. 'My stuff?'

'I'll sort it. Now go.'

I got into the car, started the engine and looked at him. Maybe I wanted to see if he really meant it. He raised one arm and pointed in the direction of the M11. He did. He was an arrogant, unreasonable bastard but he was my senior officer. I started the engine and drove along the road without looking back. As I turned the corner, my phone rang. It was Evi.

'Can you meet me at the hospital?' she said. 'I'm on my way there now. Jessica's turned up.'

64

I almost walked past the woman in the wheelchair on the second-floor corridor before realizing that it was Evi. We both stopped and faced each other.

'She's dead, isn't she?' I asked, in a low voice.

In response, Evi blinked away tears and I knew she was searching for the right words. I crouched down so my face was on a level with hers. Her lovely creamy skin looked like paper and her eyes seemed to have lost all their colour. The frown line between her brows deepened.

'She isn't dead,' she told me. 'Physically, she's not too bad. Mentally is another story entirely.'

Not dead? But that figured. Nicole had come back from her disappearance. For a while.

'What has she told us?' I asked. 'Where has she been?'

Evi shook her head. 'Let's talk when we've seen her,' she said. 'Do you mind pushing me? I'm not feeling too great.'

Given how she looked, I'd have called that an understatement. She barely had the strength to hold herself upright in the chair. I stood up, took hold of the chair's handles, and we set off.

'She was found in her room at St Catharine's first thing this morning,' Evi told me after a few seconds. 'The door was slightly ajar, one of her neighbours poked her head in and found Jessica fully dressed on the bed. She called me first. I called the ambulance.'

A little out of breath, Evi gave herself a minute.

'She was conscious for the thirty minutes the ambulance took to arrive and said nothing helpful,' she went on as we turned a corner and narrowly avoided running into a porter pushing an elderly woman along on a bed. 'She claims to have no idea where she's been or what she's been doing for the past five days. She didn't even know what day it was.'

We came to the nurses' station and were directed to a door at the end of the corridor. As I let go of the chair handles to push the door open I caught sight of the people inside. A girl with fair hair asleep on the bed, and Nick Bell standing at its foot. He'd been staring down at the girl with a frown on his face. When he looked up and saw us, his face cleared.

'Hi,' he mouthed at me. Then he turned to Evi. 'Everything stable,' he said. 'Nobody's unduly worried. They've taken bloods and salivas like you asked. They've asked for results later today if possible. And a police doctor's on her way to do an intimate examination.'

'Has she said anything?' asked Evi.

'Got very agitated when she arrived here, apparently,' he said. 'Rambling about wooden clowns or something.'

'She's scared of clowns,' said Evi. 'Did they sedate her?'

He nodded. 'Ten milligrams of diazepam intravenously. She'll be out for a couple of hours.'

I had to bite my lip. We needed to talk to Jessica now.

'I'm having her transferred to the psychiatric ward as soon as they have a room free,' said Evi.

'You're admitting her?' Nick looked surprised.

Evi nodded. 'And putting her on suicide watch. She was a serious risk before she disappeared, in my view. I'm taking no chances.'

Nick looked at the girl on the bed and then back at Evi. 'Her parents will be here later today,' he said. 'They might not be too keen on that idea.'

I opened my mouth and closed it again. An undergraduate student would not get involved in a professional disagreement between two medics.

'Tough,' said Evi. 'I'm keeping this one alive.'

Nick looked at me. 'Laura, can you give me a minute with Evi?' he asked.

I gave Evi a don't-you-give-in look and left the room. Leaning against the corridor wall, I could see Nick, through the room's window, crouched in front of Evi, arguing with her. He did it gently, though, at one point putting his hand on her arm in a concerned gesture. She seemed to be trying to reassure him. I looked at my watch. I should have been on the M11 by now, speeding towards London.

In the room, Nick straightened up, patted Evi's arm and opened the door. 'I'm already late for morning surgery,' he said to me, as the door to Jessica's room closed behind him. 'Any chance of seeing you tonight?'

Difficult to think of anything less likely. If

I wasn't in Scotland Yard arguing for my job by the time night fell, I'd be in my own flat in London looking through Situations Vacant. 'If only,' I said. 'I've got a lot of notes to catch up on.'

'I'll call you at nine,' he said. 'See if I can't persuade you over for a late supper.' He gave me a quick kiss on the cheek and disappeared off down the corridor. Pushing aside the nagging thought that I might never see him again, I went back into the room. Evi had pushed her chair to Jessica's bedside.

'We need to talk to her,' I said. 'I can stay with her until she wakes up.'

What was I thinking of? If I wasn't in London before midday, my career was probably over.

'Better if I do that,' Evi said. 'She knows me. But if there's been no improvement on an hour ago, she won't be able to tell us anything.'

I stepped closer and took my first real look at Jessica. At blonde corkscrew curls, skin like milky coffee, a slender, five-foot-seven-inch frame.

'How are they doing it?' I said. 'How do they find the pretty, vulnerable girls in the first place and then know which buttons to press?'

Evi shook her head. Too quickly, it seemed to me.

'They have medical expertise, don't they?' I said. 'You've thought of that yourself, you just didn't want to say. The drugs, the psychiatric history, it all fits.'

Evi sighed. 'I have,' she admitted. 'And there's something I haven't told you.'

I looked round, spotted a visitor's chair and sat in it. Even when my eyes were on a level with Evi's she still found it difficult to look at me.

'Fifteen years ago, when I was an under-graduate, there were five student suicides in one year,' she said. 'The only time until recently the figures have spiked at all. I mentioned it to Francis Warrener on Saturday and he remembered them. He also checked back through his old files. The authorities at the time were convinced bullying was a factor but they couldn't prove anything.'

I waited, not sure where she was going. Fifteen years was a long time.

'Three of the five were medical students,' Evi went on. 'From three different colleges, so the common denominator was the course they were doing.'

I waited some more.

'I know of four medical students from

those days who are still at the university,' Evi said. 'I'm one of them. My friend Megan Prince, like me a practising psychiatrist, is another. Nick Bell's a third. Do you see now why I didn't want to say anything?'

'You said four. Was Scott Thornton the other?'

'How did you . . . ?' Evi sighed and nodded her head.

'Another friend of yours?' I asked.

'Not really. I didn't know him at all fifteen years ago. We say hello if we bump into each other but that's all. I know it looks bad but I just can't see it, Laura. I know and trust both Nick and Meg. And Scott Thornton saved Bryony. He was the one who put the flames out and summoned help when everyone else was just in shock.'

Of course he was. I knew I'd heard that name somewhere before. I'd read it in the report Joesbury had given me the night he'd briefed me on the case.

'OK,' I said. 'Let's just pursue the medicin-general angle before we get bogged down with specific practitioners. Could it be someone here, at the hospital?'

'The girls would only be on the hospital's records if they'd been admitted,' Evi said. 'I don't remember many instances of hospitalization, do you?'

'No. What about a GP?' I said.

'There are twenty different practices in Cambridge,' Evi told me. 'Patient information is confidential to each one. We can double-check if any practice had more of the victims than others but I think we'd have spotted it already.'

She was right, we would have done.

'They're getting into these girls' heads somehow,' I said. 'Could it be someone at your clinic? A counsellor would be in the best position to know what freaks someone out, wouldn't they?'

'I've thought of that, too,' Evi told me. 'Only about half of the girls came to us for counselling. Even if someone at SCS has been hacking into his or her colleagues' confidential files, they wouldn't have found anything on the other half.'

I thought about that for a second. 'I think I sort of assumed everyone at the university was somehow on your system,' I said.

'What gave you that idea?' Evi asked me.

'Well, probably that questionnaire your department sent round,' I said. 'I thought it said it went to all new students.'

'What questionnaire?' said Evi.

I looked at her, saw what was probably my own expression reflected on her face and dug into my bag for my laptop. 'Give me a sec,' I said, finding the email with its attachment that I'd received and completed a week ago. 'There,' I said, giving Evi the laptop.

She looked at the screen. Her frown lines deepened and she tapped her middle finger on the scroll-down button a couple of times. Finally, 'I've never seen this before,' she said. 'This is nothing to do with the counselling services. There's a whole section on phobias and irrational fears.'

'Christ.' I turned, walked to the window, giving myself time to think. 'We can't rule Megan, Nick and Thornton out,' I said. 'Between them they easily have the medical and psychiatric knowledge needed.'

'Scott Thornton redesigned the medical faculty's IT system about six months ago,' said Evi. 'He's got the IT skills.'

The sky outside was the colour of unpolished silver and seemed to be pressing down closer to earth. I had a similar feeling in my head, as though there wasn't enough space for all the information trying to cram itself in. Oh boy, had I picked the right day to fall out with my senior officer.

A sudden movement made me look round. Evi seemed to be spasming in her chair, a look of intense pain on her face. 'Laura, could you give me my bag, please?' she gasped.

Her bag was two feet away from her on the floor. I picked it up and handed it over, then watched Evi fumble inside before popping two oval-shaped pills into her mouth. The second made her choke. She coughed and wheezed for the few moments it took me to fetch a glass of water from the sink in the corner. I handed it over and she drank for several seconds. When she was calmer she looked at me with tears in her eyes.

'What on earth do we do?' she asked me, and something about how vulnerable she looked helped me decide.

'You can make sure Jessica's OK,' I said. 'You're going to admit her, right? Does that mean she'll be safe? That no one can get at her?'

Evi was looking scared. 'Yes, of course,' she said. 'The psychiatric wards are secure. They're kept locked and the patients are watched all the time.'

'Then I think you should go home and rest. Later, if you feel up to it, you can try to dig up names of people who studied medicine here fifteen years ago,' I went on. 'We can go through the list together, see if anyone stands out. And I'd like you to give me Megan Prince's address, if you know it.

I already have Thornton's. And Nick's,' I added after a second.

'Why, what are you . . .'

I shook my head. 'I've involved you enough in this already. You're clearly not well.'

Evi shook her head. 'I'm fine,' she said.

'No, you're not. You're ill,' I told her. 'Listen, I have to go now but I'll come round later to walk the dog and see how you are. In the meantime, if Jessica says anything else, call me.'

Evi agreed that she would and I left the hospital. Back in my car, I dialled Joesbury's number and held my breath. After two seconds I got a recorded message.

'It's me,' I said. 'I'm still in town. I have good reason. Call me.'

I set off again, wondering if plans to do a spot of breaking and entering were going to cut it with Joesbury.

65

Scott Thornton lived in St Clement's Road, a row of brick-built terraced houses about a mile outside the city centre. The red Saab was nowhere in sight.

The whole twisted business here was finally starting to take some sort of pattern. The psychological torture and abuse of young women immediately prior to their deaths was almost certainly the ongoing crime that SO10 were investigating here. How it was all being orchestrated I still had no idea. Nor could I begin to explain why it was happening. Thank God, though, I at last had a lead on who was doing it.

After thirty minutes I decided the house was probably empty. Time to get a closer look. I climbed out of the car and walked up the street. The house had three floors, including the basement. To the right of the front door were three tall rectangular windows, each directly above the next. No lights behind any of them. No sign of movement.

At the rear were narrow, walled gardens with high wooden gates and a cobbled alleyway. When I reached 108 I took a quick look round and vaulted up and over the gate.

Snow in the small back garden was largely untouched but I managed to follow the footprints of someone who'd taken a walk to the dustbins and back. Two performance bikes were chained up near the back door. I turned to the gate I'd just climbed over. Three bolts, at the top, halfway down and at the bottom, seemed like overkill for a garden.

Through the glass of the door I could see the kitchen. Not particularly tidy or clean but otherwise a perfectly normal kitchen. The door was locked, with two deadlocks. I leaned over to look in through the window.

There was no way I was breaking into this house. The window had a state-of-the-art lock on it, and from what I could see by straining forward, so did the door. As well as the deadlocks, there were bolts top and bottom. Scott took home security very seriously. Which was interesting in itself, I thought.

'Any change?' I asked Evi.

I was back at the hospital, outside Jessica's room. From St Clement's Road I'd driven to the cottage on the outskirts of town where Megan Prince lived. Once again, impressive home security but nothing out of the ordinary that I could see. As I'd watched the cottage from a distance, a tall, dark-haired man had left the house and driven away. Megan didn't appear to live alone. After a few minutes I'd headed for Evi's house, found she wasn't home, and come straight back here.

I'd tried twice to get in touch with Joesbury and left two more messages. If he was in contact with Scotland Yard, he would know by now that I hadn't arrived. I'd heard nothing from him.

Jessica, in the meantime, had been moved to a secure floor and was being watched 24/7. She was as safe as we could make her. A woman constable from local CID had interviewed her briefly but had learned nothing other than that Jessica couldn't remember where she'd been for the past five days.

'Her parents arrived an hour ago,' Evi

said. She was still in her wheelchair. She pushed it over to a row of hard chairs so that I could sit beside her. 'They want to take her home but I've persuaded them it's not a good idea for now,' she continued. 'The blood tests showed levels of DMT in her bloodstream, which she claims she's never heard of, never mind taken. She agreed to an intimate examination but it showed nothing. She was actually very clean which, given that she's been missing for five days, is odd in itself.'

'They washed her to get rid of the evidence,' I said, in a low voice, as an elderly couple walked past.

Evi looked troubled. No sign of her disagreeing.

'What's the last thing she can remember?' I asked. 'Before she disappeared?'

'Coming to see me is the clearest thing in her head,' Evi replied. 'She has a vague recollection of going to meet someone about a study group, but can't give me any details. All a bit hopeless, I'm afraid.'

'Anything else?'

'She's jumpy, nervous as anything. Especially with men, but she knew who I was. She did say something quite odd, though: she asked me if I was real. Wasn't convinced until she could actually touch me. Then she just started talking about terrible dreams again. Terrible dreams that she couldn't remember.'

We both thought about that for a second. Dreams? Or not dreams?

Evi took a deep breath, as though bracing herself for some exertion, then shook her head. 'Tomorrow, if she's up to it and she and her parents are happy, we can try a form of hypnosis to see if we can release any memories. It's unreliable, though, and not normally the sort of thing I'd try until she's had much more time to recover.'

'And how are you? I had hoped you might have gone home.'

She managed to smile at me. She was a whole lot tougher than she looked. 'I'm much better, thanks,' she said, giving a quick look right and left to check we were alone in the corridor. 'And I did some digging around on a borrowed laptop. Nick, Meg and Scott were all at Trinity College when they studied here, so that seemed the place to start. There were twenty medical students in Trinity that year and I managed to track down most of them.'

'Blimey, that was good going.'

'Oh, it wasn't difficult. There are alumni organizations that produce directories every year, professional bodies to apply to. Anyway, four are now working abroad, two have gone into other professions and one died a couple of years ago. The rest are either GPs, working in hospitals, or teaching at other universities. They're scattered around the UK, the nearest being in Stevenage.'

'So we can probably rule them out,' I said.

A party of young doctors in crisp green scrubs appeared round the corner. We waited for them to pass by.

'The only one I couldn't find was a chap called Iestyn Thomas. He left Cambridge before he graduated and seems to have disappeared. He'd be thirty-six now, same as Meg and Nick.'

'Thin, geeky chap,' I said. 'Everyone thought he was a bit odd.'

Evi's eyes narrowed. 'To be honest, I'm not sure I ever met him. Why do you say that?'

'Nick mentioned someone like that,' I said and quickly filled Evi in with the story of the teenager who'd found his father's dead body, and then gone on to torment a school-mate, quite literally, to death.

'But Thomas, if that's who it was, was telling this story about someone he'd met,' Evi reminded me when I'd finished. 'Not about himself.'

'Supposedly.'

'Worth checking out?'
'Absolutely it is.'

It didn't take us long. We went to the visitors' cafeteria, ordered coffee and sandwiches and found a quiet table to log on to the hospital wifi on Evi's borrowed laptop.

One of the national papers had covered the story briefly, confirming what I'd already suspected, that the family was Welsh. Then it was just a question of trawling through various Welsh newspapers to pin them down. The website AberystwythOnline had archived its old footage and the story had been covered in some detail. The Thomases had been a professional family who'd lived in an old manor house not far from Aberystwyth on the West Wales coast. Both parents had worked at the university until the father was forced to retire in his late forties on health grounds.

'What's fibromyalgia?' I asked Evi.

'A degenerative muscle disease,' she replied. 'More common in women but men get it too. I had a patient once who was a sufferer. I was treating her for depression. It can be quite painful and debilitating.'

Early one Wednesday morning, when his wife was out of the house (the story hinted she'd been having an affair with a work colleague), Bryn Thomas had taken a loaded shotgun into his study and pulled the trigger. His three-year-old daughter, typically the earliest riser in the house, found him shortly afterwards. Two hours later, his teenage son had come downstairs.

'Photograph doesn't help much, does it?' I said, looking at the grainy, taken-from-a-distance shot of the mother and two children leaving the coroner's court. The son was carrying the three-year-old and only part of his profile could be seen.

'I'm not sure seeing it properly would make a difference,' said Evi. 'There can be nearly nine hundred medical students at Cambridge at any one time. I'd probably recognize most of the ones who were in my year, but the years above . . .'

'And as it was taken more than twenty years ago, the chances are he looks very different,' I said.

'So he could be here?'

'Over a hundred thousand people in the city,' I replied. 'Plenty of places to hide. On the other hand, maybe I just don't want it to be Nick.'

Evi slid her hand along the table until it rested lightly on mine.

'Neither do I,' she said. 'But even if Iestyn Thomas is here, orchestrating everything, he can't be acting alone.'

Not the least surprising thing to happen to me that day was that I found myself twisting my hand round and closing my fingers around Evi's. At the same time, nerve endings around my eyes and nose started to sting. I kept my eyes down, in the faint hope Evi wouldn't notice.

'These things never end well, Laura,' she said. 'Even if we win in the end, the wounds left behind take a long time to heal.'

I was dismayed to see a tear fall on to the keyboard. It landed, splat, right in the middle of the J.

Evi's hand gave mine a squeeze. 'Deep breaths, blink hard, then blow your nose,' she told me in a no-nonsense voice. 'There's plenty of time for therapy when the bad guys are banged up.'

I did what I was told. But when I looked at her again, her eyes were shining too.

'You're not over it, are you?' I asked her. 'That business last year in Lancashire, I mean.'

A tear shone on Evi's thick black lashes. 'I'm not sure I ever will be,' she admitted. 'Experiencing something like that is like a major bereavement. You don't get over it, you just learn to live with it.'

'What happened to the vicar?' I risked.

She smiled, let go of my hand and gave it a little pat. She didn't reply immediately, but I didn't think she minded my bringing him up.

'There was news footage of him helping you into your car,' I said. 'It looked like the two of you were together.'

Sad little shake of the head. 'We never quite made it to that stage. Harry and I were instrumental in a woman's death. She was one of my patients.'

'Instrumental how?'

'Long story, and it wasn't Harry's fault, it was mine. I thought for a while I was going to lose my practising certificate over it. In the end I just got a reprimand for a temporary lapse of judgement, but . . .'

'You can't forgive yourself?'

She sighed. 'Losing a patient in your care is hard enough, Laura. When it's because of a selfish act on your part, it's close to unbearable. I couldn't be with Harry and deal with it. And nor could he.'

She looked at her watch and pressed a button to close down the laptop. Time was running on and both of us had other places to be.

'A long time ago I made a big mistake,' I said. 'And the repercussions of it will go on for as long as I do. I know exactly what it's like to really care for someone you can't be with. I know about obstacles that just won't go away, no matter how much you want them to.'

'Sucks, doesn't it?' said Evi.

'Oh, big time. But with all due respect, what you've just told me about you and Harry doesn't cut it.'

Eyebrows up, glint in those deep-blue eyes. 'Oh, you don't think?'

'Trust me, as insurmountable barriers go, yours is strictly little league,' I told her. 'If he means that much to you, you'll deal with it. I'd call him if I were you.' I reached into my pocket, pulled out my phone. Well, Joesbury hadn't said I couldn't call a man of God. 'Fully charged up,' I told her, waggling it in her direction.

'You're nuts.' She made no move to take the phone but I could tell she was on the verge of smiling.

'I believe that term's rather frowned upon in professional circles,' I said, putting the phone back in my bag. 'Right, when this is all over and the bad guys are banged up, either you call him yourself or I'll do it for you.'

I borrowed Evi's keys and went off to take Sniffy out for a run. When the dog had settled back down I locked up carefully and took the keys back to Evi at the hospital, then jogged down a couple of flights of stairs to Bryony's floor and made my way to her room.

'Hi,' I said. Bryony's blue eyes softened and I thought perhaps she'd smiled at me. Then, before I could speak, the door opened behind us and two men stood there. The first was George, the porter from St John's who'd showed me to my room on my first day. The second was Nick.

'Hello, Miss Farrow,' said George. 'How's our patient?'

'I've just arrived myself,' I replied. 'But the nurse outside told me she's doing well.'

The two men stepped further into the room. I saw both glance down at the pad in Bryony's tent. 'Well, that's very good news,' said George, pulling up a chair and settling himself down beside Bryony. 'Hello, my dear. How are you this evening?'

Nick gestured with his head that we leave the room and I followed him out. As the door closed, we could hear George talking to Bryony is a soft, low voice.

'Did he know her well?' I asked, knowing I was getting suspicious of everyone but wondering why a college porter should be visiting a student.

465

'He's been to see her a lot,' said Nick. 'Some of the porters do get quite close to students. Surrogate sons and daughters for many of them.'

'For a GP, you spend a lot of time here,' I said, before I could think about whether it was wise or not.

'Bryony's my patient,' he replied. 'Jessica was registered with one of my partners. And I could say the same about you. What's your excuse?'

'I just said goodbye to Evi,' I said, by way of a reply.

'How are your plans for the evening shaping up?' he asked.

'Still unclear,' I replied, thinking that by the time darkness fell I might be in serious need of a bed for the night. Not that I was going anywhere near Nick's house. Not now.

66

My room was exactly as I'd left it. Except that this time Tox was there.

'You dark horse, you,' she greeted me. 'Why didn't you tell me you had such a gorgeous brother? Is he single? Is he straight? Oh God, please tell me he's not gay?'

'What?' I said, which I admit wasn't the most intelligent response in the world but I'd had a tough day.

From further down the corridor came the sound of a lavatory being flushed. Tox gave a tiny wiggle, twisted round so she could see her own arse in the mirror and tucked a straggle of hair behind one ear.

'Here she is,' she trilled at a tall, dark-haired man walking towards us along the corridor. 'I told you she wouldn't be long.'

'Hey, squirt,' said Joesbury, bending down to kiss me on the cheek and pat me on the bottom in a manner that would probably have earned a real brother a split lip.

'Yo, bro,' I replied, and yes that was lame, but, as I say, tough day.

Joesbury was wearing pale cream chinos and a pink and lilac striped button-down shirt with a lilac sweater slung over his shoulders. I'd never seen him look so wholesome. He was positively preppy.

'Mum asked me to pop in,' he said. 'Gran's had another one of her turns.'

'That's three this year,' I said, before remembering it was only January. 'Academic year,' I added, turning to Tox, who seemed unable to take her eyes off Joesbury.

'Are you going to be here for the evening?' Tox said to him. 'We could take you out somewhere, couldn't we, Laura? Unless you're seeing that delectable GP of yours, in which case I'll look after Mick.'

Good to know my brother's name, I suppose.

'Actually I need to hit the road,' Joesbury said, smiling at her in a way I swear he'd never smiled at me. Sort of cheeky and flirty and . . . 'I just came by to pick up little Laura's laptop. She's broken it again. Walk me to the car, squirt?' he finished.

'I'll give you his number,' I promised Tox, as Joesbury picked up the heavy canvas bag in which I kept my laptop and led me out of the room. 'If ever a man deserved you, it's my big brother.'

'Squirt?' I said, as we crossed the covered bridge. Below us the river had taken on the blue-grey cast of wet slate, the banks were still frosted over with snow and the fields and gardens beyond stretched white as far as light from the colleges could reach.

'Seemed siblingy,' he replied. We stepped into Third Court just as a dusting of snow fell down on us from one of the window ledges. I indicated that we needed to turn left and head north to get to the forecourt.

It was properly dark by this time and everywhere we looked, warm yellow light was shining from medieval windows. When we reached Chapel Court I decided that if I was about to be fired, we might as well get it over with. 'If you're interested in why I'm still here . . .' I began.

'I know why you're still here,' he interrupted me. 'I know about Jessica.'

A male voice, pure and light, drifted across the court from the chapel, asking God to intervene on our behalf and to do it quickly. Then the choir and congregation joined in with the response. Evensong was taking place, as it seemed to most evenings. 'O Lord, make haste to help us,' sang the choir leader.

'I sent you several messages,' I tried again.

'Didn't get them,' said Joesbury. 'We disconnected your phone this morning.' He dug into his pocket and pulled out another mobile.

Candlelight from inside the chapel was glowing through the stained-glass windows. In the few places where the snow was unbroken, the religious images from the windows were reflected in perfect detail.

'Take this for now,' Joesbury said, holding the mobile towards me. 'I picked it up at the Carphone Warehouse earlier. It's for emergency use only. Don't try to phone me with it, or Dr Oliver, or any of your colleagues on the force. And that includes DC Stenning. Is that clear?'

'Perfectly.'

'I need your old one,' he said.

I dug into my bag, handed it over. 'As it's been disconnected, not much point hanging on to it.' Joesbury wasn't looking at me any more. He was staring at the chapel, a tiny smile on his face.

'This is Haydn,' he said. ' "The Heavens Are Telling".'

'Like you've ever been to church,' I grumbled. There was something about the music that was making me feel sad, and needy. As if I wanted to go into chapel and let it wash all around me and, at the same time, to run as fast as I could in the opposite direction.

'The wonder of his works displays the firmament,' sang Joesbury, perfectly in time with the choir inside the chapel, and in a surprisingly good voice. By this time, the music had become loud and jubilant.

'I'm taking your laptop too.' He indicated the bag he'd carried from my room.

'How did you even get in here?' I said. 'You can't just drive into a Cambridge college, claiming to be a relative.'

Joesbury looked down at me. 'You think you're the only undercover officer we have in town?'

'I've just discovered you were a choirboy. Nothing will surprise me any more.'

As silence fell inside the chapel, Joesbury caught the look on my face and stepped closer. 'I'm sorry about this morning,' he said.

'I stand corrected,' I snapped, glaring at him.

A tiny twitch at the corner of his mouth. 'Setting aside for a moment the fact that you're a completely loose cannon who wouldn't know the rule book if it jumped up and bit you on the arse, you've actually done quite well,' he said.

There was a sudden need, on my part, to sit down.

'The stuff you've been emailing me about Nicole and the other girls has been pretty helpful,' he went on. 'The only reason you've been kept in the dark and why we've been telling you repeatedly not to get involved is for your own safety.'

In the chapel a beautiful, soothing voice was reading prayers. I looked up into turquoise eyes that I knew I'd never tire of. 'There's more,' I said.

Another twitch. Any second now he was going to smile at me. 'Go on,' he said.

He listened while I told him the theory that Evi and I had come up with. Sometimes almost shouting in his ear, to compete with the choir and congregation, sometimes dropping my voice when silence fell, I told him about the bogus questionnaire. That, armed with immensely private information on girls' innermost secrets, someone was devising a targeted campaign of bullying and intimidation, feeding on their worst fears. That, when the girls were close to being nervous wrecks, the abuse became physical, aided by a powerful and highly dangerous cocktail of hallucinogenic and sedative drugs.

I went on to say that I was especially worried about Evi herself, that it looked as though she too had become part of the campaign of intimidation, not because she matched the vulnerable-young-woman profile, but because she'd been poking her nose in where someone didn't want it.

As music that seemed too good for this earth rang around the court, I told Joesbury I suspected the girls were being abducted, for a purpose I couldn't begin to imagine but didn't have any good feelings about, and that, shortly after being released, they were pushed, probably again with the assistance of drugs, into taking their own lives. I told him that Bryony hadn't bought the petrol that nearly killed her.

'You're sure about that?' he interrupted me.

'Absolutely. And does it bear repeating that Nicole's wasn't the only car on the road the night she died?'

'No, I got that loud and clear. Go on.'

Only yards away, people sang of God's wonders and glory. In the real world, I told my senior officer that we were looking for a group of people with both medical and IT skills and that three such people in town had been at Cambridge fifteen years ago, the last time a spate of suicides had occurred. His face didn't flicker when I named

Nick Bell, Scott Thornton and Megan Prince as possible suspects. I told him about Iestyn Thomas.

'Bell has always taken more of an interest in Bryony than medical protocol demands. And Megan Prince is a psychiatrist, one who knows Evi very well. Thomas sounds like a twisted individual who has, very conveniently, fallen off the grid. The only one we have anything tangible on though is Scott Thornton.'

He frowned at me. 'What?'

I told him how and why I'd discovered Thornton's identity, and about seeing him going into a unit on the nearby industrial estate. When I got to my stake-out of that afternoon, he raised one eyebrow and shook his head.

'I'll have them all watched,' he said. 'And get this Iestyn Thomas character traced. I'll also have someone keep an eye on the industrial unit. That could be important.'

'I could drive out there and . . .'

His eyebrows lifted. 'Don't go anywhere near it. I mean it, Flint. Now promise.'

I'd have promised him anything. 'Is there any possibility of you telling me what's going on here?' I asked.

'Yes.' He broke eye contact to look at his watch. 'But not now. I have to get your phone and laptop to the Yard.'

'Because . . . ?'

In the chapel, the organ sounded up again. It was taking on a personality of its own for me, that instrument, swanky and loud, like an annoying boy in the school playground. 'Your cover's almost certainly been compromised,' Joesbury said. 'From what you've just told me about that question-naire, it's probably been done electronically. Someone could have hacked into your files, maybe read the emails you've sent to me. They could know exactly who we are and what we know.'

'Christ, I'm sorry.'

'Don't be. If you'd been properly briefed, you'd have been on the lookout for that sort of thing. Lacey, don't worry about it. These people are bloody clever and I may be wrong. Either way, we'll know tonight.'

'And if we are blown?'

'It won't be the end of the world. We have other people here. And, partly thanks to you, we're a lot closer than we were.'

'What do you want me to do?'

'Stay in college for a few more hours and act normal. Well, as normal as possible for you,' he said. 'An added complication is that we think the police are involved in what's going on here. We don't know yet whether it's a couple of bent local coppers or whether it even reaches the Met but you are not to trust anyone but me. Is that understood?'

I nodded. People were leaving the chapel now, the organist playing them on their way.

'There are roadworks on the M11 so I'll have to take the long way round, but I'll be back before midnight all being well and I'll call you. Do you know a hotel called the Varsity?'

Another nod. 'I think so. Just round the corner, small, concrete place. Looks very trendy.'

'That's where I'm staying,' he said. 'I'll text you with a room number when I'm back.'

One of the porters left the lodge and crossed the court towards us, nodding to a few members of the departing congregation as he did so. As I watched him approach, the choir left the chapel. They were mostly boys, some of them barely in their teens, with black robes and bright-red collars. Red and black tassels on their funny, flat little hats.

'You on your way out, sir?' the porter asked Joesbury. It was George.

'Yes thanks,' Joesbury replied, before turning back to me and lowering his voice. 'One more thing,' he said. 'About Bell.'

I'd been so caught up in the sheer joy of being on good terms with Joesbury again that for a second I thought he was talking about a large bronze thing that went ding-dong. 'If he's in the clear when this is all over, I'm fine with it,' he said. 'He seems like a nice bloke. Just stay away from him and keep your eye on the case for a bit longer, OK?'

Suddenly there was a large and heavy lump where my tongue used to be.

'I'm looking forward to finding out exactly what this case is,' I said, because I had to say something and what sprang to mind didn't seem appropriate somehow.

Joesbury put a hand behind my head in a brotherly gesture that made me want to hit him. Or weep. 'Sweetheart,' he said. 'When you do, you'll wish you hadn't.'

He got into his car, George opened the gates and he drove away.

67

Cambridge, five year earlier
'You joining us tonight, boss?'

The man sitting behind the desk shook his head. 'Got a college reunion.' He nodded his head towards the screen in front of him. 'Have you seen this, Stacey?'

Stacey, a slim blonde in her early thirties, who'd had a secret crush on her new boss for several months now, was glad of the opportunity to walk to the other side of the desk and lean over it. This close, she could smell his cologne and the warm cotton of his shirt. See the gleam of his hair.

'Good Lord, is that real?' The image on the screen, for a second, distracted her even from the fantasy of pressing her face against that broad shoulder, breathing in the male scent more deeply.

'Must be,' he replied. 'Her parents are kicking up merry hell.'

'That was here, wasn't it? She was a student

at the university.'

The video clip was just four minutes thirty-six seconds long. It showed a young woman, hanging by the neck from a tree. Her legs kicked furiously, her fingers seemed to be trying to rip her neck apart, they worked so frantically at the noose around it. The expression on her face was hard for Stacey to look at.

'I'm surprised YouTube haven't taken it off,' she said. The clip reached the end. To her surprise, her boss started it again.

'They will,' he said, 'any day now. We're among the last to see it.'

Stacey looked at the viewing figure in the bottom right-hand corner of the screen. 'Last of nearly a million,' she said. 'People are sick.' She moved away, back round the front of the desk. She was wearing her tightest skirt but his eyes didn't follow her.

'That's for sure,' the boss said. 'Have a good time, Stace.'

It was her cue to leave. To stay any longer would look obvious. She'd reached the door when her boss spoke again.

'Just imagine,' he said, but when she looked back he was still staring at the screen and she got the impression he was talking to himself now. That maybe he had even forgotten she was there. 'If every one of those punters paid a pound for the privilege.'

As Stacey closed the door, she thought she might, at last, be getting over her childish crush.

68

Spike-strips, also known as stop sticks and stingers, are used by traffic police the world over to bring high-speed car chases to an end. Typically constructed of metal teeth, between an inch and a half and three inches long and fixed to a fold-up metal frame, spike-strips are unfolded widthways across a road directly in front of a speeding car. They work by puncturing the vehicle's tyres and, used properly, bring speeding vehicles to a rapid halt whilst causing minimal damage to both people and property.

Usually, the spikes are hollow, rather than solid, and once embedded in tyres will deflate them slowly. The vehicle will be able to travel a short distance before the tyres are completely flat but the possibility of an accident is greatly reduced. Solid spikes, on the other hand, cause multiple tyre blowouts that invariably lead to trouble.

DI Mark Joesbury was a good driver.

Police officers are trained to drive quickly and confidently, with maximum levels of concentration. His aptitude behind a wheel had been spotted whilst he was still a cadet and he'd been on several advanced driving courses, including one on evasive techniques.

In daylight, he might have seen the homemade spike-strip laid across the A10 just before he reached it. Had he done so, he would have stood as good a chance of being able to avoid it as just about any other driver on the UK's roads. In the dark, driving at speed, and with a lot on his mind, it wasn't going to happen.

His BMW hit the nail-embedded steel pipe at just over sixty miles per hour. All four tyres exploded with a sound like gunshots. The BMW hit the crash barrier, broke through it, left the highway and careered down a wooded bank. It came to rest on its roof. The last thought in Mark Joesbury's head was that he hadn't passed on any of the information Lacey had shared with him.

I got back to find Tox working out ridiculously complicated equations as heavy metal rocked everything in the room that wasn't nailed firmly down. She grinned at me, mouthed something and then turned down the volume.

'I am so coming to your place for the Easter break,' she announced.

'I'll look forward to that,' I replied, wondering if Joesbury could conjure up a house in Shropshire and a plump, middle-class lady in her fifties to be our mother.

Tox grinned at me. 'Do you mind Guns N' Roses?' she asked.

'Louder the better,' I replied and, when she took me at my word, went into my room to read and wait.

As the rattle and crash of the accident faded away into the night, two hooded figures emerged from the trees. One of them picked up what was left of the spike-strip and pulled it to the side of the road. The other climbed the broken crash barrier and made his way down the bank. As he reached the vehicle, his companion joined him.

The man inside was suspended upside down by his seat belt. His head was twisted at an angle that looked unnatural.

'Is he dead?' asked the first man.

'Don't know,' replied the second. 'Looks it.'

'Let's get the stuff.'

They'd brought a crowbar with them to force open the boot. It wasn't needed. The crash had disabled the lock and the boot hatch was open. Joesbury's bag was three yards further down the slope. In it, they found the laptop and mobile phone that Joesbury had taken from Lacey less than half an hour earlier. From the main body of the car they took his own mobile. They also found a jacket with a wallet inside and took that too. Then they stood back to survey the scene.

'Torch it?' suggested the first man.

The second shook his head. 'Too obvious,' he said. 'They'd find the match. And he looks dead to me. Come on.'

They turned and made their way back up the slope. At the sound of another car they ducked low. It carried on, having no idea of the devastation just a few yards away.

'They'd find a match?' said the first man. 'You're kidding me. Won't it just burn up?'

'Nope. Match heads contain silica. Very tough compound.'

'You learn something new every day.'

The two men crossed the road and made their way through the trees to a farm track where they'd left their own vehicle. They climbed inside and drove away. Since they'd left the ruined BMW, neither had looked back.

■ ■ ■ ■

Nine o'clock arrived and Tox went off to find her boyfriend. Nine thirty followed and I'd heard nothing from Joesbury. My heartbeat went into overdrive at nine forty-five when there was a knock on the door. I shot across the room to open it. Nick Bell stood in the doorway. 'Hi,' he said.

'What's wrong?' I asked him. I'd never seen him look so serious.

He put a hand on my shoulder. 'Can I come in?' he asked.

I didn't want Nick anywhere near me but I had a sense something had happened. I stepped back and let him come inside. He came close and looked down at me, as though he wanted to kiss me but wasn't quite sure about himself.

'I'm afraid I've got bad news,' he said.

Joesbury was the first thought in my head. Ridiculous. Nick didn't know Joesbury, had no idea I was supposed to have a brother. I told myself to get a grip and nodded at Nick to go on.

'Bryony died two hours ago,' he said. 'She took her own life.'

I could not overreact. Laura would be sad, sympathetic, nothing more.

'I'm sorry,' I managed. 'I know she was important to you.'

Nick held out his arms. I stepped into them and hugged him, knowing I had to play my part to the end. 'What happened?' I asked.

He pulled away from me and crossed to Talaith's desk. 'There was an emergency in the unit,' he said. 'Everyone was occupied. She managed to get out of bed, pulled away all the lines and tubes. All the alarms went off, of course, but it was just chaos. By the time someone got to her, she'd opened the window and jumped out.'

I couldn't think of anything to say, because the only thought going through my head was that they'd got her, after all.

'There was blood around the sink,' Nick went on. 'We think she went to the mirror, saw herself properly for the first time and couldn't deal with it.'

They'd got her. They were winning, on every front.

'She was a medical student,' Nick was saying. 'She knew the score about her injuries, about what the future held. Sorry, you don't want to hear all this.'

I wasn't interested in the possibility that it might be for the best, that Bryony would have had no sort of life, as damaged as she was. All I could think about was that keeping these girls alive had become my job. And I'd failed.

'I've got a lot to do,' Nick said. 'There's always a lot of admin when someone dies. And I've left messages for her parents so I need to be around if they get back to me. Can we do supper another time?'

'Of course,' I said, relieved not to have to come up with an excuse. 'I've got a lot on myself. Why don't I walk you to the gate?'

How had they done it? There had been some final trigger, something that had pushed her over the edge. I had to find out who'd visited her that day. Apart from George and the man at my side. I couldn't go back to the hospital, though. I had to wait for Joesbury.

Snow was beginning to fall again as we crossed First Court.

'Do roads round here get blocked in the snow?' I asked Nick. Joesbury had been gone for four hours already.

'Only when it takes the authorities by surprise,' said Nick. Then he looked up. 'These flakes are tiny,' he went on. 'I doubt we're in for another big dump.'

'Good,' I said, wanting to look at my watch. At that moment, a nearby church clock struck the hour. We stepped through

487

the tiny wooden door into the street and he turned to face me. I forced a shiver that quickly turned into a real one.

'You need to get back inside,' he said. 'See you soon.'

I let him kiss me and tried not to pull away too quickly. Then I watched him walk a few paces down the road, giving him a cute, girly wave when he looked round, before turning back towards First Court.

I walked quickly across and through into Second Court, pulling my new phone out of my pocket, even though I'd have heard it if there'd been any sort of message left. Where the hell was Joesbury? Four hours! He should have been back by now.

By ten o'clock, Evi knew there was nothing more she could do for Jessica that night. She'd been transferred to a secure psychiatric wing of the hospital, her parents were with her, and she'd been given sedatives to ensure a good night's sleep. With a bit of luck, it would also be a dreamless one.

As she was making her way out through the hospital's main reception, her phone rang. Megan Prince. Conscious of her heartbeat picking up pace, Evi gave herself a second.

'Hello, Meg.'

'Evi, hi. Can you talk?' Megan's usual breezy voice seemed to be pitched lower than normal.

'Of course. What's up?'

'Can we meet tomorrow, first thing? I've no appointments till ten. Can I swing by your place at nine?'

No. Somewhere there'd be people.

'I have to be at the office early tomorrow, but I can see you there at nine. Will that do?'

'Yeah, that'll be fine. Great. See you there, Evi.'

She'd gone. OK, what was all that about? Megan had never just asked to see her out of the blue before. Should she tell Laura? Maybe have her on hand?

Evi wheeled herself across the car park, thinking perhaps that she wouldn't tell Laura until afterwards. It might be nothing, and in any case, what could happen in an office full of people?

She drove home, exhausted and hurting but, oddly, in better spirits than she'd known for some time. She told herself it was finding Jessica alive and OK. Deep down she knew it was because of the conversation she'd had earlier with Laura. *I'd call him if I were you.* Suddenly, Evi could no longer remember why calling Harry was impossible.

The dog was waiting just inside her front door.

'Hey, Sniffy,' Evi said, and was rewarded with a softly nuzzling nose and a brown-eyed look that told her she was the only important person in the world. Sniffy followed her into the kitchen and Evi opened the back door to let her out. For the first time, she realized that handing Sniffy back to her owners, when they showed up, was going to be quite hard.

She switched on the kettle and her computer. Just as the water came to the boil, a series of pinging sounds told her she had several new emails. Most were work related, one a jokey round robin from her cousin. The one that caught her eye was from a woman in Lancashire, whose young son Evi had treated the year before. It had an attachment. Alice never sent her emails. Letters occasionally, phone calls from time to time, but this was the first email Evi had ever received from her. She only knew one Alice Fletcher, though. Evi clicked it open. The attachment was a newspaper article, a cutting from the *Lancashire Telegraph*.

Dearest Evi,
     I expect you've heard the terrible news.

I don't doubt you were as shocked and saddened as we were. We can tell ourselves that God takes to himself those he loves the best but, ultimately, I'm not sure there's any meaning to be found in such events.

Anyway, I thought you would like to see the story that appeared in this week's *Telegraph.* Doesn't do him justice, of course, but what would? There's talk of a memorial service in the church. I'll keep you posted.

Love and miss you still,

Alice

A minute later, a cold dry hand had reached inside Evi's chest and taken hold of her heart. Any second now she was going to open her mouth and howl, but how could that happen when there wasn't any breath left in her body?

The newspaper story talked of a wonderful man, a man of God, who had been deeply loved and respected by all who'd known him; a man who'd been taken too soon, in the very prime of his life, by a freak climbing accident. There were details of his career, the various ecclesiastical and research posts he'd held, there was even a photograph. Evi took in none of it. At the

same time, she understood everything.
Harry was dead.

69

I left St John's, walked along bridge street and turned into Thompson's Lane where I knew I'd find the Varsity Hotel. There were two young night porters at the desk.

'Hi,' I said. 'I'm Laura Farrow. Has anyone left a message for me?'

One looked blank, the other cast his eyes over the desk in front of him. 'I can't see anything,' he said in an eastern European accent. 'What was the name of the guest?'

Very good question. I had no idea what undercover name Joesbury used.

'Mr Johnson?' I tried, because I knew initials usually remained the same. The boy looked at the screen in front of him. 'We have a Mr Jackson,' he told me.

'Is he in?' I asked, grasping at straws. The boy turned to the key hooks on the wall behind him. 'No,' he said, turning back to me. 'His key is here.'

Thanking the boys, I went outside again.

Joesbury had hinted there were more under-cover officers in the city but I hadn't a hope of tracking them down. If I phoned Scotland Yard and told them who I was they would probably put me through to SO10. But that could be completely the wrong thing to do. Don't trust the police, Joesbury had told me.

OK, I wasn't going to panic. Joesbury was more than capable of taking care of himself. Sniffy was looking after Evi. Jessica was safe in a secure psychiatric ward. Bryony was beyond our help. It looked like I was next on the list and I certainly wasn't about to take my own life. I just had to sit tight.

Back at college, hot tea felt very appealing but mindful of Evi's theory that I'd been drugged I wasn't taking any chances. I brushed my teeth, drank some water from the tap and got ready for bed. I switched the light out and wondered if I'd ever fall asleep. Then a thought hit me.

According to Talaith, Bryony had been most scared of losing her looks. She'd dreamed about disfigurement. What if the fire had never been meant to kill her? What if that was just the last stage of the physical and psychological torture? What if all some-one had done earlier today was to make sure the window of her room wasn't locked and show her a mirror?

The beeping of a text message coming into my phone nearly made me leap out of bed. I grabbed it from the bedside shelf. Joesbury. Oh, thank God.

Delayed, it said. *Sit tight. Don't contact anyone but me.*

Oh, thank God, thank God. As I muttered it over and over in my head, the world slipped away.

The man who now had Mark Joesbury's mobile phone put it down softly on the desk in front of him. 'We have another twenty-four hours maximum,' he said. 'Is she out yet?'

A screen on the computer in front of him flickered to life and he was looking at a picture of a young woman in bed, apparently asleep.

'Should be,' he was told. 'There was enough stuff in there to knock out an elephant.'

'Are we going in?' asked the third man in the room.

The man at the desk shook his head. 'Not sure.'

'Last chance, and at least we know that ruddy dog's out of the way.'

'Too risky. There's someone else sniffing around. We'll finish her off tomorrow.'

'What about Evi Oliver?'

'She's had no real pain relief for three weeks now and we've been playing with her head till she hardly knows what day it is. According to Meg, she's on the verge of losing it.'

'Is that good? We haven't had her to the unit yet.'

'We may have to pass on that. There isn't time to use them both and getting her out of the way was always the priority.' He leaned back in his chair. 'Besides, Laura is the one I've set my heart on.'

70

'Laura! Laura, I need you to wake up.'

A voice, a hand reaching down to me through the darkness. I had to get up there. Just wanted to sleep.

'I may have to call an ambulance. Can someone get me my bag?'

A hand, lightly slapping my cheek. Evi's hand. I could almost see her pale heart-shaped face above mine. It was shimmering, in and out of focus, and I knew she really wanted to talk to me. Oh, but sleep felt so good.

'Thanks,' said Evi's voice again. 'Stay with her, keep talking to her.'

A different person with me now. One of the girls in the block. I could see her long dark hair and creamy skin. Brown eyes looking into mine. The room was slowly coming into focus.

'I'm OK,' I told her and, with her help,

discovered I could sit. I was in my room in
St John's. Another girl was hovering in the
main room. No sign of Tox. Then Evi appeared in the doorway.

'I'm OK,' I repeated, not sure I could
manage much more. It felt like I was talking
through a thick mesh screen. A fly screen,
or some of that frosted glass you see in
bathroom windows. I was sinking again. 'No
ambulance,' I forced out.

Evi looked as though she were about to
argue then turned to the other girls.
'Thanks, both of you,' she told them. 'Can I
give you a call if I need you again?'

Puzzled but obedient, the girls accepted
their dismissal and left the room.

'I've been phoning you and phoning you,'
Evi told me once we were alone. 'I was
nearly frantic when you didn't call back.'

I pulled the covers back and swung my
legs round. The room started spinning and
I had to close my eyes for a second. When I
opened them, the bedside clock told me it
was nine thirty in the morning.

'What's happened?' said Evi. 'Do you
want me to call someone?'

'Give me a minute,' I said. Jesus, I had to
get a grip.

Working on autopilot I found a tracksuit
and trainers and pulled them on. Evi started

498

to say something and then thought better of it but from the look on her face she wasn't going to stay quiet for long. Just getting dressed practically exhausted me. When I was done I sat back down on the bed again.

'Looks like you were right,' I said. 'About the drugs. I've taken something. Don't ask me how or when, but . . .'

'We need to get you to hospital . . .' Evi began.

'No time,' I interrupted. 'And I think I'm OK. I just feel seriously hungover. Fresh air, coffee, something to eat, I'll be fine.' To prove a point, I managed to stand up without swaying. 'Buttery?' I suggested. I really needed to get out of that room. Evi, though, was showing no inclination to leave.

'How are they doing it?' she said, looking round. 'Tell me everything you did last night.'

Leaning against the door, I did, including the fact that I'd eaten nothing and drunk nothing but tap water all evening. She wheeled her chair closer to the sink.

'Tap water's impossible,' she muttered to herself. 'And if they'd let themselves in and stuck a syringe in your arm, you'd have woken.'

She reached out, picked up my toothpaste and sniffed it.

I shook my head. 'Toothpaste? You're kidding me.'

'LSD is typically taken on small pieces of blotting paper that sit on the tongue,' she told me. 'Drugs are absorbed very quickly in the mouth,' she went on. 'Did you use mouthwash?'

I nodded.

Evi put both toothpaste and mouthwash into her bag and zipped it shut. 'OK,' she said. 'Let's get out of here.'

We made our way to the Buttery and found strong coffee for both of us and toast for me. I was feeling better all the time. Still pretty bad, but improving. Evi, though, didn't appear to be. It was as though her rescue of me had worn her out. Her face was pink and swollen, her eyes bloodshot. Every wrinkle in her face told me she was in pain and her voice was that of a woman who was seriously ill. Or one who'd spent the night crying.

'You heard about Bryony?' I asked her, when we were both settled at a table some distance from everyone else.

She nodded. 'This morning.' There didn't seem much more we could say.

'How's Jessica?' I asked.

'Alive,' she replied. 'I guess everything else is a bonus, right now.'

'Has she talked at all?'

Evi nodded. 'That's why I've been trying to contact you. She got quite agitated late yesterday evening. A lot of it was just the usual stuff about clowns, clowns chasing her, clowns attacking her, clowns hanging by the neck from trees, the sort of stuff she's been having bad dreams about.'

The world still seemed to be operating in slow motion. Or maybe that was just me. I closed my eyes for a second, took a few deep breaths.

'And a dog. She kept talking about a dog. How she'd managed to get away and hide in a ditch but the dog had found her.'

The room was spinning. I opened my eyes again, and realized Evi had stopped talking and was just staring into space. It was as though she'd left the room. Her body was still sitting across the table, but Evi herself had gone somewhere else entirely.

'Evi?' I said. Her dark-blue eyes flicked back to me. They were swimming with tears. 'You were talking about Jessica?' I prompted.

Evi gave herself a little shake. 'Yes, then she started talking about her room at St Catharine's,' she said. 'How it was her room but wasn't her room, how they'd changed it, turned it bad, and how they were watching her all the time.'

'Sounds just like Bryony.'

'That's what I thought. That's why I needed to see you. The other thing is that Megan Prince phoned last night asking to see me today. I went to meet her at nine o'clock but she didn't show. She's not answering her phone either but I don't want to make it too obvious I'm chasing her.'

'No,' I agreed. 'Let her get in touch with you again.'

She nodded. 'Yes, that's what I figured.'

'Evi,' I said, 'has something else happened to you? Frankly, you look like I feel.'

Evi stared at me for a moment, then shook her head. 'Bad news from home,' she said. 'I can deal with it. I'm fine.'

She wasn't, but it was hardly the time to get into an argument. Especially as what she'd just said had finally filtered through. Blimey, I was slow.

'Evi, what did you just say about trees?'

'When?'

'About Jessica. What did she say about clowns hanging by the neck from trees?'

'Well, she was rambling,' said Evi. 'A lot of stuff about running through a forest, and bats and clowns having a tea party. She said there had been clowns hanging by the neck from trees. It just struck me as a particularly

502

bizarre image.'

'The sort of thing you wouldn't forget,' I agreed. 'Right, there's something I need to do. Are you on your way home now?'

'What is it?' said Evi. 'What have you thought of?'

'Probably nothing,' I said. 'Just something I need to check out. I'll come round later, if that's OK. Just to walk the dog.'

I walked Evi to her car and waved her off.

As soon as she'd gone I went to my own car and looked at the map. The day I'd had my close encounter with the buzzard, I'd found myself in a small wooded area that not only had given me the serious heebie-jeebies but was also very close to an industrial estate that Scott Thornton was connected to. An industrial estate that still had an old foundry bell. *Bell*, Bryony had written. *Bell.*

Jessica had talked about a dog finding her. The industrial estate wasn't far from Nick's house. On Friday night, when I'd been at his party, Jessica had been missing. I'd heard a woman scream. A minute or two later, Sniffy had appeared.

Joesbury had told me to sit tight. And feeling better or not, I was still in no fit state to go driving around Cambridgeshire. But I had no idea when he'd be back and I couldn't help a horrible feeling that we were running out of time. I pulled out my mobile and composed a text message.

Bell Foundry Industrial Estate 11am, I wrote, then pressed Send. On the off-chance that something went wrong, Joesbury would know where I was.

The tall, dark-haired man was getting into his car when the call came in. 'She's figured it out,' said the voice. 'Can you get over there now?'

'I thought Scott was there?'

'Can't get hold of him. He may have nipped out for food. Which means he won't have set the alarm or closed everything down. You know what he's like.'

'I'm on my way. What do you want me to do with her?'

'Hang on to her. They know about the drugs as well. We have to do it today.'

Evi was sobbing as she let herself in through her front door. The trip to St John's to check on Laura had sapped every last bit of her strength and now the pain running up and down her leg and back had reached her head. She felt as though her brain had swollen and was pressing against the bones of her skull.

Harry. Just to know he was in the world somewhere, maybe even thinking about her, seemed like bliss compared to what she had now. She was thirty-four years old, had maybe another forty years left to live and didn't know how she was going to make it through the next ten minutes.

Sniffy walked through from the kitchen, tail wagging, and pressed her damp nose against Evi's palm. Patting the dog on the head, Evi limped across the hall and into her bedroom. Just a bit longer, just a few more days, until Laura didn't need her any more. She lay down on the bed and pulled the quilt up around her.

It took me barely fifteen minutes to reach the industrial estate. I carried on past and travelled a few hundred yards further up the B1102 before pulling into a small lay-by. The last thing I felt like doing was standing upright, never mind moving forward. On the other hand, if I approached the unit on foot, I'd be much harder to spot.

Slowly but steadily, the fresh, cold air helping, I made my way through the woods and down towards the units, keeping a sharp lookout for Jim Notley or anyone else who might be around. When I passed the spot where he'd found me the previous week, I could see that the lights were still in position along the path, but the hanging figures had been taken down.

Clowns hanging by the neck? The hanging figures I'd seen hadn't been clowns. They'd been dolls, with horribly disfigured faces. Had they been for Bryony?

There was a wooden fence between the edge of the copse and the narrow, flagged path that rimmed the estate. I ducked down and climbed through. Unit 33 was one of the more recent buildings on the estate, made of huge vertical sheets of corrugated steel with a gently sloping steel roof. A massive air-conditioning unit lay silent on the moss-covered path and, just above it, a small window that had been blacked out with dark paint. I walked to the corner of the building, so that I could see the rear and the side elevations at once.

One CCTV camera, almost at roof height, directed towards the front of the building. I couldn't afford to be recognized on film, but I'd tied my hair back and brought the hood of my sweatshirt up. As long as I kept my head down, I wouldn't be identifiable.

Two windows very high up at the front suggested there might be an upper floor. The front door was locked, as were warehouse doors on the next side I came to. There wasn't going to be an easy way in.

Back at the rear, I gave myself a couple of minutes to get my breath back. Then I searched round on the ground, found a piece of old concrete, pulled my sleeve down over my fingers and drove it through the blackened window pane. In my delicate state the crash seemed unnaturally loud. I waited a moment for an alarm but there was nothing. Knocking the broken glass free of the window, I scrambled up.

At first I was trapped. Not a metre from the window was a tall, flat sheet of something blocking my way. It was slanted towards me too, leaning against the rear wall a few feet above my head. It gave slightly when I pushed against it but I didn't want to send the whole thing toppling so I moved sideways and stepped out from behind tall plywood boards.

I counted twelve in total, stacked against the wall, four to a stack. The ones at the front had been painted to resemble brickwork. As artwork went, it was pretty crude, knocked up in a hurry, but still clear what it was meant to be. Old, crumbling, damp brickwork, the sort that would line Victorian cellars or tunnels. The boards had a look of theatrical scenery. The rest of the room wasn't the cavernous space I'd expected but quite a confined area and the resemblance to the backstage of a theatre was increased by some large black floodlights, mounted on tripods in one corner. Coiled black extension leads stood at their feet. Could I be in a theatre? There was one door. It opened silently upon a vast, dark space. I raised the torch I'd brought from the car and stepped through into the very last thing I'd expected. A fairground.

71

DI John Castell was on Evi's doorstep, looking down at her. Suddenly unsteady on her feet, Evi reached out and took hold of the doorframe for support.

'I've afraid I've got bad news, Evi,' he told her. 'Megan died last night.'

Directly in front of me was a carousel. Like something from a Victorian funfair, the painted horses reared on poles, ready to prance their way around the ride when the music began. In the torchlight the carousel shone with gilt and its fluted red and white striped roof rose above me. To one side of the ride was a small fortune teller's tent and a Test Your Strength machine. Further into the warehouse was another carousel. Much smaller than the first, this was designed for young children and in place of the horses were red, blue and yellow elephants, trunks held high and gleaming with painted jewels.

The edge of my torch beam caught something and I jumped round to see a hideously scary clown looking right at me. I'd opened my mouth to yell before I realized it was a painted image. With clawing hands and a face that was half wolf, half demon, this wasn't like any clown I'd seen before. Behind it were more of the same: hideous plywood clowns that, seen quickly and in poor light, by someone high on hallucinogenic drugs, would appear very real.

Clowns were what Jessica was most afraid of. This freak show had probably been created with the sole purpose of terrifying her. As I set off again, not wanting to stay too close to those horrible images, I couldn't help but wonder what they'd done for Nicole, Bryony, Jackie, for all the others, here in this psychological torture chamber.

And what they had planned for me.

Towards the far end of the warehouse, my torch beam picked out a narrow staircase leading up to a mezzanine level. At the top was a closed door. Ten steps up and the door wasn't locked. This was a bad idea. I was a long way from my exit route if something happened. On the other hand, I would hear if a vehicle approached.

The room beyond was in darkness. There were four windows but blinds on each kept out the light. I had to rely on the torch.

A large television screen sat on a low glass table against the far wall and, facing it, in the middle of the floor, was a single chair. Desks ran along both sides of the room and the computer equipment on them looked state-of-the-art. On one desk sat two large objects concealed by thin plastic covers. I had a feeling I knew what they were, but wanting to be sure I stepped over and raised the first cover. Same thing beneath the second. Film cameras. Not simple hand-held video recorders, the sort most house-holds own these days, but the kind I'd seen news teams use when making outside broad-casts. Heavy, powerful, with huge lenses.

On the small dust-covered TV table lay a single DVD. The photograph on the case was of a girl with long dark hair in some sort of cellar, bound at her wrists and ankles. It could have been the case image of any commercially made thriller. I knew it wasn't, because I recognized the girl. The title on the case said simply *Nicole.*

Suddenly it all made sense. Unit 33 was a film studio.

Castell and Evi were in the kitchen. She had no recollection of getting there. Had John taken her arm and led her through the hallway? Possibly. Had he pulled out the chair and steadied her until she was sitting in it?

'Megan's dead?' she repeated.

Castell dropped his head, ran a hand over his face. When he looked at her again, his face was perfectly composed. 'I know,' he said. 'I really can't take it in.'

He was waiting for her to ask the inevitable questions and she had no idea what they were.

'It's too early to say for certain,' he went on, after a few moments. 'But we think she tripped at the top of the stairs. The carpet wasn't nailed down properly, and she was wearing those ridiculous heels.'

Evi told herself not to react, to let nothing show on her face. Because Meg was tall, and she walked with a long-legged stride. In summer she wore sandals, new-age-style strappy things. Pixie-boots in winter.

She never wore heels.

Movement in the corner of my eye. The screen of one of the computers had just gone into sleep mode. Someone had been here recently and they were probably on their way back. A quick check behind the nearest window blind told me no vehicles were anywhere near.

512

When the screen sprang back to life, it was to reveal the frozen image of a piece of video footage. A semi-naked girl was putting make-up on, leaning over a basin towards the camera, which had to be concealed behind the mirror. Sliding the mouse along the desk, I clicked on the arrow button that would start the video.

The girl ran a brush over her lips before stepping back and fluffing up her long hair. Then she cupped one hand into her bra, to pull her breast up higher. Same thing on the other side, the way women do to give themselves a better cleavage. She pushed back her shoulders and gave her image one last glance before turning to clothes she'd laid out on the bed.

I felt sick. The video had been shot in my room. The girl was me.

I closed down my little home movie, making a mental note of its file root, then opened up Finder. Knowing where I was heading made finding the rest of the files on me a little easier. Conveniently, someone had labelled them all with my name. Laura 001 showed the episode on the green outside St John's. This clip was nearly seven minutes long and I had to fast-forward through it. I got the gist though. Most of the time the camera had been focused on my wet, shivering body, even when it had been sprawled on the ground, covered in mud. 001 was bad enough. Laura 002 was worse. It was just twenty-two seconds long and showed me asleep.

It looked harmless enough at first. Except I was rigid. I lay like a corpse, flat on my back, legs straight and close together, arms by my sides. Everything still except for my head.

My face was quivering with effort. In small, jerking movements I threw my head from side to side and I knew, because in some part of the back of my mind I remembered, that I had been trying to wake up.

The window next to my bed opened and in my half dreaming, half waking, heavily sedated state I heard it. I stopped fidgeting and froze. Then I started tossing again, like a helpless cripple trying to flee, unable to move more than a fraction of an inch at a time. I could hear the whimpers coming out of my own throat as the dark figure climbed through the window and leaned over me on the bed.

As the sweat ran down between my shoulder blades, I remembered this happening. The dream when someone had been in my room, looking down at me, while I'd done everything I could to move and had been paralysed. I'd never felt more helpless in my life and now every second of that terrifying dream had turned out to be real.

The dark figure — impossible to say for certain who it was but the hair looked too short to be Thornton — took hold of the quilt and began to pull it down. I didn't think I could watch any more and was actually reaching out to close it down when something hurled itself at the intruder. The masked figure turned in alarm, raised an arm to defend itself and then kicked out. My rescuer — Sniffy the dog, God bless her — had backed off and was out of view but I could hear her barking and growling. The intruder glanced out of the window, climbed through and vanished. The film ended.

I went back to Finder. So many familiar names: Bryony, Nicole, Jackie, Nina, Kate, Jayne, Evi, each with several files. I didn't want to look at any of them, but there was something I had to know for certain.

I chose the file labelled *Nicole* that appeared to be the last, Nicole 010, and pressed Play. The scene had been shot at night, using some sort of night-vision equipment because the footage had the monochrome appearance of nocturnal wildlife footage. Nicole's Mini convertible was parked at the side of a quiet country road.

She was in the driver's seat and appeared to be unconscious. As I watched, a tall, masked figure (this was Thornton, judging by the hair) adjusted the seat belt around her so that it was tight while another masked man checked the knot of a rope that had been tied around the nearest tree. Thornton was pushing up the sleeve on her right arm when his companion slipped the noose end of the rope over Nicole's head. Thornton had something in his hand that looked like a syringe. He injected something into the unconscious girl and pulled her sleeve back down in place. The other turned the key in the ignition and the Mini's engine sprang to life. Both men walked out of shot.

I had to fast forward the next part. It took Nicole maybe two minutes to wake up. Her head swayed, fell forward and raised itself again slowly a couple of times before she came round properly. Her right hand went up and felt the noose around her neck. She glanced round to see where the rope finished.

Do you know what? I actually found myself hoping she wouldn't do it. That, at the last minute, she'd see sense, slip the noose from her neck and press her foot down hard on the pedal to get herself the hell away from those monsters.

She didn't, of course. She sat still for several moments, then in a flurry of activity checked the mirror, released the handbrake, clutched the steering wheel and shot forward.

The camera followed her all the way, caught the severed head bouncing along the road like a lost football, and only switched off when approaching headlights warned that another vehicle was getting close.

'And it looks as though she'd had quite a lot to drink,' said Castell. 'I was working last night. I usually try to keep an eye on her when I'm there, but . . . anyway, she broke her neck. It would have been instant. She wouldn't have known anything.'

'I didn't know Meg had a drink problem,' said Evi as Sniffy slinked over and leaned heavily against her.

Castell was nodding his head, slowly, sadly. 'Well, they get very good at hiding it.'

'Megan's dead?' said Evi, running a hand over Sniffy's head and along her velvet-soft ears.

Castell narrowed his eyes and seemed to lean towards her. 'Can I get you anything?' he asked. 'Would you like a drink? A glass of brandy?'

Evi shook her head. 'I'm not supposed to

drink alcohol.'

Castell's face was all sympathy. 'No,' he said, 'but you do though, don't you? You drink quite a lot.'

'Excuse me?'

Sniffy nudged Evi for more attention.

Castell stretched across the table, as though he were going to touch her. Evi drew her hand back. His eyes flicked down and back up again.

'Evi, this isn't easy for me to say, but Megan was concerned about you,' he said. 'Specifically, she was worried about you continuing to work in your current state of ill health. She'd written a letter to your GP, copied to the university authorities, setting out her concerns.'

Evi put an arm round Sniffy's shoulders and pulled her a little closer. 'Rubbish,' she said. 'Megan wouldn't discuss me with you. That would be completely unethical.'

Castell shrugged. 'The letter's on her computer,' he said. 'I can print it off in a matter of moments.'

It took a second, for what he'd just said to sink in. 'You can access Meg's computer?'

Eyes narrowed. 'What are you getting at?'

Castell had been at Cambridge fifteen years ago. Not studying medicine, but he'd known several people who had been. Castell had been dating Meg for months now, often stayed over at her house. If he could access Meg's computer he could have seen all the files she kept on Evi. He would know everything about her. Everything that had happened to her, everything she was afraid of.

'Can I give you some advice, Evi?' Castell was saying.

'Please do,' said Evi, wondering if the fear was visible on her face.

'Hand in your resignation today. Say you need some time to yourself for a few months. That way, the letter Meg wrote to the authorities can stay exactly where it is. No one need ever know.'

Don't argue, let him think he's won. She put her head in her hands, took a moment. 'You're probably right,' she said after a few seconds. 'Thank you.'

'And I'd hate to have to charge you with wasting police time,' said Castell. 'What with the skeleton toys and the masked men in the garden and the blood in the bath and the disappearing emails. So many calls, nothing to substantiate any of them. Your credibility could be completely undermined. You'd struggle ever to work again.'

Agree to everything. She wasn't on her own. Laura would know what to do.

'You're right,' she said, forcing herself to look straight at him. 'It's been a very difficult few months. Thank you, John.' She pushed her chair back and reached for her stick. She needed to signal this conversation was over. 'And I'm truly sorry about Meg. I know how close you two were.'

Castell got up to leave.

'Nice dog,' he said, as he headed for the door.

I had to get out of here. Not only was watching these sick film clips threatening to send me over the edge, but there was a risk I could seriously compromise Joesbury's investigation. I was conducting an illegal search. If it became known I'd done so, everything in this room might become inadmissible. And then Joesbury really would kill me.

I opened again the first clip of me and ran it to the point where I'd found it. Then I pressed Pause. I took one more minute to open up the list of files recently accessed and to delete the record of the ones I'd looked at. Someone who knew what they were doing would soon find evidence that I'd been on the computer, but with a bit of luck no one would have any reason to be suspicious.

One more second, though, to walk back to the TV table and pick up the DVD case labelled *Nicole.*

I certainly didn't have time to play it, nor did I need to. I knew exactly what I'd see. There would be footage of Nicole in her room at college, when she'd thought she was alone. I'd see her getting undressed, walking around in her underwear or night-clothes. I'd see her sleeping, someone going into her room, touching her, abusing her, when all the while she was powerless to stop it, even to remember it clearly the next day.

At some point, she would disappear from college and be brought here, where a scenario based on her worst nightmare would be played out. It would almost certainly involve some sort of sexual abuse, even rape, and it would all be captured on film.

The concluding scenes, of course, I'd just watched, albeit in their unedited state. Nicole, now a physical and mental wreck, was placed in a situation where taking her own life would be simple. The death was the conclusion the whole film was building towards. These people were making snuff movies.

'When you find out what's going on here,' Joesbury had told me, 'you'll wish you hadn't.' He'd been right about that.

By this time, my heartbeat was racing and the headache was back with a vengeance. I had to find Joesbury and get Scott Thornton, Megan Prince and Nick Bell arrested. If they were innocent they could prove it once they were behind bars. Iestyn Thomas had to be found and Jim Notley could well be involved too. I'd get back to my car and text Joesbury again. If I got no reply, I'd call Dana Tulloch.

I'd got halfway to the door when I heard movement on the floor below me. A second later, someone turned on the big warehouse lights and I was trapped.

72

'We need you to wake up now, big fella. Can you hear me? Can you tell me your name?'

The light was hurting Joesbury's eyes. He really didn't want to open them.

'You're in hospital, love. The Lister in Stevenage. You were involved in a car accident. Do you remember anything about it?'

'Rita, we've just heard that the car is owned by a haulage company in Dagenham. The registered keeper is a Michael Jackson.'

'Really?'

'That's what they told me.'

'Mr Jackson? Michael? Is that your name?'

'Mick,' managed Joesbury. 'And when people start humming "Billie Jean" at me I usually thump 'em. Will I live?'

I went for the closest window. There was nowhere in this room I could hide and if the window didn't open it was all over. I could hear more than one set of footsteps below and the occasional word being exchanged. They weren't exactly making a row but they weren't trying to be silent either. That could mean they didn't know I was in here. It could also mean they knew I couldn't escape.

If I thought about that, I'd lose my head completely, so I jumped on to the desk and ducked beneath the blind. Opened, the window would tilt to a horizontal position, allowing plenty of space for me to climb out. Trouble was, it had a lockable catch on the frame and no key in sight. From the bottom of the steps, I could hear someone speaking quietly. I had about ten seconds.

I made sure the key wasn't hung from or taped to the window frame, then shimmied along the desk to the next window. Footsteps on the top two steps. No sign of the key on the second or the third window and I had about a second left. The door handle twitched beneath the pressure of someone's hand.

Half my attention was looking round for a weapon, the other half gave one last glance to the fourth window. The key was there, sellotaped to the wall.

The door handle hadn't moved again and whoever was on the other side of it was talking to someone below. I peeled the tape from the wall and freed the key.

The handle was pushed to vertical and the door began to open as I put the tiny gold key into the window lock and turned. Cold air rushed inside. No point being silent any more. I swung myself out as a man's voice cried out, 'Shit!'

Had I been at the first window, he'd probably have caught me. As it was, he grabbed my wrist but didn't get a firm enough grip to hold on when my full weight and the force of gravity were against him. For a second I hung there, looking into a face I knew.

Tom, the maintenance man with kind eyes and broad shoulders, who'd carried my bags the day I'd arrived, who'd fixed my burst pipes, who had access to my room, probably to every student room in Cambridge, any time he liked. Tom. Thomas? As my eyes opened wide with shock, his narrowed in amusement. Then I slid through his hand and landed hard, but unhurt, on the snow.

Without looking up I set off. A second later a thump told me Tom had leaped from the window too. I ran on, head down, arms pumping, a twitch in my ankle telling me that dropping from a height hadn't been entirely without consequences, but knowing that if I could reach the main road through the estate, there'd be units with people in them.

Thirty yards ahead was a delivery van. The driver was standing outside the nearby unit, looking down at paperwork. Hearing heavy breathing behind, I reached the van and jumped inside, pulling the door shut and pressing down the lock.

I'd meant only to lock myself in for long enough to call for help. I hadn't thought about whether the keys would be in the ignition. They were. Without stopping to think about whether it was a good idea, because nothing I'd done so far that day was, I switched on the engine, released the handbrake and pressed the accelerator just as Tom pulled open the tailgate and the driver himself grasped hold of the driver's door.

I pulled away, determined not to give my pursuer a chance to climb in the back. In the rear-view mirror I saw the driver gazing after me in disbelief. Tom was already running back towards Unit 33 and, by the front door, I could see Scott Thornton.

I pulled out on to the main road and turned in the direction of my car.

Over a hundred and seventy-five miles away, the Triumph motorbike growled its last and fell silent, like a large jungle cat settling down for a nap. The rider, a tall man, switched off the engine, kicked down the stabilizers and climbed off.

All light seemed to have fled the day and the rain to have increased in intensity as he walked up the path to the house. It was cold, hard-as-nails, northern rain, just a fraction more liquid than hail. As the rider turned the key in his front door, he could hear the phone ringing in the hall. He stepped inside, pulled off his helmet, scratched short, honey-blond curls and picked up the receiver.

'Harry Laycock,' he said. Bloody hell, it was wet. He'd only been inside five seconds and he was standing in a puddle.

'Harry? Is that you, Harry?'

'Last time I checked,' he replied, pressing the receiver against one shoulder as he tried to shrug himself out of his wet jacket. A stream of rain ran down his neck. From the back of the house appeared the large ginger cat that had adopted him just over a year ago and that he'd given up mistreating in the hope it would eventually go away. 'What's up, Alice?'

'And you're OK?'

The cat inserted itself between his legs, either not minding or not noticing that they were encased in wet leather. 'Freezing cold, wetter than an otter and in serious need of something I've given up for the entire month of January,' Harry replied. 'Otherwise, not so bad.'

'Jeez, what the hell is going on?' said Alice, as though talking to herself now, or to someone in the room with her.

Harry got one arm free and transferred the phone. 'Well, why don't you tell me?' he said, as his wet jacket landed on the cat. His friend Alice was American, a little more given to wearing her heart on her sleeve than most of his British mates, but it was a long time since he'd heard her this agitated. 'Are the family OK?' he asked quickly, to quell his own sense of unease.

'They're fine. Harry, have you heard from Evi?'

And there it was, all it took to remind him that a piece of him was missing.

'I never hear from Evi,' he said. The cat slipped out from beneath the wet leather, gave him a look of disdain and stepped daintily down the hall.

'She emailed me a couple of hours ago,' said Alice. 'I've been calling you ever since. Her too, and neither one of you has been answering.'

'Is she OK?'

'I'm going to forward it on to you. Switch your computer on. You need to look at it right away. Something is very wrong.'

Officially, a snuff movie is defined as visually recorded and commercially distributed material, primarily for the purpose of sexual gratification, in which a principal character is genuinely killed. The subject had come up as part of a course I'd done at police training college, on illegal images and video material. I'd even seen short extracts of films purporting to be snuff. *Cannibal Holocaust* was one I remembered. *The Flower of Flesh and Blood* was another. Towards the end of the session, when even the blokes had been feeling queasy, we'd been told they were fake.

The sergeant running our course had been very clear. Snuff movies are an urban myth, he'd said, and not a single known film has ever been proved to be genuine. We'd nodded wisely. It was obvious when you thought about it. The special-effects capabilities accessible to film-makers these days, even to amateur ones, have rendered real violence redundant.

Whilst huge sums of money can be made from extreme pornography, our sergeant had insisted, people who make and distribute such material are businessmen, running professional, if unsavoury, operations. They would not take the risk of committing murder just to make a film.

'What about child pornography?' a fellow student had asked. 'The penalties for that are pretty severe, but people continue to make it.'

'Harder to fake,' had been the reply. 'You can fake a sadistic murder, you can't fake a kid.'

So, the official line from police authorities the world over is that snuff movies are the cinematic bogeymen. A scary idea, nothing more. They don't exist.

As I drove my stolen vehicle back towards my own car, I had a feeling that that theory was about to be challenged. What I'd just seen in Unit 33 was a commercial operation, no doubt about it. There were facilities there to make thousands of copies of their films. Thousands more would be distributed online through untraceable accounts.

I had no idea of the size of the market for illegal porn, but given that the legal variety produced on the outskirts of Hollywood nets its producers several billion dollars a year, I figured it had to be pretty sizeable.

I swapped the van for my car and drove away quickly, trying to call Joesbury as I headed back to town. An anonymous voice invited me to leave a message and I suggested he call Laura urgently. Back on the outskirts of town, I pulled off the road to think.

Evi's beautiful Queen Anne house was a university-owned building. Tom would be able to get in. When she'd asked to have her locks changed, he'd probably been the one who'd done it. When she'd had her tank checked after the blood-bath incident, Tom could have been the one who'd gone there. Every time she tried to make her home safe from stalkers, the stalker himself was one step ahead of her. I dialled in turn every number she'd given me. Home, office and mobile. She wasn't answering any of them and that didn't feel good. I needed to find her.

Before anything else, though, it was time I took out a small insurance policy.

I fished a notebook out of the glove compartment (never met a copper yet who didn't travel with one of those things) and jotted down notes of where I'd been the last couple of hours and what I'd seen. I folded the note and pushed it into the crease of the driver's seat.

If anything happened to me, my car would be searched by expert crime scene investiga-

tors. They'd find the note in minutes.
Whether it would be admissible as evidence
was a moot point — I'd been in the warehouse illegally — but they would know what
I knew.

I was just about to set off again when my
phone rang. Thank God. I grabbed it so
quickly I almost dropped it.

'Laura, it's Nick Bell.'

All air seemed to have been sucked from
the car. Bell could not have this number.
The phone was new and I hadn't given the
number to anyone. Only Joesbury knew it.

'Hi,' I managed.

'What're you up to?' he said, and he
sounded so normal that for a second everything that had just happened seemed unreal.

'Been out for a run,' I told him. 'Just heading back now.'

'Any chance of you coming by?'

'You're at home?' I glanced at my watch.
Just after one o'clock.

'Vet's coming out to see Shadowfax,' he
told me, and he sounded like he was stifling
a yawn. 'He's had me up half the night. I
have to be around to suck my teeth and look
horrified when I'm presented with the bill.
Thing is, I've got something for you.'

'Oh?' I said.

'Bryony left you a note. It fell under her

bed. Your nutty room-mate found it this morning when she went to the hospital to pick up some books. She asked if I could pass it on. Seemed to think I'd be likely to see you before she did.'

Bryony had left me a note. Or had she? No way of knowing. What the hell did I do?

'To be honest,' Nick was saying, 'I rather jumped at the excuse to call you. It's been a tough couple of days.'

Tell me about it. 'I've got a couple of calls to make. Let me get back to you in five minutes.'

As soon as the line disconnected, I tried Joesbury again. Come on, come on. An anonymous voice told me to leave a message. I told it to have him call me immediately.

Shit, shit, shit. Well, no way was I going to Bell's house. I wouldn't even call him back. Evi's then.

I'd just started the engine when a text came in. Well, speak of the devil.

Can't talk right now, Flint. What's up?

What was bloody up? My fingers wouldn't move fast enough.

Snuff movies is what's up. Unit 33, Bell

Foundries Industrial Estate. Nick Bell
has this number. He wants me to go to
his house now. I'm heading to Evi's instead.

I pressed Send. Waited. Had no idea how
fast Joesbury could type. Quite fast, it
turned out.

Bell's kosher, Flint. Been working with
us. On my way to his place myself, with
the boys. Meet you there in 15.

73

West Wales, twenty-three years earlier
'All the king's horses and all the king's men.'

Iestyn realized that his young sister was in their father's study. He pushed open the door and stepped inside. His dad was lying on the floor, face down, his sister sitting beside him. Iestyn's first thought was that they were building something together. He opened his mouth to grunt. He'd leave quick, before he got drafted into babysitting duties.

Then he realized his sister was sitting in a shiny pool of thick, gelatinous liquid, the colour and consistency of runny strawberry jam. Her hands were the same shade and her hair sticky with it. Her cute, pale face glanced up at him once before she went back to her task. She was in the process of rebuilding their father's head, picking up bone fragments from where they lay on the carpet, and trying to fit them together again like a three-dimensional jigsaw. And as she worked, she sang.

'Couldn't put Humpty together again.'

74

Nick's Range Rover was parked close by the side door when I arrived ten minutes later. There was no sign of any other vehicle.

Bell's kosher. Been working with us.

Good God, what else was the bugger going to throw at me?

You think you're the only undercover officer we have in town?

Nick Bell could not be an undercover police officer. A GP was far too complicated a cover story. But covertly working with SO10, in the same way Evi was? That wasn't impossible. So did he know who I was? Or had he been covertly investigating me while I'd been . . . oh, Lord, it didn't bear thinking about.

The back door was open and a handwritten note had been stuck to it with a drawing pin.

Upstairs, it said.

We'd almost had sex. Christ, this was going to be embarrassing.

A musical tone told me I had another text. Joesbury again.

ETA three minutes. Don't let me catch you snogging.

It was beyond me. I was handing over to Joesbury and his 'boys' as soon as they got here and then I was never having anything to do with SO10 as long as I lived. I might even apply to join Traffic.

I pushed open the door and went through into the kitchen. No sign of the dogs. The room was warm but the house had an empty feel about it.

'Hi!' I called from halfway up the stairs. 'It's me.'

There was no response. Nick could be outside with the animals but the note had definitely said come upstairs. I stopped at the top. Still no sign of him. The master bedroom where I'd slept the other night was at the front of the house, behind me, as was the main spare bedroom. Both doors shut. The bathroom was to my left. Door shut.

'Hey, gorgeous, I'm in here,' he called.

I stepped forward, pausing on the threshold of a room I hadn't seen before. I'd just registered that Nick was leaning over an old desk with a tin of polish in one hand and a leather bridle in the other when I heard the creak of a stair behind me. Joesbury.

I turned just as Nick straightened up and we both looked towards the door, the goofy smile freezing on my face. The man blocking our way out wasn't Joesbury.

'Good God,' said Nick, over my shoulder.

I could have cut off my own arm for being stupid enough to get trapped in an upstairs room. The man in the doorway, whom I'd last seen running after a stolen van at the industrial estate, ignored me. 'Hello, Nick,' he said. 'Long time no see.'

The room wasn't brightly lit, the hallway quite dark, but even so Tom's eyes seemed to have lost all their colour. They were like millponds at night, black and empty, and I couldn't remember why I'd ever thought them kind. Then I was sizing up the situation, checking the room for ways out, weapons, distractions, anything. All I really had to do was to stay calm and stall them. Joesbury and the cavalry would be here any second.

'I take it you're Iestyn Thomas?' I said. There were any number of hard objects I could introduce to Thomas's head given the chance.

'Laura, what on earth . . . ?' began Nick, his eyes going from me to the man in the doorway.

Then Thomas stepped into the room and any hope I'd had that he was alone was quashed. Scott Thornton was with him, his blue eyes gleaming at me the way they had through the ninja mask the night he'd half drowned me. And then another man appeared. This one I didn't know, except that I'd seen him leaving Megan Prince's house the day before.

'John?' Nick knew him, then, but from the tone of surprise and growing alarm in his voice it was obvious he was completely in the dark. 'What's going on? Has something happened?'

'Nick knows nothing,' I said. 'Let him go. Or tie him up and leave him here. Either way, he's not a threat.'

A nervous laugh that was more like a choke from Nick. 'Laura, don't be ridiculous. John is DI Castell. He's a police officer. Local CID.'

John Castell, the man in charge of the suicide investigations. Oh, there weren't words.

No, actually, there were. 'I'm a police officer,' I said. 'He is a twisted, psychotic piece of shit.'

They moved forward at that. Thornton and Thomas took hold of Nick and, ignoring his increasingly alarmed protests, pulled us apart. Castell and I glared at each other and I was praying I'd have the nerve to do some serious damage before he overpowered me. Or before help arrived, and on that subject, where the hell was Joes—

'Nick, how did you get my number?' I asked without taking my eyes off Castell. 'You phoned me just now on a new number. Who gave it to you?'

'Will you lot get the fuck out of my hou—'

I'm not sure who hit Nick, I only saw him sink to the carpet, before someone else appeared on the landing outside and all I could do was stare like a halfwit.

Your nutty room-mate found it this morning when she went to the hospital to pick up some books.

Talaith Robinson, my nutty room-mate, sidled up to Castell and wrapped herself around him like a bad smell around rotten meat.

'Hello, Lacey,' she said.

75

Bank of the River Cam, five years earlier
A recent summer storm had shaken millions
of leaves from the willow trees. They were
floating in the still backwaters of the river,
looking almost solid enough to walk on. They
adorned the moored punts lining the river's
edge and covered the banks like a dappled
green carpet. Already the heat was building
again, making the damp earth steam.

DI John Castell took off his jacket and slung
it over one shoulder. He loosened his tie. The
air was thick with sugar stealers and tiny
green flying insects. Several of both clung to
his shirt and his hair. He left them where they
were, rather enjoying the unusual experience
of being garlanded by nature.

As he stepped beneath the canopy of one
of the larger trees he felt as if he were entering an enchanted tropical forest. Here, hidden
from the world by a sphere of green, a woman
was waiting.

Her dress was long and made from a light, floaty fabric that managed to cling to her curves and sway in the breeze at the same time. Her hair was long too. She was like a creature from another time. Little more than twenty years old, she was far too young for him and it just wasn't going to have to matter.

'Hey, buddy,' said one of the two men with her, the men he'd come to meet. 'I'd like you to meet my sister.'

76

The high-pitched beeping of a text message woke Evi from an uncomfortable slumber at around four o'clock. She turned over on the bed and picked up her phone. It was from Laura.

Called back to London and transferred to another case. Powers that be don't consider this one worth pursuing further. Suggest you refer any ongoing concerns to local CID. Good meeting you. Take care. Laura.

Not fully awake, Evi read the text again. Laura had gone. Evi sat upright on the bed. Most of the light had gone from the day outside and her bedroom was filled with shadows. She realized she'd slept through the entire afternoon, missing two supervisions and a two-hour stint at the clinic. And yet no one had phoned her. It was as though no one had even noticed she was missing.

She got up and made her way to the kitchen, knowing something else was wrong, just unable to put her finger on what it was. Only when she saw the empty space in front of the cooker where she'd put Sniffy's rug did she realize. The rug was no longer there. Neither were the food and water bowls that she'd put by the sink. And neither was Sniffy herself. All traces of the dog were gone from the house. She might never have existed.

The fresh cold air of the early evening stung Joesbury's face but helped to clear his head. A little way ahead he could see a wooden bench where a solitary smoker sat huddled in his dressing gown. Sitting down felt like a very good idea, except he wasn't sure he'd ever get up again.

Getting out of hospital before the doctor in charge was willing to release him hadn't been easy but Joesbury had insisted. He'd waited till just after his prescribed dose of painkillers and had managed to dress himself. Now, he needed a phone.

Conscious of bloodstained clothes and a bruised, battered face, he turned and made his way to the corner of the street. Two hundred yards away was a row of public telephones. There was no response on the first number he tried. He tried again, gave up after the third attempt and dialled Scotland Yard.

'Jesus, Mark, what's going on?' DCI Phillips said, after the phone call to SO10 had been accepted. 'We expected you twenty-four hours ago.'

He listened while Joesbury explained about the accident, how both his and Lacey's laptops and mobile phones were missing, even his cover ID.

'Were you ambushed?' Phillips asked, when he'd done.

'Traffic officer who came to see me said all four tyres were in ribbons. Draw your own conclusion.'

'Looks like we're into damage limitation. I'm pulling everyone out.'

'Hang on, guv. DC Flint had information for me. Names and a possible location. Shit, it's gone.'

Heavy sigh down the line. 'You didn't write it down?'

'There's nothing wrong with my memory when I'm not concussed,' Joesbury said. 'We had a trace on her vehicle. Is it still operational?'

'Give me a sec. And I'll organize someone to pick you up while I'm at it.'

Joesbury waited, whilst the world around him became less focused. He closed his eyes, opening them only when he knew he was about to fall over.

'I've got it,' Phillips told him. 'What do you need?'

'Can you give me her movements since yesterday first thing?'

Another second passed. Then, 'She spent the night at Endicott Farm, between Burwell and Waterbeach. Did you know about that?'

Joesbury felt his headache press down. 'Yeah. She was back at St John's just before nine, then she went to the hospital. What next?'

'Went to St Clement's Road just off the town centre. Stayed about forty minutes.'

'That's it,' said Joesbury. 'Scott Thornton, number 108. I was going to have it watched. Shit, we've lost twenty-four hours.'

'Want me to organize a search warrant?'

'I think so. She's also worried about Nick Bell and Megan Prince, two local medics. And somebody called Thomas. Ianto? Iestyn. That's it, Iestyn Thomas. Where did she go after that?'

'A five-mile trip out of town to a village called Boxworth. Stayed in the high street for ten minutes, then went back into town and parked outside Evi Oliver's house for a few minutes. Back to the hospital and then on to Queen's Road. Didn't move from there for the rest of the night.'

'Guv, can you have someone find out who lives in Boxworth near where she parked? See if any names ring a bell?'

'Anything else?'

'What's she been up to today?'

'This morning, no movement until 10.17 a.m., when the car was driven out of town,' continued Phillips. 'She went towards the Bell . . .'

'Bell Foundries Industrial Estate. Unit 33,' said Joesbury. 'She saw Scott Thornton going inside earlier in the week. Please tell me she didn't.'

'She parked on the B1102, about half a mile away. Stayed there for eighty minutes, so it's anybody's guess what she got up to. After that, she drove out to Endicott Farm again.'

Bell's place again. Could she not stay away from the twat for five minutes?

'Then what?'

'It was there for nearly thirty minutes, then went back to St John's. Which is where it remains.'

'She's at St John's?'

'Car is.'

'Can you get George looking for her?'

'He's already on his way to pick you up. I'll get someone else to do it.'

'Guv, I need something else. That phone we gave her yesterday. Can you give me its recent use?'

'You're stretching my technical skills, buddy. Hang on.'

Joesbury waited, hearing Phillips call to one of the clerical staff. Then, 'One incoming text late last night,' said Phillips. 'Can't give you the details, just the number it came from.'

'Nobody should have been texting her. Nobody had that number but me.'

'It was from you.'

Joesbury leaned back against the Perspex wall of the kiosk, telling himself that throwing up right now would do nothing to improve the situation. 'Late last night I was bleeding on to a hospital pillow,' he managed. 'Somebody was using my phone to text Lacey. Anything else?'

'An outgoing text late this morning, that one also to you. I assume you didn't get it. And one more, a couple of hours later. An incoming call this time from a listed number.'

'Nobody had her number. No one could call her but me.'

'Hang on, I've got it. Here we go. She was called by a local GP. A Dr Nicholas Bell.'

Silence.

'You still there, Mark?'

77

What I remember next is being in my room at St John's. I was in bed, my arms wrapped tight around Joesbury's teddy, wearing my usual night-time jogging pants and vest. For a second, everything felt so normal it seemed the only crazy thing in the whole world was me. I felt tired, seriously hungover, and as though my limbs would shake if I tried to move, but otherwise OK.

Without thinking, my eyes went up to where I knew the camera that had been filming me had to be and that's when I knew everything had changed. The camera wasn't there. It couldn't be. The pipework that must have hidden it wasn't there. The cosmetics around the washbasin were mine but the mirror was different. The one screwed to the wall of my room had a tiny chip in it at the top right-hand corner. This one was whole and perfect.

I pushed back the duvet and sat up. The

floor wasn't right, either. It looked cleaner and newer and the wall behind the bedhead wasn't plaster but a much softer, warmer substance. Plywood.

I was not going to panic. I was going to think. Difficult, with such a thick, fuzzy head, but not impossible. Just take it slow.

Nick! What the hell had they done to Nick?

I couldn't help Nick if I panicked. Take stock. I was in Unit 33 and they'd recreated my room out of plywood, just as they'd done for Jessica. What had she said? My room but not my room?

I was going to hold it together.

This was about scaring me, about getting more gruesome footage for their sick films. They didn't want me dead yet. I had a massive advantage over the other girls who'd been here. I knew where I was and how to get out. And these bastards did not know me. They could not know what scared me. They'd have something in store that would be unpleasant, but I could deal with it. I'd squeal a bit, pretend to be more freaked than I was. Let them get their footage. And all the while I'd be looking for my chance.

First things first. What had they given me? I remembered being held from behind by Castell and Thornton pushing the needle hard into my neck, then a vague recollection of being carried down the stairs. Nothing after that. A powerful sedative would be my best guess, and it had to be starting to wear off now that I'd woken up. I'd be slow and sluggish, far from my best, but still basically OK.

I got to my feet and felt the room tilt. When I felt I could handle it, I reached over the bed towards the window. The curtains were drawn and I just knew there was something behind them I wouldn't want to see. Telling myself I could deal with it, I took hold of one curtain and pulled it gently back.

Oh, Jesus!

I'd fallen back against the wardrobe door. There was a dark space in my head that was swelling like a balloon. I was not going to lose it. I was not. It was going to take more than a horrific photograph to make me do that. When I could face it, I made myself look again at the dreadful image they'd fastened on the wall of this fake room, exactly where the window should have been.

It was easier the second time, when I knew what was coming. In fact it was nothing I hadn't seen many times before. They'd found and blown up a post-mortem photograph, taken over a hundred years ago, of a murdered woman. The poor creature lay on the bed of her rented room in London, hacked beyond recognition.

Three months earlier, I'd worked a big case in London in which women were killed as coldly and as brutally as the one in this photograph had been, and now these bozos thought this was what would scare me the most.

They weren't even close.

I walked back to the bed and sat down for a while to get my breath back and clear my head. I was going to have to leave the room. See what they had waiting for me outside. I would do it in a second. Just another second.

There was blood, trickling down the wall.

I'd closed my eyes. It's not real blood, it's not real blood, they did this to Evi, freaked her out with fake blood. It will be paint, theatrical blood, whatever. I was going to walk over there, run my finger through it, write FUCK YOU in very large letters on the wall and when I got my hands on that bitch Talaith Robinson I was going to show her exactly what a great quantity of blood looked like and it would be her own.

I opened my eyes again to find the blood had gone. I got up anyway and walked over to check. The wall was white and clean.

OK, this was more serious than I'd thought. They'd given me some sort of hallucinogen. I pulled the curtain back again. The photograph of the murdered woman was still there. I reached out, touched it. It was real. The real image had sparked a connected hallucination. Well, at least I knew how it was going to work.

Jesus, to have been through this without the knowledge I had.

No time now to worry about what the others had gone through. I was prepared. I was going to cope. On legs that felt weak and shaky, but did what I told them, I crossed the room, pulled open the door and looked outside.

I saw a dimly lit space, narrow and disappearing into blackness. The walls were of old brickwork, the ceiling low. The painted plywood boards I'd seen in a storage room earlier had been for me.

Bring it on, I muttered as I stepped out, knowing the bravado was to make myself feel better and that it wasn't really working. It's one thing to tell yourself all they can do is scare you, but being scared can feel pretty bad when you're alone in a dark space, at the mercy of people you know to be psychopathic, and without the first clue about what's going to leap out at you next.

Somehow, I held it together. I walked forward, reached a corner and turned into a narrow, fake-brick-lined alley. It was like something an art student had knocked up in a couple of hours and it was not — not — going to get to me. Neither was the little surprise a few yards ahead, where a spotlight in the ceiling picked out a form on the floor. As I drew closer I could see it was a human figure. Closer still and I knew it wasn't real. This was a clothes-shop dummy, stripped naked and smeared with fake blood. Joesbury and I had found a very similar one when we'd been investigating the case last year. This was all public knowledge for anyone who looked hard enough and, OK, I was scared, really scared, useless to pretend otherwise any more, but I could deal with being scared. I was getting out of here.

Then the dummy opened its eyes and smiled at me.

When I came to myself again, I was leaning against one of the plywood walls, muttering it's not real, it's not real, it's not real, into hands that were damp with sweat.

Shit, it had looked very real. Fighting back the fear that the dummy had risen from the floor and was even now peering over my shoulder, I made myself look. Exactly where it had been, eyes closed, lips still, but for the first time I wasn't sure how much of this I could cope with. What they had to throw at me, possibly. What my own mind was chucking in for good measure was another matter entirely.

At that moment, the dim lights went out and I was staring into darkness so thick and heavy it could have gone on for ever. Then, some way ahead, a beam of light shone down from the roof. In the pool it made on the dusty warehouse floor stood a man in dark clothes holding a long, gleaming knife.

Ridiculous, I said to myself, as something cold trickled down into the small of my back. Ridiculous, ridiculous. The figure before me — I couldn't take my eyes off it even to blink — would be nothing more than a plywood cut-out, like the clowns I'd seen earlier in the day.

The figure was moving. OK, real or hallucination? Real or not? I couldn't tell but I really had to make my mind up fast because he was coming for me. I closed my eyes. Still there when I opened them. Real enough. I turned and ran into blackness.

A second later, I stopped dead. Another spotlight had appeared in the ceiling and a second dark-clad figure was standing right in the middle of the tunnel. Everything about him was in shadow, except the steel of the knife blade that shone in his right hand. I turned again, just as darkness fell once more.

I ran on, arms outstretched, knowing I'd lost all thought of finding a way out. I didn't care. I just had to get away from the men with knives.

Suddenly, I could see my room. To either side of the door were brick walls — that I knew weren't real. I stepped up to one, pushed it hard and felt its feet slide along the floor until there was a gap large enough for me to squeeze through.

The first thing I saw on the other side was the carousel. Close by and on its side was the fortune teller's tent. The Test Your Strength machine had been dismantled and lay in pieces on the floor. This was definitely somewhere I wasn't meant to be.

'Laura!' called a voice, masculine but high-pitched and giggly. 'Lacey-Laura! Where are you?' Then the dim lights went out again.

Instinct wanted to run, common sense told me to take it slow, get to the wall and follow it. The window I'd broken that morning might not have been repaired. If I could find that, I'd be out of here.

I crept forward. To my right I thought I

could make out one of the scary clowns. It was leaning backwards, as though against . . . yes, I'd reached the wall.

As I made my way along the side of the building, I wondered why they hadn't turned on the big warehouse lights. Expecting to be flooded with powerful light any second I made it to the corner. Keep going. While the lights were out, I had a chance. A doorframe. The door opened, I slipped through and couldn't believe my luck.

I was back in the storeroom that I'd broken into earlier. Light was shining in from street lights outside. Against the window I'd smashed was a piece of heavy cardboard and it took less than a second to pull it from the wall.

It was dark outside. I landed on the flagged path just as Scott Thornton appeared at the corner of the building, blocking my escape. He was dressed exactly as he'd been when he'd burst into my room just days before, naked from the waist up, ninja mask covering his eyes, his long dark curls unmistakable. I looked the other way, more in hope than expectation, to find one of the others at the opposite corner, similarly dressed. Impossible to go back inside. No choice but to go over the fence and into the woods.

I wasn't able to run fast. Or far. The sedative they'd given me still had too hard a grip. And the hallucinogen really kicked in when I hit fresh air. All around me, colours glowed, the stars were great lanterns hanging close enough to touch and fabulous creatures watched me with huge eyes. The trees took on twisted, torturous shapes, branches reaching down for me as I passed. And with every step I took into those woods, it seemed I was going back in time. My years as a detective slipped away; the new life I'd built for myself from the wreck of my past existence vanished.

I wasn't Lacey Flint any more, I was that terrified sixteen-year-old girl again, in an open space at midnight, and they were coming.

My last thought, as a hand caught hold of my hair, was that somehow, completely impossible although I knew it to be, they knew after all what scared me the most. Somehow they'd managed to unearth the one memory that I could never allow to come to the surface because everything good and normal and safe that I hold on to would shatter.

I screamed once, a shrill cry that went up through the treetops. Somewhere, from way up high, a bird of prey echoed it back to me.

78

The dark-blue saloon car pulled up and the passenger door opened as if by itself. Joesbury climbed inside. The driver was dressed in the uniform of a porter from the college of St John.

'Thanks, mate,' said Joesbury. 'What's happening?'

George indicated and pulled out into traffic, causing the driver behind to jump on his brakes and throw both hands in the air.

'Hammond's been on to the local chief constable requesting immediate uniform back-up,' replied George. 'Locals aren't happy but they're going along for now. We've put warrants out on Nick Bell and Scott Thornton but no sign of either of them yet. Our application for a warrant on Megan Prince was turned down on the grounds that she died last night. Accident at home, according to the CID report. Fell down the cottage stairs with three-quarters of a bottle of red wine inside her. Interestingly, though, her boyfriend is a fairly senior member of the local CID himself. Bloke called John Castell, another Cambridge graduate. Ring any bells?'

'Can't say it does but you're right, that is interesting. Anything suspicious about Prince's death?'

'Not according to initial reports, but it makes you think, doesn't it?'

Joesbury agreed that it did, indeed, make you think. 'So they still have us on the run?' he said.

'The only one we've picked up is Jim Notley, DC Flint's psycho farmer. He's in the local nick now, insisting he did nothing more than rent out a piece of land, that he knows nothing about anything and he wants a solicitor. He could be telling the truth. To be honest, he doesn't seem that bright. We have cars outside 108 St Clement's Road, Notley's farm and Dr Oliver's house. They can't go in until the warrants are signed. Same at the industrial estate and Bell's farm. We've also got a call out on Talaith Robinson, DC Flint's room-mate.'

The sharp sideways glance sent a spasm of pain through Joesbury's head.

'Your car was ambushed less than an hour after you turned up at college claiming to be related to Flint,' said George. 'Who else saw you together?'

'Jesus, she's just a kid.'

'She's twenty-six, Sir, older than she looks. And she wasn't born Talaith Robinson, either. She was born Talaith Thomas. Robinson was her stepfather's name. Her own father blew his brains out when she was three. She and her elder brother, the Iestyn Thomas you asked us to trace, found the body.'

'You're going to have to tell me about Lacey sometime,' said Joesbury, and her name seemed to cling to the inside of his mouth.

George took his eyes off the road for the first time. 'Her car's still parked in the Backs,' he replied. 'No sign of her anywhere in college, but her car keys and bag are in her room.'

The traffic lights in front of them changed to amber. George pressed the accelerator and the car shot through as they flashed to red.

'No one's seen her since this morning,' George continued, turning the corner and picking up speed. A wave of nausea washed over Joesbury. He closed his eyes, opened them and focused on the night sky rather than the headlights speeding towards them.

The moon was low and a pale orange, almost full.

'She wasn't well, according to a couple of the girls on her corridor,' said George. 'About half past nine, a doctor turned up at her door — off her own bat, as far as we can judge, nobody called her — and they had to wake Lacey up. The doctor was young and female, in a wheelchair, so we can assume it was Evi Oliver. They both went over to the Buttery for breakfast and we lose track of them after that. Dr Oliver hasn't been seen at the clinic she works at, or in her college rooms. Her colleagues have been trying to contact her all day and she isn't answering the door at her house.'

Joesbury's brain felt like an engine in need of a major overhaul. He wasn't taking this in fast enough.

'DC Flint and Dr Oliver could be together,' continued George. 'Hiding out somewhere.'

'Lacey's with Bell,' said Joesbury. 'We need to get into that farm. Where's your phone?'

'In the glove compartment, if you must, Sir. But with respect, if she is in there and we go in half-cocked, we could put her in more danger. DCI Phillips has requested hostage liaison.'

Detective Constable Richards of the Cambridgeshire Constabulary was sitting in his unmarked police car outside Evi's house. He'd been there for forty minutes when the roar of a motor-bike engine startled him out of the daydream he'd been having about a recent skiing holiday, a chalet maid from Blackburn and a Jacuzzi in the snow. The large performance bike pulled up behind his car and he watched in his rear mirror as the rider switched off his headlight, climbed off and marched up the path. He was hammering on the door before Richards was out of his vehicle.

79

There are times when just waking up can feel like the hardest thing anyone could ever ask you to do. The first morning after your child has died, perhaps. Or after the man you adore has walked out. You would give anything, certainly the rest of your life, to stay down in the darkness of not knowing.

It never happens, though, does it? You always come back to yourself. The world is still there. You are still there. But death has taken root inside you and you know it will grow, like a cancer with a voice, from now until the day it consumes you whole.

I took a deep breath, just to check I still could. I was in pain, they'd been pretty rough, but it wasn't too bad. Through my eyelashes, I could see the outline of my room at St John's. There was light. I was hot and wet and sticky, and that would be sweat. The drugs they'd given me had worn off and now absolute clarity like silver light was flooding through my head.

I could not be in St John's, I knew too much. They couldn't risk sending me back. I was still in Unit 33, in the replica of my room they'd mocked up, and it was where I would stay. I would not survive to tell anyone what they'd done to me. Sometime in the next few hours they would kill me and I would never tell anyone about the hour I'd spent in the woods behind this building. If I were lucky, I might not have time to relive it for myself.

I opened my eyes, saw the whitewashed ceiling. My real ceiling at St John's had been Artexed.

Perhaps they would let me write a letter, as long as it seemed like a real suicide note. I could do what I'd thought I'd never be able to. I could tell Joesbury what he meant to me. Dear Mark, I'd write, and the name would feel so unfamiliar, so separate from the man in my head. Dear Mark, and then I'd probably leave it at that, because what I felt for that man I could never put into words and it would have to be enough that the very last thought in my head had been of him.

The room was cold and the sweat on my body cooling down, starting to itch. Instinctively, my hand went down to my stomach.

I touched something solid, slick and wet. A split second later I was sitting up, staring at the mass of bloody tissue in my hands. My whole body was covered in blood. I could hardly see my skin, and strewn around me, around the bed, were organs, intestines, bodily tissue, a heart, even what looked like lungs. They'd hacked me open and pulled out my insides and left me, still alive, to see what they'd done.

I hit the floor hard and it was cold beneath me. There was a keening noise in the room that could only have been me but it seemed to be coming out of the walls. Right by my blood-slicked left foot was a triangular piece of tissue that I knew was my own uterus and a long-handled, steel-bladed, gleaming sharp knife.

End it now.

I think I might have spoken out loud, the thought was so clear.

A bit more pain — you've gone through so much already, what difference can a few seconds more make — and it's over. They can never hurt you again, you'll never have to think about what they did to you. You know you can do it, you did it once before, you held a knife in your hand and you held out your wrist and . . .

. . . the knife was in my hand. I was on

my knees, shivering with cold, or maybe shock, and the knife handle felt warm and smooth in my palm. Five letters had been etched crudely into the blade. LACEY. My knife.

A moment's courage and it's done. Deep breath now.

A thought. A tiny, half-hearted protest, barely able to make itself heard. If I'd been ripped open, why wasn't I in agony?

I was staring down at the scar on my left wrist. I remembered the white-hot searing pain of the moment when flesh parted and blood burst out, I remembered the screams ringing in my ears.

You can do it again. You won't even feel it, your body's already full of sedatives and anaesthetic, the cut will be little more than a tickle, a mother's kiss, sending you sweetly to sleep.

My arm was outstretched, my palm facing upwards like an offering, the knife handle felt like an old friend, and I was ready.

And yet, like a late-night knock on the door, there was that nagging thought struggling for attention. If I could feel the floor beneath me, cold and hard, and the wood of the knife handle, and the wet stickiness of the gore covering me, why couldn't I feel any pain?

Do it! It's over. Your life was nothing anyway. Has there been a single day that wasn't cold and heavy and lonely? Who will even know you've gone?

Could a sedative take away pain yet leave other sensations? Somehow I didn't think so. I made myself look properly at my mutilated body for the first time. What I saw gave me the courage to touch.

I was unhurt. Oh, Jesus, I was absolutely fine. I put my hand to my left breast and felt my heart beating. And I was breathing, of course I was, my lungs were exactly where they'd always been. Beneath the blood that I knew now wasn't mine, my stomach was whole and unmarked. They'd laid me naked on the bed, covered me with gore that probably wasn't even human and hoped it would be the final straw that sent me over the edge.

You could still do it. It's always easier the second time.

'No,' I said, and put the knife down on the floor beside me. It lay in a crimson pool, its blade gleaming with promise. And a tiny voice whispered inside my head: *Are you sure?*

80

DC Richards gained entry to Evi's house by breaking a small bathroom window. A few seconds later, he opened the front door.

'Stay in the hallway, please, sir,' he told Harry. 'Don't touch anything.'

Harry could hear Richards speaking softly into his radio as he opened first one door and then another. He caught a glimpse of a kitchen, in which everything seemed lower to the floor than usual, and then what looked like a bedroom.

Evi's house. Alice had given him her address months ago. He'd looked at it many times on Google Earth, had tried to picture its interior. He'd imagined it cosier, some-how, wide hearths and soft gold light, not this cold, tiled, grand hallway.

There was a slender-framed wheelchair to one side of the door. He reached out to run a hand along the armrest but remembered in time. He wasn't supposed to touch anything. Directly in front of him were stairs. There was a stairlift. He couldn't imagine her ever using such a thing. The Evi he knew would climb the stairs herself if it killed her.

A sound from upstairs. A scuffling. Then a low-pitched whimper.

'She's upstairs,' he called out. He took the stairs two at a time. At the top, he stood listening.

'Don't go any further,' came the instruction from below. 'In fact, come down now.'

Hearing the sound again, Harry ran along the carpeted corridor. Guessing, he pushed open the last door and stopped dead.

Staring up at him were scared, bewildered eyes. The whimpering sounded again. Footsteps behind told him Richards had caught up.

'What the bugger?' said Richards, who was peering over Harry's shoulder.

Harry stepped forward, knelt down and unfastened the muzzle from the dog's face. Free to pant again, the dog didn't move, just lay still, its mouth hanging open, tongue dry and furry. Harry pulled at the knots and managed to loosen the bindings around the dog's front legs enough to slip them off. He did the same thing with its back legs and the dog scrambled to its feet.

■ ■ ■ ■

George and Joesbury arrived at Endicott Farm just as the sergeant in charge of the attending special operations team received news that a warrant had been signed and he was authorized to enter the property. He was hammering on the front door, shouting out a warning to anyone inside, as Joesbury and George climbed out of their car. George produced his warrant card and vouched for Joesbury to the constable who met them.

Properly handled, a tubular steel police enforcer can deliver three tonnes of pressure to a locked door. The centuries-old, half-rotten wood of Nick Bell's front door would have crumbled under the pressure of a strong shoulder. The young constable wielding the enforcer broke through with his first attempt and half staggered over the threshold.

As George and Joesbury, kitted out in protective clothing, followed the sergeant through the front door, they heard the shattering of glass that told them other officers were entering the property elsewhere. A dog began barking.

The search team fanned out through the house, calling out warnings, kicking open doors, switching on lights, checking each room before moving on. As instructed, Joesbury and George stayed at the rear.

'Casualty upstairs.'

Joesbury stepped forward; George's hand on his shoulder held him back. The sergeant ran heavily up the stairs and disappeared into a room on the right. A second later, they heard a radio call summoning an ambulance. Joesbury set off again and this time he wasn't stopped.

The air at the top of the steps seemed denser somehow, pressing closer, holding him back, as though trying to prevent him from seeing the prone form. He saw it anyway. A spreading pool of blood steadily making its way across the faded carpet. Bright-coloured hair dark and sodden. A serious head wound. Long, jean-clad legs. Blue sweater. Nick Bell.

81

After I'd kicked the knife away from me, I scrambled to my feet and tried the door. Locked, of course. There was no way out of this wooden box short of kicking the walls down and I really didn't think I had the energy for that. So I pulled the gore-covered top sheet away from the bed and dropped it into a corner. There was no water in the taps but I cleaned myself as much as I could with a towel. On the bed was a blanket that was largely clean. Naked and freezing, I climbed beneath it, grabbed hold of Joesbury's teddy and did the only thing possible. I fell asleep.

The phone woke me. My own phone, close by. I followed the sound and found it beneath the pillow. They'd missed my phone. How they'd been so stupid I had no idea but seconds were all I needed to tell someone where I was. The screen was bright. Joesbury! Joesbury was calling me.

'It's me. They've got me. I'm at the industrial estate. Unit 33.'

'Easy, Flint, keep your knickers on,' replied Joesbury in his distinctive south London accent. 'Now, do you have anything serious to report? Because I'm about to finish for the day.'

'I'm at the industrial estate. They're going to . . .' I stopped. This wasn't Joesbury. And I could hear him in stereo, over the phone and from directly above me. At that moment I became aware of light getting stronger, flooding the room and coming from overhead. I heard a stifled giggle and looked up.

The false ceiling of my 'room' had been removed, and behind the powerful spotlight that shone down on me I could see right the way up to the roof of the industrial unit. Then the spotlight shifted a little, to pool its light against my fake wardrobe, and I could make out a narrow gangway about ten feet above my head. Standing on it and leaning against a safety rail were Talaith Robinson and John Castell. Talaith's hair trailed down around her face like weed in a stagnant pond.

Then I heard clanging, the sound of two sets of footsteps walking along the gangway.

Scott Thornton and Iestyn Thomas making their way towards Castell and Talaith. When the two newcomers reached the couple, they all looked down at me.

And there they were at last, the three men who'd singled me out as their latest victim on my very first night here, and the woman who'd probably tipped them off in the first place.

They were about to try again. I hadn't walked into their trap earlier and I'd known they wouldn't give up. This was where I had to be calm and clever. Play for time. Don't give them what they want but don't wind them up too much. I raised my left wrist, and looked at the spot where my watch would normally be.

'Anyone got the time?' I asked.

No reply. Talaith's shoulders shook a little, as though she was almost, but not quite, laughing. Castell had a phone in his hand. It had been he imitating Joesbury just now.

'Because I think you people might be running out of it,' I went on. 'Scotland Yard know all about this place and all about you. They've been watching you for months now.'

'Is that so?' said Castell.

'There's water at the foot of the bed,' Talaith told me. 'It should still be fairly warm.

And some clothes. Get washed and get dressed.'

Being washed and dressed seemed like a very good idea. Doing it in front of these guys another matter entirely.

'You left one of those rat tails you call hair in the editing suite upstairs,' I told her. 'It's probably being analysed by the Met's finest forensic minds as we speak. If I were you, I'd be running very fast.'

Talaith shot a sideways look at Castell. He gave the smallest shake of his head. 'She's lying,' he told her. 'And even if she isn't, she's been sharing a room with you for a week. She could have brought any number of hairs in here herself.'

'If you don't get washed, Lacey,' said Iestyn Thomas, 'we'll hose you down. That always goes down well with the punters.'

Talaith had recovered from her brief moment of alarm. She leaned even further into Castell. 'What is it about wet female flesh?' she asked him.

'Works for me,' he replied, looking directly into her eyes.

'Take the money and run,' I said. 'You might even get away with it. But if you kill a police officer, they'll never stop hunting you.'

All four looked steadily down at me. None

seemed even remotely moved by my threats. It wasn't going to be that easy. I began casting my mind around the room, for any possible weapon, any place to hide.

'Oh, we won't kill you, Lacey,' said Castell eventually. 'You'll do that yourself.'

'You know, boys,' said Talaith, 'I'm not sure that scene we shot of you guys in the woods really came out that well. What do you say we go for a second take?'

'Are you listening to me?' I was yelling now. I could not go through that again and stay sane. 'I told my senior officers about you lot at seven o'clock last night. They've had, what, twenty-four hours to put their plans in place. You psychos have got seconds, if that!'

'Oh, I knew there was something we should have told her.' Talaith clicked her fingers and looked up at Castell in mock annoyance before leaning over the guard rail at me again. 'Sorry, love. That cute boyfriend of yours is dead.'

She was lying. She was an evil, manipulative bitch and lying was second nature. She had to be lying. And yet my ribcage was shrinking, squeezing everything inside it like a juicer crushes the flesh of an orange. Nick had called me earlier that day; he'd called a number that nobody knew but Joesbury.

How had he done that?

'He had an accident on the A10 last night,' said Castell. 'Tyres blew out. He left the road and cartwheeled down a bank.'

'Oh, I'd love to have seen it,' Talaith told him.

'It was quite a sight,' he agreed, before turning back to me. 'He was taken to the Lister in Stevenage and pronounced dead on arrival.'

'He phoned me last night,' I told them, but I think I was really just reminding myself.

'No, don't tell lies now,' said Thomas. 'He sent you a text, saying he'd been delayed and that you were to sit tight and contact no one but him. I wanted to add a little personal message but John said that was going too far.'

Minutes earlier, Joesbury's name had flashed on to the screen of the phone they'd left beside me. How could that have happened unless they had his phone? The only way they could have got my new number and given it to Nick was if they had Joesbury's phone. I'd heard nothing from him since he'd left the evening before. Just text messages. He'd have called, surely, if he'd been OK. No. They could not be telling me the truth.

'Would you like to reconsider the knife, Lacey?' asked Castell.

82

Harry sat on Evi's kitchen floor, occasionally running his hand down the long, slim flank of the dog lying beside him. He was vaguely aware that he was hungry. He'd lost track of time but hours had passed since he'd set off on his journey south. He had no idea what he was waiting for. Only that there was nothing else he could do, and nowhere else he wanted to go.

The uniformed police team who'd arrived shortly after the discovery of the dog had been fast and thorough. They'd probably known what they were looking for. Within minutes, they'd found hidden surveillance and broadcasting equipment in several rooms. Someone had been watching Evi in her own house.

'Sir.'

The detective sergeant was in the kitchen doorway. In his right hand was a clear plastic wallet containing a single sheet of white paper.

'Your name is Harry, is that right?'

Harry nodded. 'Harry Laycock,' he said, getting to his feet. The dog whimpered beside him, not wanting him to leave.

The sergeant held the wallet out. 'I need you to read this, sir,' he told him. 'And then help me work out where she might have gone.'

Harry took the wallet as the dog got unsteadily to its feet. Evi's handwriting was large and neat, with intricate loops on the tails. She'd used a fountain pen and violet-blue ink. The note was just five words long.

Gone to be with Harry.

'What does it mean, sir? Where would she go to look for you?'

'She thinks I'm dead,' said Harry. 'This is a suicide note.'

Mark Joesbury watched the paramedics slide the unconscious Nick Bell into the ambulance. An oxygen mask covered his face to help him breathe, an IV line was already starting to replace some of the fluid he'd lost and shiny silver blankets were stopping his temperature from falling further.

As the ambulance set off, forced to go slowly along the unlit, potholed track, a liver and white pointer followed it a few paces before sitting in the middle of the track to watch it disappear. Joesbury felt the world around him slip further away.

He turned back to the house, more because standing still for any length of time made him dizzy than because he had any reason to go in there. In the harsh artificial lights the police team had brought with them he could see blood on the snow.

The first time he'd seen Lacey Flint she'd been covered in blood. She'd arrived at a murder scene just as the victim died. The victim's blood had spattered across her face, stained a deep scarlet patch on her shirt. The paramedics she called had thought she was badly hurt too.

Over by his car, George, his back to Joesbury, was talking on a police radio. He flicked the radio to receive and spoke to the detective at his side. Joesbury caught the last few words as he approached.

'Can't tell me what?' he asked.

George's shoulders stiffened, and when he turned to face Joesbury his avuncular face had clenched itself into tight lines. 'She's not at the industrial unit,' he said. 'SOCs are going in now.'

Two things had struck him the instant he'd laid eyes on her. The first, that she was almost certainly the most beautiful woman he'd ever seen. The second, that she was probably a cold and calculating killer.

'What can't you tell me?' he repeated.

George held out one hand, as though to keep Joesbury at arm's length. 'Guv, it's too soon to know anything. We should get back. We can check her room again. We've got people searching her car. Come on, you know her as well as anyone. You'll be in the best position to spot anything.'

Joesbury didn't move. The two officers exchanged a look. The other detective dropped his eyes to the mud.

George sighed. 'It's pretty clear someone left in a hurry,' he said. 'They didn't have time to clear up. There was a lot of serial-killer paraphernalia, apparently. Not difficult to see where they were going with that. And the team that went in found a pretty good mock-up of her room at St John's. It's possible something happened in there but it's too soon . . .'

'What did they find?'

'A lot of blood, Mark. And body parts. Organs.'

She'd looked directly at him, with those hazel-blue eyes that could turn so cold, as if daring him to challenge her. She'd looked at him the way he'd only ever seen the guilty look.

'And a knife, I'm afraid,' continued George. 'With her name on it.'

The dog was standing at the door of Evi's kitchen, whining to go out.

'I'll take her,' said Harry.

'Stay near the back door,' the constable who'd been waiting with him said. 'We'll need to search the garden before we're done.'

Harry opened the door and kept his hand on the dog's collar as it stepped outside, sniffed the rear step and climbed the small stone wall edging Evi's patio. Harry went too. Light from the house reached about a quarter of the way across the lawn. Beyond it was the soft twilight that snow brings to the darkest of nights.

The garden was large, longer than it was wide, and flanked on either side by high stone walls. It sloped downwards to a much lower wall, with a central gate. Beyond the lower wall was a line of pollarded willow trees.

The dog began to whine at the exact moment that Harry spotted the footprints in the snow. He took his hand off her collar.

The footprints led across the lawn, around the cedar tree, to the gate. Small prints, made by small feet. Uneven footsteps, the one on the right much deeper and firmer than the one on the left, made by someone who walked with a pronounced limp. A few inches to the side of the left print were small indentations, left behind by a light, aluminium walking stick.

The dog made it to the gate a second before Harry did. She stood on her hind legs, barked once and then fell back on to all fours. As Harry pulled the gate open, she leapt the wall in a single bound.

Beyond the wall was a short stretch of snow-covered ground that sloped to the riverbank. A wooden pier leaned out across the water. On the bank beside it was a canoe that looked silver against the snow. Sitting close by the canoe, one arm wrapped around her knees, the other cradling the dog, was Evi. She looked round and her face was spectral pale.

'Hello, Harry,' she said.

They were approaching Cambridge again. Joesbury had a sense of tall old buildings rising up around them. He'd taken Lacey out for a meal that first night, practically forced her into going with him. She'd sat opposite him in a restaurant on the Wandsworth Road, in an orange jumpsuit, her face shiny-pink from the shower, and he'd thought, how can this be happening? How can I be falling for a killer?

'Nothing in the St Clement's address either,' said George, who was at the wheel and seemed to have some idea where they were going. 'Just a whole lot of computer gear. The hard drives appear to have been wiped but it looks as though most of the surveillance was done from there. The industrial unit was for the more advanced filming and the editing.'

'They're gone, aren't they?'

Joesbury couldn't summon the energy to turn his head. He couldn't feel any pain, he realized. He felt dizzy and nauseous, and as though every second the real world was slipping further away from him, but no pain. Whatever they'd given him at the hospital was strong stuff. Perhaps they'd let him take it for the rest of his life.

'Looks that way,' agreed George. 'But they can't have gone far and if they're in their own vehicles there's a good chance traffic will pick 'em up.'

She'd been with him at one of the worst crime scenes he'd ever come across and hadn't flinched. She'd calmly and quietly followed him round the corpse, done everything he'd asked her to, and then, even though she'd seen exactly what the killer did to women, she'd agreed instantly when he'd asked her to make herself bait. She'd walked off into the darkness without looking back and he'd told himself that he was never going to put her in danger again.

Attention all units, attention all units.

George increased the volume on the police radio. They were almost back at the college.

Any cars in the vicinity of St John's College, I need you to report there immediately. We've received a phone call about a potential suicide on the chapel tower. White female, early twenties. Believed to be a student called Laura Farrow.

One of the porters appeared beyond the gates ready to open them. Joesbury didn't wait. He jumped out of the car and sped across the short stretch of grass to the main student entrance. He raced past the porter on duty and was in First Court. The tower was immediately ahead of him.

'Alice called you, didn't she?' said Evi. 'I'm sorry I scared you.'

Harry slipped his jacket off and wrapped it round her. He'd forgotten how her hair gleamed in the dark, how it reminded him of polished walnut. He hadn't forgotten how soft it was.

She reached up, maybe to pull the jacket

more securely on to her shoulders, maybe to touch him. Her hand against his felt like the snow, damp and cold.

'We need to get you inside,' he said. As he sat down beside her, his foot caught the edge of the canoe. It slid a little further down the bank. Harry stretched forward to catch the rope.

'Leave it,' Evi told him.

There was a hammer on the ground in front of them, a fragment of pale-blue wood clinging to its claw foot.

Evi leaned a little closer to him, the side of her head resting lightly against his shoulder. 'I knew you couldn't be dead,' she said. 'I worked it out, once the pain went away. If you'd died, Alice would have phoned me, not just sent a newspaper cutting. There would have been some mention of it on your Facebook page. I realized they were just messing with my head again.'

The canoe slid a little further towards the water. Evi put her hand on Harry's arm, to stop him getting up. 'Let it go,' she said.

'Who?' he asked her. 'Who's been messing with your head?'

'I'm not entirely sure. But I know one of them's a senior police officer. He's going to make trouble for me, if he's still around.'

'He's got to get past me first, pet.'

The tiny lines on the side of Evi's face appeared slowly, almost reluctantly, as though she hadn't smiled in a while and her muscles couldn't quite remember how it was done. 'I'd forgotten you used to call me that,' she said. 'I think it all started with a very damaged young man, who found some relief from his pain by tormenting and terrifying others. And then somewhere along the line more people got involved and the whole dark business began to feed on itself until it was almost unstoppable.'

The canoe had reached the water. The river, sensing a prize within its grasp, began to tug at it. Harry blew out through pursed lips and put his arm round Evi. On the other side of her, the dog licked his hand. He had no idea what she'd just been talking about but it hardly mattered. They had plenty of time. 'What was the hammer for?' he asked her.

'To break a hole in the bottom of the canoe,' said Evi. 'And the canoe was for me to float away in, like the Lady of Shalott. The heavy dose of liquid morphine I gave myself just before I came out was to stop me struggling to the bank when it went down. If I sound a bit spacey, that's why.'

'Evi —'

'It saved me, Harry. The morphine. For

the first time in weeks, I couldn't feel any pain. I could think again.'

They watched the canoe drift downstream, sinking lower in the water.

'They've been playing around with my medication as well,' said Evi. 'Coming into my house, taking the pills I rely on, replacing them with something else, probably just some sort of placebo. And playing all sorts of weird tricks to freak me out.'

'The police found surveillance equipment in your house,' said Harry. 'And broadcasting stuff too, did you know that?'

'I guessed,' said Evi. 'They've been watching me for a while now.'

The cold of the snow was seeping up through the leather Harry wore. The canoe had sunk very low in the river now, had almost vanished in the darkness. Water began to spill over the sides.

'There I go,' said Evi. They watched the canoe disappear, then Evi turned to face Harry. He saw her hand move up towards him, felt her finger stroke the skin of his cheek, and then the wind on his damp skin.

'It's the cold, pet,' he said. 'Makes my eyes water.'

'We should go inside.'

'That'd be good.'

Harry got to his feet and lifted Evi. Leaving her stick where it lay in the snow, she took his arm and they walked together, back through the garden, towards the house. The dog ran ahead, pausing only at the end of the lawn to make sure they were following. With a last hurry-up-will-you yip, she ran in through the back door.

'Is she yours?' asked Harry.

'Yes,' said Evi.

'How does she get on with cats?' asked Harry.

83

Tuesday 22 January (a few minutes before midnight)

Joesbury feels the cold air at the same moment he spots the door at the top of the tower. He's outside before he has any idea what he's going to do if he's too late and she's already jumped. Or what the hell he'll do if she hasn't.

'Lacey,' he yells. 'No!'

The roof is empty.

From behind comes the sound of footsteps on stone and heavy breathing. Someone else has reached the top of the steps and a second later is outside.

He'll never know what it would be like, to wake up beside her.

Joesbury sees a man half stop, gasp for breath and then race to the edge of the roof, leaving a wake of footprints in the unblemished carpet of snow. He watches him lean over the parapet, shine a powerful flashlight down, before standing up again and moving round to another side of the roof. Someone else is on the roof now. Both men are moving around, leaning over the parapet, shining torches down, their footprints spreading across the roof like a cobweb. There are people on the ground shouting up at them.

He'll never see the look on her face when she meets his son for the first time.

There are uniformed police officers on the tower, speaking into radios, asking if there's any other way off the roof. The mood is urgent, confused. All the snow has been disturbed now. Piles of it collect in corners. It clings to boots. Then a man barks out an order. The sense of urgency increases. Radios crackle. People leave quickly. One by one the tower empties, until only he and one of the porters are left.

'Guv.'

He'll never see the tiny lines appear at the corners of her eyes. Never tease her about her first grey hair.

'Mark!'

Joesbury turns to George, who is ashen in the dim light. 'Have they found her?' he asks, and has a moment to hope that her face hasn't been too badly damaged, that he'll be able to look at her one last time. At her perfect, unblemished face. And then he realizes that when he opened the door to the roof the snow was complete, unmarked by footprints of any kind.

'Not here we haven't,' says George. 'That phone call was a hoax. But we do know where she is. Confirmed this time. They've put her on a different tower. Great St Mary's, about half a mile away. Hold it!'

George's hand has shot up, palm out, holding Joesbury back. 'She's hanging over the edge,' he tells him. 'Constable in attendance says she looks out of her head on drugs and she's threatening to jump if anyone goes near her.'

'Out of my way, George.'

George takes a step forward, to plant himself more firmly in Joesbury's way. He is holding up a phone and hands it over.

'PC Leffingham,' he says. 'He's with her on the tower. Good luck, guv.'

84

A falcon can feel sensation through every one of its thousands of feathers. As it takes to the air, energy will pulse through its wings, stoking its heart; as it glides on thermals, it will feel a soft, buffeting warmth, and when it dives for prey the feathers on its wings and its back will feel as if they are on fire.

I can feel all of that now, here at the tip of the world, with only stars above me.

And stars like I've never seen before. Huge, silver dinner-plates, casting out light from one to the next, until the whole night sky looks like a vast, illuminated spider's web and not a single one of them seems out of reach.

I take a step forward and know I'm weightless. Another step and I almost leave the tower behind. Enough to make you giddy, this sudden knowing; this startling realization that flying is easy. Flying is just a matter of thinking the right thoughts and believing. I can let my mind soar and my body will follow.

I'm up, on the wall, the wind teasing, tugging at me like the hands of a dozen children. Come now, come and play.

Then a voice. Hard and grating. I spin round and snarl. It backs away.

The city looks so beautiful, as though someone has thrown gold dust over a black velvet cloak, and I think I'll visit it, one last time. I'll dive down, faster than a falcon, swooping up at the last second to float like a ghost along the streets and over the rooftops.

'Laura! I'm coming a couple of steps closer. Just so we can talk to each other. No, steady on, love. Look, I'm not moving.'

My name isn't Laura.

'Sorry, Lacey. I've just been told your name is Lacey. I'm Pete. PC Leffingham. Can I come a bit . . . OK, OK, I'm staying here.'

Lacey? Is that my name? There is a tree directly below me that still has leaves and I wonder if they'll tickle, those leaves, when I glide past them.

'Lacey, I'm talking to a friend of yours. Says his name is Mark. Mark Joesbury.'

Those leaves are dead. They won't tickle,

they'll tear my flesh open as I hurtle into them. The branches will pull out my hair, stick into my eyes, impale me.

'He wants to talk to you. Can I just hand over the phone so Mark can talk to you?'

'Mark Joesbury is dead,' I tell him.

A short pause, while PC Whoever-he-is tells his caller the news of his own demise. 'No,' his voice calls up to me again. 'He's very much alive and wants me to tell you to get down from there now or he'll have you on traffic duty till you get your twenty-two-year long-service medal.'

'Joesbury's an arsehole,' I say. 'Joesbury set me up.'

I hear PC Leffingham's mumbles and tell myself they are nothing to do with me. I look at the shining silver saucers that used to be stars and I swear, if I just bounce, I can touch them.

'He says he knows. He says he's very sorry. He says please just come down and let him tell you he's sorry.'

The wind feels like a blanket, like a soft bed, like a quilt wrapping itself around me.

'I don't think she's listening to me, sir. I don't think it's going to work. She's leaning into the wind now. Christ, if it drops . . . what? OK, hang on . . . Lacey!'

Oh, will he not leave me in peace? I am

about to fly.

'Lacey, Mark says they found the note in your car and they've put out an all-ports warning on three different cars. He says they'll catch them. It's over.'

'Have you ever watched a falcon dive?' I ask. 'Do you have any idea of the speed it reaches?'

'Lacey, he says he loves you.'

'Tell him he's full of shit!'

'Steady, steady on, Lacey. Don't let go . . . let me just . . . OK, I won't come any closer. Sir, I really don't think . . .'

Leffingham's voice fades and I sense him back away from me. Good. I can see a moonbeam, shining directly down upon the pavement, its light spreading along the stone like a soft, warm pool.

'What? Sir, I . . . OK, I'll give it a go.'

The moonbeam looks like a trail, sent for me to follow.

'Lacey.'

I sigh. I am going to have to jump just to get the hell away from this pest.

'Lacey, Mark says he's on another tower. He says he can see you and if you look in the right direction, you can see him. Over there, look, to the north. He's got a torch. He's waving it around. Oh, Christ, he has too.'

I have no interest in where Mark Joesbury is. And yet one of my huge round stars has shrunk, it seems, and fallen lower, and is dancing around like a dervish because I can see what is getting PC Leffingham so excited. Across the city, where I judge the tower of St John's to be, I can see a powerful light being swung around in a constantly repeating arch.

'Tell him I'll see him in hell,' I say, and get ready to jump — I mean, to fly.

'He says he heard that and you're absolutely right you will because he's going to jump too — what?'

What?

I'm not looking at the sky, any more. Or at the city, or even across the vast dark space to St John's tower. I am staring at PC Leffingham and at the phone still clamped to his ear. He's arguing with the man on the end of the line. Well, now he knows what it's like.

'Sir, this is getting beyond . . . no, I'm not telling her that . . . who's with you? OK, OK, Jesus wept.'

Leffingham runs a hand over his face and for a second I think it crosses his mind that he might push me himself and bring the whole farce to an end. 'Mark says if you jump, he will too,' he calls up to me. 'He swears it on his son's life because this whole business is his fault and if you die he won't be able to live with himself and — yeah, yeah, I've got it — and when he jumps he's going to take the torch with him . . . and the last thing you'll see is that torch. And he says he'll hit the ground first because he's a lot heavier than you.'

'Tell him to go fuck himself.' I'm up on the ledge. I'm going.

'Lacey!'

I swear that voice wasn't PC Leffingham's.

'Lacey, he says he can't live if you don't.'

I look up, for my big dinner-plate stars and the silver silk streamers that I will fly among. They're gone and in their place are just tiny dots of light, millions of miles away. Below me, my black-velvet city strewn with gold has gone too. All that's left is a town that is beautiful but cold. Over to the north, where the light from a flashlight hasn't stopped waving, I can picture the man who's holding it, a man who is up on the edge of a parapet, just like me, and I know that he and I are on the verge of a pretty big adventure. Whether we jump, or whether we don't.

My call.

Without taking my eyes off Joesbury's

torch, I give PC Leffingham my hand and let him lead me safely back down to earth.

ACKNOWLEDGEMENTS

Grateful thanks to my kind and clever friends and colleagues, without whose help I could not write my books: Sarah Adams, Jessica, Peter and Rosie Buckman, Lynsey Dalladay, Anne Marie Doulton, Matthew Martz, Sarah Melnyk, Kelley Ragland, Kate Samano, Denise Stott, Martin Summerhayes, Adrian Summons, Jess Thomas, Mark Upton, Claire Ward and Geoff Webb. Any remaining mistakes are mine.

AUTHOR'S NOTE

There have been a few cases of student suicide in Cambridge in recent years but their details are unknown to me. My research for this book has been general, not specific, and any similarities to real events are entirely coincidental.

I have long considered Cambridge to be one of the most beautiful cities in the world, and feel nothing but wistful envy for those lucky enough to live and study there. *Dead Scared* is a work of the imagination, nothing more.

References

Burn Unit by Barbara Ravage, *The Suicidal Mind* by Edwin S. Shneidman, *Why People Die By Suicide* by Thomas Joiner, *November of the Soul* by George Howe Colt, *Dark Journey* by Ronald L. Bonner, *The Lucifer Effect* by Philip Zimbardo, *Training Birds of

Prey by Lee William Harris, *Falconry for Beginners* by Jemima Parry-Jones and *The Night Climbers of Cambridge* by Whipplesnaith.

ABOUT THE AUTHOR

S. J. Bolton is the author of four previous critically acclaimed novels, *Sacrifice, Awakening, Blood Harvest* and *Now You See Me,* all available in paperback.

Sacrifice was nominated for the International Thriller Writers Award for Best First Novel, and voted Top Debut Thriller in the first ever Amazon Rising Stars. *Awakening* won the Mary Higgins Clark Award for Thriller of the Year in the US.

In 2010 *Blood Harvest* was shortlisted for the CWA Gold Dagger for Crime Novel of the Year, and in 2011 S. J. Bolton was shortlisted for the CWA Dagger in the Library, an award for an entire body of work, nominated by library users.

S. J. Bolton lives near Oxford with her husband and young son. For more information about the author and her books, or to check out her addictive blog, visit www

.sjbolton.com. Or join her on Facebook at www.facebook.com/SJBoltonCrime